THE LIGHT BEARER

THE LIGHT BEARER

ANNIKA GOODWIN

Hidden Hollow Publishing

Published by Hidden Hollow Publishing

ISBN 978-0-9998642-0-3

Typesetting services by BOOKOW.COM

for Grandpa Goodwin
the strongest, gentlest man I have ever known. . . .
pilot, artist, author, adventurer,
gardener, builder, teacher, motivator.
In allowing me to "help" you build things,
you were actually building me.

Many thanks to:

Virginia Pinnell, who has inspired so many by her faith, love, and her reliance upon God.

Pastor Bruce Haynes, who has a vision for restoration and reconciliation.

Danny and Christy Burd at New Life Restoration Center, who daily show their love for the Lord in the ministry of discipleship and restoration.

Women's Minister Vicki Curry, whose prayers and encouragement have been invaluable to me.

Mom, Dad, and Lee, who never gave up.

Matt, who continually reminds me that with God, all things are possible.

All those who gave me feedback and helped with the editing and revision of this book: Mom and Dad, Matt, Cori Busenitz, Danny Burd, Aunt Barbara, Pastor Bruce Haynes, Lora Gwin, and Dorothy and Edith Chastain.

My Lord and Savior, Jesus Christ, who loved me and gave Himself for me. Without Him, this book would not exist.

For thou wilt light my candle: the Lord my God will enlighten my darkness. –Psalm 18:28, KJV

CONTENTS

Part I

Ekklesia

1

SELAH tugged the tattered, olive-green chore coat closer to her body. The coat had belonged to her grandmother and was missing a button about midway down the front. "I still have the button," her grandmother used to tell her with a smile, "but I don't ever intend to sew it back on. If I hadn't lost that button, I might have stayed caught on that fence I was trying to climb over to get away from John Breedon's cranky old bull."

So a gap stayed in the front of the coat. Most winters, wind wasn't too sharp in the valley where Selah lived. The surrounding hills and ridges of the Ozarks kept it at bay. But days like these, when the wind came from an unusual direction and moved in gusts like an icy slap, Selah thought about breaking with the old family tradition and just sewing a button back on. She reached a finger experimentally into the front zipper pocket and grinned when she felt the cold metal roundness of the button. It was still there, in the seldom-used pocket, after all these years. She pulled it out and looked at it as she walked down the wagon path that served for a road through the snow. Grams had kept it there, just for the sake of remembering the incident. Every time she had told the story, Selah lived it with her—the old Santa Gertrudis bull pawing in the dusty ground, dipping his head in warning, the sound of the bull's hooves as they pounded across the pasture, the terrifying feeling of being caught halfway over the fence, and the frustrated snorting and bellowing of the bull when Grams had gotten away. Selah poked the button back in the pocket and zipped it shut. The memory brought back by the gap in the coat was worth the little bit of cold that crept in once in a while.

The path of snow packed down by boots and hooves and sleigh runners turned slightly to the right. Selah stopped and looked to her left at the edge of the trees that had crept closer to the road in the last half-mile. Snow-laden cedars bowed toward the center of a lane that wound its way into the woods. A small finger of smoke curled its way above the trees in the distance. Selah frowned thoughtfully as she noticed a lone set of footprints that veered off the road and through the lane. They didn't belong to Miss Genevieve, because she was getting too unsteady on her feet to venture out in the deep snow. Besides, the boot prints were large, and whoever made them had a long, steady stride. Who else would be visiting Miss Genevieve besides Selah, herself?

"Guess I'll find out soon enough," Selah said into the stillness, and turned to follow the path under the drooping trees. Her parents had suggested she check on the older woman when the family had awakened to yet another five inches of snow that morning. She had planned on taking her some cheese later in the day anyway, after her morning chores were done, but her father was concerned she might have run out of split wood. "I'll milk Maggie this morning," Jackson Merrit had told his daughter, "You just go and check on Miss Genevieve. You may have split what seemed like enough wood the other day, but that's before the temperature dipped down into the teens yesterday afternoon. And even though it warmed up some before daylight, with this heavy of a snow, it could be that some branches may have broken and fallen onto that old trailer." Selah hadn't thought of that until her father had said it, and worry had given her a quick pace. Warmer temperatures meant a wetter, heavier snow that stuck to the trees like thick, globby icing. She had noticed several of the larger cedars with branches and trunks snapped in half. Apparently, she and her family weren't the only ones who were worried, she thought as she glanced again at the set of prints. Maybe things were changing, she thought to herself as she

trudged through the snow. Maybe the rest of the community was coming to its senses and would start treating Miss Genevieve with the respect she deserved instead of the patronizing attitude they had adopted
since that fateful day last summer. Maybe children would once again
gather on her front porch, learning to read and listening to stories. She
doubted they would ever approve of her reading anything from the history books like she used to; but then again, if history wasn't taught, how
would future generations ever understand why the community came
here in the first place, and why it would never leave?

Her thoughts were interrupted by the sight of a tall figure in a red
trapper hat. Selah's skin tingled from more than just the cold. She had
tried to forgive him, but the mere sight of Payton Hamby still put her
on edge ever since the day she had been questioned at the community
hall.

"Well, hello, Selah," Payton said in his tight-lipped manner. "What
brings you out here?"

Selah was instantly glad her father had asked her to come. She
wouldn't have to search for reasons to defend her presence in the vicin-
ity. Even though most of the valley's residents seemed to trust her
again, Selah was certain that Payton was an exception.

"Dad asked me to come check on Miss Genevieve, to make sure she
had enough wood and that no trees had fallen on the roof." Selah tried
to sound trustworthy and cheerful, but fear made her words come out
haltingly, as if she had to think about how she should answer.

"Well, that's very neighborly, but I wonder why he sent *you* and didn't
just do it himself?"

Selah bristled at the insult to her father's judgment, or her believabil-
ity—or both—but kept silent. She had learned not to contradict an elder, even when she felt like screaming inside. It never used to be like
this, she thought. She had always trusted all of them, trusted their judgment, even defended them to her friend, Garrison, when he used to rage
about them out of their earshot. But that was before she fell out of favor
with the community. Now, she was the black sheep, the only member

in Genevieve's once plentiful flock. And although she wouldn't contradict him verbally, she wouldn't stop coming to see her friend, either.

Except Payton was acting as a roadblock. Selah shifted her weight from one foot to the other and decided to try to be as civil as possible and ignore the insult. "I'm really glad someone else thought of checking on her. She can't really get out in the snow much anymore, and we wanted to make sure her wood box was full."

"I've made sure of that. There's really no need for you to go now," Payton said, without budging.

Selah wished she could slap him, tower over him...could somehow intimidate him. And then, in the middle of her anger, she remembered to ask for help. *Help me to get past him,* she prayed silently. Suddenly, she remembered the cheese. "Well, actually, Mom made some of her favorite cheese," she said, as she pulled the bundle out of a coat pocket. "She wanted me to take it to her."

Payton's eyes narrowed. "Once again, Jackson could have done that himself. But I guess if you're telling the truth, you're just obeying your parents."

"I am telling the truth," Selah bit the words off in the cold. Her civility was wearing thin.

Payton stepped out of the middle of the path. "I want to believe you, Selah. But I think I'll drop by your folks' place, on the way home, just the same—to set my mind at ease."

"Well, if you're still there when I get back, I'll make you some of my famous brewed chicory. You know, I've learned to roast it so it really tastes close to coffee. At least, that's what Shawna Beardsley says." Selah surprised herself with the burst of generosity.

Apparently, Payton was surprised, as well, because he almost seemed confused for a moment. Regaining his composure, he smiled stiffly and said, "Well, Shawna ought to know. She's been around long enough to remember what the real stuff tasted like."

Selah managed a smile. "See you, Brother Hamby. And I really mean it when I say I'm glad someone else was checking on Miss Genevieve. I'm sure it means a lot to her, too."

Payton looked momentarily confused again by her display of solidarity, but nodded and smiled slightly as he made his way back to the main road. Selah glared after him. She had meant all the kindnesses she offered, but it had drained her vat of good will down to the last dreg. She pushed through the snow until she saw the little trailer peeking through the trees.

2

DESPITE his suspicious nature, Payton still went through the motions of Christian charity, Selah considered, as she walked up the newly shoveled steps to the porch. She knocked on the door and waited as Miss Genevieve came to answer. "Well, my goodness! Two visitors in one day!" she crowed, her face gathering into the maze of wrinkles that was her smile. "Come in, child, come in! I'll bet you'll never guess who was just here. Unless you met him on his way out, that is."

"I met him, alright," Selah grumbled. "I wasn't sure he was going to let me come the rest of the way."

"Now, don't be too hard on him. He's just trying to protect the community," Miss Genevieve said.

"From your evil influence?" Selah snapped. She was instantly sorry she'd said it, but her friend didn't seem to hear.

"He even filled my wood box," Miss Genevieve said. "Although, I'm afraid he didn't realize I need my firewood a little smaller than most. I didn't want to say anything, though. Didn't want to look a gift horse in the mouth."

Selah walked over to the wood box and lifted the lid. It was filled with huge chunks of wood the older woman would never be able to manage. Selah had been splitting Genevieve's wood smaller since the elderly woman had pulled a muscle in her back picking up a larger piece. Genevieve was fiercely independent, not wanting to be a bother to anyone, but she knew her limitations. Selah sighed. She would have to carry the wood back outside and split it.

"Now, don't you worry about it. I think I can handle it. They aren't really that big," Genevieve was saying.

"It won't be any trouble at all to split these," Selah told her. "Just leave it to me. I don't charge much." She winked at the old woman, who smiled gratefully. A half hour later, the wood box was filled with smaller pieces of wood, and Selah was sitting by the stove, drinking a cup of hot cocoa.

"Is this real cocoa?" she had asked wonderingly when Miss Genevieve handed her the cup.

"Shhh. Don't tell anybody. I usually just save it for Christmas, when the little ones come around for my annual Christmas party. Of course, I didn't use as much this year," she stopped sadly. Selah remembered. She and her parents were the only ones who had dropped by. "Anyway," she began, with her customary decision to look on the bright side, "since I didn't use as much, it means I can have some with my dear friend. Meager wages for all the work you do around here, but it's all I have to offer today."

Selah grinned and drank in the hot, creamy smoothness she usually only got once a year. "I'll take these wages any day!" she said, and settled back into the quilt-padded chair.

"Now, you get good and warmed up. And then you'd better be on your way. Out of the harm of my 'evil influence,' as you call it," Genevieve chuckled.

So she *had* heard her comment earlier. Selah hoped someday to have the older woman's gift of self-control. Genevieve's power of speech rested not only in what she said, but in what she didn't say, and when she did or didn't say it. "Speaking of evil influence, did you know some of the villagers have been worried there might be illness because of what Garrison did?" Selah asked.

"Let me guess. No, I won't even say who it was. It doesn't matter. I think they're wrong. People say stupid things when they're afraid. And fear has been building in this community for some time, now. Even in the older ones who should be more mature—who should know better.

But then again, a few of them are old enough to remember the deaths. A few of them saw parents and brothers and sisters die. Of course, there weren't any grandparents left. They were all dead," Miss Genevieve said with cold finality.

Selah shuddered. "What was it like, not knowing where it would show up next? Weren't you scared? Wasn't everybody scared?"

The old woman settled back in her chair, her eyes fixed on some point in the past. "Even as a little girl, I remember going to the doctor, and the apprehension on my mother's face as she waited for my test results. We were all tested regularly to try to catch it early." She paused, sifting through years of memories. Her voice took on an oratorical tone Selah had come to love. "When we left the Old Country, the victim count was at an all time high. It didn't take us by surprise, or catch us off guard. It was something we could only accept, because acceptance seemed less frustrating—less devastating—than raging against an enemy we couldn't see. We had lived with it for years, tolerating its proximity, enduring its advances into our territory, because we weren't certain how to deal with it. It showed little or no weakness to our pathetic attempts at resistance. It showed no preference for young or old, healthy or sickly, active or sedentary. It would mark its victim and diminish the individual in stages, leaving the initial area of contact when we fought back, only to reappear in another location, stronger than before. It seemed unstoppable. We thought it would kill us all." The gray-haired woman was suddenly silent. Worried creases between her eyebrows softened as she stoked the fire in the small stove that served as the trailer's sole source of heat. Her spindle-like arms lifted one of the pieces of wood Selah had split to a manageable size. "Now, that's a proper piece of firewood," she bragged, to let Selah know she appreciated it.

Selah waited patiently as Genevieve closed the stove door and placed the poker back in its stand. She knew about the sickness, even though she had never known anyone who had it. She had heard stories from her father, passed down from her grandfather, and from some of the older members of the community, of the horrible deaths and the treatments which were just as horrible as the sickness, itself. Those who had seen its effects firsthand still seemed to be walking in a daze of amazement that their community was left unblemished by its deathly grip. They spoke of it in hushed tones, as if not to awaken a sleeping monster.

"Genetic manipulation."

Selah blinked out of her reverie. "What?"

Genevieve smacked her lips together. "I'm so thirsty I could spit cotton," she said as she began to get out of her chair.

"Just stay put. I'll get you some water," Selah insisted. Elderly folk never seemed to get in a hurry about anything, especially storytelling. Right when she felt she was on the cusp of learning something fascinating which she had never before considered, they would change the subject, or lose their train of thought. She grinned as she poured a glass of water out of the jug Genevieve kept by the front door. They were worth the extra time it took to listen. There was a shortage of books in the community, and obviously no computers or phones or access of any sort to what the old-timers referred to as the Internet. In Selah's world, information was stored in the memory of the oldest computer known to man—the mind. The elderly were held in great regard and had an extraordinary responsibility to the younger generations. It was like having a computer that gradually lost the ability to access its files. They were walking libraries that everyone knew would someday burn down. Handing Genevieve her glass, she coaxed, "What were you going to say about genetic manipulation?"

Genevieve shifted her position to ease the ache in her old bones. "Everyone was excited about the new advances being made in mapping genomes and tweaking chromosomes. They thought the New Science was the new messiah. I just wonder if that's how they did it — if that's how they're surviving. They said they had the answer, and maybe they did. But the cost was too great. We would not have been warned to leave if it had been otherwise." She leaned back in her chair, her fingers tracing the edges of a hole in the brocade armrest. "How many have died never knowing the Truth? How many have grown up with only a twisted version of history—a collection of half-truths? How different are they now, genetically and socially?"

"Surely they couldn't be *that* different. You were old enough to remember what it was like. Things don't change *that* quickly," Selah reasoned.

"They don't change that quickly around *here*," Genevieve said. "But in the Old Country, things were changing at an ever-increasing rate."

The Old Country. Genevieve liked to refer to it as that, even though whenever she talked about it, it sounded like it was full of things that were modern, shiny, clean, and convenient. Electricity—that amazing, ancient invention which allowed you to have light at the flip of a switch or to heat things up without the use of fire—was taken for granted in the Old Country. Here in Selah's small community, it was obtained only by solar panels that charged batteries capable of running appliances for only a few hours. The community was totally off-grid. Whatever power they had, they provided themselves. The Old Country, with electric and hydrogen-powered vehicles that could drive themselves, and houses with running water and electricity, sounded like a dream to Selah, especially when she was splitting wood or hauling water. She had to remind herself during those times that there was a solid reason the families of her community had left in the first place.

3

THE events of the past few months played over in Selah's mind as she made her way back home. Until Garrison had left, Genevieve had been the librarian and history teacher for the community's children. Selah's father, Jackson, had used stories told to him by his parents to explain to his daughter why the founders of the community had decided to leave their original home. But it was the memories of Genevieve that made the Old Country, with its fascination and its danger, come alive for Selah. For years, youths had gathered on the front porch or around the wood stove in inclement weather, learning where they had come from, why their ancestors had left, and why they could never return.

Selah's friend, Garrison Scoffield, had taken a keen interest in the stories when he reached his teenage years. Whatever time he had which was not spent working with the crops or the livestock was spent asking the elderly people of the community about the Old Country. Genevieve had been only too happy to oblige, telling him everything she knew, including the threats to personal freedom. "Christians had become a small minority," Genevieve told him. "The government told us that everything sacred to us was superstition carried over by our ancestors. They said we were holding up progress and denying our children the right to make up their own minds about what to believe. They said if we really wanted to advance, we would let our children grow up unfettered by the bonds of any particular belief system. If they wanted to believe in a higher power, that was okay, as long as it was understood that the higher power was simply the collective energy of humanity seen in many guises throughout the ages and most recently in the will of the State."

"But what difference does it make what they want you to believe," Garrison countered, "when you can believe whatever you choose? Just don't tell anyone about it. We could teach what we want to in our homes, and be model citizens to the outside world. In the meantime, we could be living in modern houses, with modern transportation and communication. We could see the world, instead of just this little valley."

"Children have loose lips," Genevieve said. "And school officials have ways of asking questions that can trip up even the most careful of children." After that, the discussion was over. Although Garrison pressed her for more information, Genevieve was done talking that day.

Selah, who had been witness to that conversation, often wondered what had happened in her past to make Genevieve stop talking. Whatever it was, she reasoned, was an unpleasant memory she had tried to forget, because normally, Genevieve could go on for hours about the things of the past. And Selah also knew about the growing antipathy toward people who made a stand for Biblical teachings. Saying you were a Christian had aroused no hostility in the Old Country, because society valued diversity of faith. It was when people stood by the claim that Jesus was the only Son of God and the only way to God that you began to raise eyebrows. Claiming that His gruesome death was a sacrifice for the sins of humanity–that was preposterous in the Old Country, for several different reasons.

First, society found the idea of "sin" to be offensive. They argued that people didn't sin, and they didn't need to be redeemed from a state of depravity. They just made bad choices or reacted to things as a result of abuse in their past or a chemical imbalance in their brain. "Which could be true, of course," Genevieve had explained. "But *Christians* said those bad choices were a result of the sinful nature of man. Some Christians claimed that even chemical imbalances would not have existed if sin had not entered the world. To have a chemical imbalance was not a sin, but to suffer from its existence was the result of living in a fallen world." This view was antiquated and had no grounds in scientific fact, according to the sociologists of the day.

Secondly, the idea that Jesus is the only way to God was completely offensive and at odds with the popular view that there were many roads to God. To believe that humanity's sin required a payment in the form of the blood sacrifice of God's Son to appease Him and rectify man's relationship to Him was simplistic and barbaric. Opponents of Christian mission work saw no contradiction as they argued against interference in the beliefs of native peoples' ways of life, even where people were obliged to offer animals or even humans in sacrifices to placate the gods of the spirit world. The teachings of Jesus would bring an end to such sacrifices since only one Sacrifice was needed to appease one God, and this would be a threat to a unique cultural belief system.

To claim that Jesus was the only way to God was an offense to the beliefs of every other religion in a society that prized tolerance. Over the years, many other religions were willing to say there was only one God, but He was called by many names. Even some Christians professed this belief. Selah wondered how they could believe this, if they really believed in the Bible. Part of the trouble, Genevieve said, was that many did not read it, and sometimes those who did read it did not really believe what it said.

And then there was the argument that if God is love, as claimed in the Bible, how could He send anyone to a place called Hell? Selah had asked Genevieve this question, herself. "God is holy," Genevieve explained. "Holiness cannot stand the presence of sin. They are opposites. That's where Jesus comes in. In that one event on the cross, He accepted upon Himself all the sins of humanity—past, present and future, and then died as a sacrifice. Our sins died with Him. He exchanged our sins for His righteousness, so that when God looks upon those who have asked forgiveness and believe in the power of that sacrifice, He no longer sees their sin. He sees only the perfect blood of His son. 'For he hath made him to be sin for us, who knew no sin; that we might be made the right-eousness of God in him,'"[1] Genevieve quoted. "You see, Selah, no one is sent to Hell. They make a choice to go there. God is all about free will. He won't force us to do anything. Indeed, it may be as the author C.S. Lewis proposed. 'There are only two kinds of people in the end: those who say to God, "Thy will be done," and those to whom God says, in the end, "Thy will be done."'"[2]

More and more, society's intellectuals were purporting the belief that there really was some sort of source of all life which was the result of the energy released by all living things. The argument seemed circular to Selah, for how could it be the source of all life if it was the result of the energy of those things for whom it was supposed to be the source? The idea made her dizzy. She understood Garrison's curiosity about the Old Country, but did not share his desire to experience it. It seemed a dangerous place to her, where values were turned upside down, and everyone's personal lives were monitored for signs of ideas that went against the flow of political thought. That was why her community had chosen to leave. They were safe here, and they could openly live what they believed.

---

[1] 2 Corinthians 5:21 KJV
[2] THE GREAT DIVORCE by CS Lewis, ©CS Lewis Pte Ltd 1946

4

THE idyllic, pastoral setting of the valley was in direct contrast to the fast-paced life of the Old Country. Most of the community's residents would have found life in the State a bewildering whirlwind of change. But Garrison Scoffield was drawn to the idea of it. He had attempted to set aside his curiosity, because, at first, he had believed the stories told to him by his elders—stories about the consequences of leaving the community. He didn't want to put anyone in danger. But the idea of leaving the valley chewed at the corners of his mind like the rat that occasionally gnawed on the rafters in the attic above his room. It kept him awake at night, and like the rat, it wouldn't be silenced until he did something about it.

He grew increasingly restless. When reprimanded a few times for what was seen as a dangerous fascination for the Old Country and its citizens' questionable lifestyles, he stopped seeking out the elders and began going for long walks along the wooded fringes of the valley. He happened upon Selah one day last summer when she was picking the wild blackberries that grew along the edge of the woods. "What are you doing out this far?" he asked.

Selah frowned. "What does it look like? I'm picking blackberries. And what do you mean, 'this far?' I'm still in the boundaries." Selah had always had a bit of a crush on Garrison, but his behavior lately had been a little unnerving.

"Sorry, Selah. I was being sarcastic," he said.

"You've been that way a lot lately. It's hard not to be defensive with you when you always seem to be picking a fight." There. She had finally said what had been bothering her for such a long time.

Garrison reached over Selah's head to pick some of the berries that were out of her reach and plopped them into her bucket. "I know. It just seems like every day my parents get a little more nervous about my long walks. They want to know where I am and what I'm doing every minute of every hour. The old timers talk about personal freedom and how they left society to keep it. But what about *my* personal freedom? What about the future of people *our* age?"

Selah began chewing on her lower lip and trying to think of a way to change the subject. She disliked conflict and tried to avoid it.

Garrison stopped as he noticed Selah becoming uncomfortable with the turn in conversation. "I know a better berry-picking spot than this," he said. "Come on." He grabbed Selah's berry pail with an ornery chuckle and bounded away through the tall switch grass.

"Hey!" Selah yelped. She had been picking for the better part of a morning, and had the scratches to prove it. "Get back here, Gary!" she yelled, calling him by the nickname he hated. But he kept running… through the native big bluestem, Indian grass, and switch grass that sustained the valley's small herd of cows…around the edge of Payton Hamby's wheat field, and over a large, smooth outcropping of gray sandstone that plunged into a deep thicket of wild river cane interspersed with cedars and sycamore trees. Selah stopped at the sandstone, out of breath as she looked for signs of movement in the cane below. "Gary-son, when I get hold of you, I—"

"Mmmmm. These are the sweetest blackberries!" Garrison said as he jumped into view onto a boulder in the middle of Bear Creek. A trickle of juice ran down his chin as he grinned like a grape-stealing possum. Selah had to laugh. This was the Garrison she was accustomed to and had missed for the last few months. "Come on. It's not much farther now," he called.

"You're thinking of gooseberries," Selah yelled to the boulder where Garrison had been standing. "I've never seen any blackberries over here. And gooseberries aren't in season, goofus!"

There was no reply, but Selah could hear him splashing in the creek. She sighed and slid down the rock into the cane thicket below. He was headed upstream, and it was easy to follow him, but she hadn't planned on making a day of berry picking. She kept following the sound of the splashes, expecting any minute for his game to be over. The trees around the creek grew thicker as the fields gave way to forest. Selah stopped as a strange sensation grew in the pit of her stomach. It was a feeling of warning she had felt only a few times before, whenever she had wandered close to the boundaries.

"What's wrong, Selah? Are you lost?" Garrison was standing behind a large sycamore tree. In its bark had been carved an X with a circle around it. Selah's blood ran cold.

"That's not funny, Garrison."

The playful expression on her friend's face was replaced by a scowl. "It doesn't mean anything. It doesn't hurt anything," he huffed. "It's just a mark they put on an arbitrary tree of their choosing. God had nothing to do with it."

Selah was silent for a moment. The unsettled feeling in her stomach was getting worse. "Don't you feel that—th-that *warning feeling?*" she stammered, her voice quavering. "We're not supposed to be here. It's for our protection. It's for the valley's protection."

"Do you really believe all that stuff? Look, I'm not getting struck by lightning or *anything!*" Garrison sneered.

"They never said we'd be struck by lightning. They just said this was where they felt led to put the boundary marks. They felt very strongly about it. That's why they teach us from an early age that to pass them is forbidden."

"Actually, they never said it was forbidden," Garrison quipped. "They said that to pass them would put our community in danger."

"Well, do you want to do that? Do you want to do that for a few stupid berries?" Selah was so angry, and yet doubt was beginning to pull at the edges of her mind.

"I've done it a dozen times, and nothing has ever happened. There's so much to see beyond these boundaries. Are you going to let an old superstition rule your life? This berry patch I'm taking you to is like nothing you've ever seen. It's only a quarter mile further. I promise. Now are you coming, or not?"

Selah gritted her teeth as she looked at the half-full pail of berries she had planned to use for blackberry cobbler. "Give me back my berries!" she said with all the authority she could muster, but it came out as a whiny squeak.

"Come and get them," Garrison challenged, and splashed further upstream, beyond the boundary tree, around a bend in the creek and out of sight.

Selah did not move from the spot. *"God, I know You gave us free will, but sometimes, I just wish You would make us do what You want,"* Selah prayed. She had talked to God like this—as a friend–her entire life, whether she felt He was listening or not. In moments like this, she wondered if He really cared what they did, after all.

But surely He did, she reasoned. If God didn't care about what people did, sin would not have existed, and no sacrifice for sin would have been required. It wouldn't have mattered if Adam and Eve had broken God's commandments. In fact, there would have been no commandments to break, because no moral boundaries would have been set.

Selah marveled at the concept of free will. Freedom to make their own decisions was a God-given gift to humanity, even though it had resulted in the price paid at Calvary. He hadn't forced the church members from the city of Rolla, Missouri, to pick up their lives and leave everything they knew for an unknown destination and an unknown way of life. And He wouldn't force Garrison to stay within the boundaries, either. It was a choice, just like the initial choice of believing in a God who created the universe.

Selah waited a full fifteen minutes for Garrison to come back, but he didn't. She was certain he was just playing a trick on her, trying to get her to follow him, but the unsettling sensation she referred to as "warning feelings" were too strong to ignore. She wearily got up from the rock she had been using as a chair and headed back toward home. A sense of peace and assurance began to wash over her. She knew she had made the right decision, and she somehow knew Garrison would be okay. When she passed Genevieve's trailer, she was almost tempted to stop and ask her advice; but the desire to protect her friend made her keep going. She wasn't sure what the old timers would say to him if they found out. And if he had been doing it for a while now and nothing had happened, maybe it was okay for some people to go—just not for others. She knew it was not okay for her. That much had been made clear.

It was an hour later when a knock came on the door of the cabin. Selah put down the bowl of beans she had been snapping and opened the door. There stood Garrison with a sheepish look on his face and a pail brimming full of berries. "I told you it was a patch like no other," he said triumphantly. "But I really thought you would come with me."

"Shhhh," Selah said as she came out onto the porch and guided him over to the smokehouse. Her mother was in the back bedroom mending clothes, and her father was working with Silas Johnson, cutting hay. But there was no need to take chances of being overheard. "Where did you get these?" she asked. It couldn't have taken him more than twenty minutes to pick them all, because that particular boundary tree was at least an hour and a half away at a good pace.

"I told you. You should have followed me. There are so many of them. And look...not a hair of my head is singed." Garrison tipped his head and rubbed at his dirty blond hair.

"That's not funny. Why are you doing this?" Selah asked.

"To see what's out there. And to prove it can be done," Garrison began. "Selah, with all their technology—all of *our* technology which we left behind—it's impossible that the State could not know about us. They're just allowing us to live as we please. It's part of the rights to religious freedom in the original Constitution. We live without all the modern conveniences because we live in fear. And it's not even a legitimate fear—it's a fear we've been taught by the previous two generations, formed on some emotional impulse of someone who claimed to be a spokesperson for God."

"It wasn't just one person. It was confirmed by at least a dozen people who were given the same message, some by dreams—"

"And one by a vision, and one heard an audible voice, yes, I know, I know," Garrison interrupted. "Selah, when emotions run high—and they *were* running high during the social tensions of that time—people can easily fall prey to emotional sensationalism. Especially in the world of charismatic Christianity. They can get so hyped up on the emotion of the moment that they confuse it with direction from God. And don't think ego wasn't involved. I mean, face it—who *doesn't* want to hear from God? That puts you in a position of power, to be on speaking terms with the Almighty."

"We are all on speaking terms with the Almighty," Selah said evenly.

"But we are not all on *hearing* terms with Him, are we?" Garrison said cattily.

"We are not all on *listening* terms," said a voice from around the corner of the smokehouse, and then Miss Genevieve stepped into view and settled her squat little body onto an old hickory stump nearby.

5

GARRISON looked as if someone had just punched him in the stomach.

"The Almighty is always speaking to us, but we are rarely in a position receptive enough to listen," Miss Genevieve continued. "He most often speaks to us through His written Word, but through the ages, there have been times when He used other methods. Still does. I was only five, but I know what I saw. I had my little suitcase all packed up with my clothes and my games, and I was ready to go. Couldn't understand why my folks weren't ready. 'Why aren't you ready to go?' I said. 'The man who was here this morning said it was time to get ready to go to the new place.' 'What man?' they asked. 'The one who was just here,' I told them. 'The one with the funny bag on a stick.' About that time, there was a knock on the door. It was a friend of ours from church. He had this bewildered look on his face and said he had come by to tell them about a dream he had just had the night before. 'In the dream, there was this man who came knocking at my door,' he said. 'He was dressed in old fashioned clothes that looked like they could have been from the 1800's or early 1900's. He had an old hobo's knapsack—the kind they carried on a stick resting on their shoulder. He asked me if I was ready to go, because it was almost time. I asked him where we were going, and he just said, "To the new place, where you will be safe."' And then, before he was done with his story, he got a text. It was someone else who had had a dream with the same man in it. He was trying to get them to follow him. Mom and Dad called the pastor to tell him what was happening, but before they could say anything, he told them he had just had the most incredible experience in which he heard a voice telling him it was time to go. So we all held a meeting at my folks' house, because they had suspected for a while that the church building and the pastor's house were being monitored by the government. And you know the rest. Everyone packed up the things we thought we would need for living in the time period portrayed by the clothes worn by the mysterious man. Tools, seeds for planting, solar cells, solar powered batteries, candles, flints, matches, kitchen items, and books to help with all the old ways of life which we had never experienced…I'm surprised it all fit in the back of John Breedon's pickup and the van and trailer we used to take to church camp. Some of the people who were new to the faith and had been mixed up in some weirdness earlier actually thought we might be going to travel back in time." Genevieve stopped to laugh, her belly heaving up and down over her stick-like legs. "But most people figured the man we saw was dressed in clothes from another time to show us the way we would have to live. And they were right. If you're going to live off-grid and undetected, it *is* a lot like living back in the 1800s."

"Don't you think some of them could have been making it up?" Garrison could hold it back no longer.

"Well, that's what some of the church thought. Even though the people who had the dreams were solid, older, steady people not given to being overly excited, some people thought we had gone off the deep end of reality into cultic madness. And I don't blame them. Our story sounded ridiculous.

"But we didn't just jump up the minute we had the dreams and visions. As you have been taught, not all spiritual experiences are from God. So we sought the Lord about it in prayer and fasting. And in reading His Word, we were reminded that there was even precedent for it in the Bible, where an angel appeared to Joseph in a dream, telling him to go to Egypt for the protection of Mary and the baby Jesus. During that time of seeking clearer direction from the Lord, a few more people who had thought we were crazy were visited by the same mysterious hobo.

They ended up joining us. And then, when we were headed out of the city, we saw him—the man I had seen in the vision—walking along the side of the road. We *all* saw him; it wasn't just a few of us. You can't make *that* up."

Selah and Garrison had heard about the hobo before. The group had picked him up and continued down the highway. He didn't say much, except to give directions, and no one even asked him where they were going or where he was from. One time when Selah was listening to the story, she said she couldn't believe no one had asked him anything.

"Oh, I asked him lots of things," Genevieve said with a grin. "Real important things, like, 'Do you like bubblegum?' and 'Do you have a puppy in your bag?' He was so kind to me. He answered my questions and accepted my offer of a piece of bubblegum.

"The only time an adult asked him a direct question was when we stopped at a rest stop. We came out from using the restroom and saw him crawling out from underneath one of the vehicles in our caravan. Pastor wanted to know if there was something wrong, and he shook his head. But when we got back on the road, the GPS in the van we were riding in wasn't working. The grownups all got real quiet, because it was a felony to operate a vehicle that couldn't be tracked. Whenever someone tried to tamper with a car's GPS system, the computer would give one warning. If the driver did not acknowledge it and attempted to bypass the car's command center, the computer would eventually win control, keep the driver locked inside, and carry the "driver" to the nearest authorities.

"We were all waiting for the computer to give the warning, but it never did. We just kept on driving, turning where the hobo told us to turn, and stopping where he told us to stop. Several policemen passed us on the highway, but no one ever suspected anything. It was as if we were invisible."

6

THE small group continued its trip from interstate to back roads skirting a national forest, to gravel roads that bumped and rattled the 15 passenger van crammed with 20 adults and children. Finally, when discomfort of the cramped conditions and the rough ride began to wear on even the most stoic of souls, the hobo held up his hand and said to stop and get out. Gratefully, the tired and bone-weary travelers piled out of the van and the pickup and looked around. The gravel road had led them over ridge tops with towering shortleaf pines into the gradual descent of a hardwood forest of oaks and hickories. They had come to rest near what appeared to be the edge of a large clearing. The hobo walked toward the edge of the clearing and looked back at them. "Ahead is your destination. You will be safe here, provided you stay within the boundaries. It is protected. You will have everything you need to live here. It has all been provided." He stopped and made a point of looking every individual in the eye as he continued, "You are greatly loved. Do not be discouraged, and remember the source of your strength. Remember to whom you belong. Be strong, and of good courage, for the Lord your God is with you wherever you go."[3] He then turned away from the clearing and walked without hesitation into the woods, as if he knew exactly where he was going.

"Hey, wait!" called one of the younger men. "Aren't you going to stay and help us? I've never even been camping before!"

But the mysterious man kept walking. "Is that guy for real? He's just going to leave us?" the young man asked in desperation.

---

[3] See Joshua 1:9

The pastor of the bewildered flock of believers stepped forward and placed a comforting hand on the man's shoulder. "Cameron, he said we had everything we need. That includes the knowledge to survive. It isn't a coincidence we have Veronica Hamby, who is a horticulturalist, and Ernest Rogers, who builds houses, and Jessica Beardsly, who taught weaving and spinning at the Wall School of Art and Design. We even have John Breedon, who managed the Stavesville Historical Farm and was able to bring some chickens, pigs, and a few head of cattle. And you heard the man. We'll be safe here. We won't ever have to worry about someone implanting a tracking chip in our heads, or taking our children away if we teach them that life isn't just the result of some cosmic crapshoot. And I don't know how we'll go undetected, but if God can keep the computers in our vehicles from driving us to the nearest police station when our GPS systems stopped working, I have a feeling He's got all the other details worked out, too." Pastor Coffelt stopped and smiled reassuringly as he looked at the little group. "Besides, everything the hobo said God would do is already promised to us in God's Word. 'And my God shall supply all your need according to his riches in glory by Christ Jesus,'[4] and remember 'Those who dwell in the secret place of the Most High shall abide under the shadow of the Almighty.'[5] It's right there, in Philippians 4:19 and Psalm 91. Let's keep trusting the Lord, as we have learned to trust Him in the past. He said He would never leave us nor forsake us.[6] He hasn't yet, and He won't now."

As the group made their way to the edge of the clearing, the pastor pulled the worried young man aside. "Cameron Scoffield, it's not an accident that you decided to come on this journey. God has a purpose for you and your family in all of this. We need you. Everyone here needs each other. With God's help, we're going to make it. Just considering where our society was heading, I'd rather take my chances here, in this wilderness, than back in Rolla."

---

[4] Philippians 4:19 NKJV
[5] Psalm 91:1 author's paraphrase
[6] See Hebrews 13:5

Cameron smiled begrudgingly. Pastor Coffelt had an infectious enthusiasm and a genuine warmth that melted the iciest resolve. "Thanks, Pastor. Don't worry. I'm not going to take off, or anything. I'm here for the long haul." The two men followed the rest of the group down the barely visible road into the clearing.

What they saw took them by surprise. Before them stretched a valley which appeared to be at least two miles long and a half mile wide. Along one side of the valley ran a river, its passage marked by gatherings of oaks, cedars, witch-hazel and frequent glimpses of the white bark of sycamore trees peeking through the leaves of early summer. A gray, weathered barn leaned precariously toward a collection of old corrals and chutes for working cattle. Overgrown apple trees lined up in the straight, if unkempt, rows of an abandoned orchard. Further exploration would reveal that what appeared to be the end of the valley was actually an area where the forest had bottlenecked the clearing. Just beyond the encroachment of trees there were more open fields interspersed with stands of river cane and thickets of blackberries. One of the clearings even had a mobile home that had probably been used as a hunting cabin. Most of the valley was skirted by a rusty barbed wire fence that leaned over on its side in places where old trees had blown over in the wind. It was a scene from a simpler, yet more rigorous way of life into which they were about to be initiated.

7

"THAT was the busiest summer of my childhood," Genevieve reminisced. "I didn't have time to miss my friends on social media, or any of my shows I used to like to watch, although the first week or so, I did ask why I couldn't see them anymore. It would have been pointless to bring any of that electronic stuff with us. Not only did we not have the means to keep it running, but it would have led the government straight to us. The adults had more trouble adjusting to the lack of technology than the kids. For us young'uns, it was a big adventure. There were crawdads and fish to catch in the river and berries to pick and gardens to tend. We were doing more hands-on projects with our families and with our community than we ever had before. Since there wasn't any entertainment to speak of except what we could come up with ourselves, people began to discover the talents they never knew they had. Don't misunderstand, we didn't ever have a lot of time on our hands, but Sunday was always a special day to rest up and enjoy ourselves. Even back then, folks met on my front porch, told stories and played what instruments we had been able to bring with us. And thank the good Lord that the old fashioned books had never completely been replaced by e-books. We were able to squirrel away a surprising amount in the carrier on top of the van.

"So you might think our little valley is like some show about pioneer families going out west or something. But I never saw any such show where they always used a cow to pull the plow," Genevieve shook her head and chuckled. Selah never understood why this was humorous to her. Cows and steers had always been used to pull wagons and plows and cultivate between rows in the valley, because the community didn't have any horses or mules. Selah had never even seen a one of these animals. But she was always patient with Genevieve and loved hearing her recall the old days.

Garrison's patience, on the other hand, was worn threadbare-thin. "For all we know," he began, "the government is recording us and we *are* one of those reality shows people watch in the State because they can't believe anyone is *stupid* enough to live like this!" He ran his fingers through his hair and paced back and forth between the smoke house and the stump where Genevieve sat. "I was just telling Selah that with all their technology, there's no way they couldn't know about us. What about all the satellites? What about the drones? If we had anything to fear from the State, they would have come and gotten us by now. I'm telling you, they don't care that we live this way. They don't care what we believe. If they did, they would be on our doorstep, and we would all be in jail or a mental institution."

Genevieve watched Garrison through narrowed eyes, a slight smile playing on her lips. "Young man, if you really believe everything you just said, then not a single detail of our lives would go unnoticed by the State, am I right?"

Garrison nodded, but said nothing. He knew Genevieve was about to make a point, and although he didn't agree with her on everything, he still respected her enough to keep quiet and listen.

"If they know everything about our community, then they would know that shortly after arriving, John Breedon's skin cancer began to fade and finally disappeared. The swelling in Paula Moore's lymph nodes went down, even after she ran out of the medication. Doctors had told Dad he only had a year to live six months before we left. He lived to be 89, and when he died, it wasn't from the pancreatic cancer. We haven't had a single case of cancer since we came here." Genevieve stopped and leaned toward Garrison with such a serious expression that he stopped his pacing in midstride. "Now, if they knew that, they really *would* be on our doorstep, begging for the answer. And what would we say? They wouldn't believe us. Who would believe the story of our beginning—that God said He would protect us and provide for us if we would believe Him and go to a place we didn't even know existed? It's just like Abraham and Sarah in the Old Testament. Abraham believed God, and picked up and left his kinfolk and his home, just because God told him to. And God blessed him because of it. And God has blessed us and kept His promise to us, as well. We are healthy. We have everything we need."

Garrison stuffed his hands in his pockets and leaned back against the smokehouse with a smug look on his face. "Everything except the ability to fulfill the Great Commission," he said pointedly.

Selah looked from Garrison to Genevieve to see the old woman's reaction. To "go into all the world and preach the good news to all people"[7] was a scripture Genevieve had always mentioned with wistful tones.

"Not much missionary work when you have to stay within the boundaries," Garrison added.

Selah waited for Genevieve to answer. Her wise reputation gave her words weight. Selah pretended to scratch her nose so she could hide a smile. Garrison's cockiness was about to get the best of him, she thought. The length of time it took Genevieve to answer a question often preceded a conclusion so obvious it embarrassed the inquirer with its simplicity.

Genevieve sat absolutely still, and her eyes had a faraway look. "Young man," she began, "if your motives were not in question...." she trailed off, and suddenly her eyes grew bright and alert again. "You are young and inquisitive. It's natural for you to question things. But it's inconceivable the State would leave us alone if they knew cancer was just a memory for our community. Every oncologist in the world would be fighting for a chance to study us, our diet, and our environment. No, son, I'm afraid you're wrong about that."

"You're changing the subject. What were you about to say?" Garrison asked excitedly.

---

7 See Mark 16:15

"About to say? I done said it," Genevieve winked.

"No," Garrison said, exasperated. "What about my motives? What do you mean, if they were not in question? If my motives were, say, *admirable* to you, *then* what?"

Genevieve looked at Garrison, and scrunched up her eyebrows. "I am afraid my brain is going fuzzy, son. Too many cobwebs for me to remember."

"But you were about to say something," Garrison insisted.

"Well, if my brain would stop following rabbit trails, I could probably remember what it was." Genevieve stood up with some effort and stretched her back. "I've been sitting in one place for too long. You kids have a good evening," she said, and toddled off in the direction of her home.

Garrison watched the hunched figure disappear down the road. "You see, Selah, it's answers like that, where the old timers just change the subject, that make me think they really don't know if they made the right choice or not. It's just pride that keeps us here—*their* pride. Just think…they probably wonder if their parents or grandparents made a mistake in coming here. This hard life will have been for nothing. It's fine for the ones who made the choice in the first place, but what about us? We don't get to make a choice." Garrison was fuming. "And that old woman is hiding something. She can use forgetfulness for an excuse if she wants to, but she deliberately changed the subject."

"Genevieve wouldn't lie," Selah protested. "I've never known her to lie. Not any of the other old timers, either. Why do you hate it here all of a sudden? What makes you want to risk everything?"

"I risk nothing by going past the boundaries. Like I said, the government *has* to know about us. I'm probably just an interesting segueway on an otherwise mundane reality show." He paused with a sidelong glance at Selah. "Who knows…maybe I even have a following of women and teenage girls who are watching my every move, just hoping I'll leave this backwards commune and crossover into their world."

Selah rolled her eyes. Garrison was exasperating, but he could be extremely charming. He took a few steps toward her until she could smell the cedar trees he had pushed through to get to his secret berry patch. "They're probably jealous of you right now, being so close to me," he said as he picked off a bur that had lodged in her shirt during the berry-picking escapade. "I wonder what they're thinking right now," he said, but his eyes were on Selah's. She knew whose thoughts he was really wondering about, and it made her want to slap him. It wasn't so much that he was full of himself. It was the fact that he knew the effect he had on her. She was mad at herself for being so vulnerable, and she decided that she was the one who really needed to be slapped back to reality.

Garrison leaned a little closer with a smile in his hazel eyes, but it was just so he could pick up the pail of berries which he had set down. "There's a whole world out there, Selah. Next time, you ought to come with me."

Selah got a grip on her pounding heart and managed a "Not interested," as she turned around to avoid those eyes.

"Are you that afraid of them?"

Selah didn't like being baited. She wanted to yell at him, *"What do you think you're doing, putting us in risk of detection by the State? Don't you know you're not just gambling with your life, but the life of the whole community?"* But she was also concerned. If she was combative or judgmental, he might stop listening to her altogether, so she chose her words carefully. "I want to protect our community. I want to do what I know is right. I know that I do not belong on the other side of that boundary."

Garrison's eyes darkened. "Enjoy your berries," he said curtly, and shoved the pail into her hands before striding away down the dirt road toward the Scoffield place.

So much for diplomacy.

Selah's caution was not without warrant. All her life she and the other members of the community had been trained to stay within the boundary marks of the valley or risk exposure of their community by the constant monitoring of surveillance drones and cameras that were utilized as personal privacy had dwindled to nearly nothing. With the advancement of a United Nations proposal called the Free Land Initiative, private property had been abolished, and drones kept the countryside under constant surveillance to ensure no one was "infringing upon the rights of others" by using public lands for private uses. The citizens were informed that only the State knew how best to use the land so that the environment was the least impacted for the good of the planet.

Which led to another argument against Garrison's insistence that the State knew about them. Knowing how much the Old Country valued entertainment, Selah could actually believe the State might let the community go unbothered if they were somehow bringing in revenue through unwittingly being a part of a reality show. As long as the citizens thought the community had left with permission, what would be the harm? But such a reality show, where the community practiced small scale agriculture, hunting, and fishing, was a direct violation of land usage as laid out in the Free Land Initiative. Somewhere, someone in the world would take offense at the unfair use of land. Selah wondered what it would have felt like to recognize a family farm that had been taken away from you and given to a group of people who got to use it however they wanted, simply for the entertainment value of the masses. And how many people in the crowded, impoverished slums of some south Asian city would find the community's comparative wealth of food and space entertaining? No, she didn't believe that the push toward what Genevieve called "economic equality for all people" would have allowed for such a disparity of lifestyles. No matter what Garrison said, Selah knew that compared to some, the community was doing very well. To allow some to flourish while others floundered in poverty would fuel unrest. No matter how far removed they were from the reality of the politics of the outside world, she couldn't imagine a State policy condoning that.

8

SELAH pulled her straight brown hair back out of her face and tucked it up into the sun hat she wore when she was in the garden. The heat and humidity of the mid-July morning was making her sweat, and the sweat was making her hair stick to her face. She wished her hair would do something more than just hang about her face in limp, stringy strands. Come to think of it, if she could have had a choice in the matter, she would have made a lot of changes to the way she looked. Her mother, Asha, had thick, golden hair that danced in bouncy, age-defying ringlets which would have reached to her waist if it had been straight. Her father had eyes the color of a cloudless October sky. The least God could have done was to give her green or blue eyes. But instead she had her mother's snappy brown eyes and her father's straight brown hair. At least they matched each other, she mused, as she bent over another stubborn weed.

It had been at least two weeks since the conversation at the smokehouse, and Garrison hadn't spoken to Selah in all that time. She hadn't seen much of him, either. *Fine*, she thought. *I don't need all the drama anyway.* Even though she considered him to be her best friend, lately she felt like she was on unsteady footing whenever he was around. His exploits outside the valley were bad enough, but the other feelings she felt about him were almost more unsettling to her than the risks he was taking. After all, nothing bad had come of his excursions. She was almost inclined to believe nothing would ever happen because of them. But the way her stomach flip-flopped when he grinned at her—that felt dangerous and delightful, in the same instant. She wanted to run and hide in the cornfield and stay to listen to his every word, all at the same time.

"You're not going to get anywhere, at that rate," said a voice from behind her.

Selah raised up from the bunch of foxtail grass she had been tugging at and twisted around to see Garrison grinning from ear to ear. "Why do you always have to sneak up like that?" she sputtered, a blush spreading across her face.

"Why does your face have to turn so red whenever I talk to you?" Garrison countered.

"My face is red because it is hot and I have been bending over, weeding." Selah did her best to scowl.

"Okay, okay. You don't have to give me the old evil eye. Next time, I will try to announce my presence," he said, and began to help pull weeds. He waited until he had pulled a sizeable bundle of wood sorrel and peppergrass before continuing. "I haven't seen much of you lately."

"You're one to talk. I thought maybe you were never going to speak to me again. In fact, I was beginning to wonder if you had gone for good," Selah replied.

"Did ya miss me?" Garrison asked with a flirtatious smirk.

"If you want to know the truth, everything was so peaceful, I was beginning to hope I was right," she responded with feigned snobbery.

Garrison was quiet for a moment as he dug out a particularly stubborn dandelion by the root. "Well, if *you* want to know the truth, I haven't been anywhere, except over to Seth Beardsly's to help with building his barn. We've been busy pretty much from morning to evening. I'm sorry I haven't had time to come by."

Suddenly Selah felt guilty for thinking he had been avoiding her.

"That Sadie sure makes a good piece of pie," he said with a wicked grin. Sadie was Seth's oldest daughter. She had blond hair that was wavy and a figure to match. All the guilt Selah had felt earlier disappeared in burst of jealousy.

"If all I had to do was cook and bake all day, I'm sure I would have plenty of time to get good at it," she snapped. Sadie had three brothers and a sister, while Selah was an only child. Aside from doing her school-work, Selah was expected to milk the cow, work the garden, fish, hunt and find whatever wild edibles were in season so that her mother would have time to can fruits and vegetables, wash and mend the clothes, and prepare the meals. She was trying to learn to cook in her spare time, but there wasn't much time to spare. Her father, who worked out in the fields all day at the Hamby place, tried to give her extra time by doing the milking in the evening. But by then, heating up the whole house by using the cook stove was the last thing anyone wanted to do at the end of a sweltering summer day.

"If you'd just make a little more effort to be friends with her, I'd bet she'd give you some tips," Garrison continued. "You could have at least come to her birthday party last Tuesday. Then you would have known where I've been all this time.'"

"I wasn't invited. And even if I had been, I wouldn't have had the time," Selah said crossly. Why was she so irritated? This was exactly the instability of emotion she had been thinking about earlier. She decided to change the subject. "So you haven't been doing any exploring lately, then?"

A shadow passed over Garrison's face. "No. Like I said, I've been busy. No time for fooling around. But we'll be done by Friday, and I was wondering if you'd like to go catch crawdads with me Friday night. I took a lantern down to Bear Creek the other night, and those big ones with the blue pincers were all over the flats below the falls."

Selah's face lit up. Catching crawdads had been one of her favorite things to do since she was a little girl. "Are you sure you wouldn't rather take Sadie?"

Garrison's smile broadened. "Come on, Selah. Sadie doesn't even like to touch them after they're boiled. I'm not sure I've ever seen her wading the creek anyway. She's scared of snakes."

"And well she *should* be, considering all the cottonmouths down there this time of year." Selah knew her main job would be holding the lantern, but she would have her gig with her, too, to fend off any of the venomous water snakes that came too close. "I suppose I could come along," she said, trying to sound nonchalant.

"Good. I'll come by Friday, after evening chores. Be ready!" he said, as he hopped through the maze of cucumber vines toward the garden gate.

Selah watched him as he headed home, her stomach full of butterflies.

9

SELAH thought Friday would never come, even though it was only one day later. She flew through her chores that day and set to work making a snack for the gigging trip. She was taking some of the deer jerky from the buck she had killed that winter, and had talked her mother out of one of the special cheeses made from Maggie's rich milk. Now she was pulling biscuits out of a Dutch oven on a fire in the yard. "Mom, do you think I could take some of that blackberry jam, too?" she asked.

"Good grief," her mother remarked. "Are you grabbing crawdads or going to a harvest picnic?" She smiled as she said it. "Oh, alright. Go ahead. But surely you don't need to use the whole jar."

"What else am I going to carry it in? I'll bring it back. We won't eat it all!" she exclaimed as she stuffed the jar in her knapsack. She hung the pack on a nail by the back door before heading out to the barn. Maggie was already there waiting, her udder swollen with milk. Being almost all Jersey, she had plenty of milk for her calf and much to spare. Selah's father had been too busy in the fields to do the milking tonight, but she didn't mind. She didn't know how she could have stood the slow passage of time between now and dark if she hadn't had something to do. She poured the mixture of cracked corn and oats into the trough and Maggie eagerly walked into the stanchion for the treat she always got during milking. By the time Selah had finished and turned Maggie out to pasture, the sun was casting long shadows across the fields. She went back to the house to retrieve the knapsack and caught a glimpse of herself in the mirror in the hall. Her hair was all fuzzy and scrunched up from leaning into Maggie's flank while milking. Every time she looked in a mirror, Selah almost wished she hadn't.

"Would you like me to French braid your hair?" asked her mother from behind her.

"Aw, Mom. We're only going to catch some crawdads. It'd just get messed up again anyway," she protested, while secretly wondering what it would look like. "I wouldn't want Garrison to think I was doing it just for his benefit. He might get an even more inflated opinion of himself."

Asha smiled as if sharing a secret. "You don't want your hair hanging down in the way while you're down at the creek at night. It's hard enough to see the cottonmouths coming anyway, even without *that* blocking your view." She pulled up a stool for Selah and quickly brushed her tangled hair. A few pieces of hay fell to the floor. "What did you do, share a bale with that cow?" Asha joked. She began to pick up the strands of hair closest to Selah's face, and in no time had fixed it so that the strands which usually strung down like a mop were braided into a woven crown reaching to the back of her head. She tied it off with a blue ribbon that hung down with the rest of the hair that was left loose about her shoulders. "There. No self-respecting cottonmouth will sneak up on you tonight," Asha said as she handed Selah another mirror so she could view the effect from behind.

Selah had to admit, it looked good. She glanced out the window and could see Garrison coming down the dusty road from the Scoffield place, a large pack on his back and a lantern and gig in his hand. "Thanks, Mom. You're right. It'll be much safer this way." She grabbed the knapsack from the nail and stepped out onto the back porch. "I'll be back close to midnight. If there are as many as he says there are, it may not take very long."

Garrison seemed to be straining a little with the pack he carried. He stepped up to the porch and seemed to study Selah intently. Selah blushed under his scrutiny. "You didn't need to bring any food. I packed a nice snack," she said to break the awkward silence.

"I'm sorry, ma'am," he cleared his throat and tipped his hat. "I'm looking for a little farm brat I promised to take crawdaddin' with me tonight. Could you let her know I'm here?"

Selah glared, but could not keep from laughing. "Mom just did my hair like this so I would be able to keep on the look-out for snakes. It keeps it out of my eyes this way."

"Snakes, huh? Too bad we don't go to one of those snake-handlin' churches," Garrison teased. "I bet that hairdo would look really good in combination with a dress."

Selah's face reddened even further. "Are we going to stand around and chat all night, or are we going to catch some crawdads? And how are you going to catch anything, dragging that load around with you?"

"It never hurts to be prepared," Garrison said as he patted his pack. "I brought you a gunny sack for your crawdads, too, in case you forgot, like last time."

Selah shouldered her pack and grabbed her gig and her lantern. "I remembered. Mom thinks I brought everything except the kitchen sink."

Garrison laughed. He seemed to be in an especially good mood. Selah smiled to herself as they started down the road and through the fields in the direction of the creek. Sadie had good looks, but what difference did that make if you never knew how to have any fun? The thought that it was she, and not Sadie, who was the one walking through the fields with Garrison kept her smiling all the way to creek.

Even though it was midsummer, Bear Creek still had plenty of water because it was spring-fed. Not that anyone in the community had ever seen the spring—that was somewhere beyond the boundaries—but they could tell it was spring-fed by the colder temperature of the water and the fact that it always had water, even in the hottest part of the year.

"Well, here goes," Selah said as she headed for the bank, bracing herself for its icy coldness.

"Wait, Selah," Garrison said as he grabbed her by the arm. "Let's not go in just yet."

"It's almost dark. They'll be moving around soon enough," Selah said, confused.

"It's just, I wanted to talk to you about something first."

Selah felt a warmth growing in her stomach and spreading to her arms. Maybe the effort to look a little more presentable had been worth it.

Garrison took the lantern out of her hands and set it by her pack on the bank. "Let's sit down for just a minute," he said as he steered her toward a large gray boulder shaped like a slab of bread. They sat down, and he smiled at her hesitatingly. Selah's stomach had progressed from flip flops to cartwheels.

"I know you haven't much liked my little excursions out of the valley, but in the process of my exploring, I've discovered a few things," he began.

The cartwheels tumbled to a stop like a piece of lead that dropped into her gut.

Garrison went on. "There are miles and miles of wilderness out there, but *Selah*, I found a *road!*" His eyes shone with excitement. "It's a paved road, like in those old books at Genevieve's. So far as I can tell, no one travels it anymore, but it's got to lead to somewhere eventually." He stopped and put his hands on her shoulders. "Selah, I'm going. I'm going out there. I have what we need to survive. We know how to live off the land until someone finds us and takes us back to civilization. If we just keep walking, they'll realize we're serious about leaving and—"

"What are you talking about?" Selah squeaked. "What do you mean, *we?*"

Garrison's eyes softened. "I want you to come with me," he said calmly. There was a pleading look in his eyes.

Selah was speechless. This was not a good idea.

"I've been thinking about it, and this is the best time of year to go—in the summer, when there's plenty of food and time before cold weather sets on—you know—in case it takes a while for them to come get us."

"I can't believe you're telling me this," Selah said, in a daze. This evening was not turning out at all like she had thought it would. "So just exactly when were you planning to leave?"

Garrison took her hand and pretended to study the calluses she had from hoeing in the garden. Then he suddenly looked into her eyes. "Tonight. Now."

Selah looked at him in disbelief. How could he expect her to just pick up and leave everything and everyone behind? She thought of her mother and father and Miss Genevieve. The thought of leaving them and all she had known as home was unbearable. She was loved here. She was safe. Out there, who knew what would await them?

"I know I kind of sprung this on you, unexpected-like. And I really wish I could have given you time to adjust to the idea, but I couldn't take the chance of telling anyone before the fact," Garrison said. "Selah, I can't stay here anymore. I can't live not knowing what's out there. I want more out of life than this."

"I understand," Selah said, even though she didn't.

"So are you with me?" he asked.

The sun had completely disappeared behind the western ridge above the valley. As darkness crept closer, fireflies blinked on and off through the trees. There were thousands of them, sparkling like diamonds. Selah had spent many evenings outside, just watching them as she listened to the katydids sawing out their incessant chorus. It was little things like this that made her feel like she belonged in the valley. Firefly dances and the drone of cicadas and the sound of Bear Creek trickling over stones were all things which were woven into the fabric of who she was. She took a deep breath. "Garrison, I can't leave. This is my home. I don't want to leave, anymore than you want to stay."

Garrison's face fell, and then grew set like stone. "Then I guess this is goodbye," he said. He got up and picked up his things. Selah got up with him, her stomach twisted into knots. She wanted to stop him, but knew it was no use. Once he had an idea in his head, there was no changing his mind. He had been like that since they were children.

"I'm really going to miss you, you know?" he smiled bravely, and then turned and headed upstream in the direction of the boundary tree where he had led her the day he had stolen her blackberries. She watched him go in the deepening gloom, picking his way around rocks and fallen logs and scrubby witch-hazel until he was out of sight. Suddenly she grabbed her pack and her lantern and tore through the brush after him. "Garrison, wait!" she called. It was growing fairly dark, but she could see his lantern bobbing ahead through the trees. Selah was out of breath when she caught up to him. "Here, take this," she panted. "There's some biscuits and jelly and jerky and cheese, and a flask of water." She couldn't believe she was helping him make this terrible mistake. But there it was. He was her friend, and maybe he was right, after all. Maybe they would take him in. In the mean time, this would keep him from going hungry for a little while.

Garrison set down his gear and reached for her, pulling her into a bear hug. "Thanks, pal," he said, giving her one last squeeze before he let go. "Don't worry. Remember, 'Be anxious for nothing . . .'" he began the verse in Philippians that they had all been taught as children. And then, with that cavalier smile of his, he was once again headed out of sight, this time beyond her reach.

"…but in everything by prayer and supplication, with thanksgiving, let your requests be made known to God; and the peace of God, which surpasses all understanding, will guard your hearts and minds through Christ Jesus."[8] Tears welled up in Selah's eyes as she finished the quote. She stumbled through the rough footing of the creek bank toward home, with the knowledge that peace would elude her for a long time.

---

[8] Philippians 4:6-7 NKJV

10

"EXACTLY how long had you known about this?" Payton Hamby, who was normally a calm man with an even temper, was right up in Selah's face. Selah could see a vein begin to stand out on his forehead. The questioning had been going on for about an hour in the community hall. People had foregone their chores that morning when Asha and Jackson Merrit had learned of Garrison's departure and gone to the church to strike the "bell" that was made from a piece of pipe and a little hammer. Usually, the bell was rung for special occasions, like Christmas, Easter, the harvest picnic, or the birth of a child. Ringing it at other times signaled an emergency, and people dropped what they were doing and came running to find out how they could help.

Selah tried to choose her words carefully. She had always been honest. Telling the truth was easier than lying in the long run, because you didn't have to try to remember what story you had told to which person. But without actually admitting it to herself, she had been participating in the ongoing lie that everything was as it should be in the valley. Now she worried about how her story would sound– if it would make it seem as if her parents or Garrison's parents had not kept a tight enough rein on their children. She had given up worrying how *she* would look in all of this, knowing she already looked like a fool. But she certainly didn't want to make Garrison look like a villain, and she didn't want their parents to be blamed, either.

"It's been going on for several months, but–"

"Several *months!* And you never said anything to anyone?" Payton looked at her incredulously.

"I talked to God about it. But I didn't tell anyone else because nothing ever happened, and I thought Garrison might change his mind about wanting to leave here. I didn't want to get him in trouble."

"Get him in trouble? Do you have any idea how much trouble he may have brought on the whole community by leaving here? You know we aren't supposed to go beyond the boundaries. All of our protection rests on our compliance to that rule. You have been taught *that* since you were old enough to understand right from wrong. You are just as guilty as he is, by keeping your mouth shut all this time!" Payton's eyes were filled with something Selah had never seen in an elder before. It was fear. He was more afraid than angry, she realized.

But he couldn't be more afraid than she was, she reasoned. What would happen to Garrison? What would the State do if they found him? In all of their questioning, they had never mentioned anything about what might happen to *him*. They only seemed to be concerned about what would happen to themselves.

Selah had the sensation of being detached from her surroundings, as if she were a bystander watching the proceedings unfold. As she answered, she was surprised at how calm she sounded—how mature and reasonable. "If God has truly hidden us, then Garrison is the one we should be concerned about. They'll think he's crazy, talking about some community no one has ever seen, where no one has any serious illnesses and we all live without electricity and computers and smart phones and walk everywhere we go. They'll lock him away so he won't be able to harm anyone."

"Which is what we should have done, if we had only known about his little escapades beyond the boundaries." Payton, Selah noticed, had seemed to make the transition from fear to anger.

"What is this, the Salem witch trials?" said a quavering voice from the middle of the room. The crowd parted as Genevieve hobbled her way to the front of the church. Selah was grateful as her old friend caught her eye, and then turned to face the audience. "The boy was wrong to leave without telling anyone, but I'm not certain he was wrong to leave." She paused as a murmur arose from the crowd. She held up her hand in a plea for silence, then continued. "He knew the rules. Those many years ago, we were instructed to stay within the boundaries. But we were never given definite instructions as to the location of those boundaries. So we prayed about it. And, guided by the Holy Spirit and common sense, we placed those boundary markers where we felt led to place them. At the time of their marking, I believe those were the boundaries for our community. But who is to say those boundaries might not change over time?"

More murmuring from the crowd. Selah watched and it seemed to her that men and women she had known for years were changing. It wasn't a visible change. It was something deeper, like a shift in the current of the creek when you moved a big rock under the surface of the water. Their eyes were somehow different when they looked at Genevieve, and when Payton Hamby spoke again, he had a funny tone to his voice.

"Miss Genevieve, you've been standing up for a long time," he looked over at Seth Beardsley, who was standing nearby. "Seth, would you get her a drink of water?" he said, as he attempted to usher her away from the front.

But Genevieve would not be swept away. "The Great Commission," she said simply.

"Thank you, Miss Genevieve," Payton said firmly, and nudged her toward Seth.

Genevieve did not budge. "That's what Garrison mentioned the last time I spoke to him. I told him we had everything we need here. And he said, 'Everything except the ability to fulfill the Great Commission.' And he was right. We can pray for the outside world, but for three generations now, none of us has ever attempted to do the last thing that Jesus asked us to do before He left this earth. He said, 'Go ye into all the world and preach the gospel to every creature.'[9] Now, I know we were led here. But our guide never said we were to stay here forever.

---

[9] Mark 16:15 KJV

The way I see it, this little valley is like the ark was for Noah and his family. They didn't stay in it forever. It just kept them safe for a time. Maybe that time is over now. Maybe it's time we ventured out of the ark, because the floodwaters have receded, and the air can get pretty stale when you're cooped up with all those animals."

Selah bit her lip to hide a smile. Payton looked at Genevieve in shock at her apparent insult, but her straight face convinced him she meant nothing by it.

Some of the other board members of the church, who had been talking in low voices in a corner, now looked their direction. One of them, Clive Coffelt, came forward with a gentle smile at Genevieve. "Sis, why don't you come sit down for a while. It's hot in here, and I'll bet you're thirsty," he said.

"I'm not, but I bet this little gal is," Genevieve replied, as she gestured toward Selah. "She's been answering questions for over an hour."

There it was again, Selah noticed—the difference in their eyes as the board members looked at Genevieve. "Would someone run get Selah a drink of water?" Seth said calmly, his eyes still on Genevieve. If the old woman's shoes had sprouted roots and grown into the plank floor, Selah would not have been surprised. She seemed rooted there as stubbornly as any cedar tree clinging to a rocky hillside.

To Selah's chagrin, it was Sadie Beardsley who returned with a tin cup of water from the well out front. "Thanks," she said as she took it. Sadie looked at her with the same look of compassion she had given to a coon Selah had shown her in one of the traps she set by her garden. Selah was grateful for the sympathy, but she did not need anything to make her feel weak right now. After what Genevieve said, she was beginning to think Garrison was not so much in the wrong, after all. She wanted to be strong for him. She tried to imagine herself as a steel fortress. Her eyes were the windows that were sealed shut, and no amount of force would allow any emotions or tears to escape.

"My parents and your grandparents made the choice to come here," Genevieve was saying. "Every generation since then has stayed because they were told it was the right thing to do, because it was what we were told was necessary for us to keep safe. We have simply been following in the footsteps of those before us, who took a mighty leap of faith to leave everything they knew without even knowing where they were going." She looked around at the crowd and walked over to a stand used for communion trays where a large Bible was kept as a centerpiece. She opened up the Bible and shuffled through its pages. "It's just like chapter eleven of Hebrews. Why, if we lived back in those times, we would probably be mentioned in the 'Hall of Faith.' Just listen to this:

> By faith Abraham obeyed when he was called to go out to the place which he would receive as an inheritance. And he went out, not knowing where he was going. By faith he dwelt in the land of promise as *in* a foreign country, dwelling in tents with Isaac and Jacob, the heirs with him of the same promise; for he waited for the city which has foundations, whose builder and maker *is* God....These all died in faith, not having received the promises, but having seen them afar off were assured of them, embraced *them* and confessed that they were strangers and pilgrims on the earth. For those who say such things declare plainly that they seek a homeland. And truly if they had called to mind that *country* from which they had come out, they would have had opportunity to return. But now they desire a better, that is a heavenly *country*. Therefore God is not ashamed to be called their God, for He has prepared a city for them."[10]

Everyone was listening now. "But, folks, this is not *the* city. This is not *the* homeland. We're not home yet. And I know God protects His children in many ways. But sometimes He allows them to go through things so that they can grow, spiritually. And sometimes sacrifices are made for the good of the kingdom of God. There is nothing wrong with

---

[10] Hebrews 11:8-10 and 13-16 NKJV

being safe. But why do you think we were sent here in the first place? What was it that the Lord was trying to protect? Was it our physical bodies, or our spiritual state? 2 Corinthians 4:7 says 'But we have this treasure in earthen vessels, that the excellence of the power may be of God, and not of us.'[11] Is it right for us to hide this treasure? Did the people in the eleventh chapter of Hebrews hide it to protect themselves?" She began to read again.

> "Women received their dead raised to life again.
>
> Others were tortured, not accepting deliverance, that they might obtain a better resurrection. Still others had trial of mockings and scourgings, yes, and of chains and imprisonment. They were stoned, they were sawn in two, were tempted, were slain with the sword. They wandered about in sheepskins and goatskins, being destitute, afflicted, tormented—of whom the world was not worthy."[12]

That does not sound to me like a people who were so concerned with their own safety that they would not risk venturing out to bring their message to the world."

The crowd was silent. Suddenly the tears Selah had been holding back began spilling out and trickling down her cheeks.

"Thank you, Miss Genevieve," Payton Hamby said firmly. "You may sit down now." Several board members came forward to usher Genevieve down from the front. As Selah watched, she could tell they would never view her in the same way again. The doors of the library of knowledge that was Genevieve Gutierrez were being shut, and a lock labeled "senility" was being snapped into place. No matter the sharpness of the woman's mind, the men and women of the board had made their decision.

Suddenly Selah became conscious of singing. "This little light of mine, I'm gonna let it shine! This little light of mine, I'm gonna let it

---

[11] 2 Corinthians 4:7 NKJV
[12] Hebrews 11:35-38a NKJV

shine. This little light of mine, I'm gonna let it shine, let it shine, let it shine, let it shine!" sang Miss Genevieve as she went through the crowd and out the back door. Some of the younger children began to take up the song, as their parents tried to shush them.

The tears came harder for Selah. There was more discussion about the repercussions of Garrison's actions, but the questioning was over after that. The board released her to her parents with a strong recommendation not to leave her alone for the next few weeks.

11

Long after those weeks were over, Selah could not help feeling she was no longer trusted. The community believed in forgiving, but sometimes forgetting is another matter. As for the boundaries, there was talk of forming a patrol that would walk the outskirts of the valley daily to make certain there was no change and to keep on the lookout for Garrison.

Selah worried about Garrison's parents, and she wondered if he had given any thought as to how his leaving would affect them. For several days after his disappearance, people tried to reassure them that he would be back in a few days, when his food ran out. The Scoffields had endured all the attention with tight-lipped smiles and nods, but it was easy to see that Megan was barely holding things together, emotionally. And as the weeks dragged by, with still no sign of their son, it was difficult for members of the community to know what to say. Selah overheard many of the things which were meant to be a kindness, but came out sounding less than genuine. The Scoffields began to miss a Sunday service here and there, and the more gossipy members of the congregation began to talk. Miss Genevieve put a stop to that whenever she was around, but as soon as she left, people would begin to say things about her, as well.

"Well, bless her heart, she's just not all there anymore," said Gracie Ferrel, after one such incident. "I don't send my kids over to her anymore."

"No one does," shot Jannica Breedon. "Not after they advised against it."

"Who advised against it?" asked Selah, who had been picking up some chunks of dried mud someone had tracked in underneath a pew nearby.

The ladies jumped like a couple of vultures startled off of a carcass. Jannica glared. "What are you doing down there, Selah? You seem to be going to an awful lot of trouble to eavesdrop."

"I wasn't eavesdropping. I was just cleaning up some dirt. It seemed like a better thing to do than throwing it." Selah's cheeks burned as the two ladies' eyes opened wide and Gracie's mouth dropped open. It was the meanest thing she had ever said to an adult, and even though she knew it was true, she wished she had kept the thought to herself. She turned and left before they could say anything and ran to catch up with Miss Genevieve.

She found her outside in the churchyard, surrounded by a cluster of children reaching for the molasses candy chews she liked to hand out to them every Sunday. "Are you keeping up on your reading, Logan?" she asked a small boy with ginger colored hair and a mass of freckles. He wrinkled his nose at her, causing his freckles to bunch up.

"I don't like to read. It was more fun when you would read to us," he replied.

"Yeah," said a boy a little older, with chocolate skin and sparkling dark eyes. "I liked the stories about the wars. Not the Cyber Wars, but the old World Wars, when people actually shot at each other with real bullets and real guns. People back then had to be really brave."

"They have to be brave nowadays, too, Andrew. Just in different ways," said Miss Genevieve, her eyes following Paul and Megan Scoffield as they left for home.

"Miss Genevieve, can I talk to you for a second?" asked Selah.

Genevieve's face crinkled up into a smile. "Why, sure, gal. If it's alright with your folks. It seems I've been placed on the list of banned books."

"Well, actually, that's what I wanted to talk to you about," Selah replied. "But not here. Could we go to your house? I haven't been over in a while because Mom and Dad have been keeping me busy at home. But they never said anything to me about not going to visit you." Asha and Jackson Merrit had always held Genevieve in the highest regard and had sent Selah over often to help her around her place. She couldn't imagine them doing anything to hurt her.

"Why don't you come over after you eat dinner with your folks," she said. "If it's alright, of course," she added quickly. She pressed a bag of the molasses chews into Selah's hand and made her promise to give some to her parents.

It pained Selah to see her old friend exercising so much caution to avoid offending anyone. Genevieve, who had been treated as a pillar of the community, was now being swept into a corner. Selah had seen it happen before to older people who really were beginning to lose their cognitive abilities. But Genevieve was perfectly fine, except for an occasional lapse of memory about which stories she had told to which people. And most of the time, Selah suspected she really knew she had told them before, but liked the telling so much that she just kept going. The ruse that Genevieve was "losing it" was a story cooked up, she was sure, by Payton Hamby and some of the other board members.

12

Aᴼᴛᴇʀ Sunday dinner, Selah asked if she could go see Genevieve. Asha and Jackson exchanged glances. "I just want her to know she still has a friend in this valley," Selah pleaded. "Did you know some of the parents have been advised against sending their kids over to her house?"

"Yes," said Jackson. "They told us it would be best if we didn't teach our kids as much about the Old Country. And that is Genevieve's specialty. She's the only one who is still alive who has actually been there. As much as she loves teaching, can you imagine her leaving out whole chunks of history?"

"Or not telling stories about the Old Country?" Asha added.

"It's part of who she is," Selah agreed. "Which is why I think it's so unfair."

Jackson got up from the table to scrape the sweet pepper seeds from his plate into the compost bucket. "But Garrison did spend a lot of time asking her for information about it, from what they found out after talking to her. They think her enthusiasm for the subject was a bad influence on him."

"Little kids have been going over to her house to listen to stories for years, and now that one of them leaves, they go and blame it on her!" Selah fumed.

"I know it isn't right, but people are scared right now," Asha tried to explain. "Obviously Garrison made his own choices. Remember, we grew up listening to her stories, too, and we're still here."

Jackson gathered up the rest of their plates. "You don't have to try to convince us, Selah. Genevieve does need a friend. That's why I took a load of wood over to her for her cookstove just a few days ago, to let her know we weren't going to treat her any differently. Which reminds me, she's going to need it split a little smaller, if you don't mind."

Selah jumped up and hugged them both. She had never been so proud of them before. "I know I can split it some other day besides Sunday, but I want to go over there now. I told her I would, if it was alright with you."

"Take her over a piece of cobbler. Lord knows I don't need anymore of it," Asha said as she scooped some into a bowl.

Selah put the bowl of cobbler in a lunch pail and was out the door in a matter of seconds. The trip to Genevieve's usually took her twenty minutes, but today, it took ten. Selah was surprised the old woman wasn't out on the porch enjoying the breeze of the warm summer day. When Selah knocked on the door, a voice from inside said, "Come in, Selah. It's a little too hard for me to get to the door right now."

Upon entering, she could see that Genevieve had pulled out several tables she used to use to teach crafts to the younger children. They were arranged in a U shape, and Genevieve was standing in the middle. Spread out on the tables were pages of handwritten notes and drawings of old photos from history books and magazines. A map of the state of Missouri was unfolded on one table. Genevieve looked up from her project and grinned. "Come in, come in. Come see what I've been doing with all this time I have on my hands now."

"Mom sent over some cobbler."

"Oh, God bless her. She's such a thoughtful little thing," Genevieve said.

"What is all this?" Selah asked. Some of the drawings she recognized, but many were faces of people whom she had never seen before. "Who are these people in the drawings?"

"I suppose you wonder why I would waste good paper on something like this," Genevieve began. Paper was a rare commodity in the valley.

When people had used every last inch of a piece of it and it had been erased to the point of no longer being usable, they put the scrap into the paper bin in the community hall until enough was collected for recycling. Most of the paper Selah had seen was the lumpy, dingy, recycled kind. But this paper was the good stuff. Some of it had never been used before.

"These are the faces of the people I see in my dreams. I have been seeing them in my head for years, but it's only now that I've put them down on paper." All the children in the community knew that Genevieve could draw well. They were always begging her to draw animals from the Old Country. This is the first time Selah had seen her drawings of people, and they were good. Each of them looked as if they were caught in the middle of saying something, and she mentioned this to Genevieve.

"They *are* saying something," she replied. "These people are all from the Old Country, but not from when I lived there. In the dreams, these are the ones who live there now, and they are all asking me the same question they have been asking me for years."

"What are they asking?" Selah said, her interest piqued. Most of Selah's dreams were boring ones that involved a mishmash of the events of the previous day, or an occasional old memory which was especially vivid. She had never had a dream about someone she had never met before, from a place she had never been before. It sounded fascinating.

"They're saying, 'When are you coming? When are you coming?'" Genevieve said, and suddenly began to cry.

Selah had never seen her look so vulnerable. She reached out and touched the knobby hand and Genevieve squeezed hers in return. "Selah, I am called to be a missionary. I've known it for years. But it didn't make sense. Not with the rules our community has about leaving."

Selah tried to soak in the gravity of what had just been said. Genevieve, who for years had taught children the dangers of the Old Country and the importance of staying within the boundaries, had been called by God to leave the valley and take the gospel back to the Old Country.

"But the people there don't want anything to do with it," Selah said. "Why would God ask you to leave the place He had led you to years before, only to ask you to leave it and to go and take the gospel back to a place where the government was doing everything in its power to snuff it out or make it seem like a fairytale?"

"Did you just hear what you said, Honey?" Genevieve asked. "Who would need the message more than a people who were denied access to it?" She shuffled through the pages of handwritten notes. "It's all here. Every message I ever dreamt I preached. Here's one that begins in the very beginning—at creation. Here's one that explains who Jesus is and why He had to die—and that He rose again. This is one that simply goes into depth about God's love." There were at least twenty different sermons, most of them short and to the point, but some of them going into picturesque detail. All of them relied heavily upon scriptures, with the references included.

Selah frowned. "How long have you known you were supposed to be a missionary?"

Genevieve walked over and sat in her chair. "Since Sunday, August 17, 2052." She settled deeper into the lumpy cushion and seemed to stare back into time. "It was one of those extremely hot summers, the kind where the air is so heavy it feels like you're smothering under a blanket. I was 30 years old—it had been three years since Carlos had the accident. My friends were down at Bear Creek that afternoon, playing with their children and trying to stay cool. Carlos and I had tried to have children, and I used to really let it bother me that God didn't give us any. Now I wonder if it was better He didn't, since Carlos passed away. Anyway, I just didn't feel like going down to the creek with them. It wasn't that I was feeling sorry for myself; but sometimes, being around all those children made me ache inside for one of my own. Instead, I went to a quiet place on a shady gravel bar down by the river and stuck my feet in the water. It felt so good, I laid back and put my sun hat over my eyes.

"I was just about to drift off to sleep when I had this dream, except that I wasn't asleep yet. I don't know if you would call it a vision or not, but I saw all these images in my mind. It wasn't a daydream, because I had no control over it. I saw people's faces, and I could feel what they were feeling. They were all in the hot sun, in a dry, dusty place. Face after face passed by, all looking at me with parched lips and dry throats. I wondered how they were moving by me when they all seemed to be standing still; and then I suddenly realized I was walking past them. One little boy in the line of faces stood out to me. He held out his hands and tried to ask for water, but his throat was so dry he couldn't say anything. I wondered why he was asking me for water, and then I realized I was carrying a jug of it. I had been walking by all those poor people with life in my hands. So I stopped to try to give the people some of the water, even though it looked like so little among so many, when I saw that there was a fence between us. It discouraged me at first, but after looking around, I saw there was a gate. I hurried over to the gate and was about to open it when all of the sudden there it was right on the gate—the mark."

"A boundary marker?" Selah interrupted.

"Yes, the circled X. I hesitated, and said in my heart, 'Lord, I'm not supposed to go past this mark.' And plain as you are speaking to me, I heard a voice say, 'Go ye into all the world, and preach my gospel to every creature.' After that, I opened the gate and walked through it. The people gathered all around me from everywhere, and I began to give them the water. The wonderful thing was, as many people as there were, and as small as the jug was, it never ran out. It satisfied them completely, and they ran to get their own jugs to fill them from mine. While all this was happening, I felt a great joy and peace such as I had never experienced, and have never again felt since that time. I knew in that moment I was doing what I had been born to do." Genevieve fell silent, her eyes resting on the sketches of the faces.

Selah didn't know what to say. What would it be like to know you were born to do something *that* important, something of that magnitude, and not to be able to carry it out because it went against all the rules you had been taught would keep your community safe? She imagined the guilt and frustration Genevieve must feel. "But you couldn't leave and endanger the community," Selah reasoned. "That would have been irresponsible. Even if you had left, how would you have known where to go?"

"God wouldn't have asked someone to leave here without providing His continuing protection for those who stayed," Genevieve said. "As for knowing where to go, how did the apostle Paul decide where to go next?"

Selah thought about it. "He prayed. Sometimes he wanted to go certain places and God's Spirit wouldn't let him. One time, he had a dream about people in a specific place asking him to come," she looked meaningfully at Genevieve, "much like the dream you had."

"If God really called me, then all I would have to do is do all I could to prepare, then step out in faith. He would have provided the means, the direction, the protection, and the words to say. But I lacked the courage. I was afraid of the unknown and afraid of the fear and unrest it would create in the community. So I played it safe. I began to tell myself I had the vision because I was merely supposed to pray for the people in the outside world—to intercede on their behalf. And I did. I prayed for their hearts to be opened to the good news of Jesus Christ. I prayed for their eyes to be opened to the truth. I am certain that this is *part* of what I was supposed to do. But the main thing—the actual sharing of the gospel face to face with a world saturated in lies—remains undone. I stayed in my little cocoon of safety while people I was supposed to reach died without the Living Water I was supposed to bring to them. And now, instead of their cries being 'When are you coming?' they are cries of 'Why didn't you come?' reaching up from the flames of hell." Genevieve's eyes bore into the sketches and with a sweep of her hand she scattered them across the floor. "It all boiled down to my own selfish desire to stay safely where I thought I belonged, to keep the status quo, and my refusal to trust the God who called me to walk into the unknown. But none of that matters anymore. If there ever *was* any risk to us from someone leaving, it is irrelevant now, because the community has already been compromised by Garrison's departure. And now, I know what I must do." Genevieve drew herself to her full height, which wasn't much more than five feet. But somehow in that moment, she seemed taller than Payton Hamby.

"I am going out there, Selah. And I am asking you to help me."

Selah's mouth dropped open. "But, uh, I –"

"Oh, I don't mean to come with me, child. I just mean I need help to get ready to leave. There is a lot of preparation that needs to be made. I can't do it alone."

Selah looked at Genevieve's determined expression and wondered if her friend realized how ridiculous her proposal sounded. With renewed attention to detail, she observed Genevieve's bony frame. The print dress was draped over her body as if she were a scarecrow without enough straw to stuff it. She thought of the dress catching on brambles, the spindly legs slipping on slick rocks. If Selah had been worried about Garrison, she was terrified for Miss Genevieve. It was preposterous. She was an old woman who could barely carry her own firewood anymore.

Selah suddenly realized Genevieve was staring back at her. "I know what you're thinking," she declared. "You're thinking I'm too old and that I'll never be able to make the journey. But I tell you, nothing is impossible with God."[13] The gray eyes sparked with a fiery determination.

Selah tried to choose her words carefully. "I know nothing is impossible to those who believe,[14] but how do you know God still wants you to do this? What if there was a window of opportunity, and it is no longer opened? Do you want to do this because you think it is what God wants, or are you doing it out of a sense of guilt?"

Genevieve's face fell. Selah hated the way the words had come out, even though she felt she needed to say them. She took her friend's hand

---

[13] See Luke 1:37
[14] See Mark 9:23

and stooped slightly so she could look into the downcast eyes. "You have often warned me that people sometimes mistake their own emotions for the leading of the Holy Spirit. I just want you to really think this through…to make sure it's God's agenda, and not yours."

Genevieve seemed momentarily deflated, but then her eyes sparked again. "If I'm not supposed to go, then why do I keep having the dreams? Why do the people keep asking me to come? I feel restless, like I'm just about to go on a magnificent journey. For years, I've had this message burning inside of me, and everybody here has already heard it. I want to reach the lost—those who have *never* heard."

"In that case, a little more soul searching and prayer shouldn't change your resolve. Why don't you do what you always tell *me* to do—pray on it and sleep on it, before you do anything," Selah pleaded.

"Well, I wasn't going to jump out of bed and hit the road tomorrow morning," Genevieve chuckled. "Like I said, I need to prepare, and I need help preparing. But you're right. The biggest preparation we make should always be in prayer."

Selah sighed in relief. Some people would have simply humored the old woman and even encouraged her, never dreaming she was doing anything more than telling fantastical stories and passing the time with an elaborate daydream. But Selah knew Miss Genevieve was serious and felt strongly about leaving; and usually when she felt strongly about things, it was next to impossible to change her mind about them. She felt certain if Genevieve prayed about it in earnest, really seeking God's will, then she wouldn't attempt it. After all, how could God expect one so old to do something so rigorous and dangerous?

Miss Genevieve's gaze shifted to the window and beyond to the rusty orange leaves of the oak trees surrounding her home. "Those old white oak trees," she mused. "Every other tree has just about dropped all their leaves, and they just keep hanging on." She turned to Selah with a look of wonderment. "Have you ever noticed that long into the winter, they still have their leaves? In fact, the stubborn things hang on until the new leaves push them out."

Thinking back, Selah remembered walking through a moonlit night in snow that muffled every sound and being startled by the clattering of brittle oak leaves caught in a puff of wind. "I guess I never gave it much thought, but they do seem to keep them into the winter. I didn't realize they didn't drop them until spring, though." She wondered what this had to do with going on a missionary journey. Maybe Miss Genevieve was just trying to change the subject.

"*Marcescent.*"

"What?" Sometimes Selah had difficulty keeping up with Genevieve's train of thought. It was as though the old woman's train ran on a different track than everyone else's. Sometimes the track ran parallel to popular thought, and sometimes it chugged merrily up difficult mountain passes while Selah's train ran sluggishly through the boggy valleys of self pity or self righteousness. But this was one of those times when Genevieve's tracks veered off into a tunnel. Selah knew it would come out somewhere, but it would be a while before the light dawned on her comprehension. "I'm afraid I don't follow you," Selah admitted.

"Marcescence is the quality some trees have of retaining their leaves until spring, when the new growth pushes them out," Miss Genevieve said matter-of-factly.

"Oh."

The wrinkled face beamed as Genevieve warmed to her subject. "There are several theories of why they do this. When leaves fall to the forest floor, they provide a source of nutrients to the surrounding vegetation as they decompose. But if they fall right before winter, much of these nutrients just leech away when everything is in a state of dormancy. If they wait until spring to fall, then the nutrients are available for the trees when they need it." She paused to scratch a patch of dry skin on her forehead. "And there is another theory that they fall in the spring to hide young, sprouting saplings from the mouths of hungry deer." She stopped and suddenly chuckled. "Now, why did I think of that?"

Selah couldn't answer. This train was still in the tunnel. Then she brightened. "Maybe God put it into your head because He wants you to wait until spring to start your journey."

"Nice try, Honey," Miss Genevieve crowed. "Now, you'd best get back home. I won't have any suspicion aroused about you being a rebellious little spitfire. Sometimes they can be so ridiculous, God love 'em." She always added the "God love 'em" part when she couldn't find anything nice to say and realized she had just said something derogatory about someone.

13

THE week following their conversation, Genevieve devoted herself to praying and fasting to seek God's will about her decision to leave. She had asked Selah if she would pray about it, as well. Selah feared Genevieve was only asking the Lord the proper time she should leave, and not even bothering to ask if she should even leave, at all. Normally, her old friend was careful to search out what she felt was the right thing to do in God's eyes through scripture, prayer, and fasting food. But Selah was concerned the dreams had troubled her for so long that she might be allowing her emotions to color her perceptions of the way God's Spirit was trying to lead her. So she was dedicated to seeking God with her friend on this matter.

Although Genevieve had not asked her to do so, Selah also decided to fast every other day of that week. She didn't have much experience with fasting, but there were enough references to it in the Bible in instances where people were either trying to discern the will of God or seeking Him for help that she believed there must be something to it. She remembered a time when she was around eight years old when there had been a long dry spell during the growing season. The elders of the church had called a fast for those who were willing. She had thought it strange that her parents fixed meals for her but would refrain from eating anything, themselves. As a little girl, she hadn't understood and had tried to get them to eat. Asha had smiled and said, "We just aren't eating right now. Instead, we're going to use the time we would have spent eating to ask God to send us the rain we need for the crops."

Selah had scrunched her eyebrows together thoughtfully, trying to understand the logic behind it all. "Oh, I get it!" she said suddenly. "If you stop eating, God will see how hungry you are, and will send rain so the garden will grow and we won't starve."

Jackson smiled gently. "Not exactly. Jesus said that the Father knows our needs even before we ask."

"Then why do we even ask for anything?" Selah wondered.

"Why do you ask *me* for things?" Jackson countered.

"Because you're my dad, and you can get me what I ask for." Selah answered.

"Do you always get everything you need?"

Selah thought awhile before answering. "You never gave me the rabbit I asked for on my birthday."

Jackson grinned. The rabbit was a point of contention. "I didn't ask if I gave you everything you *wanted*. I asked if I gave you everything you *needed*. Did you fall over dead because I didn't give you a rabbit?"

Selah glared. "Almost."

Jackson couldn't keep from laughing. "What are you going to get instead of a rabbit?"

Selah jumped up and down. "Daisy's next heifer calf!"

"You are more excited about that calf than I've ever seen you excited about any rabbit."

"That's because I've always wanted a milk cow, ever since the Scoffield's have been letting me help milk Daisy."

"Then why didn't you ask for a calf in the first place?" Jackson continued.

"Because I never even dreamed I could own a calf! A calf is a *huge* present. I asked for a rabbit because I thought I would have more of a chance of getting one," Selah explained.

"I guess we really didn't need a milk cow, because we could just keep trading our produce for milk. But I knew you really wanted one. And since everything around here has to earn its keep, I didn't figure it would be very fun for you when it came time to eat the rabbits. So

I made arrangements with Paul Scoffield to get Daisy's next calf. That way we can always have our own milk, and we can butcher her calves or trade them if we want," Jackson told her.

"Oh, Daddy, that's so smart!" Selah exclaimed. "I never would have thought about all of that. I asked for something small and furry and cute that would have made me feel bad when we had to kill it. You gave me something big that gives us milk and a lot more meat, and keeps on giving it. I'm glad you didn't give me what I wanted. You knew the best thing."

"Exactly, Selah. And that's just how our heavenly Father is with us. We ask Him for things, even though He already knows what we need. But we still ask Him, because He's our Father. He knows what we need better than we do."

"But I didn't have to stop eating for you to give me a calf."

Jackson sighed. "I'm not certain you'll understand this yet, Selah, but fasting doesn't change God. It changes *us*. It helps us see things more clearly. It humbles us, so we can get our own selfish desires out of the way and see what is important to God. It helps us to get our prayers in line with what God wants to do, and it gets us ready to receive the answer."

Selah twisted her mouth around in a thoughtful expression. "Like you say, maybe I'll understand someday, Daddy."

And now, years later, Selah wondered if she was finally getting ready to understand the difference fasting could make. She remembered that the community had finally received a good rain after most of the crops had failed. It had actually come when most people had decided to trust the Lord and thank Him and praise Him even if He didn't send any rain. The moisture that did fall that year came at a time to help produce a bumper crop of persimmons and wild grapes and a late crop of beans. The persimmons brought in a larger amount of deer than was normal in the valley, so that meat was in abundance. What wasn't made into jerky or summer sausage was canned to preserve it in the warmer weather. Meat from deer harvested during the colder months was pre-served with the snows and ice of winter. And although a few people joked about being tired of persimmon preserves and persimmon bread and the tartness of wild grape juice, few could deny that the Lord had provided in a way no one had expected.

14

SELAH didn't tell anyone except her parents that she was fasting. She didn't want them waiting on her to come to the table. So that week, if it was a day when she was fasting, she would go to her room or out into the woods during mealtime and ask the Lord for guidance for Miss Genevieve. As the prayer time wore on, she found other things to pray about. Garrison always came to mind. She prayed for his safety and a change of his heart. Part of her had always thought they might get married someday, so she prayed about God's will for her life in that area, as well.

After the second prayer session, Selah was sure she was doing something wrong. She was having such a hard time staying focused. Sometimes thoughts came into her mind, and she had no idea how she ever could have thought them. At one point, she started thinking about how much she would really like to see Payton Hamby trampled by his own bull. She found herself smiling as she daydreamed about the bull tossing him up into the air and his body landing on the hard dirt with a thud. She was enjoying the sight in her mind of the bull's hooves stomping him as he tried to crawl away, when suddenly she became aware that she was daydreaming. Selah shook her head in disbelief. She was fasting—doing something really spiritual. So why should she be having hateful thoughts about Payton Hamby? If anything, she should be having daydreams about baking a pie and taking it to him and his wife, and everyone forgiving each other and eating pie together. Where did these other thoughts come from? She determined in her heart to refocus, and began to pray. It almost seemed like she was talking to a brick wall.

So many times throughout her life, Selah had sensed God's presence. Now, it was as if a door had been closed between her and heaven, and there was no communication either way. Surely this couldn't be right. Fasting was supposed to have the opposite effect.

Then the next day came, a non-fasting day, and she was amazed at how different things were. Her prayer time was dynamic. She was excited about talking to Jesus. His presence seemed so near to her. It was the most wonderful time she had ever spent with the Lord. She was filled with anticipation when she lay down for the night, because the next day was a day of fasting. The breakthrough she had made today would surely carry over into tomorrow.

But that day was even worse than the first day. She was in her room, sitting on her bed and reading her Bible, when the scene flashed through her mind—it was from the day Garrison brought her back the pail of stolen blackberries. He set the bucket down and leaned closer to her. She could feel his breath on her face. His lips brushed against her cheek, and her heart began to pound wildly. Suddenly, his arms were wrapped around her waist, and she was being pulled so close that his chest was pressed up against hers. His hazel eyes looked deeply into hers, and he was just about to say something, when a crow in the tree right outside her bedroom window let loose with a barrage of caws that shocked her back into reality. What was happening? She had been so sure this was the day she would really hear from God, and she found herself daydreaming about Garrison!

Selah got up from the bed and went into the kitchen where Jackson and Asha were finishing the noon meal. "I'd really like to go see Miss Genevieve, if it's alright," she said. "I need to ask her some questions about...about fasting."

"That's fine," said Asha. "I know you're caught up on your chores."

"Is there anything you'd like to ask us?" Jackson offered.

Selah hesitated. How could she tell her parents the kinds of things that had been going through her head? She was ashamed and embarrassed to even mention them. Somehow, she thought it might be less embarrassing with Miss Genevieve. "Maybe later," she said. "I'm just having a little trouble focusing, and I thought maybe she would understand."

"Oh, that's normal with fasting," Asha said quickly. "But you learn to fight through it."

Selah hesitated. Maybe her parents would understand after all. But she couldn't bring herself to talk about it with them. Not focusing was one thing. Having violent and suggestive daydreams when you were supposed to be praying was another thing, altogether. She smiled meekly and excused herself.

Miss Genevieve grinned from ear to ear when she saw Selah coming down the path. "My dear, how good it is to see you!" she exclaimed. "And right around lunch time, too. There are some nice apples and cheese in the cellar, if you haven't eaten yet."

"Well, I'm not eating, actually," Selah said.

"Oh. You already ate."

Selah shifted her weight and looked down uncomfortably. "No, I'm fasting. I know you're not supposed to tell anyone when you're doing it, but I've never done it before, and I think I'm doing something wrong. I could use your advice."

"Well, have a seat here on the porch, child. It's a nice day, for November. Might as well enjoy it when we have it." Miss Genevieve eased herself back into her rocking chair and motioned for Selah to sit down on an oaken bench across from her. "So you think you're doing it wrong, eh?" she asked, once they were settled. "And what makes you think that?"

"Well, my mom and dad said it was normal to have trouble focusing when you pray during fasting, but it's more than that. I keep having these thoughts go through my head while I'm trying to pray. I don't even know where they come from! They're violent, and...I had this one about Payton Hamby getting trampled by a bull, and then there was this one about Garrison that...." Selah stopped short. She couldn't bring herself to say it. "Well, anyway, it's not stuff I ever think about on purpose. And it just started happening when I was fasting. The *weird* thing was the day *after* I fasted for the first time, I had the most wonderful prayer time, ever! But the days I *do* fast, it seems like I can't feel God's presence, and I don't get anything out of my Bible reading. I have these horrible daydreams. I've got to be doing something wrong."

Selah looked over at Miss Genevieve to find the woman smiling at her knowingly. "Welcome to spiritual warfare, Honey. And it only gets more intense from here."

"You mean this is normal?" Selah asked incredulously.

"Yes, indeed."

"But I've never had this problem before," Selah protested.

"You've never gone this far out onto the battlefield before. You've only stayed in friendly territory. Now you're advancing into enemy lines. And guess who doesn't like that?" Miss Genevieve asked with an intense gaze.

"The devil?" Selah was confused. "But all I'm doing is praying. It's not like I'm snatching souls from the pits of Hell and dragging them back to safety."

"Oh, really? What makes you so sure? How can you know for certain the effects your prayers have?" Miss Genevieve was leaning on the edge of her seat, and her eyes were as fierce as any warrior's. "Selah, up until now, you've been playing defense. Now you're on the offense. That changes things."

Selah thought about the basketball games she had played in Seth Beardsley's barnyard. They had a homemade basketball hoop on the side of their barn, and there was quite a competition there at one time. The team that didn't go after the ball and just tried to keep the other team from making any baskets rarely won. If you wanted to win, you had to steal the ball and go for the basket. But sometimes that meant getting knocked around a little.

"You know what I like to do when Satan tries to put those thoughts in my mind?" Miss Genevieve said with a wry grin. "I like to quote him scripture. Sometimes I put it in first person, so it makes it really personal."

"What scriptures do you use?" Selah asked.

"Well, 2 Corinthians 12:9 is a good one. It says *'And he said unto me, My grace is sufficient for thee: for my strength is made perfect in weakness. Most gladly therefore will I rather glory in my infirmities, that the power of Christ may rest upon me.'*[15] So I change it to first person tense, like this: *'His grace is sufficient for me, for his strength is made perfect in weakness.'* Then I say, 'So, devil, you may as well know the weak spot you're attacking in me right now is an area I have turned over to Jesus. I know I'm weak in that area. That's why Jesus is fighting for me there. Just thought you might like to know.' Then I do something the devil really hates." Genevieve grinned like a possum.

"What's that?" Selah asked, intrigued.

"I just start to praise the Lord. I tell Jesus how wonderful He is. And every time Satan puts a mean thought in my head about someone, I make a decision not to dwell on that thought. Instead, I replace the thought by saying something wonderful about Jesus. That makes the devil so mad, he doesn't usually stick around for long. Then Jesus and I can have a wonderful prayer time together."

Selah thought for a moment about what Genevieve was saying. "So, when the devil comes against you in your prayer time, you use God's Word and a time of praise to fight him."

"That's right, Honey. Praise and the spoken Word of God are two of the most powerful weapons we have against the enemy. You know *that* from Ephesians 6:10-18. The armor of God. We've got to put it *all* on to be able to stand against the wiles of the devil.

"I didn't know you were going to fast with me, or I would have warned you about some of this stuff. We are wrestling against the rulers of the darkness of this world and against spiritual wickedness in high places. In order to fight these things, we have to wear truth and

---

[15] 2 Corinthians 12:9 KJV

righteousness like a garment. We have to shield ourselves with faith and remind ourselves that we've been redeemed—we have the helmet of salvation. And of course, the only offensive weapon mentioned in that passage, besides prayer, is the sword of the Spirit, which is the Word of God."

Selah listened thoughtfully and went over the scripture again in her mind. She liked the New Living Translation, and had memorized it in this version:

> Stand your ground, putting on the belt of truth and the body armor of God's righteousness. For shoes, put on the peace that comes from the Good News so that you will be fully prepared. In addition to all of these, hold up the shield of faith to stop the fiery arrows of the devil. Put on salvation as your helmet, and take the sword of the Spirit, which is the word of God. Pray in the spirit at all times and on every occasion. Stay alert and be persistent in your prayers for all believers everywhere.[16]

"But it doesn't say anything about praise," Selah said after thinking it over.

"No, it doesn't," agreed Miss Genevieve. She leaned forward until her rocking chair tipped her onto the porch and she was on her feet, toddling into the trailer. She returned momentarily with a Bible.

"Do you remember the story of Jehoshaphat and the army of Moab?" she asked.

"I remember the name Jehoshaphat, but I don't remember anything he did," Selah admitted.

"Jehoshaphat was the king of Judah. Someone brought word that the army of Moab and the Ammonites and some others were coming to do battle against them. So Jehoshaphat 'set himself to seek the Lord, and proclaimed a fast throughout all Judah.'[17] Then when all of Judah

---

[16] Ephesians 6:14-18 NLT
[17] 2 Chronicles 20:3 KJV

had gathered together, he prayed. He affirmed his belief that God was in control of all the nations, and that God had said He would protect His people. He admitted their weakness against such a mighty army, and he even admitted they didn't know what to do. But—" and at this, Genevieve held up her crooked index finger and opened her eyes wide for emphasis, "he said, 'Our eyes are on Thee.' And that was exactly the right attitude to have. He came to God humbly, admitting his weakness and telling God they knew that the Lord was their only hope. And in their weakness, God was able to show His strength."

"What happened?" Selah urged.

"Basically, God told them not to be afraid. He told them to go down to the battlefield, even though they wouldn't need to do any fighting, 'for the battle is not yours, but God's.'[18] So that's what they did. They got up early in the morning, and as they went, Jehoshaphat reminded them to believe the word of the Lord. Then he got together a big choir to go out in front of the army."

"What? A choir? Why would he do that?" Selah asked. Then she grinned. "You're just kidding me, to see if I know anything about this story. You just threw that in."

But Miss Genevieve didn't crack a smile. "If you don't believe me, read it for yourself. He sent out a choir in front of the army. Their job was to praise the Lord for His beauty and His mercy. Now, I want you to sit here and read the rest of it, so you can see for yourself that I'm not making it up." Genevieve passed the worn-out King James Version of the Bible over to Selah. It wasn't the easiest version to read, but she could understand it. And she could barely believe what she was reading. As soon as the choir began to sing, before they even arrived on the battlefield, the Lord set up "ambushments" against the foreign armies. The different factions of the army began to fight against their allies and utterly destroyed each other. By the time the army of Judah arrived at the battlefield, it was all over. Not a soldier was left alive. There was

---

[18] 2 Chronicles 20:15 KJV

so much plunder, it took Jehoshaphat and his people three days to cart away the spoils of the enemy army.

Selah looked up from her reading and imagined the scene from beginning to end: the enemy threat, the frightened king, the fast and the plea for deliverance. And then the words, "Don't be afraid. The battle isn't yours, but God's. You don't need to fight in this battle. Stand still, and see the salvation of the Lord." The army assembled, and as their journey began and the choir began to sing, Selah imagined herself as one of the singers. Would her voice have quavered in fear, or would she have belted out the notes like a volley of arrows? The scene continued in her mind, with the choir advancing and the army in tow. Suddenly the scene shifted to the battlefield. As the choir sang, the three nations making up the army began to be suspicious of their allies. Distrust and tension mounted, until with a cry of fear, one soldier lunged at another with his sword, slashing out and cutting down one of his former allies. Mass hysteria broke out as soldiers fought against each other with spear and sword until not a single one remained alive. Then the army of Jehoshaphat made their entrance. In shock they looked out over the valley of dead bodies below. The words echoed through the wind that swept over the battlefield: "The battle is not yours, but God's."

Selah felt something rising up inside of her. It made her feel like hopping right off the porch and running as far as her feet could take her. She jumped up from her bench and whirled around to Miss Genevieve. "Who can stand a chance against someone who is fighting for the Lord, if the Lord is fighting for him?" she said, her eyes wide with wonder.

"If God be for us, who can be against us?"[19] quoted Miss Genevieve. Then she took out a little pad of notebook paper and a pencil stub which she kept in the pocket of her dress and began to write. When she was finished, she ripped out the page and handed it to Selah. "These are some scriptures you may find helpful this week, and anytime you face opposition from the enemy, for that matter."

---

[19] See Romans 8:31 KJV

Selah took the page and slipped it into her pants pocket. "Thanks, Miss Genevieve," she said gratefully. The next time she encountered spiritual warfare, she would be ready. She turned to go and had reached the path through the overgrown yard when Genevieve called out to her.

"Selah! It's best if you memorize those passages, so you'll have them at a moment's notice. You won't always have a Bible beside you when the enemy attacks. Having them in your memory is like always carrying a drawn sword—you'll be ready for anything."

"I understand," Selah answered, and as she headed toward home, she looked through her mental files for all the scriptures she knew by memory to see what kind of an arsenal was already at her disposal. With the wonder of the story of Jehoshaphat's army coursing through her body like adrenaline, she sang songs of praise all the way home.

Part II

Parakletos

15

GARRISON shifted the weight of the backpack to a better position. With a lantern in one hand and the addition of Selah's pack in the other, he was not going at a very quick pace. He wanted to be miles away from the boundary by daybreak. Not that anyone would follow him. He imagined there would be a group of them at the boundary when they found out, calling for him to come back. Well, they could yell all they wanted to. He wasn't turning around. It was just the thought of the sound of his mom and dad's voices calling that made him want to increase his speed—he didn't want anything to melt his resolve.

Climbing up the wooded slopes of the valley was difficult enough in the daylight, even when unencumbered by heavy packs. At night, the green briar vines that hung at varying levels acted like God's own trip wires…a last ditch effort to keep him there. Garrison smirked at the thought. As if God cared—if He even existed, that is. Suddenly Garrison felt almost sick to his stomach. He wasn't sure he had ever admitted that suspicion to himself. He had prayed when he was little, but now that he was older, he wasn't sure why anyone prayed. What was the point of talking to someone you couldn't even prove existed, who never answered back? It was basically like talking to yourself, he had decided. Everyone else in the community had seemed so sure about their relationship with God, almost as if He were an old friend.

"Have you ever asked Jesus into your heart, Gary?" he could hear the voice of his Sunday school teacher asking him as she blocked his view to the window with her face.

"No. Why?" he had answered, irritated she had interrupted his daydream and called him by the nickname he couldn't stand.

"Well, because He loves you. God loves you so much, He sent Jesus to die to pay the price for your sins. Then Jesus rose again—He came back to life—because He won the victory over death. He did all of this so we could become God's friends and live with Him forever."

Garrison had thought this over before. It sounded fishy to him. "Why didn't God send someone else? Was Jesus bad?"

Miss Madison smiled. "No, not at all. He was the only one who lived a perfect life. He was the only one who could have been a sacrifice for us, because He was perfect. If someone loves you that much, don't you think you could make room for Him in your heart?" she continued.

Garrison considered it. "You know, I really don't think there's much room in there. If Jesus is God's son, He could pick any place to live. Why would He want to live in some nasty old heart?" he asked, remembering butchering day, and how hearts always had all those strange looking arteries coming out of them.

"But Jesus can make even the nastiest of hearts white as snow," the teacher was explaining earnestly.

"Does He use bleach? We don't have any bleach here."

"No. His *blood* is what makes us clean. His perfect blood washes away all of our sins," she was explaining.

Garrison looked at her in disgust. Even as young as he was, he knew the realities of butchering day. Being an only child, he didn't have the luxury of being squeamish, because he was expected to help. After the animal was killed, he helped remove the organs, saving the liver and heart in a tub and being careful not to puncture the stomach or the intestines. It had taken him a while to get used to the smell and the sight of his own arms scarlet red up past the elbows. "Blood is red. It doesn't make things white. It makes them red, and when it dries, it gets brown and crusty. That's not clean. That's nasty. The only way you can get it out is with really cold water."

The teacher smiled and sighed patiently. "I don't think you understand what I mean. You will when you're a little older, though. And when you do, I hope you make the decision to let Jesus come into your heart."

Garrison imagined his heart, all hollowed out with little windows and a door. Grown ups were so weird sometimes. Why would God want to live in a muscle that pumped blood through your body?

Looking back on the incident, he smiled at the misunderstanding. Of course, Miss Madison had been talking about his true self, the core of his very being– not his anatomical heart. But even when he had come to understand that, Garrison had doubted there would be room in there for Jesus. He guarded his heart carefully, and let very few people near the real him. Letting people in there would influence his way of thinking. He didn't want anyone getting close enough that their opinion would make a difference. There were things he wanted to do that he was certain would not meet the approval of anyone in the community. People here didn't want him to voice his interest in the things beyond the valley. They usually interrupted him to tell him he should focus on something else.

Selah was the exception. She might not agree with his ideas, but she usually kept it to herself and let him vent all his frustrations. It made him wonder if she, too, had the same feelings about exploring the world beyond the boundaries, but was just too intimidated by her upbringing to risk voicing her desire. She had been trained to believe certain things —things that made up the very center of their society. Admittedly, it was frightening to entertain the possibility that the foundations of their way of life were built on nothing but an irrational idea cooked up by grandparents and great grandparents. But Garrison found the possibility—even the fear— invigorating.

His fascination had started when he was very young. He remembered an incident with his parents. They had gone on a picnic and he had begged and begged to carry the picnic basket. His father had looked so important carrying it, swinging it slightly as they strolled along to the spot down by the creek. Like most boys his age, he wanted to be just like his dad. He copied his facial expressions, the way he walked, and hung on his every word. So naturally, when Garrison saw Paul was in charge of carrying the basket, he simply had to have a try. When they were almost at their destination, his father had finally relented and handed the basket down for Garrison to carry. He had wrapped the fingers of one hand around the handle and waited for his dad to let go. "You'd better use both hands, partner," Paul Scoffield said gently. "It's heavier than it looks."

"I do it, Dad!" Garrison insisted. Paul smiled and lowered the basket even further, until it was a few inches from the ground.

"You got it?" Paul asked.

"Got it!" Garrison replied. Paul let the basket go and it landed with a thunk on the ground. Garrison tried with all his might to pick up the basket with one hand, just like his father had done it. When that didn't work, he used both hands, and ended up dragging the basket unceremoniously the last few remaining feet to the creek bank. It had looked so easy when his dad had done it. He looked up to see if his mother was impressed. She smiled at him as she spread the blanket on the gravel bar.

It was a wonderful picnic, with fried chicken and rolls and apples. Garrison splashed rocks in the water when they were done eating, but he always kept one ear to Paul and Megan's conversation. Much of what they said was grown-up talk and not very interesting, but the warmth in their voices was comforting. He had scooped out a little bay in the creek gravel and was building a miniature jetty to use as a holding pen for baby crawdads when he noticed the conversation had changed. There was a sharpness to his father's voice that Garrison hadn't heard before. He looked over at his parents and noticed that his mother looked worried.

"Don't you ever wonder, Meg? The world might be different now," Paul was saying.

"Of course it's different. It's worse! The Bible said there would be persecution, famine, disease…"

"I'm not talking about the tribulation or the apocalypse. The Church will be in heaven before that all starts."

"Tell that to the Christians throughout the ages who have been tortured for their faith. You know the way things were headed. Back when the State was the United States, some people still talked about the way our country started out. But we strayed so far from that. How could God keep blessing a nation that had wandered so far from His laws? We went from being the most powerful nation on earth to a nation that was scared of its own shadow. Our foundations were rocked by terrorists. Everyone was suspect. Little by little, for our own protection, our personal freedoms were taken away. Anyone who questioned the State was taken into custody for reconditioning. And you think things might be better now?" Megan's eyes were wide, and although Garrison didn't understand what she was talking about, he understood that she was upset and afraid.

Paul's eyes softened and he took her hand. "The truth is, Meg, we don't really know what happened since we left. All I'm saying is, there's a chance it could be better, instead of worse. Think of all the things our children will miss because we were too afraid to try to adapt, or worse yet, too afraid to try to reach out to a people who had lost sight of their God. What if God wants us to go back—to be missionaries to our own people?"

Megan was quiet for a moment. Then she looked up at Paul with fierce determination. "Alright, Paul. Let's just say you're right. If you are, God would surely confirm what you've said out of the mouths of two or three witnesses. You pray about it. Ask Him to somehow confirm it through one of the elders. If He really wants us to leave, if this is actually His idea, He will confirm it. It will be like the fleece Gideon put out to decide if God was really telling him to go into battle."

Paul grinned. "Ok, Meg. I'll put out the proverbial fleece. If one of the elders confirms it, then would you consider making plans to go back?"

"If they confirm it, without you bringing it up, then I *might* consider making plans," Megan agreed.

Paul rolled his eyes and sighed. "I'm still not sure what you're so afraid of. They're human, just like we are."

"Hitler was human. Nero and Stalin were human. Chairman Mao was human."

Paul laughed. "Oh, Megan. You're so dramatic." He pulled her into his arms. She stiffened and tried to scowl, but the corners of her mouth were turning up despite her efforts. "That's not very convincing. Maybe you need to take more drama classes."

"Don't worry, Daddy. I go," said a confident little voice right behind them.

Paul and Megan stopped their tussling to look over their shoulders at the little boy. "Where are you going, Little Man?" Paul asked.

"I go with you. To the better place."

Paul's smile faded and he took Garrison up in his arms. "If we go anywhere, Little Man, we'll all go together," he said.

Looking back on the whole incident, Garrison realized how uneasy his behavior in the next few weeks had made his parents. Of course, they had no idea he was paying attention to their conversation at the picnic until he had made his declaration. Afterward, explaining away the things he said in public about "the better place" proved to be a lesson in diplomacy for Paul and Megan.

As he trudged through the leaves on his way out of the valley, Garrison realized a song had been playing through his head for the last few hundred yards of his trek. "Be careful little ears, what you hear. Oh, be careful little ears what you hear! There's a Father up above, looking down in tender love. Oh, be careful little ears, what you hear." There was more truth to that song than he had ever realized—not to mention some of the other verses: "Be careful little eyes, what you see," and "Be careful little mouth, what you say." He stopped to put the packs down for a minute and stretched his back and arms. It was crazy to think that this very moment, this exodus, all began from a seed that was planted from a conversation between his parents that he had overheard when he was barely old enough to talk.

He looked to the terrain ahead of him. He had almost reached the area where things began to level off. The road was not far away. When he reached it, he could snuff out his lantern and have one less thing to carry when it had cooled enough to pack away. There was enough moonlight in the open area of the road to allow him to see any snakes underfoot. Besides, he wasn't certain he wanted to attract too much attention to himself yet by brandishing a light down what was probably a forbidden road. He shouldered the packs again and began to softly sing as he went. "Be careful little feet, where you go...."

16

THE sun was a white-hot smelting pot in the sky as Garrison clomped through the woods next to the old road. He was beginning to question his decision of leaving in late summer. He had sweated through his clothes in the Ozarks humidity, and his feet felt squishy in his boots. *A swim in the creek would feel good about now*, he thought to himself. But modern society would have running water for bathing and pools made just for swimming. He would be able to taste foods he had never known existed and see all sorts of different types of people. He grimaced as he wiped a spider web out of his face. *If you're so excited about going there, then why are you hiding in the woods off the side of the road?* The question taunted him. It was true. When dawn had come, he had felt the need to continue, but had decided to stay relatively hidden from the sight of the drones he had heard about by staying under the canopy of the forest. When he had been back in the valley, it had been his plan all along to intercept a drone—to be discovered and rescued. Now that he was out on his own, he was having second thoughts. What if they viewed him as a terrorist threat? Would he be shot on sight? Suddenly he laughed out loud. An eighteen-year-old boy with a couple of backpacks, viewed as a threat? Then he remembered the stories of the bombings. The bombs were often hidden in backpacks. Yes, he would remain hidden until he figured out the safest way to announce his presence. That is, if he was still undetected.

Toward the middle of the day, he made his way deeper into the forest and set his packs down for a rest. It might be best to sleep in the daylight, anyway. Less movement in the daytime might mean less chance of being detected. Traveling during the evening instead of sleeping also meant he would be more alert for any nocturnal predators that might come around. He piled up some leaves at the base of a tree, and using a pack as a pillow, tried to make himself comfortable. His eyes were closed for only a few moments when he became aware of a burning sensation around his ankles. He groaned as he realized he could have been walking through stands of poison ivy in the dark. "Oh well. What's done is done," he said to himself. But then he realized poison ivy couldn't be the culprit, for the burning was underneath his socks. He peeled them back to reveal what looked like minute grains of pepper scattered on his leg. Some of the pepper grains were moving. "Seed ticks!" he cried in disgust. He had encountered them once in a while in the valley, but that was right after he had run into them, when the tick nymphs were still in a large wad on his pant leg. All one had to do then was to find a cedar branch and use it as a switch to clean off the infested area. It was too late for Garrison to avoid most of their nibblings, for they had already scattered out, and most of them were attached. He stripped off his pants and began the long, tedious work of picking off the parasites that were almost too small to see with the naked eye. His pocketknife helped to scrape some of them off. As he worked, he noticed an adult tick on a nearby sapling, its legs stretched toward him to grab on in case he would venture too close. He had never seen so many ticks! Maybe the community had been protected from more than just sickness and detection by the state. He wondered what other things he might encounter before he reached civilization.

Water would hopefully be one of them. His canteens were running low already, and most of the creeks he had seen were dry due to late summer's low rainfall. Once he found water, would it be fit to drink? He could make a fire and boil it, but what about chemicals like mercury or lead? He wasn't sure the filtration system he had made out of a couple of canning jars with sand and a modified lid would be able to extract all the impurities. On any account, he had tested it only once, and it took an incredibly long time for the water to make it through the sand and the mesh and drip out into the receiving jar. He smashed a few more ticks against his knife blade. It would probably take less time to pick off the ticks than it would take for the water to filter. He sighed. The sooner he got to civilization, the better, he decided as he looked over his pants for any ticks that might be there. A switch from a nearby cedar helped with that task.

He was switching away at the pants when he became conscious of a slight humming noise.

"Are ya off ya chip, or what?" said a voice from behind him.

Garrison spun around, his pants in one hand and the cedar switch in the other. Hovering twenty feet away was a machine that looked a little like the old pictures of motorcycles in Genevieve's books, except that this machine had no wheels. He had heard of hovercrafts, but only the larger ones used on oceans or rivers. This one was only big enough for one or two people. Perched atop the craft was a girl wearing a skin-tight bodysuit that reflected her surroundings like a mirror. It had an effect of blending her in with the trees. Even her milk chocolate skin and her dark, almond eyes seemed to help her camouflage with the tree trunks. But there was no hiding that hair. One half of it was a shock of silver white, and the other side was blood red. On the white side, a small streak of royal blue curved around to help frame her face. The effect was both startling and stunning. Suddenly Garrison was very aware that he was standing out in the open in his underwear.

"Come on, man. Are ya chippin'?" she spoke again.

"Uh, I don't know," he answered truthfully, as he tried to cover himself with the tick-infested pants.

"What are ya doing this far out from the stream docks? Is that why I don't see ya bike? It ran out of charge and ya were too far out to ge' back?"

"Well, I—"

The girl continued before he could finish his sentence. Her words spilled over each other so quickly that he could barely make them out. "Ya stupid chipper. Were ya so blinked out ya didn't remember that if ya stay wid ya bike, they'll come pick y'up? Tracking devices, ya know. Plus that monstrosity in ya head. Oh, they'll come for that, soon enough. If they figure out ya won't work with it, they can find someone who will, believe it, now."

She brought the craft a few yards closer and leaned toward him for emphasis. "But God's mercy on the blinker that tweaks his chip."

Finally. Some common ground. "You believe in God?" Garrison asked.

The girl sat up straight on the bike, causing it to rear back for an instant. "I suppose ya think ya can hold that over ma head. But look whose chip is tweaked," She said smugly.

"No, I'm not trying to threaten you. I believe in Him, too. At least, I did at one time," Garrison said.

The girl seemed to look at him differently. "Ya don't look like a Way Man."

"A what?" Garrison had no idea how difficult it would be to understand someone who spoke his own language. But the rapidity with which she fired her words, coupled with the accent and the jargon, made it almost impossible.

"A Way Man. A man of the Way. I mean, the chippin' part follows through, but the clothes... and ya talk like someone in an oldie flat screen." She cocked her head to the side as she studied him. "Where ya dock, eh?"

"I'm sorry, I don't know what you're asking me. Could you please slow down a little?" Garrison felt helplessly exposed, both physically and mentally. He must look and act like a complete idiot to this girl.

She smiled, and the severe look of her face was transformed in an instant. "Where...are...you...from?" she said slowly and loudly, as if he were deaf as well as stupid.

"I'm not from around here," he began.

The girl laughed so hard she nearly fell off her bike. "As if that's on my news feed, eh?" She settled down enough for Garrison to continue.

"I'm looking for a new place to stay," he ventured.

"Aren't we all, blinker? And ya'd better find one, too, if ya really tweaked ya chip. Oh, sorry," she said as if suddenly remembering something, and began to speak more slowly. "I can take you to a new place, but not with that chip in ya head."

"What chip?" Garrison asked.

"Whattaya mean, what chip? THE chip." She moved the craft a little closer to him, until she was only five feet away. "If ya don't have a chip, I can give ya a ride to a safe place. But ya gonna have to flash me."

Garrison blushed and shifted uncomfortably behind his pants. "I think I may already be doing that."

The girl shot him an exasperated look. "Listen, blinker. I need to know ya status. I'm only coming close enough for ya to flash me. But if ya try anything funny, I'll blast ya over with ma bike, ya savvy?"

"I'm sorry, I don't know what you want," Garrison said, frustrated.

"Hold out ya hand, ya stupid blink!" she practically yelled.

Garrison stretched out one hand while clinging desperately to his pants with the other. "Palm out. Jovies, it's like ya never been flashed before."

Garrison complied, and the girl waved her hand in front of his. She waited and frowned and waved it again.

"What are you doing?" Garrison asked.

The girl's eyes were wide. She jumped off the bike and grabbed his hand, feeling of his palm. "You *are* a Way Man. But I would remember you! I know them all! Where are ya from? Did ya parents hide ya somehow? Ya got no Palmscan! That's been S.I. for years!"

"S.I.?" Garrison was hopelessly confused.

"Standard Implant. You really *aren't* from around here, are ya? Or anywhere anyone knows about, eh?"

"That's what I've been trying to tell you. I come from a place that's… hidden." Garrison's heart was beating wildly. Was he putting the community in danger by even saying that?

"Oh, Jovies! We gotta get ya somewhere safe. And I know just the place. What's ya name? 'Cause I can't keep callin' ya blinker. Ya don't even know what I'm talkin' about," the girl said excitedly.

"And that's news to me?" Garrison laughed. "I'm Garrison Scoffield. And you are?"

"Viviana Delacruz. But you can call me Viv." She slipped on a pair of goggles that had been hanging around her neck and climbed aboard the bike again. "Now, hop on. And would ya mind puttin' on ya pants?"

"Love to," Garrison said sheepishly. After he was back in his pants and boots, he grabbed the packs and looked at the bike. He had once jumped off a fence onto Martin Breedon's bull. That had been a wild, short ride, and he had barely escaped without getting stomped. He figured this hover bike would be no challenge in comparison with a lurching, bucking bull.

He took a couple of large strides and tried to hop onto the bike. It tipped and veered away like a canoe in the Beardsley pond, and Garrison ended up on his back in the leaves. Viv laughed and turned down the air on the craft until the humming noise stopped and it touched the ground.

"Try again, Garrison," she said, and once again flashed him her beautiful smile. He climbed aboard. After securing his packs in some storage compartments from which she also procured him a pair of goggles, Viv turned to him and said, "I guess ya never been on one of these, then?"

Garrison shook his head.

"Well, no sudden moves. Hold on with ya legs, and lean when I lean." Viv turned on the bike, and it rose off the forest floor. Soon, they were floating gently through the trees. They continued like that for five or ten minutes, with Viv occasionally weaving around trees and boulders and over logs. "Are ya gettin' it then?" she asked over her shoulder.

"Yeah, it's not too bad," Garrison answered.

"Good. Hold onto me," she ordered.

"What?"

"We can move now. No more wasting time," she said. And with that, the bike increased in speed until their surroundings became a blur. Garrison held on as Viv zipped around the trees like a damselfly zipping through the witch-hazel branches on Bear Creek. He was scared that at any moment he would fly off and hit a tree, but at the same time, he was exhilarated. This was just the sort of thing he had dreamed about doing his whole life. He was grinning like a monkey when Viv cast a glance back at him.

"Better keep ya mouth shut," she clipped.

Garrison opened his mouth to ask why just in time to inhale a bug. He could feel Viv's body shake with laughter as he choked and sputtered behind her. And then—he wouldn't have thought it possible—she leaned forward and the bike went even faster. The trees became smears of color on their left and right. He couldn't understand how they were able to avoid hitting them until he ventured a look below and realized they were skimming over the top of a small river. He hadn't even realized when they came across it, but it seemed an exceptional way to cover a lot of ground as quickly as possible. Except for the occasional tree fallen over the water, the way was clear.

After about twenty minutes of dizzying speed, the river narrowed. Tree branches reached closer to the middle of the waterway, impeding their progress. Viv slowed the bike to accommodate the new landscape, and eventually left the river altogether. Garrison wasn't sure how she was navigating unless it was through one of the GPS screens he had heard about. When he glimpsed over her shoulder at the bike's control panel, the only screen he saw was dark. There was, however, a compass and an odometer which seemed to be operational. "I notice your GPS unit isn't working. Are you just using the compass to navigate?" he finally asked, since the wind noise had died down with their reduced speed.

"I use the rivers to navigate—and my compass and landmarks," she seemed to answer with as little explanation as possible.

"Does the State still require every vehicle to have a GPS unit that can both navigate and be tracked by satellite?" Garrison decided to risk the question.

Viv slowed the bike so she could look back from time to time as she swerved between the trees. "Listen, Way Man. I don't know where ya from, but it's not safe for ya to be out here where the drones might see ya, savvy? I'm givin' ya a ride to a safe place. Keep the questions down, eh? The less ya know, the less ya can get me in trouble if they catch ya."

"If who catches me?"

"The State, man! The Administrators. They watch everything. I can't believe I found ya first, ya being so close to the road as ya were. But if we're careful, they won't find ya where we're goin'."

Garrison suddenly had an urge to launch himself off the bike. He might have, if his packs hadn't been securely stowed in the storage compartments. How could he know that this girl he had just met wasn't some criminal or a delusional lunatic who was taking him to a place no one would ever find him?

"Where are we going?" he asked.

"I told ya already. A safe place. Do ya know what the Administrators would do if they found ya?" Viv asked, without pausing long enough for him to answer. "First, they'd run a buncha tests, because ya look terrible healthy for a man that doesn't have a chip or an implant. Then, they'd ask ya a lot of questions, like where ya dock an' all. They'd wanna know if there was anyone else where ya came from. And if ya didn't answer, they'd chip ya right then and there and just dig it out'ya brain. And if there *is* anyone ya left back where ya came from, they'd find 'em, believe it now. No free radicals allowed in the perfect societal model. Too volatile. Too convenient for discontented citizens. If the Discards found out they could make it on their own, I'm tellin' ya, it'd be a mass exodus from the outer docks."

Garrison felt numb. He didn't understand exactly what she was saying, but it seemed the fears of the old timers were not unfounded, after all. Unless the girl was delusional. He suddenly realized that his greatest hope was that the girl who was taking him who-knows-where was clinically paranoid. Momentary panic caused a short little laugh to escape his throat. He clamped his mouth shut, hoping Viv hadn't noticed. A jump off the bike might be possible at this speed without being seriously injured, but if she really was crazy, she might try to run him down. He sat very still, trying to quiet the panic rising inside of him. *What would Selah do in this situation?* He wondered to himself. *For starters, she would never have found herself in this situation. She would never have wandered beyond the boundaries.* The next thought that came to his mind left his stomach feeling queasy. *Selah would pray.*

The thought of calling for help to Someone Who was supposed to be in control of everything, Someone Whose strength and knowledge and ability knew no bounds, seemed incredibly appealing right now. He felt a strange sensation in his chest that he had been feeling over the past few months. It felt almost the same as when his grandpa had died and he had known with such finality that he wouldn't be able to take walks with him anymore, or go fishing, or make things with him in his shop. It was like being homesick for a person, except in the reverse, as if someone were homesick for him.

Garrison tried to shake off the feeling. He couldn't pray. That line of communication had been cut off, he was certain. If there was a God, Garrison didn't think He would appreciate His existence being doubted. What was that verse Genevieve had him memorize? "Without faith no one can please God. Anyone who comes to God must believe that he is real and that he rewards those who truly want to find him. Hebrews 11:6,"[20] he quoted under his breath. For most people, Genevieve gladly divulged her stories of the Old Country. But for Garrison, who came to her often, asking for something—anything —she could tell him about where they had originated, her price was scripture memorization. She would pick out a scripture, he would pick out the translation he liked, and when he had learned it, she would

---

[20] Hebrews 11:6 NCV

tell a story, or a fragment of a story. It used to infuriate him when he would memorize a long or particularly difficult passage and recite it, and she would repay him with a fractured memory consisting of only one or two sentences. And now one of the passages tucked away in his memory bank seemed to confirm that, in his present state, he was in no condition to ask God for help.

"Hebrews. Some of my favorite writings are in that book," Viv was saying.

"You heard me?" Garrison asked, dismayed that he had spoken loud enough for her to hear.

"I have a hearing implant that can filter out and focus in on specific sounds," she explained. "I got several implants, before my second birth date."

"They put implants in babies, before they're even old enough to make a choice?" Garrison asked incredulously.

"Well, of course, there's the standard implants, like Health 1 and 2, and Palmscan. Those are put in at birth. I'm talking about the optionals ya can put in once ya reach 16, like Optical Correct and 2nd Sight—the vision implants. One corrects ya vision if ya have any vision problems. The other gives ya the ability to see farther and microscopically. Some people claim that after having 2nd Sight for a year or so, they can train themselves to see *through* things. But I don't know if that's the truth. I can't imagine the State allowing that kind of ability, unless ya were an Administrator."

Garrison pondered this for a moment. "But you said you got your optional implants before you were two years old."

Viv grinned. "Nah, nah. Before my second *birth date*, not my second birth*day*."

"Your second birth date? What are you talking about? Do people go through some sort of second birthing process where you come from?" Garrison imagined people going back to the hospital and climbing voluntarily into an oversized, artificial womb. "Do people get some sort of genetic improvements after a certain age?" he asked.

Viv looked at him strangely. "Are ya a man of the Way and ya still don't understand? Nah! They must not call it the same where ya dock. Everyone gets born, eh? But if ya wanna be of the Way, ya have to be born a second time. It's like something inside of ya that was dead comes alive. And God, he puts His Spirit in ya, when ya believe in His Son, Jesus."

"I feel like Nicodemus," Garrison said with a smirk.

"Who?"

"I tell you the truth, unless you are born of water and the Spirit, you cannot enter God's kingdom. Human life comes from human parents, but spiritual life comes from the Spirit,"[21] quoted Garrison. "John chapter three. Nicodemus, the Pharisee who came to Jesus by night so he wouldn't be seen. Even with all his education, he couldn't understand what Jesus was talking about."

"I can't remember the Word like *you* can. It almost makes me wish I could have the chip. But that won't be happenin'. Anyway, I don't see what's so hard to understand about the second birth. Ya don't need the chip to understand that. Fact is, I think they might be working against that part of ya brain with their techno." She paused and looked back at him, as if trying to see into his soul. "Ya know all the words, like a Way Man, but ya talk them like a hollow pipe. Ya spit 'em out like ya know 'em. But ya don't know 'em, do ya? Ya don't really know what they mean. It's like ya don't feel 'em for real."

Garrison swallowed. She was reading him like a book, and it was unsettling. No one back home had ever accused him of that—of being a phony. He had been called rebellious and disrespectful and half a dozen other things people said about him when they thought he wasn't in earshot. But for them to think he didn't actually believe...that was unthinkable.

Viv had brought the bike to a turtle's pace at the base of a hill and was studying him intently. "I think ya lied to me," she said, finally.

---

[21] John 3:5-6 NCV

"I promise, I've told you the truth. I really do come from a place that's hidden. I'm looking for a new place, and—"

"Nah! Not about that," she interrupted him. "Ya said ya believed in God, at one time, leastways. But I don't see how anyone could ever believe, could ever *really* know Him, and just decide to stop believin' in Him...to stop lovin' Him. I mean, I guess it's possible, 'cause He gave us free choice. But ya'd have to be dock-drained to really know Him and say goodbye. Jovies, man! How do ya make it without Him?" The look of disbelief in her eyes was quickly replaced by a sadness that made him feel as hollow as she claimed he was. But before he could think of anything to say, she had the bike moving at a faster speed. They crested the hill, which turned out to be a bluff overlooking another river. It was beautiful, with gray sandstone walls and outcroppings.

"Hang on again, Garrison. We're gonna cover some ground," she said. And suddenly, with no warning, she rushed the bike to the edge of the bluff and angled it down.

Garrison didn't realize he was screaming until he found it difficult to breath because he had run out of breath. His attempts to inhale were complicated by the wind tearing at his face. It seemed to steal the breath right out of his mouth. The river bank was rushing toward them with incredible speed, and his body wasn't staying on the seat of the bike very well at all. He wasn't sure what difference it would make at this point whether he stayed on or fell off. Viv, on the other hand, was stuck to the seat like a cocklebur in a cow's tail. Her colorful hair whipping in the wind was the only thing that moved. When they were twenty feet away from the bank, Garrison could hold it back no longer. "God, help us!" he screamed. Abruptly, Viv pulled up on the bike and angled it over the water so that it was headed downstream. Water sprayed in a wide arc to the side, and Garrison tumbled head over heels into the river. He broke surface to see Viv turning the bike around to come pick him up. Her face was beaming with excitement as she threw out a towrope to take him ashore. *"Whew!* Wasn't that amazing?" she said, and whooped a couple more times for good measure. "I can't believe ya fell off, anyway, the way ya were digging ya fingas into m'ribs."

Garrison was speechless. He felt like kissing the ground.

"And I knew ya were lyin'," she continued. "But ya weren't lyin' to me. You were lyin' to y'self," she smiled.

Garrison's brow furrowed. What in the world was she talking about?

"Ya still believe in God, you Tab-a-ras!"

"What makes you think I still believe? And what was that you called me?" Garrison asked.

"Tab-a-ras. Tabula Rasa. It's what they call the chippers that get their chips wiped."

"Meaning...?"

"Meaning you're empty-headed, ya goof!"

Garrison grinned. Selah used to call him a goofus all the time. It wasn't exactly the first impression he had hoped to make here, but he was glad to hear something familiar, even if it was an insult.

"And I know ya still believe, even if you're on the outs with Him right now." She smiled from ear to ear. "You called out to Him, Way Man. 'God, help us!'" she mimicked his scream in a comical, wavering voice.

Garrison glared. "Just because I did that doesn't mean anything. I panicked. They were just words."

"*Death and life are in the power of the tongue,*"[22] Viv quoted. "And whether ya like it or not, your *spirit* chose *life*."

Garrison stood on the riverbank, dripping wet. He was tired of being sized up. "Look, Viv, I'm really grateful you gave me a ride, but maybe you should just give me my packs and I'll be on my way," he said.

Viv seemed shocked. "We're almost there. It's just half an hour over the river. You've gotta meet Dawson. I think when ya do, you'll understand things better."

"Who's Dawson?" Garrison asked warily.

---

[22] Proverbs 18:21a KJV

"Come with me and find out," Viv said, and flashed him her amazing smile.

"I'll come as long as you promise not to go over any more cliffs."

"Nah, man! It's just down the river. No more cliffs."

For some reason, he trusted her. He got back on the bike, and soon, the sycamore trees on the banks were blurs of white and green. Half an hour later, true to her word, Viv slowed the bike and turned into the woods. Once they were deep in the forest, she stopped the bike and turned it off.

"Grab ya packs, man," she said. "We walk from here."

17

GARRISON wondered at first why Viv had left the bike behind, but after walking a mere twenty feet farther away from the river, the vegetation had thickened to a nearly impenetrable wall of green briar and honeysuckle vines. "I always hafta use ma knife fa this mess," she explained. "It doesn' matter how recently I been here, it always grows back like no one was ever here." She reached into a pocket of her body-suit and procured a small pocketknife.

Garrison's expression betrayed his doubt, but in a show of good faith, he pulled out his own knife and began sawing at the nearest bramble. "What're ya doin'?" laughed Viv.

"I just thought I could help, unless you want to do it all yourself," Garrison said, confused.

"Way Man, ya need a new knife," she laughed again, and suddenly a blue line of light appeared from the end of the hilt of her knife, where a blade should have been. She held it up to a mass of honeysuckle and began slicing through it as if it were warm butter. Garrison watched in fascination and disbelief as the leaves and vines fell away. Viv stopped to look at him gawking at her progress. "Well, if ya wanna help, ya could at least drag summa this stuff outta the way," she said, kicking a wad of vines to the side.

"Oh, yeah, sure," he said, and shook himself out of his daze to began clearing the brush from the path she was making.

They worked steadily for half an hour or more. Garrison could easily understand why no one would look for them here. The scratches he was getting from just hauling the vines out of the way crisscrossed his forearms, and his sweat ran into the cuts, making them sting. The only sounds he heard were the slight sizzle of the beam of light as it cut through the vines, the shuffling sound their feet made in the leaves, and the incessant buzzing of the cloud of mosquitoes that hovered around their heads as they worked. The brush was so thick and undisturbed that it didn't look like anyone had been here for a long, long time.

Suddenly, Viv stopped and tilted her head. She turned and smiled at him. "I can hear it. So will you, in a bit," she said.

"Hear what?" Garrison asked, swatting at a mosquito.

"The sounds of Adullam," she said, with no other explanation, and went back to work.

"Adullam? Like the cave where David went to hide from Saul?"

"Yeah, I think that's where they got the name."

"I wonder why they named it that?"

"Ya can ask Dawson when we get there. But it seems obvious to me. Don't ya think this is a good place to hide?"

Garrison looked around. Through the fog of mosquitoes, all he could see was walls of leaves. The underbrush was so thick he could see no farther than three feet in front of him. "I could do without the mosquitoes and the jungle, but I can see it would be a good hideout," he finally said.

"Well, it's not all like this, Tab-a-ras," she chided him. "Just wait 'til ya see it. I wanted to stay when I first came here, but Dawson wouldn't let me."

"Why not?"

"He said I had a job to do, an' I couldn't do it if I just stayed in Adullam. Before I came, they didn't know there were any Way people left in the State. He said they were still there for a reason, that God didn't leave a remnant by accident," she explained. "I didn't wanna go back, but when I thought about it, I knew he was right. But I come back to visit, 'cause I'm only about one year old in the Way, an' I wanna learn all I can. The only religious meetings they allow where I come from are ones that have been sanctioned by the State, and the only Bibles they have are the ones that have been *edited* by the State. They aren't even real Bibles at all. They take writings from the Bible, the Koran, the Up-anishads, the Tao Te Ching, an' whatever else they wanna throw in an' wrap them all up in one book an' try to tell ya that they're all the same thing, just from different points of view. The download changes every three months or so, because any time anyone has a new idea or a new way of sayin' somethin', they try to incorporate it."

"You mean your Bible changes every three months?" Garrison asked in disbelief.

"It's not a Bible. It's a corruption of what was once the Bible, added with the Koran and writings of Buddhism an' Hinduism an' a lotta other philosophical mumbo jumbo."

"So why do you come back to Adullam? Couldn't you just pick out the parts that you know are from the Bible and study them? I mean, isn't this an incredible risk you're taking to come to a place where people aren't following what is sanctioned by the State? You could just take what you wanted from the State's Bible and disregard the rest."

Viv looked at him as if he had lost his mind. "Nahh, man. It's all blended together. It's so jumbled up, ya can't separate it anymore. And even if ya could, how would *I* be able to tell the difference? Like I said, I'm only a year old in the Way. The Word isn't always just stuff that makes ya feel good. It's stuff that teaches ya how to live, an' that isn't always easy to hear. It's easy to swallow the syrupy glop the State pours down ya throat about how everyone is born good, but the goodness gradually fades away, so ya just need to get the implants and the chip to fix it all an' become *'the enhanced person you were always meant to be.'"* Viv said this last part with no trace of her strange accent and an eerily placid smile. "It's not so easy to swallow *'For all have sinned and come short of the glory of God,'*[23] and *'the wages of sin is death.'*[24] Who wants to know that? But we have to, ya see. If we don't see how we really are,

---

[23] Romans 3:23 KJV
[24] See Romans 6:23 KJV

if we think the lies spread by the State are true an' everyone is basically good, then why would we think we ever needed savin'? The funny thing is, everyone deep down knows somethin' is wrong. Otherwise, why would they be gettin' the implants an' chips? They can reprogram their minds if they want to, but they can't reprogram their soul. So they get a new implant an' feel good for a while. Then the hollow feeling comes back, so they get another one. I have some friends who have so many implants, I don't even know how to act around 'em anymore. Almost nothing is left of who they used to be, inside an' out; an' they're still looking for somethin' to fill the hollowness. It never ends!"

The laser knife had been slashing through the brush during her whole monologue, but suddenly she stopped and turned to him, her gaze gripping him with its intensity. "The chip . . ." she stopped and cleared her throat, and Garrison was surprised to see her eyes suddenly red with tears. "The chip is different. I have a friend who got the chip when it first came out a few months ago. She goes back every few weeks to get the next download. I tried to talk her out of it, but she was so unhappy. She had tried every implant. Before the chip came out, she even talked about donating herself."

"Donating herself? What's that mean?" Garrison asked.

"It's where, if ya tired of livin', ya can just go an' they put ya to sleep an' take ya organs an' all the good parts of ya for the hospitals that treat the Discards who don' want the implants or the chip. Anyone who is desperate enough can buy 'em, if they can afford it. Most can't, though."

"So does your friend like the chip?"

Viv swallowed and looked away. When she finally spoke, it was with difficulty. "She loves it. She thinks it's the best thing that ever happened to her. She's tryin' to talk me into gettin' one."

Garrison carefully put down a stickery wad of multiflora rose branches. "So what's the problem?" he asked. "She's happy now. Aren't you happy for her?"

Viv's eyes flashed with anger, and he flinched as she stepped toward him. He imagined the laser knife slicing through his arm. She stopped short when she saw him flinch and glance at the knife.

"I'm not gonna hurt ya, ya stupid chip-wipe. An' ya don't hafta worry none about this knife. When it comes in contact with human flesh, it's programmed to shut off, see?" She took the blue blade and made a slashing motion through her hand. The laser beam disappeared and there was only a slight redness where it had first come in contact with her skin. "*I'm* the one that should be worried about *you*. What ya carry around with *you*, that's the real danger."

Garrison reached in his pocket and pulled out his little pocketknife. "This? This isn't a weapon. It's more of a tool. I just use it to open things and to skin squirrels and gut fish–that kind of thing. I don't use it for self defense."

Viv just looked at him and shook her head. "Nahh!" She put her head in her hands in exasperation. "The crazy idea ya got in ya head. It's like ya think ya don't need Jesus in ya life. It's like ya think ya don't need savin'. Where'd ya get those ideas, if ya came from a place that walks in the Way? My friend that I been tellin' ya about, she doesn't believe in Jesus, ya see? I tried to tell her, but she got so tired of me tryin' that she even threatened to report me for instability. And now she has the chip, an' she thinks everything that was wrong with her is fine now. She doesn't think she *needs* anything else, see? I can't get to her now. I'm too late!" Viv sobbed and leaned her colorful head up against the rough bark of a black oak.

"It might not be too late, Viv," said a gentle voice from behind the wall of vines.

Viv froze and then smiled and wiped her eyes. "Dawson? How'd ya sneak up on us like that?" She got out the knife and sliced through the last few feet of honeysuckle. On the other side stood a man of small stature who appeared to be of Asian descent. It was hard to tell his age, but he looked to be in his thirties.

"I didn't sneak up. The Lord told me you were coming, so I came here to wait. While I waited and prayed, you came to me," he said simply.

Viv stepped through the opening to clasp the man's hand and smile at him. She looked back at Garrison. "I found someone who needs a place to stay. He doesn't have anything that could be tracked. Says he's from a place that's hidden—like Adullam."

Garrison still stood within the thickness of the underbrush, swatting at the hordes of mosquitoes, uncertain of how he would be received. As far as he could tell, Viv had just assumed he would be welcome here. But what if they didn't trust him? What if they were hesitant to let him leave if they thought he might expose their community?

"Welcome to Adullam," the man spoke. "I'm Dawson Manaba."

"Garrison Scoffield," Garrison replied, still rooted to the makeshift trail.

"Well, are ya gonna just stand there gettin' eaten alive by all those mosquitoes, or are ya comin'?" Viv asked impatiently.

Considering his options, Adullam seemed like the best choice. They had let Viv come and go. Hopefully they would do the same for him. He stepped through the threshold of vegetation and accepted Dawson's extended hand. Suddenly, the mosquitoes dissipated. He looked back through the leaves and could see them hovering around in bloodthirsty little clouds, but none passed beyond what must have been the boundary of this community.

"That's some boundary," Garrison commented. "All we have are trees with a circled X cut into them."

Dawson grinned. "I am very interested in learning about where you come from," he said. "But first, you must be tired and in need of some rest. Let me show you to our guest quarters." He turned and led them down a path that opened up into a meadow. Garrison could see a small herd of brown and white animals grazing in the distance. Every once in a while, he could hear a high-pitched bleating sound coming from their direction.

"Are those goats?" he asked. "We don't have goats where I'm from."

"Yes. Goats and chickens are all the animals we have," Dawson replied. "Except for wildlife, and fish, of course. But we don't eat too many fish because of mercury levels that build up in them."

The group continued through the meadow and came to a stand of giant cottonwood trees. Garrison couldn't stop thinking about the goats. He had read about them. They were voracious animals, and would eat anything. People used to use them to clear pieces of land that were thick with underbrush. "What stops your goats from eating right through the boundary?" he suddenly asked.

"Goats don't like mosquitoes or deerflies any more than we do," Dawson replied. "But even in the wintertime, they stay within the boundaries. I can't really explain it. It's well known that you need a good fence to keep a goat in or out of a place. But we don't have any fences, except around our yards, and our goats stay within the boundaries. It's as if they know where they're supposed to stay."

"Sounds like people back home," Garrison commented under his breath.

"Ya don't have a lot of love for the people back where ya came from, do ya?" Viv said. Once again, she had heard something he wished she hadn't.

"A guy can't even *think* his mind around you, much less speak it," Garrison said.

"I've thought of havin' Audio-boost removed," she replied, "but there are always the questions that come with havin' somethin' removed. 'Can you explain your dissatisfaction with the implant? Would you like to try the next generation of its kind?' And on and on. Besides, I'm not certain they might not slip somethin' else in ya if they thought ya behavior was suspicious and that ya needed monitored. So I just keep it an' the others. They come in handy sometimes, anyway. Look ahead up there through the trees," she abruptly changed the subject.

Garrison looked and could see the sides of a few buildings. Viv turned to him, her eyes shining. "There it is. That's the main settlement."

The three of them wound their way down the path through the cottonwoods and came out in a clearing. They seemed to be on the back side of the houses, which were laid out in circular rows. A woman hanging out her wash looked up and smiled broadly when she saw Viv. "Viviana! You're finally back!" she said, and put down her wash basket to come meet them.

"Julie! I've missed all of ya so much!" Viv said, and grabbed the little woman in a bear hug. To Garrison's surprise, Viv started to cry, and the woman patted her shoulder as she held her. His first impression of Viv had been of someone who was strong and sure of herself, but as he watched the scene and remembered her tears for her friend earlier, he realized she was as tender-hearted as a child. Suddenly he was aware of Dawson watching him.

"Let's go ahead and I'll show you to your cabin," Dawson said. "Viv has many friends here whom she will want to visit. I'm sure you will want time to settle in before dinner."

18

GARRISON followed Dawson through the curved rows of houses. As they passed by, people who were in their yards stopped to watch and wave and smile. None of them seemed frightened or surprised by his arrival. "Do you have many visitors?" Garrison asked.

"No. You and Viv are the only people from the outside to have visited in the twenty-two years that we've been here," Dawson replied.

"Twenty-two years! That's all the time you've been here?"

"Yes. That's when the State began rewriting the Bible," Dawson explained.

"The founders of my community left two generations back. But it wasn't because of any new major development like that. They just left because...." Garrison's voice trailed off as he realized how crazy it might sound to tell someone here about the hobo. He glanced at Dawson, who was listening intently. "Well, it's kind of hard to explain," he finished.

Dawson smiled. "Being led of the Spirit is often difficult to describe or explain," he offered. "God's riches are very great, and his wisdom and knowledge have no end! No one can explain the things God decides or understand his ways."[25]

Garrison grimaced. "That sounds like something from the Psalms," he commented.

"Romans 11:33."

Garrison tried to ignore the irritation he always felt when someone started quoting scripture. "So, your community—Adullam—do people here believe in the gifts of the Holy Spirit?" Garrison asked.

---

[25] See Romans 11:33 NCV

"Yes, we do."

"May I ask what denomination you are?"

"We don't actually belong to any denomination," Dawson explained. "We are Christians who believe what is written in the Bible, both Old and New Testaments. We believe scripture is relevant for today and is used to strengthen, teach, enlighten and encourage all who will receive the Truth. Oh, and it is also a powerful weapon against the forces of our enemy."

"You mean the devil, not the State, right?" Garrison asked.

"Yes, I am referring to the devil. Although he has been using the State as one of his tools."

"Viv told me she comes and visits here so she can learn more about the Bible, since the State is constantly corrupting it and rewriting it."

"Yes. I don't know how many uncorrupted versions of the Bible there are left in circulation, but the version sanctioned by the State is too corrupted to be trusted in the teachings of young Christians, or any Christians, for that matter."

"Don't you worry she will lead the Administrators right to you?"

"Viv doesn't have a chip, so she can't be tracked that way. And the GPS unit on her bike stopped working not long after she became a Christian," Dawson explained.

Garrison smirked. "Coincidence, I suppose."

Dawson smiled and glanced at Garrison as the two arrived at what appeared to be a smaller cabin tucked between two of the original homes. "I give very little credence to coincidence," he said. "The God who sees every sparrow that falls to the ground and knows the numbers of hairs on our heads certainly knows the intricacies of a GPS unit." He opened the gate to the yard of the little cabin. "This is where you will be staying," he announced.

Garrison looked at the beautifully laid stonework of the front walk that led through a tidy flower garden to the front door. Solar panels were elevated on a wooden framework to the height of the roofs of the adjacent houses. "I guess you built this for Viv, when she started coming?" Garrison asked.

"We started work on this cabin a year before Viviana came to us," Dawson said.

"Why? What made you just decide to start building a cabin?" Garrison asked, but he had a feeling he already knew the answer.

"I have always had a desire—a calling, if you will—to teach young Christians. God placed this desire on my heart many years ago, before we left the State."

Garrison studied Dawson more closely, wondering how old he really was.

"After I left," Dawson was saying, "I continued teaching here in Adullam, but I always felt I was supposed to reach out to more than just those in our community. I saw this cabin one day, during one of our praise and worship services."

"What do you mean, you saw it?"

"I had my eyes closed, lost in the presence of God as I worshipped, and suddenly, I saw this cabin in my mind. Then I began to see people coming out of the cabin. They were new faces that I had never seen before. They poured out of the door, much more than could have actually fit inside. They all began crowding around me, asking me questions, begging for Bibles," Dawson stopped and looked from the cabin back to Garrison. "Something tells me this story isn't all that unusual to you."

"It sounds just like something Miss Genevieve would have told us about back home," Garrison explained. "Our community used to have visions and dreams, although I haven't heard of anyone having one in years."

Dawson considered this thoughtfully for a moment. "I would very much like to meet the members of your community. I always suspected there were more people who broke away from the State to pursue religious freedom and escape religious persecution."

"I sure didn't suspect it!" Garrison exclaimed. "I thought we were the only bunch of people insane enough to leave behind society and technology and everything that goes along with it." Suddenly he noticed

Dawson grinning broadly at his outburst and hastened to apologize. "I didn't mean people here were—I mean..."

"Crazy?" Dawson finished the sentence for him. "No offense taken. I can see you have had your doubts about the decision made by your ancestors. I, too, have had misgivings."

"You? But, aren't you the leader of this community?"

"Yes. And I know we made the right decision to leave. But I often wondered about those we left behind. Where would young Christians receive solid biblical teaching without a proper Bible? I didn't know that God's plan was to bring those young Christians to us. But come, now," he said as he led Garrison up the little stone walkway to the door. "I know you are tired. Your eyes have a journey behind them. Get some rest now, and someone will come by later to bring you to dinner." With that, he bid his farewell and left Garrison to explore the guest quarters.

The cabin was sparsely furnished, but cozy and inviting. The front door opened into a room with a fireplace. Three chairs with soft-looking cushions sat in the room. The cushions were made of a slightly fluffy material Garrison didn't recognize and were of a color unavailable to the dye-makers back home. A hand-woven rug with more familiar colors covered most of the polished wooden floor. Garrison turned from the rug to study the fireplace more closely and gasped at the elegant writing he saw carved into the mantle: *"He who has begun a good work in you will complete it until the day of Christ Jesus"*[26]—*Philippians 1:6*. Carvings of delicate wildflowers graced either side of the scripture verse, as if to emphasize that if the Creator took this much care in the design of a flower, He would in no way neglect the development of a human being's spiritual growth.

Garrison left his study of the fireplace to investigate two rooms leading off of the main living area. One turned out to be a bedroom with a double bed, a desk and a chair. He turned to open the door to the other room and what he saw made his eyes open wide. "An indoor toilet?"

---

[26] Philippians 1:6b NKJV

he muttered aloud. He wondered how people could stand the stench in the house, but upon further investigation, he discovered it was some sort of composting unit. There was also a pitcher of water, a wash basin, and a large tub which had been filled with water that was warm to the touch. He noticed a cord running from the tub to a small hole in the wall. "A bathtub heated by solar power," he mused, thinking of how many kettles of scalding water it took to heat a wash tub back home. He gratefully took off his clothes, still damp from his fall in the river, and climbed into the bathtub. He wondered if the other houses had indoor toilets and solar-heated tubs.

After his bath and a clean change of clothes he had brought in his pack, he lay down on the bed to see if there were any more pleasant differences in mattress quality. It felt like a feather bed, he decided. He was wondering how many chickens existed in Adullam to provide such an extravagant mattress for a guest cabin when he drifted off to sleep.

An hour later, he was awakened by a loud banging on the door. "Garrison? Are ya in there?" he could hear Viv calling.

Garrison rolled off the bed and stumbled, bleary-eyed, to the door.

"Come on, man, I'm starvin'!" Viv said as he stepped out the door, and then she laughed. "Ya look like leftover death!"

"Nice to see you, too," Garrison grumbled. The bed was softer than any back home, and he could have slept through dinner until morning.

"Come on, we'll be late," Viv said.

"Are we going to Dawson's house for dinner?" Garrison asked sleepily.

"Nahh, man. They don't eat dinner at home here. It's a big dining room or commons area or somethin', where they all eat together as a community. And the food is *amazing!*" Viv exclaimed.

"What's so different about it?"

"It's fresh—like they just grow it in the gardens and bring it straight to the kitchen!" Viv's eyes were round and enthusiastic as she explained about the tomatoes, green beans, sugar snap peas, lettuce and turnips she had tasted on former visits.

"Oh, okay," Garrison said, trying to sound interested.

"Whaddaya mean, 'Okay'?" Viv asked, mimicking Garrison's lack of enthusiasm. "It comes outta the ground, not a can or a pouch! And that's not the craziest part." She paused for dramatic emphasis. "The meat. It comes from animals they actually *kill!*" At this, she grabbed his arm for emphasis. "I don't eat the meat."

"Do you think they'll serve meat tonight?" Garrison asked, suddenly becoming more alert. "I've never had goat."

"Ugh," Viv said, holding her hand to her stomach.

"So, where are you staying?" Garrison asked, to change the subject. "I guess I took your bed, didn't I?"

Viv brightened. "Julie and her family are puttin' me up for the night."

"Does Julie's house have an indoor toilet and a heated bathtub?" he asked.

"Yeah," Viv said, crinkling her nose. "The water in the tub never gets very hot, and the toilet is kinda nasty, but it's better than havin' to go out in the woods."

Garrison wondered what Viv would think of his community, with their outhouses and wooden wash tubs they had to fill with water heated over the cook stove. He looked around as they made their way to the center of the rows of houses and could see a few families walking together to a large building which appeared to be the dining hall. It was like their community center back home, except much bigger. They had almost reached the hall when a shaggy brown blur bound out of nowhere and leapt up on Viv, who began giggling like a little girl. "Macy, ya big lug," she laughed.

"A dog!" Garrison exclaimed.

"Yeah, or a poor excuse for one," Viv teased, as she flopped the animal's ears back and forth affectionately.

"I've never seen a dog before," Garrison said, intrigued.

"Yeah? Well, ya still haven't seen a proper one," she said, as she held the dog's front paws. Macy was the size of a German Shepherd, but the similarity ended there. Her heritage appeared to have some golden retriever, border collie, and maybe even red heeler. She was mostly brown, but mixed in with her coat were black and golden hairs that gave her the appearance of a pot of well-cooked stew. "Macy, say hi to Garrison," Viv said, patting him on the shoulder as if to introduce them.

"Hi, Macy," Garrison said tentatively. The hodge-podge of a dog moved directly in front of him and sat down, watching him intently. "He looks like he wants me to do something," he commented.

"Well, pet, her, ya goof!" Viv laughed.

"Does he bite?"

"It's a *she*. And, no, I've never known her to bite. Just pet her, ya big baby."

Garrison started to mutter under his breath, but stopped himself, as he realized Viv would be able to hear him anyway. Macy suddenly melted his fears of being bitten as she nudged her big red nose up under his hand. Her soft brown eyes looked up at him, imploringly, as if to say, "How could you possibly resist petting me?" He fell in love with her in an instant.

"I see you've made friends with Macy," said Dawson, as he came out of the hall. "I was just coming out to look for you."

"We're coming!" Viv exclaimed, leaving Garrison behind with the dog.

"I thought all you had were chickens and goats," Garrison said.

"Well, I didn't really think of counting Macy. She wandered into our community a couple of years ago. She gets along with everyone, and except for her occasionally digging in a garden, we enjoy having her around," Dawson explained.

He led the way up to the door of the hall. Garrison wondered if Macy would follow them inside, but she sat down just outside the door, waiting hopefully for scraps. "She seems to know her place," Garrison noted.

"She knows she's not supposed to come in here. She's a good dog." Macy cocked her head at the comment, and lay down with her head on her paws.

The dining hall was laid out much like a cafeteria, with food served buffet-style. Long tables were set out in rows. Most people were done eating and were laughing and talking among themselves. Garrison filled his plate, complete with roasted goat meat, and sat down by Viv to eat.

"Oh, yuck, Garrison! Do ya have to eat that sittin' right next to me?" she squawked.

"It's delicious, and it's something different I've never tried before," he said, stuffing another forkful of the meat into his mouth. Viv turned a shade paler and scooted her chair farther away. "So I've gathered from what you said earlier and from your reaction now that the State doesn't have meat on the menu?" Garrison asked, with his mouth full.

"Killing animals for any reason other than euthanasia has been illegal for years," Viv said.

"Then you're all vegetarians?" Garrison asked.

"No, we still eat meat. But it's not from animals. They grow it in factories, from cloned protein cells. No animal has to die in the process," Viv explained.

"Does it taste the same?"

"How would I know? I'm not gonna eat somethin' that was up walkin' around a few minutes ago!" Viv said irritably, and turned her chair to face a different direction.

Dawson, obviously amused, sat down across from them. "There are many things about the laws of the State which might surprise you," he began. "The idea of killing and eating an animal was so offensive to Viv when she first came, that she turned around and left when she found out they are one of our main food sources."

"She apparently overcame that aversion, since she's still coming around," Garrison commented.

"Yes. I think she forgave what she considered to be our barbaric way of life when the Holy Spirit drew her back for more teaching of the Word."

"Well, it's not like ya have much choice. And the whole world used to do it, anyway," Viv said, careful to avert her gaze from Garrison's plate. "I just can't get used to it yet."

"You would probably faint dead away if you came to my house on butchering day," Garrison said. His thoughts went back to the conversation he had with his Sunday School teacher when he was a little boy, and suddenly he remembered the image he had in his mind years ago of a hollowed-out heart. He had felt for certain that he would be able to fill that heart when he left his community. But here he was, in another place very similar to the one he left. He seemed no closer to reaching his goal of exploring modern society than he had when he left home. "Is the State really all that dangerous to visit?" he suddenly asked. "I've wanted to go my whole life—to experience the technology, the information networks they have on their computers—or just to see a computer! I want to know what it's like to have lights at the flick of a switch and water that comes out of a pipe in the wall, and to be able to heat a house without wood and drive a car, and there are so many other things I don't even know about. That's why I left home. I wanted more. But it seems you people here in Adullam are doing the same thing people back home were doing. You're just hiding out. I didn't leave to go back into hiding. I left to see the world."

The people around their table had stopped talking to watch Garrison. Suddenly he felt very exposed. Dawson cleared his throat and smiled. "I understand your fascination. There are days when I think I would do almost anything just to have a hot shower again." He was silent for a moment as he looked intently at Garrison. "Do you know why we call this place Adullam?"

"Well, I assumed it was named after the cave where David hid when he was running from King Saul," Garrison replied.

"That's right. And when his family heard about it, they all came down to be with him. The scriptures say that 'everyone *who was* in distress, and everyone *who was* in debt, and everyone *who was* discontented gathered to him.'[27] David became a shepherd to those people. He ended up with about four hundred men, some of whom became known as his mighty men. They were an unlikely group of heroes—people who were in debt and discouraged with life. With such a dismal beginning, how do you think they became known as mighty men?" Dawson waited for Garrison to answer.

"I guess because they listened to David. He was a good leader. Everyone seemed to like him," Garrison ventured.

"Ahh, yes. He had charisma. But consider the leaders in world history. Hitler, for instance, had incredible charisma. And look at the horrors he accomplished with his regime."

"Well, I guess the difference there would obviously be what led the leaders. David was led by God. He sought His will in almost every decision he made. Hitler had his own agenda, and it was an evil one," Garrison hastened to explain.

"Yes. Very true. But I am actually looking for a simpler answer to my original question," Dawson said. "How did the people in Adullam become David's mighty men? Yes, they followed their leader, and he was a good one to follow. But more importantly, they didn't stay in Adullam forever. It was a good place to hide, but it wasn't their final destination."

Garrison became aware that several members of the community had gathered around their table and were listening closely. Some looked at him and smiled, nodding their agreement with Dawson. "This was never meant to be a permanent home," Dawson continued. "It was a place to hide out for a while, to teach those who are hungry to learn in a safe environment. And we will not leave until God leads us to do so. Young Christians from the State who need to soak in the Word may do so here, and then go forth into their communities to bring the light of Truth to them. 2 Corinthians 4:6 says 'For it is the God who commanded light to shine out of darkness, who has shone in our hearts to *give* the

---

[27] See 1 Samuel 22:2 NKJV

light of the knowledge of the glory of God in the face of Jesus Christ.'[28] We didn't come here to hide forever. This is a launching pad for Truth."

Garrison looked around at the shining faces gathered around the table. He was certain none of these people could complain of having an empty, hollowed-out heart. Faith and certainty seemed to shine out from within them. Suddenly he felt something nudging against his leg and was surprised to see Macy staring up at him. She cocked her head and barked, and half the people in the gathered crowd jumped, and then laughed at themselves for jumping.

"Macy, what are you doing?" Dawson scolded. "You know you're not supposed to be in here."

Macy looked at Dawson and then back at Garrison and lay her head in his lap. "I wish Selah could meet you," Garrison said, and his chest seemed to constrict with a sudden, unexpected longing for home.

---

[28] 2 Corinthians 4:6 NKJV

19

THE next morning, Garrison awoke surprisingly early. It was still dark outside, and the community had not yet begun to stir. He turned over in the soft bed and wondered why he was awake. Then he heard it. A slight scraping sound. He sat up and quietly swung his feet over the edge of the bed. There it was again. It was definitely a scratching sound, and it was coming from the front room. Careful not to make any noise, Garrison stole to the doorway of the bedroom and tried to see through the darkness to locate the rat or opossum that must have somehow found a way inside. *Scritch, scritch.* The sound was coming from the direction of the front door. In the faint moonlight coming through the windows, Garrison could see nothing in the cabin, itself. Something on the outside was trying to get in. Well, he would simply open the door and startle it away. Just in case it was a skunk, he planned to open the door just a crack to see what type of varmint it was before booting it off the porch.

He had no more turned the knob when the door was suddenly flung open and his knees were shoved out from under him. Garrison stumbled to the floor and immediately felt something warm and moist smear across his face. He cried out in surprise and propelled himself backwards across the floor. Whatever it was, it kept coming, with its bad breath and slobbery tongue. Suddenly Garrison stopped scrambling backward as common sense kicked in. "Macy? Is that you?" he asked.

Macy answered with a friendly bark. "Well, good morning to you, too," Garrison said, his heart still thumping hard. "What brings you here so early? Did you think it was time for me to get up?"

The shaggy mutt stuck her cold nose in his face and dragged her tongue across his lips. "Enough, enough!" Garrison sputtered, and got to his feet. Macy trotted to the open door, where she was silhouetted against the gray daylight. Garrison could see her tail wagging as she looked back at him. *"Rarf!"* she barked.

"Quiet! You'll wake everybody up," Garrison shushed her, and went to the front door. Macy stepped out onto the walkway and turned again to look back at him. When Garrison didn't move, she barked again. "What do you want, you crazy animal?" Garrison said in a loud whisper, trying not to wake the neighbors. He walked up to Macy to pet her, which she seemed to enjoy immensely. As soon as he was done petting her, she went to the gate and looked back and barked again. "If I didn't know any better, I'd think you wanted me to follow you. But I'm not even dressed yet. Come back inside while I put on some clothes."

Macy followed him inside the house and watched him closely as he took off the pajamas loaned to him by Dawson and pulled on his pants and shirt from the night before. Then she turned around and headed up the stone walkway to the gate, which Garrison noticed was opened, and then stepped out onto the road in front of the house. With one more look at him over her shoulder, she trotted down the road. Garrison walked quickly to keep up. Dogs were interesting creatures, he decided, so maybe this stop at Adullam wasn't a total loss. He followed Macy around side yards on a route that led them to the big dining hall, where he assumed she was looking for an early breakfast. But the dog simply skirted the building and crossed the open area to the other side and began making her way through the rows of houses. Garrison marveled at how much more populated Adullam was than his own community. How had a community of this size escaped detection by the State? Weren't they missed when they disappeared from society? Suddenly he realized Macy had stopped in front of the gate of an unobtrusive little house. There was a light glowing from one of the windows. Macy put her paws up on the gate and shoved her nose up under the latch that kept it shut. The gate swung open, and she trotted inside and sat down by the front door. Garrison stood hesitantly by the front gate. Macy obviously wanted him to follow her, but he had no idea whose house this was. Someone was awake, but who would welcome such an early guest, and a stranger, at that?

While Garrison was still deciding what to do, Macy stood up and stepped to the side of the house, her ears cocked forward as she looked toward the back yard. She looked back at Garrison with her mouth open and her tongue lolling out with an expression that looked like a goofy grin. She then resumed her post, looking toward the back yard. "What are you listening to?" Garrison whispered. Finally curiosity got the best of him, and he moved quietly forward to stand beside the dog. He could hear someone speaking quietly from the back of the house, and when he strained to listen, he could just make out the words.

"You know my knowledge is limited. I'm depending on You to help me to make the right decisions. I know it's my place to stay here, to guide and teach Your people. You know how I feel. I've been telling You for years—I want to go myself, to see if I can find Yosi. But if that isn't the plan, then send someone else to him…someone who knows the truth. Keep him safe, Father. I'm depending on You, my God. You and Sophia are the only ones who really know how I feel. You had to let go of Your Son, too. You understand the pain of separation I feel. It seems everyone else has forgotten him—given him up for dead, or worse. I will never give up, for Your Word says that You are the God of all flesh, and there is nothing too hard for You."[29]

Garrison shrank back, ashamed to have been eavesdropping on such a private and emotional conversation. He didn't know who Yosi or Sophia were, but he knew that the voice in the back yard belonged to Dawson. As he stepped backward, the voice rose in a song of praise. Garrison stopped in his tracks. How could this man, who was in such anguish over this Yosi character, praise God when everything seemed so bleak? And it wasn't something that was faked. Dawson was unaware of his presence, so he wasn't doing it for anyone else's benefit

---

[29] See Jeremiah 32:27

123

but God, Himself. The words seemed strained at first, but the longer he sang, the stronger his voice became, until Dawson was singing joyfully at the top of his lungs. A strange feeling began to overtake Garrison. He was riveted to the spot, captivated by the overwhelming sense of joy in Dawson's voice. It was as if he could feel the same emotion Dawson was feeling, simply by hearing his song—a feeling of trust, joy, and deep, underlying peace.

The neighborhood was beginning to wake up as dawn made its way to Adullam. Objects which were unrecognizable moments ago were now obvious in the growing daylight. An angular chunk to his right became a wheelbarrow. What he had thought was a decorative cross was merely one end of a clothesline. Any minute now, someone would spot him and wonder what he was doing just standing in Dawson's yard.

Suddenly, the song ended, and Garrison heard the sound of a door shutting. He quickly walked back to the gate and was reaching to shut it when he remembered Macy, still inside the yard. "Macy! Come here!" he called. The dog took two steps toward him and barked. "Macy, so help me, I will carry you out of that yard if I have to," Garrison said as loud as he dared. Macy simply barked and smiled her goofy dog-smile and sat down, tail flopping. Garrison flinched as the front door opened. A woman in her fifties, with graying, blond hair tied back in a braid, stuck her head out and spoke to the dog.

"I'm going to get whoever taught you to open the gates," she said. Then she noticed Garrison. "Hello! You must be Garrison." She stepped out onto the porch. "I didn't get a chance to meet you yesterday. I'm Sophia, Dawson's wife."

Garrison smiled. That was one mystery solved. And obviously, they must have a son named Yosi. "I'm glad to meet you," he replied. "I'm sorry to come by so early. I didn't know who lived here. Macy sort of led me here, I guess," he tried to explain.

"Dawson was saying that Macy has really taken a fancy to you," Sophia said. "Why don't you come inside for a cup of coffee?"

"Coffee? You have coffee?" Garrison asked in disbelief.

"Thanks to Viv. Over the past few months, she has brought enough of the highly concentrated instant stuff to last the whole community for a while. We keep telling her we don't want anything, but she always feels like she has to bring something with her when she comes." Sophia beckoned him into the house and showed him to a seat at the kitchen table. "So what do you think of our little community?"

Garrison thought for a second. His first impression of the community wasn't exactly a true representation, when he remembered Dawson's words last night about Adullam being a launching pad. Until then, he had considered them just another group of paranoid isolationists. They were different, though, since they were obviously trying to reach out to the outside world in a positive, albeit limited way. "Well, when I first got here, I thought it was just like back home. But the more I learn about it, the more I see where the similarities end," Garrison said carefully.

"We always knew there must be more communities like ours, but we've never yet felt it was time to leave to seek them out," Sophia's eyes crinkled in a smile. She had the interesting wrinkles of a person who smiles a great deal.

"I didn't exactly go with my community's blessing," Garrison found himself admitting, and hesitated. Sophia was watching him, and her gentle expression didn't change with the news. "Okay, actually, I had to sneak out," he continued. "No one is allowed to leave our community, because the elders say that if we do, we might risk detection by the State. But I had gone outside the boundaries dozens of times this summer, and nothing ever came of it. I finally worked up the nerve to leave. But I wasn't leaving to try to find out if there were more people like us. I left because I thought the elders were wrong, and I didn't think it was fair to keep people in a place they didn't want to stay. Our valley was like a haven for most people there, but to me, it was like a prison. I want to know what it's like out there in the real world now. And I'm tired of people who feel they know what is best for me holding me back and making my decisions for me." Garrison stopped suddenly. He had not admitted the last thing to anyone before, even himself. It was as if someone had pulled a cork out of his mouth and released a fountain of words.

Sophia added hot water from her kettle to the instant coffee she had put in a mug that said *"Visit beautiful Yellowstone National Park"* with a picture of Old Faithful and multicolored Morning Glory Pool on the side. She quietly handed him the cup.

Garrison thanked her, marveling that she made no comment about his decision to leave or his attitude toward the elders. She seemed to simply listen thoughtfully, reserving her judgment. "Did Yellowstone National Park still exist when you left to come here?" Garrison asked as he studied the mug.

"It did. But recently, it was lost to China."

Garrison was enjoying the completely new aroma wafting up out of the cup when Sophia's words registered. "China?"

"Yes. Because the State defaulted on China's loan to the United States all those years ago, China finally followed through with the threat to collect," Sophia explained.

"So after all the effort to abolish private property to protect the environment, the State lost one of our National Parks?"

"Ironic, isn't it?" Sophia said. "What do you think of the coffee?"

Garrison grinned. "I was so busy smelling it I haven't even tried any yet. It smells wonderful." He sipped at the steaming dark liquid and frowned at it thoughtfully. "It tastes different than it smells."

"You mean, it smells better than it tastes?" Sophia ventured.

"Well, I wasn't going to say that, but, yes," Garrison admitted.

Sophia laughed. "Don't worry. Just about everyone, even coffee lovers, agree with that statement. "We can add some milk or sugar, if you like."

"Is it goat's milk?" Garrison asked.

"Well, yes. I'm sorry. That's the only kind of milk we have here."

"No, don't be sorry. I'd like to try it," Garrison said eagerly.

"You have an adventurous spirit, even with food," Sophia said, her eyes twinkling. She went to a small box on the counter. The front of it opened like a door, and she pulled out a bottle of milk to bring to the table. When Garrison reached for the milk, he was surprised at how cold it was.

"Is your spring branch nearby?" he asked

"Our what?"

"Your spring. You must have a spring nearby where you store your milk. If you've already been to the spring and back, you either got up really early or it's nearby. For the milk to be so cold, I mean," Garrison tried to explain.

"Oh!" Sophia laughed. "Come here, Garrison," she said, and went over to the box on the counter. Garrison followed her and watched with interest as she opened up the door again. "Put your hand in here," she instructed.

Garrison complied, and his eyes widened in surprise. "Is that little box a refrigerator?"

"Yes, indeed," Sophia smiled. "It's just a mini-fridge. Most houses here have them."

"But where do you get the power for it?"

"The same place we get the power for our heated bath tubs and the hot plates we use to cook with. Solar panels."

"Solar panels must have gotten better over the years," Garrison said. "We almost never use ours."

"What do you think of our lighting?" Sophia asked, as she flipped on a switch. Suddenly the room was ablaze with light. Garrison could see a cord running across the ceiling. It was dotted with tiny circles that emitted an amazing amount of light, considering their size.

"What kind of light is that?" Garrison asked, astounded.

"L.E.D.s," Sophia explained. "Light Emitting Diodes. People in the State used L.E.D. light bulbs at the time we left, but using the emitters without the bulbs took up less space, and we have some very clever people who live here who know how to step down the electricity supplied by our solar powered batteries so they will work with these emitters."

"So who are the lucky people who get to have them in their homes?" Garrison asked, thinking of the dark guest cabin and the lantern on the desk in his room.

Sophia looked puzzled. "All the homes have them. Didn't you see the switch by your front door?"

Garrison was embarrassed to realize he hadn't. He had light at his fingertips the whole time, and never thought to look for the source of power flow. "I can't believe I didn't notice that," he said.

"Don't feel bad. I would imagine a lot of people miss the light source, because they aren't looking, or they're in a hurry, or they just expect to have to do things the hard way," Sophia said with a look Garrison couldn't quite interpret.

"I didn't notice the lights in the dining hall last night," Garrison said.

"They were there. But we also have lanterns there, and with all the new things to take in, you must have missed them," she said, and turned to greet Dawson as he came in from the back of the house.

"Who is this at such an early hour?" said Dawson with a smile.

Garrison extended his hand, and Dawson clasped it warmly. "I'm sorry about it being so early," Garrison apologized.

"You are always welcome here," Dawson assured him.

"I was just explaining to Garrison about our light source," Sophia said. "He has been struggling in the dark using nothing but the little lantern in the guest cabin because he didn't know what was available to him."

Dawson chuckled and gave his wife a hug. "How funny. Isn't it like us to always try to do things the hard way?" His face seemed to beam with happiness. No matter the inner struggle he had dealt with in the prayer time, during the time of praise, Garrison could see he had been given strength.

"Why don't you join us for breakfast?" Dawson asked. "Most families eat the noon and evening meals in the dining hall, but breakfast is a uniquely family time. I would be honored if you would be our guest."

Sophia glanced at Dawson, and for a fleeting moment, Garrison thought a look of sadness crossed her face.

"I would love to," Garrison replied.

"Can I help you with anything, Honey?" Dawson asked Sophia.

"Yes. You can entertain our guest while I make breakfast," she smiled.

Dawson looked at Garrison and seemed to be making his mind up about something. Finally, he said, "Come with me to my study. I have something I'm certain will hold your interest."

Garrison followed Dawson down a short hall to a back room. In the room was a desk covered with books and papers. "I apologize for my mess. I'm always preparing for the next message." He stacked and restacked the papers, and then opened a drawer of the desk and pulled out a flat, shiny object about twelve by eighteen inches in size. He glanced up at Garrison and smiled as he opened the flat object. It stayed open at a right angle. Dawson plugged a black cord into the back of the object and plugged a pronged plug at the other end of the cord into an outlet on the wall. He rotated the object so that it was in Garrison's full view and pushed a button on the front.

Garrison watched as a void black surface suddenly came alive with light. A picture of a much younger Dawson and Sophia appeared. Between them was a boy who looked to be about eight years old. They were all smiling, and behind them was an incredible mountain vista.

Garrison couldn't believe what he was seeing. "Is this a . . ."

"Computer?" Dawson finished the question for him. "Yes. It's what's known as a laptop, and one of the last models made without the option of a touchscreen. It was a dinosaur even thirty years ago. But it still works well, and it could run all the games Yosi liked to play when we left."

"Yosi?" Garrison asked tentatively.

"My son, Joseph. We called him Yosi." Dawson paused as if he would like to say something more, and then reconsidered. He pointed to one of several little objects which seemed to float on top of the picture of the happy family. "These are called icons. They are shortcuts to different programs stored on the computer. This is the program I use the most," he said. "I can use this little pad at the base of the keyboard to select things on the screen. It's kind of like a mouse, when you don't have one."

"A mouse?" Garrison asked, trying to conceive what earthly good a rodent would be in conjunction with the use of an electronic device like this.

Dawson laughed. "Not a varmint mouse. Nevermind." He dragged his finger across the pad, and Garrison could see an arrow moving across the screen. It stopped at the icon he had gestured to earlier. Dawson tapped the pad, and the screen changed. Eventually, what appeared to be a blank piece of paper appeared on the screen. Dawson typed on the keyboard, and words appeared on the page. "This is a word processing program. I use it to write in my journal. Once in a great while, I will use it to write sermon notes, but then, of course, I have to bring the laptop with me when I preach, because I don't have a printer.

"A printer?" Garrison asked.

"A device that prints onto paper what you have created on the computer. Most people stopped using them years before we left, because they just kept the information on a tablet and could share it into what they call a 'cloud,' which is just a way for people to conceptualize a method of storing information over the internet," Dawson explained.

"But I don't understand. No one was allowed to bring electronic devices when my community left society. They were told that having things like that would alert the State to our presence."

"And well they could have. Almost every electronic device made for the past 80 years won't work without some sort of a connection to the internet. But this device is so old it doesn't need the internet to work.

It has programs stored on its own hard drive, so it can run independently. It is no more of a threat of detection for our society than, say, our refrigerator," Dawson said.

"Another wonderful item we didn't have back home," Garrison mused. He wondered why their ancestors had decided to do without so many things that would have helped ease their way of life. Then he remembered the story of the cramped van ride, and the sense of urgency they had felt. Maybe if they had had more time to plan, they would have been able to bring refrigerators and hotplates. He wondered about Adullam's beginnings. "Dawson, when this community relocated from the State, how did it escape notice? Our community started out with maybe twenty-five people—just a few families. Your community hasn't existed for nearly as long as mine, but it's probably ten times the size of ours. I can only assume it was like a mass exodus when you all left the State."

Dawson gestured for Garrison to sit down in a comfortable looking chair as he sat down in a seat behind the desk. "Actually, Adullam started with just one family," he said.

"One family?"

"Yes. Mine. Sophia and I made the decision to leave. We had talked about the possibility with our congregation—theoretically, of course. You see, I was the pastor of a large congregation in St. Louis. I had to be careful about what I said, because the congregation was so large, it was almost impossible for me to get to know everyone on a personal basis. I couldn't reveal that I had felt the Holy Spirit leading me to leave civilization, as we know it, because someone there would probably have turned me in to the authorities. But I did mention frequently that our society was becoming less and less tolerant of the Christian view. When the State began to crack down on the use of religious publications by anyone who claimed their literature was the infallible Word of God, I mentioned offhandedly how it would be wonderful if we could escape to a safe haven where the Bible we used, in its unaltered, uncensored form, could still be taught. A few members of the congregation messaged me about this, and I answered them glibly, since all of our electronic communication could be tracked. But a few people were actually serious about it and came to me privately, in person. I still had to be careful. Some of those people were informants, but it was fairly easy to spot them. I was tight-lipped, even with those who were genuine, knowing the trouble they could be in if they were brought in for questioning.

"During the whole process, I had all these questions and loose ends. I used to lie awake at night and ask the Lord things like, 'Do you want me to gather a group of people and take them with us? Should I find a replacement before I leave? Is one of my associate pastors ready to take my place? Who will take over the online ministry?' I fasted and prayed for direction, and the only answer I ever got was, 'Trust me. Leave it to me. Don't worry about tomorrow. Today's trouble is enough for today.' And even though my mind was in turmoil about all the details that weren't mentioned, my spirit was peaceful. So I turned it all over to Him and made preparations only for my own family to leave.

"Just a few weeks into the preparation process, an old friend of mine who had speaking engagements around the world called me to say he was in town and asked if we could meet. We met in my office, where he told me he didn't know why he was there. He had cancelled all his future speaking engagements because the Lord had told him he was supposed to be there. I sat there, and as I looked at him, the Lord said to me, 'There's your replacement. But don't tell him anything of your plans.' So I explained to him that I had been thinking of taking a sabbatical, of sorts, and I had been praying to find someone to fill my pulpit while I was gone. He agreed, and the transition was underway. One of his first steps was to change the focus of the online ministry by making it less of the responsibility of the senior pastor and more of a joint effort between the associate pastors and cell group leaders. The online ministry, which had seemed slightly stale before, blossomed under this new direction, and was a tremendously more effective outreach tool. I could almost hear God laughing at me for worrying. The church was running smoothly and more efficiently than when I had been at the helm.

"Then came the question of when to leave and how, and how we would live once we got to where we were going. I had been researching solar power, wind power, even the use of water wheels, and finally settled on solar power because it was the most portable equipment. I had to purchase a vehicle, because we didn't own one, living in the city as we did. Then I had to rent a storage shed, because we had no place to keep the vehicle and all the things we were amassing for our expedition. I just kept doing the things I knew to do, and let God take care of all the rest.

"Then one day, it was time to go. I woke up and I just knew. Sophia only had to look at me, and she knew it was time. We hadn't told Yosi anything except that we were going to be leaving for a while, which everyone else already knew anyway. That's what you do when you go on sabbatical—you leave to study somewhere else and hopefully come home with a fresh outlook and something new to bring to the table. We just didn't know when the return trip would be.

"Yosi looked at it as an adventure, but he was dubious about leaving all his internet-connected devices. So I downloaded all his favorite games to this laptop. 'It's not the same if I can't play online with my friends,' he said. I told him at least he could still play with the computer as his opponent. I had always had concerns about Yosi when I thought about taking him away from everything and everyone he knew, but I really started to worry about him then. He obviously had no say in this new development in his life. How would he feel about it? Would he resent us? Would he feel trapped in his new home? But God once again reminded me He had everything under control." Dawson stopped talking and leaned back in his chair.

Garrison had to ask the question that had been gnawing at him since he had first heard Yosi's name mentioned in prayer. "Dawson, I have a confession to make," he began. "This morning, I overheard you praying. I didn't mean to be eavesdropping, but Macy..." he stopped as he realized how ridiculous it would sound to say the dog made him do it. "What I mean is, I followed the dog to your house, and I could hear you praying. I heard you praying for Yosi. May I ask what happened?"

Dawson's face clouded, whether because of the news that someone had overheard him or because of the memory of Yosi, Garrison couldn't tell. Dawson leaned forward and glanced up at him and then back at his hands, his finger tracing an invisible outline on the desk. "Yosi did not adjust well to life here. It was an adventure, at first, but when puberty hit, things became more difficult."

"If he was the only kid here, I can't say I'm surprised," Garrison said as politely as he could.

"Oh, he wasn't the only child here," Dawson said quickly. "We were the first of many families, as you must have guessed. But people came in groups of one, two and three families, at the most. Little by little, our community began to grow. The second family to come here was my associate pastor and his wife and little boy. They arrived a month later. He said he felt like he was just wandering around, looking for a place for his family to stay, and yet that wandering ended up with them on our doorstep. It was much the same for all the other families. Some of them have come here as recently as ten years ago. Of course, we have had marriages and new births since then, so our community has grown quite large. But back to your question. Yosi always had plenty of friends, and many of them had parents who had found electronic gaming devices which were independent of the internet, as well. Yosi was able to link the devices so they could play their games as they always did. They eventually ran lengths of cable from house to house so that they had their own mini version of the internet. But the older Yosi got, the more restless he became. He had a great gift with technology, you see, and had always dreamed of creating and marketing his own games and starting up his own tech company. Of course, this was impossible in Adullam, with his archaic laptop and our disconnect with the outside world. He became resentful, as I had feared in the beginning. And then, things seemed to get better. He began spending a little more time with his mother and me, asking us about the very first day we started on our trip. I didn't realize until later he was trying to get directions home. One day, not long after he turned 18, he walked out with his backpack and said he was going to see his friend, Anthony. It was a Saturday. I had been struggling with the sermon, and barely looked up from my study to mumble 'See you later.' That was the last we saw of him." Dawson was quiet for a moment. "I was so angry with God at first. 'You told me not to worry about anything, and look where it got me.' I told Him. I immediately tried to go after Yosi, as soon as we realized he was gone. But it was not God's will. I would leave Adullam, and somehow always managed to find myself back at Adullam, no matter what direction I took. So since God would not let me leave, I begged and pleaded with Him to bring Yosi back to us. That was sixteen years ago."

Garrison felt a heaviness settle over him as the weight of what he had really done to his parents bore down on him. A lump rose in his throat, and he swallowed and stood up to walk to the window so his face would be hidden. Always before, he had managed to sidestep this feeling of guilt. Listening to this gentle man's story from a parent's point of view changed everything. The tears came unbidden down his cheeks and he tried to keep from sniffling, but it was no use. He was embarrassed by the onslaught of emotion he was experiencing. Suddenly he felt a hand on his shoulder, and to his own surprise, he turned and looked at Dawson instead of pulling away as he would have in the past. "I'm... sorry..." the words jerked out between sobs. "I hurt so many people. I'm sorry for everything," he said to God and to his parents and Selah and the whole community, even though they weren't there. He said it looking at Dawson, and somehow the man seemed to understand, for he pulled Garrison to him so that his head rested on his shoulder, and he just let him cry. The two stood there like that for some time.

Finally, he backed away and fixed Garrison with his eyes. "If the people you hurt were here, I think they would forgive you," Dawson said. "But more importantly, God forgives you."

"No, I don't think so," Garrison said weakly. "You don't understand. I was angry with Him for the life I was trapped in. Then I told myself that He didn't even exist. How can He forgive someone who doesn't even believe in Him?"

"How can someone who doesn't even believe in Him worry about whether or not he will be forgiven?" Dawson replied, looking knowingly at Garrison. "Besides, do you think your doubts took God by surprise? Even if all your atheistic proclamations were simply your way of getting back at Him, do you think He can't forgive you?"

"It's not that He can't. What if He won't?" Garrison reasoned.

"You mean, you think He doesn't love you anymore?" Dawson asked.

"I never gave Him a chance to love me in the first place. I never asked Jesus to forgive me for all my sins and come into my heart."

"It sounds to me like you did just ask Him to forgive you for all your sins. Not in those exact words, of course. But your apology wasn't just directed at the people you've hurt, was it?" Dawson asked. Garrison shook his head. "As for asking Jesus to come into your heart, as you say, why don't you explain to me what you mean by that?"

Garrison looked at him quizzically. "Well, I mean, when someone asks Jesus to come into their heart, it means they want His Spirit to live in them. They want to give over control of their life to Him and yield to His Spirit instead of always following their own way. It's like dying to your old self and being reborn, spiritually."

Dawson smiled. "Yes, that's right. So how about it? Are you ready to give your life to Jesus?"

"Why would He want me? I haven't done anything to endear myself to Him, that's for certain," Garrison said.

"He created you and knew you before you were born. That's what it says in Psalm 139. That psalm also says that all the days of your life were written in His book before they ever took shape. You took careful planning on His part." Dawson grabbed a Bible off of the desk. "I want you to read this, right here. Romans 8:35. Read it aloud," Dawson said, and handed the Bible to Garrison.

"Can anything ever separate us from Christ's love? Does it mean He no longer loves us if we have trouble or calamity, or are persecuted, or hungry, or destitute, or in danger, or threatened with death?"[30] read Garrison.

"Now read verses 37 through 39," Dawson instructed.

"No, despite all these things, overwhelming victory is ours through Christ, who loved us,"[31] Garrison continued, "And I am convinced that nothing can ever separate us from God's love. Neither death nor life, neither angels nor demons, neither our fears for today nor our worries about tomorrow—not even the powers of hell can separate us from God's love. No power in the sky above or in the earth below—indeed, nothing in all creation will ever be able to separate us from the love of God that is revealed in Christ Jesus our Lord."[32]

Garrison couldn't believe what was happening. All of the things he had been taught since he was young, all of the things he had made fun of since he was little, suddenly made perfect sense. The sense of longing for something that he had felt his whole life was building to an incredible crescendo inside of him. He looked at Dawson. "I'm ready. I'm ready to ask Him."

"Then just ask Him. He's been waiting for you your whole life to ask Him this one thing," Dawson said.

Garrison closed his eyes. A sense of humility gripped him, and he found himself kneeling right there on the floor. "Jesus, I know I really messed things up," he began. "But just now I realize I really do believe in You, and I'm sorry I was so angry with You. I'd really like it if You would take away this rotten heart of mine and give me a new one, a heart like Yours–a heart that would be a place You would like to live, where You can be my God and my Father, and I can be Your son. Please somehow do this, and show me how to live from now on." His words were choked with emotion, but his head was clear. He meant

---

[30] Romans 8:35 NLT
[31] Romans 8:37 NLT
[32] Romans 8:38-39 NLT

every word, and he knew that this would change all the plans he had made from now on. A nagging voice entered his mind. *"What about all your plans? Are you just throwing everything away?"* it seemed to ask. He sighed and mentally surrendered all his old plans of seeing modern society. It seemed so insignificant now, compared with the God of eternity. As he did this, the weight he had felt earlier lifted and a feeling like warmth spread through his whole body. Suddenly, he realized the feeling was God's love—the love that had been surrounding him and waiting for him to receive it his whole life. "Thank you, Jesus!" he whispered in amazement. He opened his eyes to see Dawson kneeling beside him, watching him. "He really did it," Garrison said in wonder. "He really changed something in me!"

"Therefore, if anyone *is* in Christ, *he is* a new creation; old things have passed away; behold, all things have become new,"[33] quoted Dawson.

"2 Corinthians 5:17," Garrison added.

"You see, Garrison, someone taught you God's Word. And no matter how you felt about it at the time, God's Word does not return to Him void. Hebrews 4:12 says it is 'alive and powerful. It is sharper than the sharpest two-edged sword, cutting between soul and spirit, between joint and marrow. It exposes our innermost thoughts and desires.'[34] The Word of God you learned as a boy stayed with you, working in you, helping bring about this very moment in your life," Dawson said.

"Somehow, now, I believe that," Garrison said.

A gentle knock was heard at the door as Sophia stepped into view. "Breakfast is ready," she said.

"Do you know what just happened, dear?" Dawson asked.

Sophia beamed and wiped a tear with her apron. "I've been praying for you since you two left me in the kitchen," she admitted, and they all laughed.

Dawson and Garrison followed Sophia back into the kitchen, where a table was spread with eggs, biscuits and gravy, and something that

---

[33] 2 Corinthians 5:17 NKJV
[34] See Hebrews 4:12 NLT

looked like sausage patties but smelled more like goat. They all had some more coffee, and while Sophia and Dawson listened intently, Garrison told them stories of home.

20

"My goodness, Garrison," said Dawson suddenly. "I've been so engrossed in your stories that time has gotten away from me!"

Sophia, whose chin had been perched on her hand as she listened, glanced at the antique clock on their mantle and gasped in surprise.

"I'm sorry I kept rambling on," Garrison said, a little embarrassed that he had monopolized their time.

"On the contrary, I have found your stories to be fascinating. However, I have to preach a message in less than an hour, and I need to change clothes and look over my notes again," Dawson explained as he excused himself and headed down the hall.

"Is it Sunday?" Garrison asked.

"Yes!" Sophia exclaimed as she began clearing away the dishes. "I just completely lost track of time."

"Well, *I* completely lost track of what *day* it was," Garrison mused. "I'll be on my way so you can get ready."

"You're not bothering us," Sophia hastened to reassure him. "Why don't you just wait here and we can all go together? You *are* coming, aren't you?"

Garrison grinned from ear to ear. "It's the first time I ever wanted to go to church, instead of being dragged there. I wouldn't miss it!"

While Sophia and Dawson made final preparations for the morning service, Garrison busied himself by looking through an old-time family photo book that was propped up on the mantle beside the clock. Even with all the innovations in technology, the practice of making memory books had apparently never gone out of style. This particular one was a compilation of photographs and journal entries, bound into a professional-looking book format. It chronicled the Manaba family's summer vacation to Colorado. Garrison smiled as he saw a picture of Yosi looking rather dubiously at a brook trout he was holding with Dawson. In other photos, Sophia and Yosi paddled a canoe in a lake that perfectly reflected the surrounding gray-faced mountains and white-barked aspen trees. Garrison shook his head at a picture of Yosi engrossed by something on a small computer screen, while in the background, a bull elk with an enormous set of antlers grazed just off the edge of a highway. The caption read, *"Later, Yosi found a picture of an elk on the internet and asked, 'When are we going to see one of those?'"* In other pictures by scenic landmarks where crowds were gathered, Garrison noticed that almost every individual held a small device in their hands. Many of the people seemed to be looking at their devices instead of the scenery, and most of the interactions taking place seemed to be a result of little groups clustered around a device held by an individual.

"I see you found our family vacation book," Sophia said as she came back into the living room.

"Yes. It's such a beautiful landscape. But what are these people looking at? What is that they're holding?" Garrison asked.

Sophia looked at the photo. "Oh. Those are phones. Or some of them, the larger ones, are tablets. They're like smaller versions of the laptop in Dawson's office. The people are probably looking at a picture they just took, or watching a video, or some of them are sending messages to their friends or posting their photos on a social media site."

Garrison had heard about social media from Miss Genevieve, who still remembered having friends on the internet whom she had never actually met. "I guess I'm just surprised that after traveling all that way to see something, they would spend more time looking at a phone or a little computer instead of the scenery and the people they're with."

Sophia looked thoughtful. "You know, looking back, I remember trips where I spent so much time trying to record all the memories that

I was too busy to just relax and enjoy *making* the memories I was trying to record. Getting the perfect shot to post online was such an addictive thing. It was very gratifying when people would comment on what you had posted. Some people got their sense of self-worth from the feedback they received from their on-line friends."

"I guess that's not much different from where I grew up. Whether they admit it or not, people measure themselves by the comments of others," Garrison said.

"Except that comments on the internet are not made face to face," Sophia noted. "People tend to be less tactful when they don't have to look the person in the eye as they say something. And since the comments are printed on the screen, they can be reviewed over and over again, whether kind or devastating. Various censoring programs were written with the original purpose of protecting people from bullying and tracking down offenders. But it went much farther than that. Eventually, they became the means through which online ministries were being shut down all over the web; and it was the start of the rewriting of the Bible. To insist that we are all sinners is very offensive to the people who aren't willing to admit it. *Muzzler*, the censor program ultimately adopted by the government, became a powerful tool in the hands of those with anti-Christian sentiments."

"I've never heard of such a program," Garrison said, "but it doesn't surprise me that someone came up with it. I've always wanted to learn about modern technology, but I know there are risks in using it."

"The good or the bad isn't in the tool, itself," said Dawson, as he came down the hall. "It's in how it's used and who is using it. Technology has made incredible strides in advancing the gospel. It's a shame humanity is using that very tool to undermine it now." He slid into a jacket and gathered his notes and his Bible. "Are we ready?" he asked.

"Yes, sir!" Garrison smiled. It was such a strange feeling to be looking forward to church.

As they made their way to the sanctuary, Garrison could see many families were already converging on the structure. It was a sizable building, nearly twice as large as the one used for meals. Located at the very center of the community, the concentric rows of houses used the sanctuary as their hub. Garrison, marveling at the materials used to build the house of worship, couldn't help but wonder why so much effort was put into a building having only one purpose. "Couldn't you have saved a lot of work and materials by making the dining hall a little bigger and using it for your services, as well as meals?" he asked.

Dawson looked at the structure fondly as they approached the front doors. "Of course. Since everything here has to be built without the use of modern equipment, projects such as these take even longer, so the idea of having a multipurpose building was a temptation. We did consider that in the initial planning stage. But we wanted the sanctuary to be a building that was set aside solely for the worship of God and the teaching of His Word. I know the place where we meet is just wood and stone, and I know we could meet anywhere we choose. But we wanted this place to be special—set aside for spiritual purposes. Can you imagine how distracting it would be when the smell of food began wafting into a sanctuary that would be transformed into a dining hall in a few minutes? People in the middle of worshipping would suddenly have visions of roasted chicken interfering with their focus on Jesus. Our carnal nature can concoct enough of its own distractions without having some provided from an outside source. Besides, I think it pleases the Lord to know we would go to the trouble of making a building set apart for Him. For us, the very act of planning and building this sanctuary became an extended act of worship."

Garrison considered Dawson's words as they entered the building. In his home, the community hall had served multiple purposes, including its use as the church's meeting place. He had never given it a second thought. But then again, he had never cared before. He was always looking out a window, daydreaming about what he would do after the service was over, or secretly making fun of Shawna Beardsley singing off key.

Today was different. For one thing, as he was looking around the room, he experienced a feeling of anticipation. It was on the faces of people as they found their seats in the polished oaken pews. But the faces of the people weren't the only way he could sense it. There was a warm feeling of connection between himself and everyone here. When he shook people's hands, it was almost as if a feeling of love bridged the gap of any lack of familiarity between them. Complete strangers seemed like family. "I feel like I know these people, but I've never seen them before in my life," Garrison said to Sophia as they sat down on a front row.

"There is a kinship between God's children. We are all brothers and sisters in Christ. Now that you are part of the family of God, you are experiencing the bond of love we share," Sophia said warmly.

"I've never felt this close to people, even to the people I've known all my life," Garrison mused. "I can't explain it. It's like I love them without ever having met them before."

"That's the love of God," Sophia explained. "It is unconditional. You will find you also have it for those who don't know Jesus. But the feeling of kinship you are experiencing is often so strong with others who know the Lord that you can often sense whether someone is part of the family of God without even having to ask them."

Garrison continued to look around the room. He spotted Viv and several other young adults sitting with Julie and her family. As he watched them smiling and visiting with each other, he suddenly realized how much he owed to Viv for bringing him here. He was about to excuse himself to go over and speak with her when a voice from the stage area greeted the crowd. "Good morning, children of God!" said a young man standing behind an electric keyboard.

"That's Josiah Langston, our worship leader," Sophia told Garrison. Garrison had been so busy watching the crowd that he hadn't paid much attention to the platform. He was surprised to see the man was speaking into a microphone, and the members of the band had electric instruments. But then again, Adullam seemed to have a better grasp of alternative sources of electricity. The band was completed by a middle aged woman on electric guitar, a spikey-haired young man on bass guitar, a teenage girl on the drums, and three more vocalists standing in the front.

"It's a beautiful day to worship the Lord!" the worship leader was saying enthusiastically. "Of course, you know there are only two times to worship the Lord. And when is that?" he paused, waiting for the crowd to give the answer.

"When you feel like it, and when you don't!" several voices in the crowd said in unison.

"How many of you feel like it today?" Josiah asked. A roar of enthusiastic cheering erupted from the section of the crowd occupied by Viv and her friends.

"Come on, I wanna know if God has done anything for you! How many of you in this place have been brought out of darkness into His marvelous light?" Josiah stopped playing around on the keyboard to lift both of his hands straight up in the air. Most of the crowd were shouting words of affirmation or waving their hands to indicate their gratitude. Garrison wanted to shout with them, but a feeling of overwhelming emotion flooded over him, and he found that all he could do was weep. "How many of you here today are ready to surrender all to God in worship?" Josiah asked. Suddenly, Garrison found both of his hands in the air. His knees hit the floor as he paid homage to the King he had just allowed to walk into his life. This King had created him and had always had every right to own him in every way, but had never insisted on His rights, instead allowing Himself, the Creator, to be chosen by the creation. It was too much for Garrison to comprehend. All he could do was express his gratitude, love, and surrender by kneeling on the floor and putting his hands in the air. He had seen a few people back home raise their hands during the songs they would sing at church, but he had never understood why. Now he understood completely. He wanted to show his respect, submission, and humility and to reach for

God with all his might– all at the same time. All around him, the congregation was singing a happy song of praise, and tears were streaming down his face. He briefly wondered what they must think of him, but decided he didn't care. This was between him and the One who had just saved him from his sins. As he knelt there, he found it no challenge at all to focus on the One who had died for him. The most amazing thing was that it felt as if Jesus was right there, focusing on *him*. Waves of love seemed to sweep over him as the crowd continued to sing, and though he had never heard these songs before, he was eventually able to join in on some of the simpler choruses.

When the worship part of the service was over, he reluctantly sat back down in his seat. Sophia handed him a handkerchief, which he gratefully accepted. It was time for the sermon, and once again, Garrison found no trouble concentrating. He hung on every word Dawson said.

"I struggled with the message for today," Dawson was saying. "It's such a familiar message that many of us grow calloused to it, I'm afraid. But the message of reconciliation is the core of the gospel. God knew when He created us that we would go astray. He knew in advance that He would have to send His Son to die for us to make atonement for our sin. But through Christ's death on the cross, and His victory over death in the resurrection, the bridge of reconciliation has been built. Jesus spanned the awful chasm of separation through the cross! His innocent blood reconciled us to the Father." Dawson stopped abruptly and shook his head. "I'm getting ahead of myself," he said. "Let's open up our Bibles and turn to Luke chapter 15, starting with verse 11." Some of the crowd pulled out a hard copy of their Bibles, while others used electronic media to access the scriptures. He shared a Bible with Sophia, but the scripture reference was so familiar to him that he didn't even need to read the words.

It was the story of a man who had two sons. The younger son decided he had had enough of working for his father. He wanted to see the world. So he asked to be given his inheritance in advance instead of waiting to receive it when his father died. The son then took the inheritance and spent it wastefully in a faraway land. About the time his money dried up, so did the crops in the land; and as famine set in, the boy began to know hardship. He went to work for a farmer, taking care of the man's pigs, and was so hungry he wished he could eat the food he fed to them. One day, the scripture said, he "came to himself." "It was the 'A-hah' moment," Dawson explained. "He finally awoke out of his sleep. 'My father's servants have plenty to eat, and here I am dying of hunger!' he said to himself. 'I will go to my father and say to him, 'Father, I have sinned against heaven and against you, and am no longer worthy to be called your son. Will you take me on as a hired hand?'[35] I wonder how many times he recited his speech, wondering if his father would even listen to anything he had to say. But when he came in sight of the family farm, his father could see him from a long way off. Did he tell his servants to meet his son at the gate and block his entry? No. He ran to meet him and embraced him. The boy could only get out the first few words of his long-recited speech before the father turned to his servants and told them to bring out the finest robe they could find for the boy, put a ring on his finger and shoes on his feet, and to kill the calf they had been fattening for a special occasion so they could prepare a feast. 'My son was dead, and has come to life. He was lost, but now is found!'"[36] Dawson said. In his voice, Garrison could hear the passion of a father who knows the pain of a lost son.

The implications of the story, which had always been lost on him, now hit him. He had always identified with the wayward boy, having always been the one who wanted to leave. What he hadn't realized before was that he had been lost a long time before he left home. And though he hadn't made it back to his earthly home yet, he knew without a doubt that he had been found. The love of Jesus was so real in this room that he could sense it. He was once again grateful for the handkerchief Sophia had given him as he blew his nose as quietly as he

---

[35] See Luke 15:17-19
[36] See Luke 15:24

could. *"Selah would never believe this,"* he thought to himself, and suddenly laughed out loud.

After the service, Garrison wanted to talk to Dawson and tell him the sermon had spoken directly to him. But a line of people had already formed, and somehow he was already toward the end of it. Suddenly, someone shoved herself directly in front of him, and he found himself looking straight at Viv. "Garrison! It *is* you. I didn't think it was, at first. For someone who doesn't believe in God, ya sure do get into worship," she exclaimed, and looked at him searchingly.

"I know you probably thought I was faking. I wanted to tell you before service started, but didn't get the chance. Something happened to me, Viv—something incredible that I never expected. Dawson and I were talking this morning before service," Garrison began.

"Before service? But he didn't get here 'til right before," Viv interrupted.

"It wasn't here. I was at his house."

"Ya went to visit him on Sunday morning, right before church? Isn't he kinda busy, havin' to preach an' all?" Viv seemed surprised.

"I didn't go on purpose. I didn't even remember it was Sunday. But that dog came by and got me," he began.

"Macy came and got ya? Whaddaya mean?"

Garrison sighed. "It's extremely hard to explain anything to you when you keep interrupting," he said. "So maybe I'd better just get to the point. I gave my life to Jesus this morning."

Viv's eyes opened wide and she grabbed him around the neck and squealed. "Way Man! Ya really *are* a Way Man now!" she exclaimed, practically choking him with her hug. "That explains the way ya were worshippin' down there. Tell me all about it, now! I wanna know everything from the dock launch."

Garrison told his story to Viv and Julie, who had come over to join them. "There are so many scriptures Dawson used in his sermon that I've known since I was a boy, but I never *really* knew them until now," he said when he was finished.

Julie looked at him, her eyes shining. "You knew them by memory, but you didn't know them by heart," she said.

Garrison was surprised by the simple paradox. She was right. He had intellectual knowledge of the Word of God, but until now, his heart had remained in the dark. Different scriptures he had memorized for Miss Genevieve were coming back to him, and while they had seemed to mean nothing before, he could tell just by thinking about them that they were rich in multiple meanings. A whole new world was opening up to him, and he was aware of the debt of gratitude he owed to the wise elderly woman who had often told him that "God's Word would not return unto Him void, but would accomplish what it was sent out to do."[37]

"Come on, Way Man. Let's get some lunch," said Viv as she tugged at his arm. They followed Julie and her family through the crowd to the dining hall.

They were almost finished eating when Dawson and Sophia came by with their plates of food. "So did you tell Viv the good news?" Dawson asked Garrison.

Viv jumped up and whooped and pumped her arm in the air for an answer. Dawson and Sophia couldn't help but laugh. "Viv, I hope you always stay this enthusiastic," Dawson said.

"It's not just Viv," Garrison said. "The way you worship here—it's so different from back home. Of course, we don't have many instruments, but even so, there doesn't seem to be any life in the way people sing and play there. But here, it's like God is right there in the room with you and you want to tell Him exactly how you feel."

Dawson seemed to consider his words carefully before he spoke. "It's true that we're blessed with some talented musicians and singers who are dedicated to serving the Lord in song. But I've been to many places in my lifetime that didn't have the array of instruments we have. One church just had an old, antique, out-of-tune piano. And the singing—

---

[37] See Isaiah 55:11

well, it wasn't what you'd call pleasing to the ear. But I know it pleased the Lord's ears, because you could tell those people were singing and playing from the heart, with a sincere desire to worship. I could sense the presence of God stronger in some of those types of services than I could in some of the mega churches that had a full orchestra to complement their hundred-voice choir. It's about whether or not you're worshipping sincerely, 'in spirit and truth,' although when you have both the elements of talent *and* sincerity, coupled with the anointing, it's hard to beat."

"What's the anointing?" asked Viv.

"It's when God's Spirit rests on someone to do something. It makes all the difference. I've seen extremely talented musicians and vocalists who were focused on themselves and their abilities instead of on God and what He can do. Their performances were nothing but performances, and many times, since man was lifting up himself, the Spirit of God didn't move through the service. But on the other hand, I've heard some mediocre singers—and some who were downright awful, to be honest —but somehow, God used them and souls were drawn to the Lord by a move of His Holy Spirit in the service. The difference is that one was anointed and another was not," Dawson explained.

"I want that! I wanna be anointed to bring others to Jesus!" Viv exclaimed emphatically.

"Well, Viv, it seems that you already are," Dawson grinned as he looked at Garrison.

Viv scrunched her eyebrows together. "You mean because I brought Garrison to Adullam? But I just brought 'em here. I didn't talk 'em into getting' saved or nothin'."

"What made you stop and pick him up?" Julie asked. "Didn't you tell me you had a feeling you were supposed to bring him along, even though it seemed dangerous?"

"Well, yeah," Viv said thoughtfully.

"And when he said he didn't believe in God, did that discourage you from talking to him about the Lord?" Julie asked.

"Are you kidding?" Garrison interrupted. "She wouldn't shut up about Him. She practically killed me trying to get me to call out to God for mercy when she took us over that cliff."

"I knew what I was doin'," Viv insisted.

"You certainly did," Garrison said. "I knew I needed a Higher Power at that point like I never had before!" He laughed as Viv punched him in the arm.

"What Julie is trying to tell you is that God used you for the specific task of bringing Garrison here and planting a seed in his heart," Sophia said.

"It's true," Garrison added. "That's what I wanted to tell you before the service. I wanted to thank you for bringing me here, and for showing me someone who is really alive in Christ."

"Dawson has that affect on a lot of people," Viv said.

"I was actually talking about *you*," Garrison replied. "Everyone I grew up around has heard about Jesus all their lives. Many of them are really Christians. But they've all *grown up* knowing about God. For you, in your society, it's not the normal thing. You take a risk in believing there is only one way to God. It makes everything about your life in Christ seem more intense."

Viv's eyes had a faraway look. "You have no idea," she said softly. "If they knew, they might try to force me to take the chip. That's what they do to people who seem unbalanced. 'Except for the Discards, of course. Nobody messes much wi' them, 'cause they don't live very long, anyway. I don' know what happens to ya after ya have a chip, but no one I ever met who got one ever seems the same as before. It's like they steal their soul, or somethin'."

Dawson looked at her intently. "Viv, I hope they would never force you to have the chip implant. But you know Romans 8:38 and 39 says that neither death nor life, nor angels nor principalities nor powers, nor things present nor things to come, nor height, nor depth, nor any other created thing, shall be able to separate us from the love of God which is in Christ Jesus our Lord.[38] That pretty much covers everything—even

---

[38] See Romans 8:38-39 NKJV

computer chips."

"Does it really say that?" Viv asked

"Don't take my word for it. Read it for yourself," Dawson said, getting out his Bible that he had brought with him, having come straight from the service. He waited for Viv to read the passage and then continued. "There is a reason you've never been caught coming and going here. There's a reason you haven't been labeled as imbalanced. You have a purpose to fulfill. Viv, you are anointed to reach out to others and bring them to Jesus Christ. When you first came here, you had a long way to go. But as time goes by and you study the Word of God and spend time with Him in prayer, you gain maturity. You learn wisdom as you think about what His Word really means in your life, and what it has meant to the people in this community. Someday, God may lay it on your heart to bring someone else here, as well. And someday, God may lay it on the heart of someone from Adullam to go back with you, to help you share the gospel. But if you're waiting for God to anoint you to do something, let me assure you, you've already been anointed!"

Viv sat quietly for a moment and then grinned at Garrison. "Whaddaya know, Way Man? Looks like I'm the Tab-a-ras, now!"

21

Sunday afternoon in Adullam was spent visiting with family and relaxing or napping until the evening service. Viv and Garrison stayed with Julie and her husband, Mark, and their four children, who all seemed to have the gift of hospitality. Garrison felt right at home the minute he came through the door. The front yard was full of children and teenagers playing either catch or tag. "This is a popular place," Garrison commented to Viv. "It kind of reminds me of going to the Beardsley's house back home—kids running all over the place and some sort of game going on all the time."

"Julie and Mark are like real family to me," Viv replied. "They just love on everybody. And if ya need to talk about somethin', ya can tell 'em and don't need to worry 'bout it goin' no further." She stopped and laughed as she watched Julie give a neighborhood girl a playful swat for sneaking an extra cookie. "Julie said she'd adopt me, if I wasn't so ornery. I tell ya, Way Man, this family is one of the reasons I hate goin' back to the State. I wish I could stay here forever."

"When do you have to go back?" Garrison asked.

"Tomorrow mornin'. I don't hafta go back to work 'til Tuesday. I usually come to Adullam when I have a three day weekend so I can have more time. Or sometimes I come when I just can't stand it anymore."

"What is your job in the State?" Garrison asked. "People still have jobs, right? Or do they just live for recreation because the government takes care of everything?"

"Yeah, we have jobs. I work in a food packaging plant."

"Do you work on an assembly line?" Garrison asked, remembering the pictures of factory workers from Genevieve's books.

"Not exactly. I'm a line tech. We keep the machines on the assembly line up and runnin'. We run diagnostics on equipment. I'm really lucky —I mean blessed—to have the job. Most people who work there have a college degree. They hired me with the understanding that I would get a degree in a coupla years. I'm a special case, because my dad was —" Viv stopped short, and then seemed to will herself to continue. "He was a Discard. They give special consideration to children of Discards. Makes the State look good, ya know. Shows they can fix anybody an' give 'em a good life." Viv's voice was drenched in sarcasm.

"What exactly is a Discard?" Garrison asked cautiously.

Viv shifted her position on the couch and rested her chin on a throw pillow as she hugged it tightly. "Discards are the people who don't want anything to do with havin' anything implanted in their bodies. They even give birth at home, on their own, so the State can't put implants in their babies. They don't usually live very long because they get sick with somethin' or another since they don't have the health implants to help their bodies fight off things like cancer or diabetes or heart disease. They got all kindsa things wrong with 'em, most times. Lots of 'em can't have kids 'cause of the cancer surgery they hafta have, and some of 'em need new livers or kidneys. But most of 'em can't afford to have surgery or buy spare parts. And some of the ones that do have money end up spendin' it on drugs."

"They won't put an implant in their body, but they'll take drugs?" Garrison asked in disbelief. He had learned about the Age of Addiction from the old timers. It had enslaved entire generations, costing more lives than some of the early wars.

"The reason they won't get an implant isn't because they think it's wrong or bad for ya to put it in there. It's because they don't trust the government an' they think the implants are tracking devices or experiments on humans," Viv explained.

"They feel about the implants the way you feel about the chip," Garrison offered.

"Except we don't just *suspect* the chip is a tracking device. The government told us they are. It's one of the selling points. Ol' Mother State can watch over ya an' protect ya at all times. Ya never get lost, because ya have a built-in GPS that helps ya navigate. The chip can help ya do your job better. It can help ya get along with people better. Ya can learn things faster. It's the answer for everything."

"Except an empty heart," Garrison replied.

"I used to think that, an' I still do, really," Viv said. "But the chip works better than drugs to fill the empty space. If ya start feelin' empty again, ya just get a new upgrade, like my friend I told ya about. And then there are the people that it seems like nothin' can fix. They get a chip just so they can tweak it, which is highly illegal, since a chip is always considered government property, even after they put it in ya. They call it 'chippin'. They say it's crazier than any trip from old-fashioned drugs. And some of the chippers have gone so blinked out that they make serial killers look like kindergarten teachers."

"They must know the risks when they mess with their chip. Why would anyone *do* that?" Garrison asked incredulously.

"I guess they think it's worth the risk. Some of 'em say it makes 'em think on a higher plane—helps 'em access parts of their brain they've never used before," Viv explained.

"How do they alter it, if it's inside their bodies?"

"They hafta have a lot of money just to find someone who can do the job—usually a chip tech who works dirty on the side. Then they pay the dirty tech to alter their chips with illegal upgrades. Problem is, the upgrades are always corrupted, 'cause they're pirated copies and they're never as good as the original. But that's also the excitement of it, because ya never know exactly whatcha gonna get. You could end up a genius, or permanently high, or a psycho that chops up your own dock mate. It's only the most desperate people who try it—the ones that for them, livin' is worse than dyin'." Viv was wringing the throw pillow into a twisted knot. "Anything to escape the memories they're runnin' from."

"Why don't they make an upgrade that can erase memory?" Garrison asked. "Maybe then, there wouldn't be so many people trying to alter their chips."

"I think they're workin' on that," Viv said, twisting the pillow in the other direction now.

"You're awfully hard on those pillows," Garrison commented.

Viv stuck out her tongue at him and fluffed the pillow back to normal size. "It's just that it bothers me 'cause I don't know how to stop 'em. Once they start messin' with people's brains, are they even gonna be able to understand the message of Jesus Christ?"

"They have a choice before they even get the chip," Garrison ventured.

"Not if they don't even know about the choice," Viv replied. She grabbed a strand of her silky hair from its red section and seemed to ponder it for a moment. "Garrison, why do ya think I colored my hair this way?"

Garrison was caught off guard by the seemingly unrelated question. "I just figured that the people where you live must have wild hair these days."

Viv ran her fingers through the red strands. "Nahh, man. I mean, it's not unusual to see a crazy 'do, but this one is symbolic. The red half is for the blood of Christ. The white half is how He took my darkest sins away an' made me white as snow. Whenever someone asks me about it, I can tell 'em what Jesus did for me. They don't come down so hard on ya if someone else starts it."

"And the blue?" Garrison asked.

Viv picked up the blue strands and twisted them around her index finger. "The blue is to go along with the red and the white. It shows I still believe in the possibility of a return to the America that used to exist. They try to make it sound dangerous, like all that freedom was too much for us to handle. But I gotta believe they're wrong. I mean, what they're doin' now, it can't be right!" She settled back down into the couch.

"So you've never gotten in trouble for telling someone when they ask?"

"Ya can't get in trouble for tellin' people what ya believe unless ya come across as bein' pushy about it, like ya have the inside info an' you're tryin' to get people to believe a certain way." She paused and smiled. "Which is, of course, what I'm tryin' to do. I mean, there's only one way to God—through the death and resurrection of His Son, Jesus. It's His sacrifice that makes us free, 'cause we couldn't pay for our own sins. All the other gods they teach about in that fake Bible they put out now—they're not like Jesus. Their followers claim that some of them came to earth and took on human form, or that they were already human and became like gods. But none of them gave their life for us. And when they died, none of them rose again. Jesus left heaven and lived life on earth as one of us. He knows what it's like here and what we're goin' through. An' even though He knew we'd mess up, He created us. He knew when He was hangin' on that cross that He would create someone named Viviana who would totally mess up her life and need to have His mercy. He knew it, an' He still loved me." She was silent for a moment, her eyes shining with wonder. "How do ya account for a love like that, Garrison– a love that won't quit? I know someday I might get in trouble if people get offended at what I say. I've come plenty close a few times. But if Jesus was willin' to do all that He did for me, shouldn't I be willin' to take a few risks? An' if I know the truth that will set people free from their misery, how can I hide it? On the Day of Judgment, I don't want them to come up to me and ask me why I never said nothin' when I worked beside 'em every day. We have life in Christ, Garrison. That life is the light of men. The darker this world gets, the brighter the light shines, and the darkness has never been able to put it out. It says so in John 1:5. I hafta remind myself of that when I start feelin' hopeless about it all."

Garrison felt a lump in his throat. He had suddenly remembered the conversation he'd had with Miss Genevieve and Selah beside the smokehouse. He had used the idea of the Great Commission as his justification for leaving the valley, when he had absolutely no intention of sharing the love of Christ. Here was a girl who longed for the very culture he had despised. She was immersed in a society that was sick and needed to hear truth, and she was willing to risk her freedom to share it.

"What would happen if you got caught telling someone that Jesus is the only way?" he asked.

"Anyone who claims their belief is the only way is considered intolerant. Intolerance leads to discrimination, and discrimination leads to violence against people who don't believe the way you do. If you get warned for intolerance enough times, you get a citation and hafta appear before a judge who will decide if ya need reconditioning of some sort," Viv explained.

"What is reconditioning? Do you have to spend time in jail?"

"Not jail so much as a mental health center. They check out your implants to see if everything is workin' right, and if ya have a chip, they reprogram it. I'm not sure exactly what that does—but it does somethin' to the way ya think. I've only really met one other person besides the people in Adullam who told people the truth about Jesus. I'm not sure what happened to her, but I don't think the State would bother with her. I only saw her the one time. She could be dead by now, I guess."

"What makes you say that?" Garrison asked.

"Well, she was a Discard, ya savvy? Like I told ya, they don't live very long. I met her when I went to see my dad one time. I don't go to see him 'less I hafta. I mean, I know I should, but it's hard. He's high, most times. An' the only reason I went was to get proof that he was my real dad so I could get the job I have now. I was ridin' my bike real slow-like in the outer docks, cause I was keepin' an eye up the alleys for him. I wasn't really sure where he docked anymore, but I knew his neighborhood. An' this girl in a ragged ol' jacket standin' on the sidewalk smiles an' waves real big at me like she knows me." Viv's eyes took on a faraway look, as if she could see the scene playing out in her memory. "'Hey, Miss!' she calls out to me, 'I know how to find who ya lookin' for,' she says, real confident. So I stops the bike an' I say, 'How ya know who I lookin' for, girl?' An' she smiles the prettiest smile outta that dirt-smeared face an' says, 'I knowed Him for a long time now. He's my best friend. He's the greatest. I can tell ya how to find Him.' Well, I knew then that she couldn't be talkin' about my junkie dad. The only ones who called him the greatest were the ones he shared his dope with when they needed a fix. So I told her I wasn't lookin' for who she thought I was lookin' for. But she kept insisting I was lookin' for this dude she knew. So I asked her what was so great about him, 'cause she didn't look like anyone who had used before, ya know? She was real young, and she didn't jitter or phase. An' then she told me how this one time she had been thinkin' about usin', 'cause her ma had just died an' everything felt so hopeless. She was diggin' through the trash lookin' for somethin' to sell to buy dope, an' she found a book. It was an actual book, not an electronic one. She showed it to me. It was this little bitty New Testament, all old an' worn out. She said she thought maybe it could be a valuable antique she could pawn somewhere. So on the way to the pawn shop, she starts readin' it as she walks. She just opens it up an' starts readin' in John chapter one. She didn't understand all she read, but she said it was like when she read about Jesus, a light came on inside her and she kept wantin' to read more. She got to the pawn shop and sat on the step and kept readin', cause she didn't want to give it up until she learned all she could about this Jesus dude. She sat there all day, until the shop closed, so she decided to come back the next day. She read all that night in the shelter where she slept, and all the way back to the shop the next mornin'. She sat down on the step again, 'cause somethin' just wouldn't let her pawn that book. And even though she didn't understand everything, she understood John 3:16 & 17. 'For God so loved the world that He gave His only begotten Son, that whoever believes in Him should not perish but have everlasting life. For God did not send His Son into the world to condemn the world, but that the world through Him might be saved.'[39] Right there on the steps to that shop, she prayed to Jesus—a God she had never heard of before—and asked Him to help her and forgive her and be her Lord. She said she wasn't so lonely and desperate anymore after that, because she had someone who was with her all the time who had promised to never leave her. Well, I thought then an' there that she was just touched in the head with grief about her ma and from livin' in the outer dock filth her whole life. I asked her what she thought that had to do with my dad, because that was who I was lookin' for. An' she says –I'll never forget it—she says that I'm *really* lookin' for my *real* dad, an' I jus' don't know it yet. I knew she was just a kid, but somethin' about the way she said it made me mad. I told her she was crazy an' she needed to get some help. But she just smiled like an angel and told me she had gotten all the help she needed. She said if I would ask Jesus, He would show me how to find my real Dad and give me all the help I need. I thought I had wasted enough time listenin' to the crazy, and I scooted on down the road. But I couldn't get her outta my head—not her, and not what she had said. It played over an' over in my mind even after I got back to where I dock. She started my search for the one true God. It's because of her that I accepted Jesus. I never saw her but that one time, even though I went lookin' for her later. No one I asked knew what happened to her, but they all knew who I was talkin' about, 'cause she was hard to forget. She had told everyone she knew about Jesus."

"So do you think she died of some health problem, or did the State find out about her and take her into custody?" Garrison asked.

"I don't know. The State doesn't pay much attention to the Discards, unless they go to one of the health clinics in the outer docks. If a Discard has money to pay for cancer surgery or a new kidney, they usually wanna know how they came up with it, an' then they'll check them out real close. Like I said, I don't know. But I still pray for her every day, because if it wasn't for her, I wouldn't know the Lord." Viv stood up and

---

[39] John 3:16-17 NKJV

looked out the window at a group of teenagers playing football. "Come on, Garrison. Let's do somethin' besides just sittin' here. We only have one hour before service starts." She pulled him up off the couch and shoved him toward the door.

Even though he had never met her, Garrison found he couldn't stop thinking about the little girl in the outer docks, either. There were so many people who needed to hear what he had taken for granted his entire life.

22

SUNDAY evening services at Adullam were broken into three different sections: a youth service in the left wing of the building, a children's service in the right wing, and the adult service in the main sanctuary. "I used to just always go wherever Dawson was preachin', because he's a Word man and 'e knows the Word better'n anyone I know," Viv told Garrison as they entered the left wing, "but one time Craig asked if I could come and tell how I learned about Jesus. Some of the people in the youth group really connected with me. I don't know if it's 'cause I'm their age and I grew up in the State, or if they just can't believe someone wouldn't give their life to Jesus until they were 17, or both. I think most people who grow up here decide to follow Jesus when they're just little."

"You're only 17?" Garrison asked. "For some reason I thought you were older than that."

"I'm 19. Seventeen is how old I was when I came to Jesus. Ya see, I graduated from high school early, but I didn't want to go to college just yet. I wanted to earn some money for more implants so I could be exactly the way I thought I wanted to be. I had the chance for that tech job so I went lookin' for my dad, 'cause I knew the factory would hire me if I could prove I was from the outer docks. An' then I met that girl, and whether she knew it or not, she led me to Jesus."

"She planted a seed," Garrison suggested.

"Yeah, like the story Jesus told about the farmer who sows seeds that land on all kinds of ground."[40] Viv's eyes were warm and bright as

---

[40] See Matthew 13:3-9, 18-23

the scripture unfolded in her own words. "Some seeds land on rocky ground and sprout, but dry up quick-like. Some get eaten up by birds, and some get choked out by thorns, but some land on good ground and take root. The seed that little gal sowed took root in me, and here I am. Craig asked if I could keep comin' when I'm here on Sunday nights, so I do. If it encourages other people somehow, I'm glad to help. And the way Craig explains the Word, I've really learned a lot. He makes it easy to understand. That story about the seed, I read it before, but it made more sense when he explained it."

"Viv! Sit with us!" called a red-headed girl sitting with a group of teens on the front row.

"Chat-ra, if I sit wit' ya, ya gotta promise not to talk through the whole service!" Viv said with a wink.

The girl tried to scowl ferociously but just ended up with her face twisted into a lopsided grin. "Garrison, this is Chat-ra—I mean *Chandra*." Viv introduced the two. "She has the gift of gab." Chandra elbowed Viv in the ribs and smiled shyly at Garrison. The shyness lasted only a split second, though, as Chandra quickly demonstrated how she had earned her nickname.

"So, why'd you do it?" She asked him. "Why'd you leave?"

"Well . . ." Garrison thought about how his story of leaving would spread around the community—how it must seem like news to a place that didn't get much in the way of news.

"Maybe he doesn't want to talk about it," Viv interjected, as Garrison seemed to flounder with an answer.

"There's no harm in asking," Chandra insisted. "If he doesn't want to tell me, he doesn't have to!"

"No, I don't mind," Garrison assured them. Suddenly he realized he had a small audience clustered around the front row, and he felt a little self-conscious. His reasons for leaving had been so selfish. All the more reason to tell them, he decided. "I left because I wanted to see the world. I wanted to live in a modern society, where we didn't have to work so hard. I wanted to experience technology. You see, where I come from, we don't have computers at all. We don't have much access to electricity. I wanted more than what our little valley has to offer. I didn't even care that it might risk exposing our community. The real problem was, I didn't know who Jesus was. I mean, I knew who He was in the Bible and in history, but I didn't have any connection to Him, personally. So I just went my own way, which was the wrong way." One of Miss Genevieve's scriptures suddenly popped into his head. "Isaiah 53:6 says it exactly. 'All we like sheep have gone astray; we have turned, every one, to his own way; and the Lord has laid on Him the iniquity of us all.'"[41]

"That's pretty good preaching," said a voice behind him.

"Hey, Craig! Garrison, this is Pastor Craig Goforth," said Viv brightly. The way she blushed when she looked at him, Garrison wondered if her motives for being in the youth service were strictly to help with the other teens.

"I'm glad to meet you, Pastor Craig," Garrison said as he extended his hand.

"Everyone here just calls me Craig," the dark-haired, dark-eyed man said with a smile. He looked to be in his mid-twenties, and was strikingly handsome. From the looks some of the other girls gave him, Garrison didn't doubt that many of them were never late for youth service. But later, as he was able to observe Craig interacting with different youths of both genders, he noticed they all seemed to have genuine respect and admiration for him. The man had charisma, but more importantly, Garrison could tell he truly cared about each one of the teens, and they knew it.

The praise and worship service was even louder and longer than the one in the morning service, and Garrison wondered if the others were really focused on worship or just having a good time jumping around to the beat of the music. When the last few songs were sung, his question was answered. They were songs that were slower and more worshipful,

---

[41] Isaiah 53:6 NKJV

and he could see that many of the people there seemed lost in worship. He stopped worrying about what everyone else was doing and began to focus on Jesus and all the Lord had done in his life in just this one day. The songs ended too soon for him. It seemed he had finally gotten focused when that part of the service was over and it was time for the teaching of the Word.

Craig stepped to the platform and addressed the congregation of teenagers. "Alright, everyone. Before we open the Word of God, I want everyone to do something for me. Everyone take off your shoes and socks and look at your feet."

"What?" Viv sputtered, along with fifty or more others around the room.

"Craig, my brother's in here! You got some kind of a death wish?" Chandra exclaimed.

"Come on," Craig insisted. "See, I'll do it, too." He bent over and unlaced his shoes and pulled off his socks. With a wry grin, he stood up on the platform, sticking out his feet and wriggling his toes. "Really, it's not so bad. You can put your shoes back on in a minute, but right now, I want you to get a good look at your feet."

Garrison was the first. He took off his boots and socks and stared at his calluses.

"Ya need to trim ya toenails, Way Man," Viv cackled, as she slipped off her shoes and socks. It seemed to spread from the front row where they were sitting, until all the kids in the auditorium were barefoot.

"So what do you think?" Craig was saying. "How do they look?"

"I have *ugly toes!*" an older boy announced proudly.

"Trevor, that ain't ugly, that's scary," said his friend sitting next to him. Several people around them laughed.

"Who here thinks you have beautiful feet?" Craig asked.

No one said anything.

"Do you know that everyone here has the potential for beautiful feet?" Craig asked.

"Jesus loves us even if we have ugly feet," Chandra blurted out.

"That's true," Craig said, "But does anyone here know that He wants us all to have beautiful feet?"

Everyone in the room looked around at each other as if Craig had lost his mind.

"Does this have something to do with the Church being the bride of Christ, and He wants every part of us to be beautiful?" Chandra spoke up again.

"No, not exactly," Craig said. "Ok, you can put on your shoes and socks now."

"Can we just stay barefoot?" asked a girl in the back.

"Suit yourself. As long as your neighbors don't mind the smell," Craig joked.

"Tonight," He said amidst the soft clomping sounds of 200 plus teenagers putting on their shoes, "the title of my message is *Beautiful Feet*."

Viv turned to Garrison with an apologetic expression. "His sermons aren't usually so weird like this," she whispered.

"I'd like you to turn to the book of Romans," Craig was saying. "Romans 10, starting with verse 8." Craig waited for everyone to find the scripture and then began reading.

> "In fact, it says, 'The message is very close at hand; it is on your lips and in your heart.' And that message is the very message about faith that we preach: If you openly declare that Jesus is Lord and believe in your heart that God raised him from the dead, you will be saved. For it is by believing in your heart that you are made right with God, and it is by openly declaring your faith that you are saved. As the Scriptures tell us, 'Anyone who trusts in him will never be disgraced.' Jew and Gentile are the same in this respect. They have the same Lord, who gives generously to all who call on him. For 'Everyone who calls on the name of the Lord will be saved.'"[42]

---

[42] Romans 10:8-13 NLT

At this point, Craig paused and read more slowly for emphasis.

> "But how can they call on him to save them unless they believe in him? And how can they believe in him if they have never heard about him? And how can they hear about him unless someone tells them? And how will anyone go and tell them without being sent? That is why the Scriptures say, 'How beautiful are the feet of messengers who bring good news!'"[43]

Pastor Craig looked around the room. "I know you all were wondering what having nice feet has to do with being a Christian. I mean, when we think of beauty, we usually concentrate on hair or eyes or lips. That's what songs are written about. It's easy to say, 'Your lips are like roses,' or 'Your eyes sparkle like starlight.' Are you taking notes, boys?" Craig grinned as some of the rowdier boys batted eyelashes at each other in jest. "But what do you say about the feet? They just don't lend themselves to poetic verse. What complimentary thing you can find to say about them? *'Your feet aren't that hairy'* or *'Your toes don't have any lint between them?'*"

A collective *"Ewww!"* erupted from the crowd.

"Yet here the apostle Paul is saying that people who bring the good news of Jesus Christ have beautiful feet. He's actually quoting a verse in Isaiah. It's Isaiah 52:7: 'How beautiful on the mountains are the feet of the messenger who brings good news, the good news of peace and salvation, the news that the God of Israel reigns!'[44] Think about what it was like in Israel at that time. People wore sandals, not high-tech hiking shoes with comfortable arch supports and protective material. Feet on a journey became dusty, scratched by twigs or briars, callused and blistered. But when the lowly feet become the vehicle for the most important message anyone can hear, even they can be considered lovely because of what they are carrying." Craig looked around the room. "You

---

[43] Romans 10:14-15 NLT
[44] Isaiah 52:7 NLT

may not consider yourself to be a worthy vehicle of the gospel. Maybe you're not good with words, or maybe you're shy. Maybe you don't think you're a very likeable person. But you have a message that you carry with you that can change someone's world. The beauty of that message trumps anything you think might be wrong with you. But just as Romans 10:14 says, 'How can they call on him to save them unless they believe in him? And how can they believe in him if they have never heard about him? And how can they hear about him unless someone tells them?'[45] Jesus didn't intend that we keep the message to ourselves. Which is why we have a ministry to anyone who comes from the State seeking a different way of life. And it's also why we train for being called to go forth from this community to reach the lost. I have no doubt in my mind that someday, some of you will be called by God to leave here." The silence in the room was heavy. "It won't be easy and it won't be safe. But if God calls you to do it, He will make a way," Craig said.

Garrison was dumbfounded. This was the exact opposite of the way his community operated. All their lives, they were taught to stay in the boundaries, to protect and guard their community by keeping to themselves. There was no jail in his community, but he was sure that if anyone was caught encouraging young people to leave, they would build one for the culprit. He glanced at Viv and was surprised to see her crying.

---

[45] Romans 10:14 NLT

23

AFTER the service, Viv waited for Craig to stop horsing around with the other kids so that she could talk to him.

"I'm not doin' enough," she said to him when she finally got the chance. "I was sayin' earlier to Garrison, people can't make a choice to come to Jesus if they don't even know about the choice. An' that's what that whole bit o' scripture was sayin'. How can they believe in Him if they never heard about 'im? I gotta find more ways to tell people about Jesus."

"Viv, I think you're having more of an impact than you realize. The people you work with know there's something different about you just by the way you act and how you live. Many times the message is carried more effectively by actions rather than words," Craig told her.

Garrison, who overheard their conversation, spoke up. "Remember that I had heard the message my whole life, and it never made an impact on me until I met you and Dawson. I think Craig is right. Your life is the message, even if you don't get a chance to say it with words."

Craig studied her for a moment as he gave Garrison's words a chance to sink in. "God knows your hunger to spread the good news about Jesus. Viv, if you'll ask Him for opportunities, He will give them to you. But don't try to force it. He will open doors for you to say something. He will pave the way in conversations for the subject to come up. The Holy Spirit will guide you to say the right thing at the right time to the right person. But you have to trust Him and be in tune to His leading," Craig said. "On the other hand, there may come a day when you feel very strongly that out of the blue, someone you meet needs to hear about Jesus."

"Well, how am I supposed to know what to do?" Viv asked tearfully.

"You'll just know," Craig said simply. "God will make a way for you to share the message, and He'll show you the right time to do it. Just trust the leading of the Holy Spirit."

Viv sighed deeply and then looked at Craig with an intense expression. "I know God puts His Spirit in us when we get saved. But I been readin' about the Holy Spirit in Acts," she said. "They talk about people who became Christians bein' filled with the Holy Spirit after they got saved. And anyone who was filled, it's like they were different after that. They weren't afraid to get up in front of people. They could tell when God wanted them to do somethin', an' they did it. I don't exactly know what it means to be filled with the Holy Spirit, but I think that's what I need."

A broad grin spread across Craig's face. "Viv, it's what we *all* need. If you want to receive the baptism of the Holy Spirit, we can pray for you right now."

The colorful head nodded vigorously. Craig stepped away from Viv and looked around the room. He caught the eye of one of the older girls and motioned for her to join them. "Dania, would you go get Thom and Lydia and a few of the others who are Spirit-filled? Viv wants to receive the baptism, and we're going to pray for her."

Dania's dark eyes sparkled as she smiled at Viv briefly, and then she was off to collect the others. Craig looked back at Viv. "If you've been studying Acts, then I'm sure you've noticed that sometimes people were filled with the Holy Spirit without even asking for it. In Acts chapter ten, when Peter preached to Cornelius and his friends who were seeking the will of God in their lives, as soon as they heard the message of salvation through faith in Jesus Christ for the first time, they believed. And as they listened to the message, the gift of the Holy Ghost was poured out on them.

"When the Holy Spirit was *first* poured out, the believers were all together in one place because Jesus had told them to wait in Jerusalem for the promise of the Father. That was in Acts chapter two.

"In other instances, individuals received the Holy Ghost when the disciples laid hands on them and prayed for them to receive. In all of these instances, believers were together, seeking a deeper relationship with the Lord." Craig waited as Dania, Thom, Lydia, and a few others arrived. "Viv, I've asked these people to come pray with us because they have received the infilling of the Holy Spirit."

"The infilling?" Viv asked.

"That means we've been filled with the Spirit—in other words, that we've received the baptism of the Holy Spirit," Dania explained.

"I'm sorry that sometimes we use all this jargon that we're used to hearing. We forget that it's totally unfamiliar to a new Christian, and it isn't fair that we just expect you to know what we mean. If you have any questions about what any of this means, feel free to ask us," Craig said.

"How will I know I've been filled?" she asked. "Will I speak in another language like they did in the Bible?"

"That was the evidence given in the case of the believers who first received, and in the case of Cornelius and his friends and relatives. They glorified God in other languages they had never used before," Craig explained.

"But why wouldn't God just have us speak in our own language?" Viv asked. "What's the point in hearing a bunch of stuff no one understands?"

"Well, another gift of the Holy Spirit is the interpretation of tongues, after a message in tongues is given in a service," Craig said. "But as far as a believer first receiving the baptism and as far as praying in other tongues during your personal prayer time, I think maybe it has something to do with allowing God to have total control. And the book of Jude encourages us to build up ourselves on our most holy faith, praying in the Holy Ghost. Something about it increases our faith and our spiritual strength. The important thing to remember is that Jesus depended on the Holy Spirit in His ministry, and He told us that if He didn't leave, He couldn't send us the Comforter, which is another name for the Holy Spirit. We may not necessarily understand everything about it, but if Jesus put such emphasis on receiving the baptism of the Holy Ghost, we know that it must be an important part of our Christian walk. And once you receive it, you'll understand more."

Viv seemed to ponder what Craig had said, and then looked up almost guiltily. "I do have somethin' else that has kept me from askin' for this before now," Viv said, and hesitated.

"Go on. We're listening," Craig encouraged her.

"Well, there were other spirits in the Bible besides the Holy Spirit," Viv said with a visible shiver. "Sometimes people were filled with evil spirits, and they had to be cast out of 'em. What's to keep one of those kinds o' spirits from tryin' to get in when I'm askin' for the Holy Spirit to come in?"

"That's a perfectly legitimate question," Craig replied. "In fact, Jesus anticipated that people would have this fear. That's why he addressed it in Luke chapter eleven. Starting in verse nine, He says,

> 'Ask, and it will be given to you; seek, and you will find; knock, and it will be opened to you. For everyone who asks receives, and he who seeks finds, and to him who knocks it will be opened. If a son asks for bread from any father among you, will he give him a stone? Or if *he asks* for a fish, will he give him a serpent instead of a fish? Or if he asks for an egg, will he offer him a scorpion? If you then, being evil, know how to give good gifts to your children, how much more will *your* heavenly Father give the Holy Spirit to those who ask Him!'"[46]

"Craig," Lydia said suddenly, "may I read that passage in The Message Bible?"

---

[46] See Luke 11:9-13 NKJV

"Go ahead," Craig nodded.

Lydia held up an electronic device Garrison had noticed about 50% of the people of Adullam used for their Bibles and began to read.

> "...Ask and you'll get;
> Seek and you'll find;
> Knock and the door will open.
>
> Don't bargain with God. Be direct. Ask for what you need. This is not a cat-and-mouse, hide-and-seek game we're in. If your little boy asks for a serving of fish, do you scare him with a live snake on his plate? If your little girl asks for an egg, do you trick her with a spider? As bad as you are, you wouldn't think of such a thing—you're at least decent to your own children. And don't you think the Father who conceived you in love will give the Holy Spirit when you ask him?"[47]

Lydia looked up at Viv knowingly. "I used to wonder about the same thing, before I received the Holy Spirit. I wanted to be closer to Jesus, and I wanted to receive the power that He talked about in Acts 1. But I was afraid that in opening myself up to receive the Holy Spirit, something else might come in instead. When I was searching out the scriptures, I found this passage. If we are saved, and we are asking God to fill us with His Holy Spirit, He's not going to allow a demon to step in front of Him and invade one of His children. Jesus assured us in these verses that God will not let this happen."

Viv seemed relieved. "If Jesus said it, then ya know it's true," she said.

"There's just one more thing that might help you out before we pray," began one of the younger girls who had previously remained quiet in the background, but she hesitated as she looked at her peers.

"Say on," Viv said encouragingly.

---

47 Luke 11:9-13, THE MESSAGE

"Well, it's just . . ." she looked around quickly and ran off to retrieve something. She returned with a trash can that had been sitting in a corner of the room. "Spit out your gum," she suggested.

Dania looked at her strangely and laughed.

"No, she's right!" Thom exclaimed. "I don't know how many times I've seen people praying to get the Holy Ghost, and they actually get distracted by chomping their gum. They have to stop praising the Lord every few minutes to chomp awhile. I love gum as much as the next guy, and I love it when Viv brings us more of it, but Lelah might have a point."

Craig scratched his head and grinned. "I never thought of that, but I guess it's a possibility."

Viv spit her gum into the trash can. "I'm not gonna let somethin' as small as a piece o' gum stand in my way," she declared.

Craig smiled reassuringly at her. "As we're praying for you, Viv, just concentrate on the Lord. Tell Him you want to receive the Holy Spirit that He promised was available to all those who receive His Son, Jesus. Then just begin to thank Him for it. Think about all He Has done for you and how He deserves all your praise."

Viv closed her eyes and raised her hands as if to receive something. "I love ya, Lord. I love ya, Jesus," she began. "Ya done so much for me. Ya saved me. Ya forgave me. Ya delivered me from the darkness that was all aroun' me." Tears began to flow down her cheeks as she poured out her heart to the Lord. "I need Ya so much, Jesus. I need Your Holy Spirit. Ya promised us in Your Word that anyone who believes in You can receive Him. Please fill me with Your Holy Spirit."

Pastor Craig laid his hands on Viv's head as the teenagers laid hands on her shoulders. "Just keep praising Him, Viv," Craig encouraged her, and then he began to pray. "Father, You know Viv's desire and her need for more of You. I ask that You fill Viv with Your Holy Spirit so she can receive the power she needs not only in her everyday life, but the power she needs to be an effective witness to others. I ask it in the name of Jesus."

When Craig said the name of Jesus, Viv's body jerked slightly and her hands reached higher in the air. Garrison, who had begun to back away as soon as the others moved in closer to pray, watched apprehensively. He had seen Miss Genevieve speak in different languages as she gave praise to God, but he had always assumed she was just following some old tradition of sing-song gibberish that was fading away in their society. He had never doubted she was being genuine, but he thought it was a form of prayer which was unique to her. He had heard all the scriptures Craig had brought up to explain things to Viv, but since no one in his community except Miss Genevieve had ever spoken in other tongues, he didn't think of it as something everyone needed. As he watched Viv continue to praise the Lord, he suddenly realized she wasn't speaking English anymore. She was obviously still praising God, but he couldn't understand what she was saying. He wondered briefly if she was frightened, but the look of joy on her face told him otherwise. He watched the faces of the other teens, obviously thrilled that Viv had apparently just received the Holy Spirit, as they gave praise to God in languages he couldn't understand. He wished he could share their joy, but it was a little disturbing. Why didn't anything like this ever happen in his community?

His thoughts were interrupted as Viv gave a loud whoop and jumped up and down in irrepressible joy.

"Are you okay?" someone asked from behind him.

Garrison turned quickly to see Lelah, the girl who had almost been too shy to give her suggestion about the gum. "Well, it's just…we didn't really see much of this sort of thing where I'm from," he tried to explain. "It's really strange to me. But she seems so happy."

Lelah's gaze seemed to penetrate him to his very soul. "There's no need to be afraid. Jesus is happy with her, and she can feel that happiness. She has a closer connection to Him now, and the joy she feels is real. 'For the kingdom of God is not meat and drink; but righteousness, and peace, and joy in the Holy Ghost.' Romans 14:17,"[48] Lelah quoted.

---

[48] Romans 14:17 KJV

"I just wonder why this almost never happened where I'm from," Garrison questioned.

Lelah, who had seemed so shy and tentative before, seemed almost to grow in stature as she spoke. "Many people who are Christians never know about receiving the Holy Ghost. But those who do receive Him experience the greatest joy they have ever known. That's why she seems so happy. And they also receive a boldness to do God's will. That is why I am able to speak to you so easily now. God wants me to tell you this. He wants you to know that there is no need to be afraid."

Garrison pondered what she was saying. He couldn't deny that the salvation experience he had earlier that day was real, but he wasn't sure about any of this Holy Ghost stuff. He couldn't deny the joy on the faces of those around him, or the boldness with which the normally demure Lelah spoke, but he couldn't help but wonder if this whole group he had stumbled upon was actually wandering off into some sort of false doctrine. *What about the verse in I Corinthians 13, which said that tongues would cease?* He wondered to himself. *Is this Holy Spirit actually still available to Christians today if the Bible said that tongues would cease? Or is this actually an imposter—an evil spirit that initially comes in making people feel good and then turns on its host later?*

He shook himself back to the present as Lelah spoke again. "Love never ends; as for prophecy, it will pass away; as for tongues, they will cease; as for knowledge, it will pass away. For our knowledge is imperfect and our prophecy is imperfect; but when the perfect comes, the imperfect will pass away."[49] she quoted.

Garrison's breath caught in his throat. It was the very verse he had been thinking about.

"The Holy Spirit just impressed upon me that you needed to hear that verse," Lelah continued. She looked down at the electronic tablet she held in her hand. *"When the perfect comes, the imperfect will pass away."* She repeated. "Now let me read you a little more. 'When I was a child,

---

[49] 1 Corinthians 13:8-10 RSV

I spoke like a child, I thought like a child, I reasoned like a child; when I became a man, I gave up childish ways. For now we see in a mirror dimly, but then face to face. Now I know in part; then I shall understand fully, even as I have been fully understood.'"[50]

Lelah continued with an unearthly confidence. "Has 'the perfect' come? Do we understand everything perfectly, just as God fully knows and understands us? *I* certainly don't. But someday we will, because one day, we will see Jesus face to face. In 1 John 3:2, it says, 'Beloved, now we are children of God; and it has not yet been revealed what we shall be, but we know that when He is revealed, we shall be like Him, for we shall see Him as He is.'"[51] Lelah looked at Garrison intently. "Jesus hasn't come back yet. The end of the age hasn't yet happened. Until that time, the Holy Spirit will work through people in the gifts of tongues, special knowledge, and prophecy. That is how I am able to tell you all this right now. I could never have thought of this and had the courage to say it on my own."

Garrison looked from Lelah to Viv. Her hands were trembling as she continued to speak in another language, and the smile she wore threatened to split her face apart.

"What if she can't stop?" he asked suddenly. "What if the Holy Spirit won't let her stop and she can't control herself anymore? I don't think I will ever want to do what she's doing right now. I'm afraid of losing control."

"The Holy Spirit's not like that," Lelah said. "I mean, He doesn't come where He isn't wanted. You can stop speaking in tongues at any time. It's not like you *have* to operate in a gift of the Holy Spirit. It's like you sometimes feel Him asking you to do something, and you can either yield to Him or you can ignore Him. The more you yield, the more He will use you. The more you ignore Him and turn a cold shoulder to Him, the less He will ask you. Or maybe it's more like the less you are able to feel Him ask."

---

[50] 1 Corinthians 13:11-12 RSV
[51] 1 John 3:2 NKJV

Garrison watched as Viv and the others continued to rejoice. "I think maybe I'll just watch from over here," he told Lelah, as he sat down on a pew to keep an eye on the proceedings. Lelah smiled gently and squeezed his shoulder reassuringly. Then she walked back to the others, lifted her hands, and began to give thanks to God. Garrison noticed absently that she wasn't speaking in English, either. It didn't seem like any of the teens were out of control, emotionally. Except maybe Viv. She seemed almost overcome with joy, and he wasn't certain there was any harm in that. A Bible rested on the seat next to him, and he picked it up and thumbed through its pages as he waited. He looked up as he noticed Viv had stopped speaking and was making a kind of moaning sound. That couldn't be right, could it? Was she in distress? But she didn't look as though she was in distress. Her smile had faded and was replaced by a look of intensity, as if she were trying to say something, but all that came out was a groan. Garrison frowned. This was all so weird. Nothing like this ever happened back home. He glanced down at the Bible in his lap. It was opened to the book of Romans, chapter 8. He began reading at verse 26:

> And the Holy Spirit helps us in our weakness. For example, we don't know what God wants us to pray for. But the Holy Spirit prays for us with groanings that cannot be expressed in words. And the Father who knows all hearts knows what the Spirit is saying, for the Spirit pleads for us believers in harmony with God's own will.[52]

Garrison looked around to see if anyone could have flipped the pages of the Bible to that particular passage, but no one else was near him. He looked back at Viv. She seemed calm now, and had stopped groaning. "Thank You, Jesus," he heard her say. She opened her eyes, red with tears, but shining with happiness. "Oh, isn't He wonderful!" she exclaimed. The whole group around her burst into a chorus of laughter and began hugging each other.

---

[52] Romans 8:26-27, NLT

Lelah glanced at Garrison and smiled as if to say, *"See, everything is alright."*

24

THE muggy Missouri evening had surrendered to the rhythmic, hand-saw stroke of katydid calls by the time Garrison and Viv left the church building. Macy was waiting for them, her tongue lolling out the side of her mouth and her scraggly tail wagging in delight. Garrison felt relieved to see her. He was still unsettled about what he had witnessed. Was it real, or just fanatical emotion? He didn't have to wonder about things like that with an animal like Macy. She was genuine. You didn't have to guess about how she felt, or worry about her being carried away by her emotions. Sure, she was overly enthusiastic about things sometimes, but that just seemed to fit with her personality. Suddenly he laughed as he realized that description also fit Viv. Maybe his concern about what had happened was unwarranted.

"It's hard not to be happy, huh, Way Man?" Viv said. It was the first thing she had said since they left the others.

"What do you mean?" Garrison asked.

"Don't ya feel that joy? It's like we're walkin' on air!" she gushed.

"Actually, I was just thinking about how you're a lot like Macy."

Instead of the bone-jarring punch in the arm he was expecting, Viv nearly doubled over laughing. "Which part do ya mean? The slobbery, hairy part, or always showin' up where I'm not wanted?"

"Nothing of the sort. It was much more complimentary than that. I was just thinking—" he stopped himself short. If Viv was so happy, why should he bring her down with his negative questioning?

"Thinkin' what?" Viv pressed.

"Nothing." He paused and glanced at her as they walked along the path. "It's just that... you're a really genuine person, Viv. There's nothing fake about you. It's refreshing." He blushed as Viv stared at him a moment.

"Thank you, Garrison. I try to be real. There's a lot of fake where I come from," she finally said.

"I know how you feel," Garrison replied.

"Whaddaya mean?" Viv seemed surprised. "You come from a community of believers. How can ya get any more real than that? I'd give my right arm to live where you're from."

"You might feel differently if you'd been there," Garrison said bitterly. "It's not like here. I mean, there are some really nice people there, but if someone came walking into our community, they wouldn't be welcomed with open arms. They'd probably never be allowed to leave. The whole community is obsessed with keeping it secret and safe. No one is allowed to go beyond the boundaries."

"Then how are they gonna do what Jesus said to do?" Viv asked. "How are they gonna tell everyone that they can come to God through His Son, Jesus?"

"I think they gave up on that a long time ago," Garrison said.

"How can they feel like that? Man, I wanted to tell people about Jesus before, but *now*, I'm just *bustin'* to go do it! There ain't no implant or chip can compete with bein' filled with the Holy Ghost," Viv said excitedly.

Garrison held his tongue. He didn't want to spoil her good mood, but his skepticism was becoming increasingly hard to set aside.

"Doesn't the Holy Spirit make everyone feel that way?" Viv continued. "After bein' filled with the Spirit, don't the people in your town want to go out an' preach the gospel to the whole world?"

"It's not like that there," Garrison said sharply.

Viv seemed taken aback. "Whaddaya mean? Don't they believe in the Holy Spirit there?"

Thunk! Garrison kicked a rock out of the path and it smacked into the fence bordering somebody's yard. Macy barked and chased after the rock.

"*Shhhh!*" Viv and Garrison both scolded Macy at the same time. Garrison hoped the distraction would make Viv forget her question, but she would not be deterred.

"Doesn't anyone where ya dock speak in tongues like I just did?" she persisted.

"No. Well, actually, yes. I have heard one person do it. But I thought it was just some individual quirk she had. A weird habit. I never thought of it as being the Holy Spirit." It dawned on him then. Miss Genevieve was not only the sole person from his community who spoke in tongues, but she was also the only one who ever spoke wistfully of the Great Commission. No one else seemed to think it was relevant to them, personally.

"I just don't see how ya can know about Jesus an' not want to tell others about Him. Are ya sure they really know Him?" Viv asked sincerely.

Garrison was surprised by the question. The thought had never occurred to him. He had never questioned that his friends and neighbors were Christians. He remembered his Sunday School teacher, and the Beardsleys, and Selah and her family. The love of Jesus was evident in their lives, in the way they treated others and the way they talked about the Lord. But there were others who seemed to exhibit more suspicion and fear than faith and love. And these were the people who were thought of as guardians of the community.

"As far as I know, everyone there knows Jesus," he finally answered. "But some of them seem more controlled by fear than by love. The lady I told you about who prayed in a different language—Miss Genevieve —she is the only one who ever talked about spreading the gospel to the rest of the world. She didn't talk much about it, though, because she knew the elders wouldn't like it. So she would just teach us scriptures about it. The elders couldn't very well argue against the Word of God, and…" Garrison drifted off as a sudden realization dawned on him. "Oh, no. I can't believe I didn't see it!"

"See what?"

"Miss Genevieve is the one who taught me about the Great Commission—that is, the command Jesus gave us to go into all the world and preach the gospel. She never actually *encouraged* us to do it. She couldn't, without getting in trouble with the other elders. But right before I left, we were having this conversation by the smokehouse—she and Selah and I. I was being really sarcastic with her. She was talking about how God had promised to take care of us, and that He had kept us healthy and safe. She said that we have everything we need in our little valley. And I told her we didn't have the ability to fulfill the Great Commission. When I said that, she just froze. I thought, *boy, I really got the best of her this time.* She was just staring off into space and didn't talk for so long that I thought maybe she couldn't come up with anything to say back to me. I was feeling pretty proud of myself when she said something about my motives. She said, 'If your motives were not in question,' and then she stopped and changed the subject. When I tried to get her to explain what she meant about my motives, she said she couldn't remember what she was going to say. It was almost like she was trying to hide something from me. But now I think I know what was going on."

He stopped and looked at Viv. "There's always been something different about Miss Genevieve. No one has any doubt that the Lord has first place in her life. She treats Him with reverence, but she also talks about Him like He's her best friend."

"You mean she respects Him for who He is, but she knows she doesn't have to be afraid to talk to Him?" Viv asked.

"Exactly. To her, He's not only the Creator of the Universe, Protector of the community, God Almighty, our Savior and Redeemer, but He's also her friend, her confidante, the love of her life, and her…Daddy." Garrison had hesitated as he debated about whether or not to use the familiar term.

Viv looked at him thoughtfully. "Garrison, that's kinda how I feel about Him. Even more, now that I've been filled with the Holy Spirit. Don't the people where ya dock feel the same way?"

"Well, I know they know all that stuff with their heads. But sometimes it seems like their hearts have forgotten who He is. They're more concerned with the things He told them to do than with what He means to them, on a personal level. You see, God sent an angel to lead the founding families to our valley—"

"An angel! What kinda download are ya dealin', Way Man?" Viv interrupted.

"I know it sounds crazy, but it's true. Miss Genevieve was there when it happened, and all the original families were there to see it, too."

"You mean an angel with wings and everything?" Viv asked dubiously, flapping her arms slightly.

"No, more of an angel in disguise. He just looked like an ordinary bum."

"Then how did they know he wasn't just some crazy?"

"Several people saw him in dreams before they saw him in person. He seemed to know them all and to know exactly where they needed to go. The story has been passed down for two generations now, along with what he said about staying there if they wanted to be safe. And now it's like everyone who lives there can't go beyond what they were told to do back when we first came there. We were told we would have everything we need and that if we would stay within the boundaries, we would be safe. All they think about now is protecting the community and staying in the boundaries. But the angel didn't say we *had* to stay within the boundaries. He just said that if we did, we would be provided for and protected." Garrison stopped and put his hands on Viv's shoulders. "Viv, I think she *wanted* to leave!" he said, his eyes shining. "I think Miss Genevieve wanted to, but she knew she was too old to go anywhere. She was looking for a protégé, someone she could teach as much as she could and send out in her place. But where would she find someone like that? I wanted to leave, but she knew my motives were wrong. Telling people about Jesus was the farthest thing from my mind. And even if there were someone else in the community who loved Jesus as much as she did and wanted to share Him with others, it would be against the rules to leave."

"But the rules where ya dock don't sound like somethin' outta God's Word. Shouldn't ya just focus on what God's Word says to do, instead of what man's rules are? Craig told me tonight that if I felt like the Holy Spirit was tellin' me to do somethin', I should always make sure it lined up with the Bible. If it didn't line up with the Word of God, it wasn't the Holy Spirit tellin' me to do it," Viv said.

"Yeah. The people where I dock," he caught himself and laughed. "Now you've got me saying it. Anyway, we have a board of directors. The board sometimes reminds me of the Pharisees in the Bible."

"The Fair-uh-seez?"

"The Pharisees were wonderful scholars of God's Word. Many of them had the whole thing memorized. They knew all the laws from the Old Testament and tried to follow them exactly. But they also had made up a bunch of other laws to go along with what God had given Moses on Mount Sinai. Those other laws were man's rules, and they were extremely strict—nearly impossible to follow. Sometimes it seems like the board has forgotten that the angel didn't tell us that if we left, we would be forfeiting our Christianity. He was simply telling us how we could be kept safe, physically. You only have to look at the Christians in the New Testament to know that the fear of death didn't stand in their way when it came to telling others about Jesus. Many of them were killed because they professed Christ. But the people in our community—they're caught up in following man's rules. I know they love God, but they can't see beyond what their forefathers told them to do."

"If only Miss Genevieve could see ya now, eh?" Viv mused. "She'd have found her protégé, an' I ain't chippin'!"

The two walked in silence for a while, Garrison's brow furrowed in thought, and Viv still basking in the experience she had had in the youth service. Macy snuffled along the trail beside them, snorting occasion-ally when she smelled something particularly interesting. Garrison's thoughts were still on Miss Genevieve. If this Holy Spirit thing was re-ally real, that might explain why she had been able to see beyond the rules of man and into the desire of God's heart.

"So, what's it like?" he asked suddenly.

"What like?"

"Being baptized in the Holy Ghost."

Viv grinned from ear to ear, and her step seemed to get a little bouncier. "It's amazin', Way Man. It's like, I feel closer to God, and I have faith that He can do absolutely anything. I know He's gonna show me when's the right time to tell someone about Jesus, an' He's gonna give me the words to say."

"But when you were speaking in tongues, did you ever feel out of control? Like someone had taken control of your body?"

Viv looked at him, horrified. "Nahh, Man! It's not like that at all. It was like whenever I opened my mouth to praise Jesus an' started to say somethin', it just came out in another language. I could've kept goin' all night, except I was gettin' kinda tired, so I just stopped. I felt like I was filled to the top with God! It felt like power an' love an' faith an'…" she trailed off. "I just can't put it all into words. Ya just gotta experience it for yourself."

"I'm just not sure about it," Garrison began. "I know that even if some of the people in my community may be following their own agendas now, there are a lot of good, solid Christians there, too, and they don't speak in tongues or do any of the other things that the Holy Spirit led people to do in the Bible."

"Well, they don't know what they're missin'," Viv said. "I mean, I'm sure they know Jesus. But if someone ya know gives ya a present, whad-daya do?"

"You say thank you."

"Well, yes, but what else do ya do?"

"Tell them you are really going to enjoy it?" Garrison ventured.

"Yes," Viv said patiently. "But how do ya know if ya gonna enjoy it if ya never open it?" Her face broke into a broad grin.

Garrison was quiet for a moment. "Viv, for being a new Christian, you sure seem to know a lot. Did you come up with that on your own, or did someone tell you that?"

"Nahh, Man. I couldn'a come up with that on my own. I think it was the Holy Spirit gave me that just now." She stopped suddenly as the path approached Julie's house. Her face grew serious as she regarded Garrison. "Way Man, I won't see ya at breakfast. I gotta get up before the roosters to get back in time. But I'll be back as soon as I can. You'll be safe here, but if ya ever feel like leavin', just make sure ya don't leave too soon, before God lets ya know it's time to go. I'm tellin' ya, I don't know how they didn't spot ya if ya really were walkin' down that road. They watch the old roads real close-like. It's only God that kept ya from bein' seen. An' when it's time for ya to leave, He'll hide ya again. He hides me when I come an' go."

Garrison nodded. The idea of leaving Adullam seemed premature to him now, even though yesterday he would have left in a heart beat. "Take care, Viv. Go with God."

"Always," she said with that dazzling smile, and quietly opened Julie's front gate and entered the dark house.

Garrison looked past Mark and Julie's house to the path that left the village for the grove of cottonwood trees. He didn't feel like going back to the cabin just yet. Lightening bugs blinked in the grove and the katydids continued their raspy chorus. Suddenly Macy brushed past him, her mottled fur nearly disappearing amidst the dappled shadows of the trees. She stopped and looked back at him as if to say, "You're coming, aren't you?" Garrison chuckled and followed the dog. "Well, where are you taking me this time, Mace?" The mongrel barked in response. "*Shhhhh!* I'm coming, I'm coming!" Garrison replied, and followed the wagging tail down the path into the grove.

The shadows deepened as the overarching branches of the cottonwoods obscured the light from the waning moon. Garrison couldn't see

Macy, but he could tell where she was by the occasional snorts she emitted. He was practically jogging to keep up, when he suddenly heard something off the side of the trail. He stopped and listened. Something was rustling in the grass, but it was moving away from him, he was fairly certain. He tried to listen for Macy ahead of him, but could hear nothing except the commotion off to his left. Suddenly, it was quiet. And then he heard it again, except this time it sounded like it was coming closer. *I'm still in the boundaries. This place is protected, right?* Garrison offered up a silent prayer. The noise grew louder. Garrison strained to see in the darkness, and what he saw made his blood run cold. At first, all he could see was shadows. But then, he could make out one shadow that was darker than the others. Whatever it was, it wasn't afraid of him. It seemed to be slowly, purposefully making its way toward him. "Jesus, help me!" Garrison sputtered.

"*Rarf!*" the shadow barked, and bounded toward him.

Garrison's heart skipped a beat as he realized the menacing shadow was none other than Macy. "Macy, you idiot! You scared the stuffing out of me!" he exclaimed. He didn't know whether to pet her out of relief or swat her. But since she obviously had no intentions of frightening him, he settled on scratching her ears. She leaned into his hand for a while, then turned abruptly back off the path again and continued, this time at a slower pace. Every once in a while, she would look over her shoulder at him, and once he had caught up to her, she would continue on her way. "Where are you going, you crazy mutt?" Garrison asked. It seemed like a replay of that morning. As he trudged through the lush grass and fallen limbs of the grove, he wondered if Adullam was protected from snakes as well as mosquitoes. He nearly tripped over Macy as she came to an abrupt halt, and noticed that the grove had opened up to the edge of a meadow. He heard a strange, soft, tinkling sound coming from the direction of some large boulders in the tall grass.

Garrison squinted in the dim light. The biggest boulder looked rough and jagged and had an unusual pattern of lighter colored blotches on it. Suddenly, one of the blotches moved to another part of the boulder. He realized with a start that he was looking at a herd of goats. The moving blotch settled down again onto the dark face of the boulder. It didn't seem like a very comfortable place to spend the night, compared with all that lush, soft grass on the floor of the meadow, below. But it would be an excellent place from which to see approaching predators, he reasoned, if predators could even make it past the briarwood boundaries of Adullam. The goats were taking every precaution, when in reality, they were probably never in any danger. How much more comfortable it would have been to lie down in the soft grass, grabbing a mouthful of it to eat whenever they got hungry.

Macy bumped his hand with her nose to give him a lick, and then meandered off into the cottonwood grove again. Garrison glanced back at the goats. He was surprised Macy hadn't bounded over to the boulder to greet them. Surely she knew they were there, with the lead goat wearing a bell that clinked and tinkled with every move it made. He turned back toward the sound of Macy pushing through the grass. This time, he would make certain to keep up. She headed back to the path and began trotting toward the village. When they reached the main road through the rows of houses, Macy slowed to a walk. "Listen, dog. I don't care where you're going—I'm going to bed," Garrison announced. Macy looked back at him with her goofy, slobbery grin and dropped back behind him as he walked. He was exhilarated by the events of the day, but it had exhausted him, and he was ready to get some rest.

The little cabin was a welcome sight. Macy followed him through the flower-lined, stone walk and curled up on the front porch, leaving him to stumble through the dark until he remembered the light switch Sophia had told him was by the front door. He undressed and slipped into bed, enjoying the softness of the down mattress. The momentous events of the day began to play out in his mind, but in time, exhaustion won the battle, and he drifted asleep.

25

*G*arrison pulled back the covers and sat up in bed. He thought he had heard something. There it was again. "Garrison," a voice called from outside the cabin on the front porch. He slid off the bed and went into the living room. The front door was open. He cautiously approached and peered out onto the porch. The path in the yard was sharply outlined in the moonlight. It looked so inviting. "Garrison," the voice called warmly. He followed the sound of it out onto the porch and into the night. The brightness of the moon made everything easily visible. It was so light he could almost distinguish color. The grass was almost green, the flowers almost red and yellow; the grayscale world of night was being usurped by the moon.

Garrison walked silently down the path and through the gate to the main road. It wasn't as if he had to get up early and do chores. What would it hurt to take a little walk? The road seemed smooth and clean in the moonlight. His bare feet felt good on the warm dirt. He could hear the voice calling again, and his pace quickened. He knew that voice from somewhere. It was hard to ignore.

He passed house by quiet house, wondering absently what time it was and realizing he didn't even care. Nothing seemed more important than following the sound of that voice. Minutes later, he found himself passing Mark and Julie's place. He stopped at the edge of the cottonwood grove. Overhead branches obscured most of the moonlight, and he wondered if anything other than goats could be wandering in the undergrowth. Shadows of the trees played charades with his fear, mimicking the silhouette of a crouching mountain lion in one minute, morphing into a humanoid form in the next. Garrison could not bring himself to step into the darkness.

"Garrison," the voice called again, and at the sound of it, a small area of the path through the grove grew light as day. He rushed into the halo of light toward the sound of the voice. Shadows danced on every side, but as long as he was in the light, he wasn't afraid. As he took a step forward, the light moved with him. When he stopped, it stopped, as if it were waiting for him to gain the courage to move forward. He couldn't see very far in front of him at all, and the path behind was black as pitch. There was only enough light for him to see just where his feet were about to step. He placed one foot in front of the other and decided to ignore the shadows. The voice called him when he slowed down or stopped, and the light accompanied him as he followed the sound of the voice, until at last he was in the open meadow. Out in the distance he could see the large boulders he had noticed earlier that evening. He looked down at the lush grass at his feet and had a strange urge to kneel down and smell it. As he did so, he had an even stranger urge to bite off a mouthful of it. "Ridiculous," he said to himself, but all that came out was a high-pitched bleat. He looked in dismay at his hands as they rested on the ground beneath him. They were no longer hands, but cloven hooves. He looked to the boulders and spotted the herd of goats. "Maybe they will know what to do," he thought to himself, and with a short little bleat, he bounded over to the largest rock. "Clink, clink!" went the bell on the lead goat's collar. Its head peered down at him over the edge of the boulder. "May I join you?" Garrison asked in what he hoped was a Nubian dialect. The goat seemed to glare at him from the strange rectangular pupils of its yellow eyes. Garrison jumped onto a small rock near the base of the boulder. Several more goats had gathered near to stare at him over the steep edge. "Hi," Garrison bleated. "Isn't it a nice night?" The goats said nothing and stared. Garrison decided to take their silence as a sign of reticence. His little hooves went clippety clip as he hopped from rock to rock. Finally, he was near enough to touch the giant boulder. The first level spot seemed quite a ways up. He took a monumental leap, and his hooves barely made purchase as he clambered up onto the rock shelf. Clomp! The lead goat had landed on a shelf right beside him. "Hello, I—" Bam! Suddenly Garrison found himself upside down in the rocks at the base of the boulder. Dazed and confused, he looked back up at the rock ledge and could see the lead goat and a crowd of goats behind it. Obviously, he had misinterpreted their silence as a sign of indifference.

What would he do? The goats liked being high on the rocks so they could keep a lookout, he supposed. How would he fare, all alone on the lower rocks, unable to see if a predator was coming and without the help of others to defend him? He bleated pitifully to the stingy goats, but to no avail. They seemed determined that the rock was their territory. He looked around at the other rocks. Picking out the largest one he could find, he scrambled up onto it, wincing as he knocked against the side of it with a bruised leg. The light he had enjoyed earlier had dissipated in the open meadow and was now indistinguishable from the rest of the night. As he bedded down on the jagged rock, he wished the light would come back. Better to spend a night in the light surrounded by darkness than on a sharp, pointy rock. "I might as well be sitting on a serving tray," he thought to himself, as the rock had raised him up just enough above the grass so as to be visible to predators, but not enough to keep him out of reach. As he tried to get comfortable, his stomach (or was it stomachs?) began to growl. He looked down at the soft, thick grass. It looked so delicious. But if he left his little rock, he wouldn't be able to see if trouble was coming. He decided to stay put and wait until daylight. As the minutes passed, he began to feel miserable. He was so hungry! The rock was so rough. He sighed and looked back up at the goats and wished he could at least have a little company. Why wouldn't they accept one of their own kind?

"They don't accept you because you are not one of them," said a voice beside him. Garrison jumped to his four feet. It was the voice he had heard earlier, and it was coming from a young man standing beside the rock. "How did you get here without me seeing you?" Garrison bleated nervously.

"You don't have to be afraid," the man said. He looked back at the goats. "They don't need to be afraid, either, but they would rather go their own way than to trust their protection to someone other than themselves."

"Protection? Aren't they protected on the rock?" Garrison asked.

"They can see a little of what's coming, but they really can't do much about it. In the mean time, here you are, closer to the soft floor of the meadow. Why don't you get down from that rock and bed down in the grass. I know you're hungry. You can take a bite to eat when you want. I'll keep watch," the man with the warm voice assured him.

Garrison considered it for a moment. The voice still sounded like someone he could trust, and the grass looked so inviting. He looked up at the man. "Why are the goats so territorial? How do they know I'm not one of them? I look just like they do, don't I?"

The man cocked his head and studied Garrison. "Not exactly," he said.

"What do you mean, 'not exactly'?"

The man smiled and picked up a walking stick he had leaned up against a rock. "Follow me," he said simply, and turned away toward the open part of the meadow, picking his way between the hunched limestone forms that poked their heads above the grass. Garrison hopped down off of his rock and trotted after him, snatching a mouthful of grass as he went. The man was easy to keep up with. As they walked along, he pointed out the especially delicious varieties of vegetation. The sound of his voice was soothing as they moved farther out into the meadow. Finally, his guide slowed to a stop, and Garrison noticed the sound of something besides the soothing voice. Several yards in front of them was a stream that jumped and gurgled as it meandered its way through the meadow. He shrank back at the sound of the stream, although he wasn't certain why. "Are goats afraid of running water?" Garrison asked. The man looked at him. "They don't like not being able to hear things approach them. The sound of the water masks other noises. It makes them nervous. But I am here with you. I'll be your lookout. Follow me, and I'll lead you to a better part of the stream," the man explained. Garrison followed the man downstream until they came beside a larger pool that had been dammed up by some beavers. The water smelled good, and he was suddenly thirsty. "Go ahead and drink," the man encouraged him. "The water won't sweep you away here. It's still and peaceful." Garrison walked close to the water's edge and jumped as he saw his reflection in the moonlight. His coat wasn't short and sleek like the goats. It was thick and soft and…wooly. "I'm not a goat! I'm a sheep!" he exclaimed.

The man's laughter rose in deep, rich tones. "So you are," he agreed.

Garrison stared at his image for a while, and then drank deeply of the water until he was satisfied. The man waited for him to finish. Then he turned toward the deep meadow grass, and Garrison followed closely behind. In an area ahead, the grass gave way to a strange sort of vegetation he had never seen before. The plant had a tall bloom and rounded leaves. It looked pretty, but Garrison didn't trust it. Suddenly he noticed the man was watching him. "I know you're hungry. That plant is delicious and nutritious as well. Go ahead and eat some of it."

Garrison eyed the vegetation suspiciously. He had heard of some plants that were particularly beautiful being especially toxic. "I think I'd just like to eat the regular grass, if that's okay."

The man smiled patiently. "We have a long journey ahead of us. This plant will sustain you through the times when the other grass runs thin. You have nothing to fear."

Garrison stood looking at the plant. The man hadn't led him astray yet. But still, he hesitated. The plant was taller than he was. In the moonlight, he could see the redness of its bloom. It seemed so foreign to him.

"Don't you trust me, Garrison?" the man asked sadly. "If you asked me for a fish, would I give you a serpent? If you asked me for a loaf of bread, would I give you a stone?"

Garrison jerked awake. It was still dark outside, but an early-rising rooster crowed somewhere on the back streets of Adullam. He sat up in bed. The dream gripped his mind, teasing his memory with its vivid imagery. Suddenly he could hear Pastor Craig's voice in his head:

> "If a son asks for bread from any father among you, will he give him a stone? Or if he asks for a fish, will he give him a serpent instead of a fish? Or if he asks for an egg, will he offer him a scorpion? If you then, being evil, know how to give good gifts to your children, how much more will your heavenly Father give the Holy Spirit to those who ask Him!"[53]

A breeze blew softly through the window, carrying with it the faint scent of meadow grass.

---

[53] Luke 11:11-13 NKJV

Part III

Phos

26

WINTER dragged its icy belly wearily through the valley, as if it hadn't even the strength to surrender to spring. Even the brown nubbins of dogwood buds, which normally began appearing during the coldest months, seemed reluctant to form. "Everything is holding its breath," commented Miss Genevieve, as Selah brought another armful of wood into the little trailer. The hunched figure lifted a faded denim curtain away from the windows. "Spring is held in suspense. And so am I."

Selah brushed the crumbs of bark off of her coat into the wood box. She had a feeling her friend was referring to something in the spiritual world, rather than a mere changing of the seasons. It felt to her as though they were in a holding pattern, and like hawks or vultures circling and rising on currents of air, they were in watchful stasis.

Selah had learned more practical things about spiritual matters in the past few months than she had in all her years of Bible study and church attendance. Her studies with Miss Genevieve had taken on new significance, because Selah was becoming increasingly more aware of the unseen world she had heretofore given only a fleeting thought. She was learning how to wield the sword of the Spirit—the Word of God—spoken of in Ephesians chapter six. "You're just building on the good foundation you already have," Miss Genevieve had explained. "If it were not for you being rooted and grounded in the Word, you wouldn't be ready for all you're experiencing now."

Selah knew she was right. Until she had stepped out onto the battlefield of prayer, she had known nothing of opposition from the enemy.

Now that she was fasting and seeking God's will with new intensity, she found that it paid to be wearing her spiritual armor and to have some scriptures in the arsenal of her memory.

Most of the time, the enemy's tactics were so subtle that they were difficult to detect, even when she was expecting something. Depression, anger, self pity, self righteousness, a judgmental attitude—these were all emotions or attributes Selah had become acutely aware already existed in small amounts in her personality. Before she realized what was really happening, the enemy would use these traits to his advantage by exacerbating them to volcanic emotional eruptions.

"It's like he can read my mind and knows what's going to really get to me. And then he'll send someone along and use them to yank my chain," Selah had confided in Genevieve one day.

"Satan and his demons can't read our minds, but they can observe and predict how we react to different situations. Think of the thousands of years the devil has had to study human nature!" Genevieve replied.

"It's infuriating. I keep falling for the same old things," Selah confessed.

"Why should he try any new tricks when he already knows what has worked on you in the past? He knows where you are weakest. He knows your pressure points. One thing you have to ask is, are you allowing yourself to return to the same situation or thoughts? Are you putting yourself in a position where you will be tempted, simply by the things you dwell upon in your mind?" Genevieve asked.

Selah considered the question. "Some of the things that come into my head are just crazy. I don't even realize what's happening until I'm smack in the middle of some daydream involving someone who has made me mad in the past. Then before I know it, I'm mad at that person the next time I see them, and they're confused about why I'm acting like something's wrong between us. Later, I will see what was really going on, but not until after I've made some snippy comment and hurt someone's feelings."

Genevieve sighed. "I will pray for you to begin to recognize these attacks for what they are," her friend counseled her. "And when you do, you must rebuke those thoughts. You know, Selah, thoughts are like birds. There's nothing wrong with letting them fly over your head, but you don't have to let them build a nest in your hair."

Selah could imagine her hair piled up on top of her head, the birds flying in and out of a precarious network of nests. "So, how do I rebuke a thought?" she asked.

Miss Genevieve went over to a bookshelf where she kept several different versions of the Bible. "Let's suppose you notice you are feeling down about things. A little of this is just normal in your dealings with everyday life. But when it seems like nothing is going right and you feel like you are down in a hole you can't crawl out of, something else is going on. You can speak to that emotion, because sometimes, it's not just an emotion. Sometimes it's a spirit sent to oppress you. As you grow in maturity, you will have the ability to discern whether it is a natural emotion you are experiencing or an oppressive spirit. If it is the latter, call it by what it is and command it to leave—like so: 'Depression, I rebuke you, and I command you to leave in the name of Jesus.' As a child of God, you have the authority to do that. Since you know Jesus personally, you can use His name and operate by the power of that name." Miss Genevieve paused and gazed intensely at Selah to emphasize her point. "You have mentioned that sometimes, for no reason, you have negative, violent, or depressing daydreams or worries that won't seem to leave you alone. When that happens, take control of your mind in the name of Jesus. Sometimes I say, 'I refuse to think on that, in Jesus name.' And of course, your best offensive weapon is the Word of God. Quote scripture to the devil. Quote it to yourself. Scriptures like 2 Timothy 1:7—*For God hath not given us the spirit of fear; but of power, and of love, and of a sound mind.*[54] Miss Genevieve took a Bible out of the bookshelf. "You need to read that in the Amplified. It really makes

---

[54] 2 Timothy 1:7 KJV

it simple to understand," she said, as she thumbed through its pages, handing the Bible to Selah. Selah sometimes got lost in the wordiness of the Amplified version, but she decided it lent itself well to this particular verse as she read. "For God did not give us a spirit of timidity *or* cowardice *or* fear, but [He has given us a spirit] of power and of love and of sound judgment *and* personal discipline [abilities that result in a calm, well-balanced mind and self-control]."[55]

"I think I'd like to write that one down," she said, as she reached for the little pad of paper she kept in her back pocket. Miss Genevieve had given her the small, homemade notebook during Selah's first fast so she could write down scriptures relevant to whatever spiritual battle she was facing, and so she could record whatever things she felt the Lord was speaking to her. The notebook was already half full, even though Selah had made a point to write in tiny manuscript. In it were not only scriptures, but her thoughts about them as the Holy Spirit illuminated her mind with deeper meanings she had always overlooked, or small details that seemed tailored especially to her situation. She made it a point to memorize those scriptures she thought might be invaluable in spiritual warfare, because the more intensely she prayed about something, the more opposition she faced. The mind games increased with her new spiritual growth. Her selfish nature rebelled, and sometimes the only thing that propelled her forward was the spoken Word of God.

"You might not always have a Bible with you, so it's good to know as many scriptures as you can by heart," Miss Genevieve counseled. "If you're out weeding the garden, or chopping wood, and you start having thoughts you know will lead you down the wrong mental road, you want to be able to resist as soon as you know something is going on. You need to have your sword at hand for immediate use, much like Nehemiah and the children of Israel when they were rebuilding the walls of Jerusalem."

Selah had a new appreciation for stories such as these. Until now, she had never realized the truths she could glean from what at first seemed

---

[55] 2 Timothy 1:7 AMP

a simple historical record. The story of Nehemiah as he led the people in rebuilding the walls told of perseverance under criticism and the threat of attack. "Listen to this, Selah." Miss Genevieve said, as she picked up a tattered old Revised Standard Version and read a passage from the account:

> "And I looked, and arose, and said to the nobles and to the officials and to the rest of the people, 'Do not be afraid of them. Remember the Lord, who is great and terrible, and fight for your brethren, your sons, your daughters, your wives, and your homes.'
>
> When our enemies heard that it was known to us and that God had frustrated their plan, we all returned to the wall, each to his work. From that day on, half of my servants worked on construction, and half held the spears, shields, bows, and coats of mail; and the leaders stood behind all the house of Judah, who were building on the wall. Those who carried burdens were laden in such a way that each with one hand labored on the work and with the other held his weapon. And each of the builders had his sword girded at his side while he built. The man who sounded the trumpet was beside me."[56]

"They were ready to face an attacker, no matter what they were doing at the time. You can be ready, too. As you pray, use the Word of God. Speak life into your prayers by speaking its promises out loud. Use it to cut through the lies of the enemy. As you use it, it will reveal truths about yourself and your situation that you will be amazed to discover. Slowly, carefully, it will uncover hidden things, layer by layer, as you are able to receive them." She gazed fiercely at Selah.

"I cannot stress how important it is that you hold onto the Word of God, study it, digest it, and memorize parts of it—because just like Nehemiah, you are building a wall." At this, the old woman wandered

---

[56] Nehemiah 4:14-18 RSV

again to the window and peered out of it, raising the curtain for Selah to see. "Just look out there Selah. We are a community of isolation, protected from detection, careful to stay within our boundaries. We are so busy protecting the pathetic invisible wall between us and the outside world that we don't realize the real wall is in a state of disrepair."

"The real wall . . ." Selah said blankly.

"Yes. The real wall. The wall of true righteousness that should surround every believer in this community. The very foundation that is crumbling in neglect—our relationship with God. We are so focused on playing it safe when we should be focused on the Father's heart. What are *His* desires? What is *His* will?"

"Don't many believe it's His will that we stay here, hidden, since we were led here?" Selah interjected.

"Certainly they believe that," Miss Genevieve said simply. "But if our time to stay here was over, who do you think God would tell?"

"Anyone who would listen," Selah replied.

"And how many people would He find listening?" Miss Genevieve asked. There was a long pause as she allowed Selah to consider the question. "We stopped listening when that hobo walked away from us seventy-some years ago." She walked over to a table where she had spread out her sketches of the people she had seen in her dreams. "Ezekiel lived in a nation that had turned from God to follow their own desires. The priests were corrupt, the princes took advantage of the people, and the prophets told the people things they claimed were from God, when they were really just saying things to look important or gain power. The people of the land took advantage of the poor and needy—in short, everything was a mess. And God couldn't stand it. He went looking for someone who would "stand in the gap," who would fill the gaping hole in the wall of righteousness—someone who would intercede for the people and the land, but He found no one.[57] Selah, that is an intercessor's main job. It is to be an intermediary between two

---

[57] See Ezekiel 22:30

parties. In Ezekiel's case, God was looking for someone to pray for a people who had long since ceased to care about praying, themselves."

Selah frowned as an uncomfortable feeling began to rise in the pit of her stomach. "You think I'm building a wall of righteousness for our community?" The idea sounded tedious, painstaking, even boring. She would rather hear about pulling down spiritual strongholds or battling a demon head-on. That sounded exciting, even heroic. But praying for the righteousness of a community? "I thought everyone was responsible for their own walk with God. I can't live your life for you, anymore than I can ride my parents' apron strings into heaven."

Miss Genevieve eyed her speculatively. "True. But remember how the apostle Paul said that he travailed or labored in birth again until Christ was formed in the Christians from the church in Galatia? Paul led people to Christ, but he didn't stop there. He kept praying for them. He wrote to them to teach and encourage them—and to reprimand them, if necessary."

"But those were brand new Christians. Everyone here has known Christ for a long time. Most of them are older than I am," Selah argued.

"There is a difference between chronological age and spiritual maturity. How mature you are in Christ depends on what kind of spiritual food you have been eating. Some people only study the stuff that's easy to swallow. They keep drinking the spiritual equivalent of milk long after they should have moved on to meat. Sometimes meat is hard to chew. It's harder to digest. Spiritual meat that makes you grow isn't always easy to swallow. It's the kind of scripture that will make you take a good hard look at yourself and point out to you the places in your life that are not surrendered to God. In 1 Corinthians 3, Paul told the Christians from the church in Corinth that he had fed them with milk and not solid food because they weren't able to receive it. They were still living by the world's standards, like they used to live before they came to Christ." At this, Genevieve opened the Bible she was still holding and began to read.

"But I, brethren, could not address you as spiritual men, but as men of the flesh, as babes in Christ. I fed you with milk, not solid food; for you were not ready for it; and even yet you are not ready, for you are still of the flesh. For while there is jealousy and strife among you, are you not of the flesh, and behaving like ordinary men?"[58]

Genevieve looked up at Selah. "Selah, you have moved on to meat, while some of the people in this community are still drinking milk." She chuckled. "Even though I was only a small girl, I still remember Pastor Coffelt said he didn't mind bottle feeding a young Christian, but he thought it was a shame when you had to move a moustache out of the way in order to give him his bottle. Some of the people who live here are in a state of spiritual stagnation. They have been struggling with strongholds of fear and a lack of faith. That has led to disobedience and rebellion."

"Rebellion?"

"Oh, I don't mean the kind of rebellion you would read about in the historical accounts of government coups or rebel uprisings. I'm talking about a personal rebellion, where the Holy Spirit is trying to deal with an individual about something, and they refuse to listen and try to justify their behavior. Selah, when we first came here, we were what they call 'on fire for God.' It took a lot of faith to get up and leave everything and follow a stranger to an unknown place. But we were certain we were doing the right thing, because people had been having dreams and visions and we were sensitive to the leading of the Holy Spirit. There was scriptural precedent for what we did. We left everything we knew because we wanted to please God, and we trusted Him."

She went over to the woodstove to poke at the smoldering pieces of wood that didn't seem to want to catch fire. "When was the last time you heard anyone say anything about a dream in which they felt the Lord was trying to tell them something? When was the last time you

---

[58] 1 Corinthians 3:1-3 RSV

heard anyone operating in the gifts of tongues and interpretation in a church service?" she asked, as she moved the sticks around with a poker.

Selah thought for a moment. "Once in a while, Mom will mention a dream that she thinks is more than just an ordinary dream. But as far as speaking in tongues, I guess you're the only person I've heard do that."

Miss Genevieve levered the poker underneath a chunk of oak that refused to burn. "It's kind of like this wood in the stove. It's good wood. The tree it came from has been dead a long time, so you know it isn't green. But these particular pieces got out from under the covering that I use to keep the woodpile dry. When you brought them in the house, there was snow stuck to them. Then it melted and soaked the wood, and now it won't burn." She went over to the wood box and pulled out another chunk. "Now this piece, it's a dry one. It was under the covering," she said, as she poked it strategically over a few glowing coals in the stove. She turned and looked at Selah with a twinkle in her eye. "It stayed under the covering, so it was ready for the fire. It has been placed in position to burn. Now all it needs is a little wind." At that, she turned back to the fire and blew on the coals. The coals turned white hot and the little stick of wood caught fire almost immediately. "Now, *that* wood is a delight to burn, because it was not only seasoned, it wasn't sogged up with a bunch of leftover snow," she gestured to the wood box with the poker. "Selah, when we belong to Christ, and we stay under the covering of His love through daily fellowship with Him, we are protected from the elements of this life that would soak into us and rob us of our ability to be on fire for Him. Romans 12:1 and 2 says,

> I appeal to you therefore, brethren, by the mercies of God, to present your bodies as a living sacrifice, holy and acceptable to God, which is your spiritual worship. Do not be conformed to this world but be transformed by the renewal of your mind, that you may prove what is the will of God, what is good and acceptable and perfect.[59]

[59] Romans 12:1-2 RSV

You would think that this place, of all places, would be the easiest place to serve God and know His will. But while we can get away from the world, we can't get away from our *own* stubborn will. We carry it with us wherever we go. Until we learn to offer ourselves as a living sacrifice, stay under the covering of His love, and allow ourselves to be placed in position to serve Him, we will just sit here and smolder."

"Well, how are the people in our valley going to know they are missing the heart of God if they think they are in His perfect will? Maybe someone needs to point that out to our community—to tell them they need to move on to the meat of the Word and to really search their hearts to discern God's will for their lives. Why can't we tell them? Some of them might listen."

"I doubt it," Miss Genevieve replied. "But if we pray for them to be more sensitive to the Holy Spirit, they might listen to *Him*."

Selah looked away from Genevieve's eyes, which seemed to be boring a hole into her head, and watched the fire burning in the stove. The flames feeding on the new stick of wood seemed to be drying out some of the other sticks. A few of them even seemed past the point of smoldering and ready to burn.

"The seeds of revival are sown in prayer," Genevieve was saying. "All the great moves of God that we read about began when the hearts of a few hungry people were broken for their communities. These people who were hungry for righteousness and the presence of God sought the Lord in prayer—sometimes for months. Their hearts were broken because God's heart was broken."

"But that was for people who didn't know God!" Selah blurted out. "Why should I pray for people who know better! These people are saved. They know what the Bible says. You said it yourself—they're in rebellion. Why should I pray for people like that?" Selah's voice was shaking. She couldn't understand why she was so angry, unless it was another attack of the enemy. "Maybe this is one of those times I should rebuke a thought," Selah said suddenly.

Genevieve looked at her calmly. "It won't do much good to rebuke the thought if you don't get to the root of the problem that's causing the thoughts."

Selah sighed. She evidently did not have the gift of discernment. "What do you mean?"

"Have you ever really forgiven the people of this community for what they did?" Genevieve asked.

"You mean for how they made Garrison feel like an outsider when he kept asking questions about the Old Country? And how they made his parents feel bad by treating them differently? And what about how they treated you? They told people to stop sending their kids to you for teaching, as if you were a bad influence!" The words came rushing out, unbidden.

Miss Genevieve looked at her sadly. "And what about the way they treated *you* when they found out you knew about Garrison's little escapades beyond the borders? They didn't exactly extend the right hand of fellowship, did they?" she said.

"No. It's like they drove away my best friend, and then they stopped all chances of me being around any other kids my age. You and my parents are the only friends I have, besides the Lord," Selah said with a lump in her throat. "Whenever I feel lonely, I know I'm not really alone. But I miss Garrison. I wonder what happened to him. And then I think about the elders and the gossips and I get so angry." Selah imagined that if a kettle had feelings, this is what it would feel like, sitting full of boiling water on a hot stove. The feelings bubbled and churned inside of her, threatening to spill out and burn someone.

"Being angry isn't necessarily a sin. But harboring unforgiveness in your heart—that is a problem. Matthew 6:14 and 15 says, 'For if you forgive men their trespasses, your heavenly Father will also forgive you. But if you do not forgive men their trespasses, neither will your Father forgive your trespasses.'"[60] Miss Genevieve quoted.

---

[60] Matthew 6:14-15 NKJV

Selah tried to swallow the lump in her throat. She knew her friend was right, and she couldn't argue with the Word. But it didn't seem to make it any easier. "I'm really struggling with this," she admitted. "And I didn't even realize it."

Genevieve came close to Selah and placed her hand on the girl's shoulder. "How about if we pray about it?" she suggested.

Selah nodded, wondering how she could ever forgive the people who had hurt her and her friends. She didn't see how asking God for help with the issue could change the way she felt. She didn't feel like forgiving them. How could God honor her prayer when she could not find it in herself to want to forgive? It seemed impossible and pointless, but in respect to Miss Genevieve, she bowed her head to pray.

"Father," Genevieve began, "You know how Selah has been hurting for a long time. I ask that You would help her to forgive the people who have wronged her and the people she loves. Right now, Holy Spirit, I ask that You would bring to her mind anyone she needs to forgive, and that You would help her to forgive them." At that point, Genevieve stopped and directed her words to Selah. "Honey, you know what Ephesians 4:32 says?"

Selah cringed. She knew it all too well. "And be ye kind to one to another, tenderhearted, forgiving one another, even as God for Christ's sake hath forgiven you,"[61] she said weakly. As she said the words, "for Christ's sake," she almost lost her voice. God, in His infinite mercy, had forgiven her because Christ was willing to present His body as a sacrifice for her sins. God forgave her because of Jesus and what He did. It was nothing she had done to earn it.

Miss Genevieve watched her with a gentle expression. "It's hard to forgive people who have really hurt you, but who are we to withhold forgiveness when we have been forgiven of so much, ourselves?" Genevieve said. "Selah, I know you may not feel like forgiving these people. And even as you say it, you may not feel it in your heart yet.

---

[61] Ephesians 4:32 KJV

But you need to forgive them. Say it out loud, because you know that spoken words have power. And even if you may not feel like you have forgiven them, you have taken the first step towards forgiveness."

Selah thought for a moment. The first person who came to mind was Payton Hamby. "I forgive Payton Hamby for making me feel like an outcast. I forgive him for ostracizing Miss Genevieve. I forgive him for spreading lies about Garrison." She hesitated and looked over at Genevieve, who smiled encouragingly. "How long does it take for me to feel like I've actually forgiven them?" she asked.

"When you ask for forgiveness, does God forgive you because He feels like it?" Genevieve asked.

"What—I, uh," Selah sputtered.

"Why does God forgive us when we mess up? Is it because we deserve it?"

"Of course not!" Selah exclaimed.

"Then why does He forgive us, knowing we will probably mess up again?"

"He forgives us because of what Jesus did on the cross."

"Then it has nothing to do with how He feels about our actions?" Miss Genevieve continued.

"No. It's because of the blood of His Son, which was shed as a sacrifice for our sins."

"The new covenant. The covenant of His blood," Genevieve said. "When God looks at us, He doesn't see our imperfections. He sees the precious blood of His Son. Selah, in 1 John 1:9, it says that if we confess our sins, He is faithful and just to forgive us our sins, and to cleanse us from all unrighteousness.[62] If His Word says that, then we need to take Him at His Word. We don't rely on whether or not we *feel* forgiven. We rely on the blood covenant He made with us. We rely on His Word, which tells us that if we ask His forgiveness, He will forgive us."

"But for me, forgiveness is about how I feel about someone. When I don't forgive a person, it colors everything that I think about them.

---

[62] See 1 John 1:9 NKJV

Nothing they can do is good enough to make me forget about how they hurt me," Selah explained.

"You're right. They can't do anything good enough to make up for what they did. They can't pay for their mistake, any more than you could pay for your mistake when you asked God to forgive you. He forgave you because of the blood of Jesus and because He said He would forgive if you admitted you had done wrong. Now, I know those people haven't asked you to forgive them. They think *you're* the one at fault. They probably don't have any inkling that they have wronged you. And you know, I don't think they are losing any sleep over how you feel." She paused and made sure Selah was looking her in the eyes. "But I bet *you've* lost sleep over it. That's one reason it's so important to forgive. The one we are really hurting by not forgiving is ourselves."

Selah bit her lip and looked at the threadbare carpet. "I *want* to forgive them. I know it's the right thing to do. I just don't know if I can."

"Now you're getting the idea," Miss Genevieve said happily. "There's no way you can forgive them."

"What are you talking about? You just spent half an hour trying to convince me I should forgive them, and now you're telling me I can't?"

"You should, but you can't. Not on your own. But you can, *through Christ*," Miss Genevieve explained. "You can do all things through Christ, who gives you strength."

"Philippians 4:13," Selah supplied the reference.

"Now, try again. This time, remember Philippians 4:13. Step out in faith as you tell these people you forgive them. Go ahead and talk to them just as if they were standing right here, in this room," Genevieve suggested.

Selah took a deep breath. "Lord, I need your help with this," she began. "Your Word says that I can do all things through Christ, who gives me strength. Give me the strength to forgive."

One by one, Selah spoke her forgiveness to all the people who had hurt her, as their faces appeared before her in her mind's eye. It was a lengthy list, and it took a while. When she had finished with the last person she could think of, she stopped and directed her words toward God. "Lord, please forgive me for holding onto unforgiveness in my heart. I forgive these people with the words of my mouth, with faith that you will do the work that needs to happen in my heart." As she finished the prayer, she felt like a weight had come off her shoulders. When she thought of the individuals she had forgiven, it seemed like the anger she had toward them had lost some of its sharpness. Maybe God's work in her wasn't finished yet, but it had certainly started.

Miss Genevieve backed away from her a little and seemed to size her up. "You don't look too bad, for someone who just came off the battle-field," she said warmly. "Now, let's put some more dry wood on the fire. We'll get those soggy old logs to burn, yet!"

The two friends sat close to the stove while Genevieve manned the poker. A warmth that was greater than the fire settled on the little trailer as Selah listened to stories of revivals in Wales, America, and China. A strange sensation she didn't recognize at first began to seep its way slowly into her spirit. And then it dawned on her. It was peace.

27

THE next morning, Selah awoke to a monotonous tapping noise outside her window. The sound had invaded her dreams, taking on the form of one of the chickens pecking persistently on her head when she tried to gather eggs in the hen house. She was just about to pick up the hen and remove it from its nesting box when she woke up. She looked around the room, which seemed to be flooded with light. Surely she couldn't have overslept. Maggie would have been mooing for her hay even if Selah was only fifteen minutes later than normal. She rubbed her eyes and swung her feet over the edge of the bed. Then it dawned on her. The tapping noise was water dripping. The snow on the roof was melting.

Selah went to the window and pulled the curtains back. She was almost blinded by the morning sun reflecting on the snow. Quickly she dressed and came into the kitchen, where Asha was mixing up a batch of biscuits. "Is it finally thawing?" Selah asked her mother, as she pinched off a piece of the dough.

Asha playfully slapped her hand away. "Can't you wait 'til I take them out of the oven?" she asked.

"Your biscuits are good enough to eat raw," Selah said. She peered out the kitchen window and watched the water dripping off of icicles forming under the eaves during the thaw. "Did you notice the snow is melting off the roof?"

"How could I keep from it, with all that dripping and the water splattering onto the lid of the rain barrel?" Asha said as she kneaded the dough and rolled it out onto a portion of the counter she had dusted with flour. "I guess we might be able to take the lid off that barrel, if it really is thawing now. I thought I had overslept when I woke up, but it turns out we just forgot what sunshine looks like."

Selah thought back over the seemingly endless weeks of gray, overcast skies and subzero temperatures. Dreary weather had become the norm that winter, and the sunshine was unfamiliar– almost a shock. "Isn't it strange how we get used to something, and we begin to believe it won't ever change?" she heard herself say. "And then, suddenly, it does." The prayer session with Miss Genevieve flashed through her mind. "God is full of surprises," she added, as she took the old can Asha used for a biscuit cutter and shuffled the cutting edge of it back and forth in a little pile of flour. "Just when you think a situation is hopeless, He changes your way of seeing things, and everything that was impossible before is possible now." *Wumpf!* Selah plopped the can down onto the dough, cutting it into a plump, tidy circle.

Asha watched her daughter cut out three more circles, shuffling the edge of the can in the flour between each cut. "How is Miss Genevieve?" she asked.

"She's great. I hope someday I can be that wise," Selah said as she poked her hand through the can to free a stubborn biscuit that was clinging to its edge.

"You've been spending a lot of time with her lately," Asha remarked. "Are you sure she's okay?"

Selah looked up quickly. "What do you mean?"

Asha frowned thoughtfully. "She just seems a little preoccupied at the last few church services. And thinner."

"What? Thinner?" Selah's forehead wrinkled in concentration as she tried to remember every detail of her friend's appearance. "I haven't noticed her looking any thinner than usual."

"That's probably because you've been going to see her almost every day. I only see her once a week, and so I see a week's worth of change every time I see her," Asha explained.

Selah pushed a circle of dough through the flour, marking a wobbly trail across the counter. "Well, I haven't noticed."

"Look at the way her clothes fit her," Asha suggested. "Then you might see it. She must have lost fifteen or twenty pounds. I'm just concerned something might be wrong."

Asha took the can from Selah and deftly cut out the rest of the dough, shaping the remaining scraps into a lumpy mass that Jackson liked to call the "stepchild biscuit."

"Oh!" Selah said suddenly as she remembered the obvious. "She has been fasting lately, but I didn't think it was enough for her to lose that much weight."

Asha placed the biscuits onto a greased baking pan. "Well, at her age, missing a few meals might make more of a difference. I hope that's all it is."

"What do you mean?" Selah asked.

Asha slid the pan into the metal barrel of the homemade cookstove. "She just doesn't look well. I hope it's my imagination. Anyway, I'm glad you two have been spending so much time with each other. I don't suppose anyone has given you any trouble about it?"

Selah shook her head. "I think they've written us both off as outcasts. As long as we keep to ourselves and stay in the boundaries, we're not considered a threat to society."

Their conversation was interrupted by a loud mooing outside.

"Well, there's someone who thinks you're a threat to her supply of grain," Asha smiled.

Selah shrugged on her coat and stepped outside into the sunshine. Maggie was waiting by the corral gate and uttered a low-pitched moo when she saw Selah. "You'd think we were starving you," Selah said to the chocolaty-cream colored cow. Maggie blew her breath out in steamy puffs and began nosing around Selah's pockets. "We're long out of carrots, you greedy gut," Selah admonished her. She had wanted Maggie to be easy to work with, being a milk cow, and so had spent considerable time handling her and rewarding her with treats like carrots and apples. The only carrots around this time of year were canned, so Maggie had to make do with a little extra oats with her daily hay ration. "You seemed to fare well this winter, no matter how you complain," Selah remarked as she ran her hand along the cow's side to see if she could feel any ribs under the fuzzy winter coat. Dairy cows were always a little bonier than beef cattle, but Maggie was healthier than most, being somewhat of a pet. Selah noticed her udder was beginning to fill out, "making a bag," as the cattlemen called it when they were watching for signs of calving. "It won't be long now, Maggie. Our family will have milk and cream to drink again, and we can make cheese. I can make some of Miss Genevieve's favorite cheese to take to her." Selah stopped as she remembered her mother's words. She really hadn't noticed Miss Genevieve getting thinner. It bothered her that something might be wrong. Maybe her mother was exaggerating. She decided to make it a point to be more observant the next time she visited her old friend.

In the mean time, she was in wonder of the difference between today and yesterday. It seemed a warm breeze was blowing through the valley, speeding up the thawing process. The temperature had risen to slightly above freezing, and with the sun out, the frozen ground was drinking up what snow-melt it could hold and puddling the rest into quagmires of mud.

A bright cascade of birdsong tumbled from the top of the cedar tree in the corner of the yard. Selah could see a cardinal there, and he turned to face a different direction before he resumed his song, as if to declare to every living soul whose ears could hear him that spring was finally moving in. "I wonder if your kind are singing where Garrison is...wherever he is," Selah said to the bird. The brilliant red vocalist faced yet another direction and sang again, his song as loud and insistent as a rallying cry. *"Here! Here! Here! Start-it, start-it, start-it!"* he seemed to say.

"Start what?" Selah asked in amusement. It was a game she played with herself, answering the birds according to what it sounded like they were saying.

"Ba-*CAWK!*" cackled one of the hens in the hen house.

"Well, that was plain enough," Selah called back to the hen as she finished filling Maggie's feed trough. "I'm coming, I'm coming," she said, as she hurried to let the chickens out of their house for the day. They rushed out, seemingly urged on by the sunshine and hopes of any remaining grass or seeds that might emerge from beneath the melting snow. One old black chicken Selah called Clucky remained in her nesting box while Selah looked to see if any of the hens had started laying yet. When she came to Clucky's box, the hen puffed up her feathers. Selah thought she might get pecked as she reached under the chicken, but Clucky just stayed puffed up, her wings slightly spread out as if to protect a clutch of eggs. "It's still kind of early in the season for you to be sitting, Clucky," Selah warned her. "It's going to be cold and wet for a long time, yet. Not good for little chicks." Clucky ducked her head and held her ground. "Come on, Clucky." Selah reached in and pulled the chicken out of the box, sitting her on the floor of the hen house, where the hen remained in a docile, puffed-up state. "Get over it," Selah scolded her. She nudged the hen with her boot in an attempt to snap her out of her torpor. When hens started exhibiting brooding behavior, they often stopped laying, so Selah tried to discourage it unless they were ready for a new batch of chicks. "It's not time yet, Clucky," she said, as she reached into the box for what she hoped would be the first egg of the year. She was delighted to find not one, but *two* eggs. Although each hen usually would only lay one egg every day or so, they often used the same nesting box and would sit on each others' eggs. "Oh, great," Selah said, as she notice one of the eggs felt slightly wet. Sometimes the eggs got stepped on and broken. When that happened, it was good to get rid of the broken one as quickly and completely as possible so the hens didn't eat it and develop a habit of breaking them on purpose. She gently cupped the egg in her hand to keep as much of its contents contained as she possibly could. *"Peep, peep, peep!"* cried a chick from within the eggshell. Selah almost dropped it. The egg had felt slightly wet because a chick had begun to peck its way out. "How in the world did you stay unnoticed?" Selah asked as she put the egg back into the box. The other egg was obviously newly laid. She looked back at Clucky, who cocked her head warily at Selah as if she expected another nudge from a boot. Since laying was triggered by light and the weather had been so gray and limited, Selah hadn't been checking the nesting boxes on a regular basis. Clucky must have been brooding unnoticed for several weeks. "I guess you knew what you were clucking about," Selah told her, as she picked up the broody hen and put her back in the box with the chick. "That's an awful lot of energy to put out for one measly chick," she scolded. "You're going to be out of commission for weeks because of this." Clucky hovered over the hatching chick, watching its progress. "Good chicken," Selah said fondly, reaching in to pet the hen. Clucky rewarded her with a sharp peck. "Okay, I know the routine," Selah said crossly, and left her alone. Garrison had always wanted to tap the hens back when they pecked him, but Selah had argued they were just protecting their babies. She sighed. So many things reminded her of him, even getting pecked by a chicken.

"Where is he now?" she wondered. Was he living it up in a luxurious housing complex provided by the State, with running water and heat that came out of vents in the floor? Or was he in custody, awaiting whatever fate the State decided?

"Selah." Jackson awakened her out of her reverie. He was just outside the hen house, and she suddenly realized she had been standing in the open doorway, lost in thought for quite some time. She started to tell him about the chick, but something in his demeanor made her stop short. "What is it?" she asked.

"Payton was just here. He said he had just gone by to check on Miss Genevieve, and..." Jackson hesitated as he regarded Selah carefully, "something has happened. It doesn't look good."

"What happened? What do you mean?" Selah asked, her eyes wide with worry.

"He thinks she's had a stroke," Jackson continued. "She isn't making much sense. He found her on the floor by the stove. He's afraid she may have broken a hip. Doc Stratton has been over to see her, but he says there's not much we can do, with our limited medicine."

Selah bolted out of the doorway and toward the main road without a word.

"There's a bunch of people there," he called after her. "Asha and I will be over as soon as we can."

Selah heard him, but didn't respond. All she could think of was Miss Genevieve, confused by a stroke and in pain from the fall. "Oh, God," she pleaded as she ran. "Oh, God, please be with her, and help her, Jesus!" Selah prayed all the way to Genevieve's house. It seemed the longest run of her life. How could a day that had begun with such promise take such a drastic turn?

When she arrived at the trailer, a few people stood on the porch outside, looking up glumly as she bounded through the slushy snow in the yard. "Hey, Selah," said Seth Beardsley as she took two porch steps at a time. Selah looked at him briefly, out of breath and at a loss for words, and then opened the trailer door.

Miss Genevieve was lying on her couch, which had been pulled closer to the stove for warmth. Payton and his wife, Addy, were standing beside her, and Addy was holding her hand. They both looked up as Selah came in. "Hello, Selah," Payton said softly. Selah glanced at him without a word and walked over to the crumpled figure on the couch. Addy stepped aside as Selah knelt down to see her friend.

"She's been quiet for some time now, but she was trying to talk earlier," Addy said. "We couldn't make any sense of it, though."

The old woman's eyes were closed, but her breathing seemed steady and regular. Selah took the hand of her friend and swallowed hard. "Lord Jesus," she began to pray.

At the sound of her voice, Miss Genevieve's eyes opened up. She looked sluggishly around the room, trying to locate the source of the voice. "I'm right here, Miss Genevieve," Selah said.

Genevieve's mouth drew up into a slight, lopsided smile. "Uhh," she grunted, and squeezed Selah's hand.

Payton knelt down beside Selah. "She's been asking for someone named Marcy," he said. "We think it must have been a childhood friend from the Old Country, since there's no one by that name around here."

Selah kept her eyes on Genevieve. She felt as though her heart had been ripped out of her chest and was beating, exposed, on the trailer floor, for all to see. "We're going to pray for you, Miss Genevieve," she said bravely. "James 5:14 and 15 says 'Is anyone among you sick? Let him call for the elders of the church, and let them pray over him, anointing him with oil in the name of the Lord. And the prayer of faith will save the sick, and the Lord will raise him up. And if he has committed sins, he will be forgiven.'"[63] She looked over at Payton and Addy. "We happen to have some elders here right now, and I know they'd be willing to pray for you."

Payton looked at Selah and smiled sadly. "Addy, can you find some oil in the kitchen?" he said, without taking his eyes away from the girl. Addy somberly went into the kitchen and began searching the cabinets.

"She keeps it in the one to the right of the old electric stove," Selah said. Soon Addy returned with a quart jar of homemade corn oil. Traditionally, Christians had used olive oil for anointing purposes, but olive trees didn't grow in the valley.

Payton dipped the tip of his finger in the oil and touched it lightly to Miss Genevieve's forehead. "Father, in Jesus' name, we ask that You touch Miss Genevieve in her body. We ask You to heal her mind and whatever damage has been caused by the stroke. And heal her hip, Lord. Please take the pain away and accelerate the healing process. But, Father, we want to pray in Your will. We ask above all that You have Your will in Miss Genevieve. If it's her time to go on to be with You, we ask that she not linger painfully."

---

[63] James 5:14-15 NKJV

At those words, Selah's eyes shot open and she regarded Payton in horror as he continued his prayer. She cried out to God in her spirit, *"No, Lord! It's not time yet! He's got it wrong. She isn't finished here yet!"*

Payton finished his prayer to find Selah still staring at him. "God can heal her," Selah said firmly.

Payton nodded. "Yes, He can. But remember, she is 92 years old. To every thing, there is a season and a time, to every purpose under heaven."

Selah felt the anger at him welling up inside of her again. She started to say something in response when she felt Miss Genevieve squeeze her hand. She looked at her friend, whose eyes met hers. "For durdy do," the woman said weakly.

"For durdy do...." Selah repeated slowly, trying to decipher the phrase.

Addy stepped forward hopefully. "Floor dirty? Floor dirty too? We can clean house for you, Sis. It's no trouble at all," she said in her eagerness to find something she could do to help.

Miss Genevieve's eyes closed slightly and she looked to the side. "Feezns for durdy do," she said again.

And suddenly Selah understood. "Ephesians 4:32," she said, lowering her head as she remembered yesterday and all the people she had forgiven out loud, including Payton Hamby. She looked at him meaningfully. "She's reminding me of something we prayed about yesterday," she explained.

Payton looked at her searchingly, and Selah wondered if he could guess what they had prayed about.

"Marcy," Miss Genevieve said, looking at Selah intently. *"Marcy!"*

"There she goes again with that name," Addy said. "Maybe you remind her of whoever it is she's talking about," she suggested to Selah.

"I don't think that's it. I think it's *mercy* she's saying, instead of Marcy. She wants me to show mercy," Selah said. It made sense, considering the reference to the scripture about forgiveness.

"NO!" Miss Genevieve said emphatically. "Marcy!"

The three watched helplessly as Miss Genevieve tried to communicate, and Selah prayed silently for the Lord to heal the damaged neural connections in her brain. Finally, the old woman gave up in exhaustion and fell asleep.

The door to the trailer opened and Asha and Jackson came inside.

Payton stood up to make room for them around the couch. "Addy's going to stay with Miss Genevieve today," he said quietly. "We can all take turns."

"I'll do it," Selah said. "She's used to me being here. I know where everything is. I know the way she likes things."

Payton smiled sympathetically at Selah. "You can't do it all, Selah. And you know, when someone in the body of Christ is hurting, all the other members of the body hurt with them and want to help out."

"I know, but I just don't want to leave her!" she sobbed.

Payton hesitated for a moment and then placed a comforting hand on her shoulder. "We love her, too, Sis," he said, and Selah realized that, no matter how they had behaved toward the old woman last summer when fear was running rampant through the ranks, he really meant it. They did love Miss Genevieve. After all, who was it who had found her this morning? Payton had been checking on Miss Genevieve every other day, unwilling to leave her care solely in the hands of a teenage girl. Each time he would make an excuse for why he came, so as not to make Genevieve feel like a burden. Genevieve used to chuckle at his reasons for coming as she told Selah of them, but she never spoke of him spitefully. Looking back, Selah realized Genevieve had been trying to nudge her toward forgiving him for a long time.

"Tell you what," he said slowly, "We'll have a revolving list of people to come stay with her. But you can stay as long as you like, and as long as your parents will let you." He looked at Asha and Jackson. "In fact, if your family would rather take the first day, it'd be fine with us."

Jackson nodded. "We'll work the first day out between the three of us," he said.

"Okay, then," Payton said simply. Addy joined him and the two left quietly.

Selah could hear the rest of the crowd on the porch leaving. They must have all stopped in before she arrived. She looked around the darkened trailer. "Can't we open the curtains and let some light in?" she asked. "Miss Genevieve was looking forward to spring. We talked about it just yesterday."

Asha came close to the couch and watched the cover rise and fall with the elder's regular breathing. "Good idea," she said, and quietly went to the windows to let in some light.

Jackson checked the supply of wood and the water in the jugs by the door. "Be careful if you try to give her any water," he advised. "She may not be able to swallow."

Selah looked at him miserably. "Why did this have to happen to her?" she asked.

"Why does anything bad happen to anyone?" Jackson replied. "God didn't tell us life would be fair. If anything, he said the opposite. *In the world you will have tribulation; but be of good cheer, I have overcome the world.*"[64]

"John 16:33," Selah said, as she remembered the memory verse Miss Genevieve had stressed to her throughout the past few months.

"I know what Genevieve would say about why this happened to her," Asha said softly. *"And we know that God causes everything to work together for the good of those who love God and are called according to his purpose for them."*[65]

Selah knew that was exactly what her friend would have said, but it didn't seem to make this any easier. The three set about trying to make Miss Genevieve as comfortable as possible, and then Jackson left to take care of the rest of the chores around their place. Asha would stay during the daytime, and Jackson would return at nightfall. Selah still insisted she wasn't leaving.

---

[64] John 16:33b NKJV
[65] Romans 8:28 NLT

Asha busied herself dusting some of the things in the trailer that were on shelves too high for Genevieve to reach. Selah collected several versions of the Bible from the Bible bookshelf and began reading them to her friend out loud, even though she was asleep. Sometime in the mid morning, Genevieve's eyes opened and she watched Selah as she read. Selah smiled encouragingly. "Is there anything you'd like to hear, especially?" she asked.

The gray eyes looked slowly over to the Bible Selah was holding and she grimaced in concentration. "Uhh," she said, and frowned. She pulled her good arm out of the covers and pointed to the wood stacked by the stove. "Uhh."

"You want some more wood on the fire?" Selah asked, and got up to pick up one of the smaller logs.

"Uhhh!" Miss Genevieve demanded, pointing to the log and motioning for Selah to bring it to her.

Selah could see clearly that Miss Genevieve wanted her to bring the log over to her, but she couldn't figure out why. However, she obediently brought it to the woman, who looked up at her and smiled. And then, she made a chopping motion on the wood with her bony hand.

"You think it isn't cut small enough?" Selah asked, confused.

"Aaa," Miss Genevieve said, with difficulty, and pointed to the Bible Selah had left in the chair. She chopped at the wood again, using her hand like an axe, and again pointed to the Bible.

"Selah," said Asha, who had been watching from the kitchen, "she wants you to read from Acts."

"Mmmm," Miss Genevieve hummed in approval, and held up two fingers.

"Acts chapter two, to be specific—am I right?" Asha asked.

"Mmmm," the woman hummed again, and tried to nod.

Selah looked at Asha gratefully and set down the wood. She began reading in the second chapter of Acts, as Miss Genevieve had requested.

"On the day of Pentecost, all the believers were meeting together in one place. Suddenly, there was a sound from heaven like the roaring of a mighty windstorm, and it filled the house where they were sitting. Then, what looked like flames or tongues of fire appeared and settled on each of them. And everyone present was filled with the Holy Spirit and began speaking in other languages, as the Holy Spirit gave them this ability."[66]

Selah stopped to glance at Miss Genevieve, whose eyes were sparkling. She looked back at the New Living Translation she had been reading from and continued. When she got to verses 38 and 39, Genevieve raised her hand and held up one finger, as if to emphasize what Selah was reading. "…Each of you must repent of your sins and turn to God, and be baptized in the name of Jesus Christ for the forgiveness of your sins. Then you will receive the gift of the Holy Spirit. This promise is to you, to your children, and to those far away—all who have been called by the Lord our God."[67]

Miss Genevieve lowered her hand and smiled droopily. She turned her head slightly toward Selah and strained to look into her eyes. She pointed at the Bible and then to Selah. *"You,"* she said thickly.

Selah watched her quietly, trying to comprehend. "Do you want me to read some more?" she asked. But Miss Genevieve had fallen asleep again. Selah decided to keep reading.

A half hour later, her throat was dry. She got up for a drink of water. "Mom, don't we need to try to get her to drink?" she asked.

Asha brought a glass of water and a small sponge she had collected and sanitized earlier from the water in the kettle on the woodstove. "When she wakes up again, we can try, but we have to be very careful. We don't want her to choke," she explained. She set down the glass of water on the table near Miss Genevieve's sketches. "She is quite an artist, isn't she?"

---

[66] Acts 2:1-4 NLT
[67] Acts 2:38-39 NLT

Selah walked over to the table and looked at the desperate faces of the lost, crying out silently from their paper prison. As hopeless as her dream of becoming a missionary had seemed before, it seemed even more impossible now. *"Maybe that's why she never felt like she had Your approval to leave,"* Selah prayed silently, as she recalled to mind all the fasting and prayer, and how the two never felt a sense of God confirming to them that Genevieve should, against all odds, go forward with her plan. God had known what the future held for Miss Genevieve. But if He knew she was going to have a stroke, why had He never given her a release from her calling? Why did she still have such a drive to reach out to the lost she would never see, except in her dreams?

Asha came over to the couch, carrying a clipboard with a piece of paper and a pencil. "I know her writing hand is the one affected by the stroke, but she still might be able to write a little with her left hand to communicate," Asha suggested, and leaned the clipboard against the couch. The movement awakened Genevieve, and Asha smiled, retrieving the clipboard and holding it up for her to see. "Maybe you can write on this, to tell us what you want," she said.

"Are you thirsty?" Selah asked, reaching for the water and the sponge. Miss Genevieve looked longingly at the glass of water. "I have to use the sponge first, because we don't know how well you can swallow yet." She dipped the sponge in the glass, wrung out the excess water, and gently lifted it to Genevieve's lips. The elder opened her mouth and stuck out her tongue, and Selah moistened it for her. A drop of water from the sponge suddenly rolled down her tongue and into her throat. Genevieve's body was wracked by spasms of coughing and choking. "Sit her up," Asha said, and the two worked together to lift up the old woman to a sitting position. The coughing continued, and Asha and Selah prayed fervently as the minutes passed. Finally, the coughing stopped. Miss Genevieve swallowed slightly. "Well, I guess she can swallow, but just not very well," Selah said.

"If she hadn't been able to swallow at all, Doc would have had her sitting up, and she would have been drooling," Asha said matter-of-factly.

Selah looked dismally at her old friend, who seemed absolutely exhausted by the coughing attack. They started to lay her back down on the couch, when her eyes darted to the window.

"Marcy!" she whispered, pointing out the window. *"Marcy!"*

Selah looked out the window, half expecting to see one of the neighborhood children peering inside. "Who is Marcy?" she asked. And then, remembering the clipboard, she lifted it up for Genevieve to use, placing the pencil in her left hand.

Genevieve studied the pencil for a while, and then looked at Selah with a smile pulling at the left side of her mouth. Slowly and carefully, she began to draw as well as she could with her non-dominant hand. Selah watched as she drew. What appeared was a wobbly, lobed shape. Genevieve looked up at Selah again, her eyes twinkling. "Marcy," she said, pointing to the picture.

"That's Marcy?" Selah asked, wondering if Genevieve was actually making sense to herself.

"No," said her friend, with a discouraged tone. "Marcy," she said again, pointing to the picture, and then to herself, and then to Selah.

Selah looked at Asha helplessly. "I'm sorry, Miss Genevieve, I just don't understand."

Genevieve sighed, and then looked toward the Bible near Selah's chair. Selah brought the Bible to her. "Show me where you want to read," Selah said, opening it for her. Miss Genevieve seemed confused as she flipped through the pages. She looked up at Asha and Selah and shook her head.

"You don't want to read?" Selah asked, and started to pull the Bible away.

"Uhh!" Genevieve cried plaintively, and clung to the Bible like a squirrel to a tree trunk.

"Selah, it may be that she has lost the ability to read and organize thoughts," Asha explained softly. "Sometimes after a stroke, it can take a while to regain these abilities."

Genevieve looked at her meaningfully. She pointed to the Bible and then to a thick blanket on the back of the couch.

"Are you cold?" Selah asked, reaching for the blanket.

Genevieve grabbed her hand to stop her.

"I think she's trying to tell us where she wants you to read—like she did with the wood earlier," Asha suggested.

Selah settled down in the chair and began a guessing game. "Blanket? Like the blanket Peter saw in his vision?"

Genevieve started to shake her head, but then seemed to change her mind. Selah read the story from Acts chapter ten about Peter and the vision he had when God was telling him to go and tell Cornelius and the other Gentiles about Jesus. In the vision, Peter saw a blanket coming down from heaven. It was drawn up at the four corners like a bundle, and contained all sorts of animals which Jews considered ceremonially unclean. God told Peter to kill and eat from the animals in the blanket; and Peter refused, saying he had never eaten anything common or unclean. "What God has cleansed you must not call common," a voice said to him in the vision. When the Gentiles arrived, seeking Peter, the Spirit told him not to hesitate to go with them, for He had sent them.

Selah stopped reading, as Genevieve had closed her eyes and appeared to be asleep. When she stopped, the woman's eyes shot open and she pointed at the Bible again. Selah smiled and started reading again. When she got to verse 44, Miss Genevieve grew agitated. "Even as Peter was saying these things," Selah read, "the Holy Spirit fell upon all who had heard the message. The Jewish believers who came with Peter were amazed that the gift of the Holy Spirit had been poured out upon the Gentiles, too. And there could be no doubt about it, for they heard them speaking in tongues and praising God."[68]

Genevieve poked her knobby finger at the Bible and then reached again for the thick blanket, stroking it lovingly and pulling it to her in a hug. "The Bible is such a comfort to her," Asha said; and at that, Genevieve almost rolled off the couch.

---

[68] Acts 10:44-46 NLT

"Easy, Miss Genevieve!" Selah said, scrambling to keep her friend from falling. Genevieve winced and moaned as she rolled on the injured hip. After she had regained her place on the couch, she pointed at Asha.

"What were you saying right before that happened?" Selah asked.

"The Bible is a comfort to her," Asha repeated, and at the word, "comfort," Miss Genevieve pointed at Asha and then jabbed at the blanket with her finger.

"Comforter," Selah slapped herself on the forehead as she realized what Miss Genevieve was saying. "She wants us to read about the Holy Spirit being a comforter."

Miss Genevieve's lopsided grin was all they needed for confirmation. Asha found a King James Version of the Bible, which used the word Comforter when referring to the Holy Spirit in John chapter fourteen, and she began to read in verse sixteen. "And I will pray the Father, and he shall give you another Comforter, that he may abide with you for ever; even the Spirit of truth; whom the world cannot receive, because it seeth him not, neither knoweth him: but ye know him; for he dwelleth with you, and shall be in you. I will not leave you comfortless: I will come to you."[69] Asha skipped down to verse twenty-six. "But the Comforter, which is the Holy Ghost, whom the Father will send in my name, he shall teach you all things, and bring all things to your remembrance, whatsoever I have said unto you."[70]

Miss Genevieve nodded and poked her finger into Selah's chest. Then she touched Selah's forehead and tapped it gently. "You want me to memorize that, don't you?" Selah said, and pulled out the pad of paper she always kept with her so that she could record the verses they had just read. Genevieve nodded as Selah wrote them down, and then grabbed the pencil again. This time, she drew what appeared to be a tree. She looked hopefully at Selah. "Marcy?" she said imploringly.

"I don't know," Selah said, frustrated. "I don't know what Marcy looks like. She kind of looks like a tree, to me," Selah said, hoping she didn't offend Miss Genevieve.

---

[69] John 14:16-18 KJV
[70] John 14:26 KJV

But Genevieve nodded happily, and made a line connecting the tree-like figure to the lobed shape she had made earlier. "Marcy," she cooed, and pointed to herself again.

"Was that your nickname when you were really little?" Selah asked, grasping at straws.

Genevieve looked at her with disgust and settled back down into the covers. "I'm sorry I don't understand you," Selah apologized. Genevieve patted her hand reassuringly, and then drifted off to sleep.

28

THE day wore on, with Miss Genevieve sleeping through most of it. Selah spent the day in prayer and reflection on the past few months. She couldn't stop thinking about what Genevieve had told her just before they had started fasting and earnestly seeking the Lord in prayer. "I feel restless, like I'm just about to go on a magnificent journey," she had said. Everything had seemed so exciting then, as if they were on the cusp of something phenomenal. Selah watched the sleeping form on the couch and cried silently to God for another chance for her to fulfill her destiny. *"It's all she ever wanted,"* she said to herself. *"And since God has a heart to reach those who don't know Him, it should be something that would please Him. I just can't understand why this has happened."*

Several times she studied the picture Miss Genevieve had drawn and attempted to decipher it, but without success. As she looked at the tree-like shape and the lumpy form beside it, she pondered how it must be frustrating for Genevieve to lose not only her ability to speak, but her ability to draw, as well.

Jackson came to take Asha's post at nightfall. "Don't forget, you need to get some rest, too," Asha counseled Selah. "You might as well sleep while she's sleeping, or you won't be any help to her when she's awake."

"Good advice, Mama," Selah admitted, and gave Asha a hug before she left.

Jackson had brought some of that morning's biscuits from the house, as well as some canned peaches and cold ham they had eaten for dinner the night before. "Ham and biscuits are a fine meal, but I'll be glad when those hens get to laying again," he said between mouthfuls.

"Oh, good grief," Selah said suddenly, and went over to her coat that was hung by the door. She looked apprehensively into the side pocket. "I can't believe it."

"What?" Jackson asked as he watched from his seat at the kitchen table.

"I got an egg this morning. Actually, there were two eggs, but one was hatching. I put the other one in my pocket on the way over here. And it appears to have survived the trip."

"Did you say one was hatching?" Jackson asked, his eyebrows raised in surprise.

"Yeah," Selah muttered.

"Haven't been highly involved in poultry care lately, I take it?" Jackson teased her.

"Well, they always get fed and watered, but I really didn't see much point in checking the nesting boxes every day until our days started getting longer," Selah explained. "Anyway, Clucky is now a proud mother. What a waste of a good layer this early in the spring."

"Oh well. Get a skillet and we'll fry that egg up on the wood stove. We'll split it to celebrate the arrival of warmer weather." Jackson was a firm believer in celebrations of small, serendipitous happenings as much as the momentous occasions of life. "Might as well enjoy life as you go along," he would often say.

The two ate the egg to the soft snoring sounds coming from the direction of the couch. "You'd better follow her example and get some shut-eye," Jackson told Selah.

"It's just that I haven't done anything physical all day long. I don't think I could sleep if I tried," Selah explained.

"Well, go take a walk, then. Of course, that might just wake you up."

Selah looked reluctantly at the sleeping figure. "I don't want to be gone if she wakes up. I'll just sit here and read," she said as she got a candle out of a drawer in the kitchen.

She settled in the chair beside the couch and read silently from the book of Acts, beginning where she had stopped earlier in chapter two. Peter was one of her favorite people in the Bible, and she liked reading about the difference in him before and after he had received the Holy Spirit. In the gospels, he had declared he was willing to die for Jesus and then had ended up denying he even knew Christ. But after he had received the Holy Ghost, he preached to a crowd of over three thousand. "What a difference it makes to be filled with the Spirit!" Miss Genevieve had told her when they had discussed it. It seemed that the past few weeks, she had been increasingly focused on the importance of the Holy Spirit in the life of the believer. "He's our Guide, our Helper, our Teacher, and our Intercessor. When someone prays in the Spirit, they pray the perfect will of God. You know, so many times, we want to interject our own thoughts about the way things should be. We think we know, when sometimes, we've got it all wrong. And in some situations, we really don't have any idea how to pray. But when we allow the Spirit to pray *through* us in His own language, then our limited human intellect doesn't get in the way. Like it says in Romans 8:26 and 27, 'For we don't even know what we should pray for, nor how we should pray. But the Holy Spirit prays for us with groanings that cannot be expressed in words. And the Father who knows all hearts knows what the Spirit is saying, for the Spirit pleads for us believers in harmony with God's own will.'[71] Now, that's the best kind of intercession!" she had declared. Selah watched her once articulate friend, reduced to a few words, grunts and hand gestures. She swallowed the lump in her throat and kept reading.

Even though she wasn't physically tired, she felt mentally and spiritually exhausted. Every other thought that day had been a prayer. Without realizing it, she began to nod off.

She was in the chicken house, and Clucky was fluffed up over her nesting box. "I can't believe you are going to expend all that energy on one measly chick,"

---

[71] Romans 8:26-27 NLT

Selah scolded her again. Clucky looked up at her with a fierce gleam in her eye. "You can glare at me all you want, but you could be laying an egg every day, and now you won't do anything except babysit. That's an awful lot of effort for one little chick. I hope it's worth it to you." Clucky studied Selah carefully with her burnished brown eyes, and then stood up slightly and raised one of her wings as if she were trying to show Selah the fruit of her labors. Selah bent down beside the nesting box and peered closely at the chick. It was facing away from her. It didn't really look like a chick at all, she decided. It was wearing pants and a coat, and it didn't have any feathers. It looked more like a little person than a chicken. Suddenly, the chick turned to look at her, and Selah was horrified to see that the face looking back at her was her own.

"Marcy!" Clucky whispered in a voice that sounded just like Genevieve's, her eyes still gleaming. "Marcy!" she said, more loudly this time, and with a flick of her beak, she pushed the miniature Selah out of the nest.

Selah awoke with a start. That was, without a doubt, the weirdest dream she had ever had. She looked over at her friend, whom she could barely see in the darkness of the trailer. Her father must have blown out the candle after she had fallen asleep. Selah stood up and stretched her cramped neck.

"Well, at least you got a little sleep," Jackson said quietly from a chair in the corner.

"Yeah, guess so," Selah mumbled, still groggy and confused from the dream. "I'm going to get some fresh air on the porch for a minute," she told him, and put on her boots that had finally dried out from this morning's run. She stepped out into the damp, chilly air.

A warm breeze was still breathing its way through the woods. Selah walked down the steps and out into the sloppy slush. Her boots would dry out again in front of the wood stove, and she felt the need to move around. Sitting still for long periods of time had always been difficult for her. Even when visiting Miss Genevieve, she often got up and moved around, doing little chores or just pacing back and forth as they spoke.

The breeze picked up suddenly and Selah heard a rattling sound coming from a couple of white oak trees in the yard. She slushed over in their direction, watching the brittle brown leaves clatter like castanets as they stubbornly clung to the branches. *"Those old white oak trees,"* she could hear Miss Genevieve saying in her mind. *"Every other tree has just about dropped all their leaves, and they just keep hanging on."* Selah's heart skipped a beat. Now she knew what Miss Genevieve had been trying to say.

"Marcescent!" Selah said out loud as she recalled the conversation they had last fall about trees that held onto their leaves through the winter and into spring. "That explains the picture that looked like a tree. And the lobed figure was a leaf! But why would she bring that up? What's so important about leaves holding onto tree branches until the new leaves push them out?" She tried to remember everything her friend had told her about why some trees held onto their leaves longer than others. All she could remember was something about a theory that the old leaves fell off only after the new leaves pushed them out so that the dead ones could provide nutrients for young saplings and give them some protection from browsing animals. Selah stood under the rattling leaves, knowing she was missing something significant. "I don't get this, God. What is she trying to tell me?" she prayed.

The dream about Clucky flashed through her mind. *"Marcy!"* the protective hen had whispered as she showed Selah that she was not protecting a chick, but a miniature version of Selah, herself. And then Selah remembered how Genevieve had said "Marcy," and pointed to herself and then to Selah. And then she understood.

"No," she said, as the tears welled up in her eyes. *"NO! It's not time yet. It's not her time!"* She ripped a handful of the brown leaves off of a low-hanging branch. "I haven't learned all I need to learn from her! This must be *her* idea. It can't be Yours. You wouldn't think up anything that stupid!" Selah said loudly. "I understand why she wouldn't want to stay here, in the shape she's in, but You can heal her! You can make her want to stay! I need her. She's my friend. She's my teacher. She helps me understand things about You. Don't You think that's a good reason to keep her here a little longer? Especially if You healed her. *I mean, doesn't that sound reasonable to You?"*

"Selah, what's wrong?" Jackson said from the porch. "I can hear you from all the way inside. Why are you yelling?"

"I'll tell you why I'm yelling," Selah began, but Jackson turned his head suddenly toward the door of the trailer and motioned for her to be quiet.

"She's singing," he said, and went back inside.

Selah stood for an instant in the snow. Had God just answered her prayers that quickly? She ran as fast as she could through the sloppy yard.

When she entered the trailer, she was greeted by the sound of singing in another language. Jackson had lit the candle again, and Selah could see that Genevieve's eyes were closed.

"I think she's singing in her sleep," he mused.

Selah remembered again the verse from Romans chapter eight that told of how the Spirit helps us in our distress by praying for us when we don't know how to pray. She came close to the couch and watched. Genevieve was smiling broadly as she sang, and the droop in her face was less noticeable now. When Miss Genevieve's brain had failed to allow her to communicate, the Holy Spirit had made a way for her to communicate with the only One who really mattered. Selah didn't recognize the tune at first, since the words were in a different language. But then, abruptly, Miss Genevieve began to sing in perfect English, and her eyes opened and twinkled in the candlelight. *"Oh, I want to see him, look upon his face, there to sing forever of his saving grace; on the streets of Glory let me lift my voice; cares all past, home at last, ever to rejoice!"*[72]

Selah took the knobby hand in her own as Genevieve continued to sing. Jackson came close and held her other hand in his and began to sing in his soft baritone voice. Selah didn't think she would be able to

---

[72] From the hymn, "O I Want to See Him," by R.H. Cornelius

sing, but she managed to choke out a few words of the chorus before the song ended. Miss Genevieve fell silent, her face beaming. Selah couldn't tell if she was awake or asleep. She seemed to be looking at something neither one of them could see. Suddenly, she laughed and sighed. Her breathing sounded different. It was irregular, and each breath seemed more difficult than the last, but her eyes stayed fixed on whatever it was she was watching. Selah wondered what it was that she saw. Her face had relaxed from the broad grin she had been wearing, to be replaced by a look of immeasurable peace. Selah waited for her next breath, but it never came. "Miss Genevieve," she said, squeezing the work-worn hand. "Miss Genevieve!" she said again. There was no response. Jackson checked for a pulse.

"We can ask God to send her back!" Selah said desperately. "Let's pray now! Jesus said if we would ask anything in His name, He would do it!"[73]

"Selah, sometimes we ask amiss. Do you really think it's God's will to bring her back?" Jackson said softly.

"But it's not her time! I'm not ready for her to go yet!" Selah said between sobs.

"We may not be ready for her to go, but *she* was ready. Would you really want to call her back from where she is now? Selah, she's with *Jesus*. She is looking into the face of God. She is young and strong again, and perfectly whole. No more pain. No more stroke. No more broken hip. No more cares of this life. Now she can do forever what she prepared for her entire life—to be with the One she loves the most."

"That wasn't what she prepared for her entire life," Selah blurted out. "She wanted to be a missionary to the Old Country. God had called her to be a missionary. What does He think He's doing, taking her before she can fulfill her life's calling?" Selah demanded.

Jackson was silent for a moment as he took in this new revelation. "I don't know," he finally said, "but I do know that God is God, and we are not. Maybe His plan for her was different than she thought."

---

[73] See John 14:13

"No!" Selah said stubbornly. "She was closer to God than anyone here. She would know."

"If she would know God's will, then why was she singing that song? Why did she look so happy? Why didn't she fight it?" Jackson asked.

Selah looked at the still figure, tears blurring her vision. *"Marcescent,"* said Miss Genevieve's voice in her head. And she knew her father was right. It wasn't the journey she had originally planned, but Miss Genevieve had gone on a magnificent journey after all.

29

Bear Creek bucked and rolled with the spring run-off, rambling around the edges of its banks. Selah watched from a smooth gray boulder. Spring may have come to the valley, but it felt to her as if a different type of winter had just set in. A numbness seemed to spread to every part of her being. She went through the daily motions of getting up in the morning, doing her chores, and eating her meals, but nothing felt normal. Nothing *felt* at all.

It had been two days since Miss Genevieve's funeral. The community never wasted any time burying their dead, since they had no way to preserve the bodies. Funerals were conducted within one or two days of a death. It seemed to Selah as if she were watching the funeral from a great distance. When people had come up to her to offer their condolences, she had only been able to clasp their extended hand, or hug them stiffly, with dry eyes and a blank expression. She had wept inconsolably in her father's arms right after Genevieve's death, but all her emotions dried up after that. Like the creek that threatened to overrun its banks with the torrent of extra water it contained, Selah was overwhelmed with the onslaught of emotions rushing through her. Rather than face the threat of overrunning the banks of her emotional stability, she had shut off the flow completely. A few people tried to remind her she would see her friend someday and how wonderful it was that Genevieve was once again young and healthy, walking and talking with Jesus and her family that had gone on before her. It was at these times that Selah felt the only emotion that still occasionally trickled through the dam she had built inside. Her face would briefly darken, she would find the appropriate response somewhere, and then make an excuse to leave before the anger got any stronger. She knew that being angry with well-meaning people who couldn't possibly know how she felt wasn't fair, but it was easier than acknowledging the real target of her anger.

"She will deal with it when she's able," Jackson had told Asha.

"But it would be so much easier if she would stop being angry with God and allow Him to help her," Asha had responded.

"You know Selah. She'll come around. But it has to be in her own time," Jackson said. They gave Selah space, but they kept her busy, as well. This was the first time she had been able to slip away, just to think.

Being angry with God was something new to Selah. She had always trusted Him implicitly. Everything He had done in her life had always made sense. He had always provided for her needs. He had delighted her with the beauty of the natural world. She had always felt like she could talk to Him about anything. Even when He didn't bring Garrison back when she asked, she was willing to trust that someday, somehow, everything would work out and it would all make sense.

But how did the present circumstance make any sense at all? Miss Genevieve was gone, and with her, the dream of carrying the gospel to the Old Country. How could this be God's will? And yet He had allowed Genevieve to die with her unfulfilled calling and had left Selah feeling desperately alone. He was omnipotent, wasn't He? Why had He chosen to stand by in silence, His arms folded, like a bystander who won't help, but watches just out of arm's reach? How could she ever trust Him again?

The music of the creek had always been a source of peace for her, but today it seemed merely a tumbled mass of noise. "Some comfort you are," Selah said bitterly to the water, and the image of Miss Genevieve almost falling off the couch came to her mind. Why had she thought of that? "Comfort. Comforter," Selah said out loud. That was the word which had triggered the memory. That was the word which had excited her friend so much on her last evening on earth. Again the anger began to trickle out from under the emotional dam. "Where's the Comforter you promised to send?" Selah spat out the words. "You leave me here, with no friends except my parents, and the only promise from You that she seemed to want to keep bringing up was the promise that You would send Your Holy Spirit as a comforter. How's that supposed to work? How can I be comforted by a Spirit? And if I can, then where are you now?" Selah dug her fingers into her scalp and scowled at the water.

"Whoever drinks of the water that I shall give him will never thirst. But the water that I shall give him will become in him a fountain of water springing up into everlasting life."[74]

The scripture fluttered to the forefront of her memory like a leaf swirling to the surface of the turbulent waters below. "I have all these scriptures inside, all these wonderful things You inspired people to record in Your Word for us to remember, and now there's no one to share them with," Selah said, but her voice caught in her throat. That wasn't true. Who was she fooling, to think she could lie to God? She decided to get right to the point.

"I don't blame You for taking her. She's the kindest, wisest person I've ever known. But I miss her so much. I wasn't ready for her to go, and I am so angry with You that she's gone!" Selah nearly shouted the words, but they were swallowed in the song of the tumbling creek. She pulled her legs to her chest and rested her chin on her knees. To her surprise, she began to cry. The tears came slowly at first, but each seemed to do its work of undermining the base of the dam. Finally, she was sobbing. "Why did You do this? You could have healed her. You could have kept her from having a stroke in the first place! Why does it have to be this way?" Selah's body jerked as she drew in each breath. She sat there for a long time, the sound of her weeping lost in the voice of the waters. Finally, her crying subsided, and she was able to breath normally again. She placed a hand on the boulder's smooth surface. "You're the only thing that feels real anymore," she said to the rock. "Is

---

[74] John 4:13-14 KJV

anything real beyond what I can see? If God is real, why didn't He do anything to stop this from happening?"

It was a relief to release some of her pent-up emotion. She looked around at the lengthening shadows and shuddered involuntarily. The sun was going down, and an evening chill had settled over the low-lands. She stood up and stretched. There was nothing else to do but head for home.

The witch-hazel was in bloom, she noticed as she used a flimsy branch of the fragrant tree to pull herself up the bank. She hadn't seen it on the way down, but it had to have been all around her when she arrived, with its heady fragrance that made her sneeze. The world was coming into focus again, and with it, the sharpness of loss. It was almost like a physical pain—losing somebody—she realized, as the memory of her friend stabbed through her middle. Losing Garrison had been hard, but there was always the hope she might see him again. It might be a long, long time before she saw Miss Genevieve, if she *ever* saw her again. Sadness gripped her chest like a clawed hand. She swallowed the bitterness that welled up within her like bile, and her pace quickened as she reached the road. Maybe she could outrun grief, like a runner outdistances his competitors. She allowed the daydream to play out in her mind, fueling the power to pump her legs as she raced down the road. Grief and anger were momentarily forgotten as she pushed herself to go faster. With each intake of breath, her lungs felt stretched to the bursting point, and the pain momentarily overtook her sadness. In this moment, she could forget everything except the effort it took to breathe.

Up ahead, Selah could see the path leading to Genevieve's house. As she came to the junction of the path, she hesitated. She hadn't been there since the day Genevieve died. *"There's nothing there for me anymore,"* she thought to herself. Then what was that feeling that seemed to be tug-ging her toward the old path? Suddenly it came to her. What about all the sketches? What about the sermons? Someone had to preserve Genevieve's life's work. Surely they wouldn't just be recycled in the used paper bin. Her heart beat even faster as she turned down the lane. She would go in and get them, making sure they would be there for future generations. The idea that all of the drawings, all of the dreams, could just be tossed and shredded and mixed into a pulpy mass of recycled paper was unthinkable.

A startled squirrel shot up one of the white oak trees as she burst into the yard. She bound up the porch steps and opened the door, gasping for breath after her attempt to outrun Grief.

"Wha—" she panted as she looked around the room. Someone had been here. The big tables where Miss Genevieve had placed the sketches had been put away. Selah went into the kitchen. The kitchen table was there, but there was nothing on it except a salt and pepper shaker. One of the cabinets was opened, and someone had started filling a box with canned goods. Anger suddenly caught up with Selah again as she looked in the box and noticed a jar of peach preserves Asha had made last summer. Her eyes darted to the book shelves in the living room. Most of the Bibles were still there, but a few of them, including one of Miss Genevieve's favorites, were missing. Who had been here? Who had done this? She went through the rest of the house to see if anything else was missing. One thing was for certain. All traces of the sketches and the sermons were gone. A horrible thought crossed her mind. What if they had already been destroyed?

She rushed back out of the trailer and jumped the length of the steps. They might still be in the recycling bin. It took a long time for that to fill up, after all. Her feet pounded up the lane and down the road toward the town center. But when she reached the community hall, she found the paper bin was empty except for a few scraps. Selah leaned against the clapboard siding of the town hall, stopping to spit in the mud as her sides heaved with every breath. Whose turn was it to recycle the paper? There was a list of community duties on the inside of the pantry at her house. Asha would know whose turn it was. She turned toward home.

"Mom!" she called as she burst through the door of the kitchen. "Someone's been messing around with Genevieve's stuff!"

Asha and Jackson looked up from where they were sitting at the table. Across from them was Payton Hamby.

"Selah, where have you been?" Asha asked. "You've been gone nearly three hours."

"Payton's been trying to track you down," Jackson said.

Selah regarded Payton without a word.

He shifted his weight uncomfortably in the chair and cleared his throat. "Yes, indeed," he said in an affable tone. "And let me put your mind at ease. I am the one who has been over at Miss Genevieve's place."

Grief was left behind in the dust as Anger came down the backstretch and collided abruptly into Selah. She found herself glaring at Payton, wondering if he had read the sermons and studied the sketches. Could he have guessed her idea to take the gospel outside the valley? Would he have destroyed her work to squelch her ideas and keep them from influencing any other impressionable minds?

"I had her permission," Payton was saying in what was meant to be a reassuring voice.

"What have you done with them?" Selah blurted out. Payton looked at her blankly and opened his mouth as he fumbled for a response. She continued before he could find one. "The drawings and the sermons— what have you done with them?"

"Selah, mind your manners," Jackson said gruffly.

"No, it's alright," Payton said, with some difficulty. "Sometimes when someone is grieving, they don't know how to react."

"I know enough to know when someone has been messing around with something they shouldn't have been. You have no right to do this. You won't get away with it. I'll make sure you don't, even if God, Himself, doesn't care anymore," Selah said coldly.

Asha gasped. Jackson stood up from the table. "Selah, what's gotten into you?" he asked as calmly as possible, but there was an edge to his voice.

"I'm done with always doing everything everyone expects me to do. From now on, I'll do what is right, no matter who it upsets. I won't let you destroy her life's work. So if you think you can get rid of it by recycling a bunch of paper, you don't understand anything about her at all. Her work wasn't in paper, it was in people. And you can't destroy that, unless you're willing to kill me and all the other people she taught in this town." Selah glowered at him. No one said anything for a moment. Asha's blue eyes were wide in shock.

"Go to your room. I will deal with you later," Jackson said. He turned to Payton. "Apparently, this is not a good time. This really isn't like her, you know."

"I'm not going anywhere until I know what happened to her things. Even if you can't kill her ideas, I still want to know what you did to her work. *You're* the real danger to the community, here. I can't believe she ever got me to forgive you in the first place. It was a waste of time, because now, I won't ever forgive you for what you've done!" Selah clenched her fists and planted her feet on the kitchen floor as Jackson started toward her.

Payton held up his hand and stood up to block Jackson's path. "It's okay," he said.

"It is *not* okay," Jackson interrupted him. "Even if she's grieving, she can't be allowed to lash out at people like this. I would be in error to just let her run wild with her mouth and her emotions."

"Jackson, as your pastor, I'm asking you to err on the side of mercy," Payton began. He looked at Selah with an expression she couldn't interpret. "I do owe her an explanation for my behavior. And an apology."

Selah stood her ground. This was an unexpected development.

"An apology for what?" Asha sputtered.

"I owe her an apology for the way I treated her after Garrison left. I was afraid, and I let fear take over. Ever since I became the senior elder, I have felt such a burden and a responsibility for the physical and spiritual well-being of this community. I always did everything I could to look after everyone as best I could. When Garrison left, it blindsided me. I suddenly realized I was never really in control of anything. All my efforts had been for nothing, and I was at the mercy of a seventeen year-old boy. In my hastiness to regain a sense of control, I stepped on a lot of toes—mainly yours, Selah, and also Miss Genevieve's." He looked down at his scuffed boots. "But the Holy Spirit started working on me. I knew I had to go apologize to her. And she forgave me, of course. That's just how she was. She knew the importance of forgiveness. She not only practiced what she preached, but she practiced what I preached—which was more than I had been doing, up to that point." He shook his head and smiled. "I would go visit her every other day or so, and do you know, she gradually got me to see that I had yet to forgive Garrison for leaving like he did? One day, she and I had a 'come to Jesus' meeting, and I forgave Garrison right there in her living room."

Selah studied a knot in the hardwood floor. She still remembered the feeling of Miss Genevieve's hands on her shoulder as she had prayed for her to be able to forgive all the people who had done things to hurt her. She never dreamed that Payton had been having a similar experience when she wasn't there.

Payton looked cautiously at Selah. "After a while, I realized that my sense of control was a sham. It was a prideful thing for me to think I had any real control. That's God's job. He knew Garrison was going to leave from the day Garrison was born. He knows the end from the beginning, and He has a reason for letting things happen. It was wrong for me to take out my fear and frustration on you. I know you may not want to hear this right now, but I'm sorry for how I treated you. I've been trying to think of the right way to say it, but I can't think of anything to say, except I'm sorry."

Selah swallowed hard and tried to look Payton in the eyes, but she couldn't summon the strength. If he and Miss Genevieve had made amends and he had forgiven Garrison and stopped believing he was in control of things, why had he destroyed the sermons?

Payton was talking again, and Selah was tempted to walk out the door, even though she had declared she wasn't going anywhere until she found out what he had done with Genevieve's work. She was just about to pivot on her heel and head for the barn when his words finally registered in her brain.

"I know this is rather soon after her passing," he was saying, "but she made me promise I wouldn't delay too long in this. You see, Miss Genevieve asked me if I would be the executor of her will several months ago. It's funny—she wasn't very particular about who got the trailer and furniture, but she was very insistent that you should receive these items."

Payton retrieved a large satchel from underneath the table and held it out toward Selah like a peace offering. She looked from Payton's face to the satchel and begrudgingly took it from him.

"Go ahead and look," he coaxed her. "They're really quite good. I told her so when she showed them to me."

Selah opened the flap of the bag. One of the sketches peeked out at her from within a leather- bound folder. Nestled next to the folder was a familiar, three-ring binder notebook. Selah pulled it out and recognized it as the one in which Genevieve kept all the sermons. There were a few more items within the bag, but she was too shocked to look any further. Shame burned her face like a brand. Selah put the binder back in the satchel and clutched it to her, not knowing what to say.

"It must have been very important to her that you should have them," Payton remarked.

"I thought you had recycled them," Selah said haltingly. There didn't seem to be any way to make a recovery from the way she had acted. "Well," she nodded her head, trying to swallow the stubborn lump in her throat. "Well." Not knowing what to say, she turned to take the satchel to her room, and then stopped. "So she knew?" she asked Payton.

"Knew what?"

"She knew she was going to die?" Selah asked.

Payton thought a moment. "She did tell me the Holy Spirit had impressed upon her to get her affairs in order. So, I guess she must have known something was going to happen."

Selah was surprised Miss Genevieve would have told Payton and said nothing to her. But then again, Payton was the current pastor of the community. Genevieve believed that as much as a person could, they should do everything in order, under the blessing of spiritual leadership. Apparently that's why she had asked Payton to be executor of her will, instead of someone like Jackson. Selah couldn't understand how she could feel that way about leadership after how they had treated her. But then again, Genevieve had more practice at forgiving than she did.

"Well, I'd better get home. Addy will think I fell in a hole," Payton said with an attempt at lightheartedness. He turned and started to go out the door, and suddenly stopped to look back at Selah again. "One more thing, Selah. You said you were done doing what everyone expects you to do. You said from now on, you're going to do what's right, no matter who it upsets."

Selah stared at the floor again. Was she going to get a lecture now? She knew she deserved one, but she already felt bowed down by the weight of her own caustic words.

"I want to hold you to that. I hope it is a promise you keep," he said. Selah's head jerked up to meet his gaze. "Miss Genevieve would have liked that, too," he said, and opened the door to leave. Jackson followed him outside and walked him to the front gate, talking softly as they went.

As Selah watched him go, something Miss Genevieve said on more than one occasion came to mind. "Pray for the leadership of the church —the pastor, the teachers, the elders. They are under constant attack from the enemy in one form or another. Pray they will be led by the Holy Spirit. A church is a body of believers, and a pastor is the head that directs that body. Pray for unity in the body and God's will in the way the pastor leads his flock."

Selah looked up to see Asha watching her. She put her head down and took the bag to her room, spreading its contents out on the bed. Aside from the sketches and the sermons, there was the Amplified Bible, a Bible concordance, and a book with a homemade binding that she had never seen before. She opened the book and discovered it was a diary, complete with sketches of wildflowers, deer, and the occasional portrait.

Selah closed the book as Asha suddenly appeared at the door. "We're about to have supper, if you're interested," she said.

Selah shook her head. "Thanks, but I don't really feel like eating," she replied. Asha lingered for a moment as if trying to think of something to say, and finally left. Selah closed the door to her room and opened the diary again. The date on the first page was March 5 of 2049. Genevieve would have been in her late twenties. Selah thumbed through the pages, glancing at the sketches. One in particular caught her eye. It filled up the whole page. Down the middle was a dark canyon with sheer, steep walls. On one side was what appeared to be a company of angels and a handsome man of Hispanic descent. On the other side was a solitary woman, her hand outstretched to the figures on the other side. The word WHY was written in large, angry letters at the bottom of the ravine. Selah read the entry. "I still can't understand why You took him away from me. We never had any children. Mom and Dad are gone. Now I have no one except You. And how can I trust You after You've done this thing? How could You have allowed it to happen?" The entry went on, with Genevieve pouring her heart out, holding nothing back from the God she had trusted all her life. The Hispanic man was Carlos, of course—Miss Genevieve's husband. Selah didn't remember her friend ever telling her she had been mad at God for her husband's death. Maybe she hadn't told anyone except God, Himself.

After the angry entry, several months passed before anything else was written. The contrast between the two entries could not have been more extreme. "Oh, Lord, there is no one like You!" it began. "You are more beautiful than the first snowfall of the year, more lovely than birdsong, more precious than sunlight to me. You have turned my mourning into dancing, given me beauty for ashes and the oil of joy for mourning. I will praise You all of my days." What could have caused such a difference? Selah read on. "I can't believe I lived this long without being filled with Your Spirit! But now that I've experienced it, I'm ready for whatever You want to teach me. And now I know I am never really alone."

So Miss Genevieve had received the baptism of the Holy Spirit not long after Carlos' death. She remembered how her friend had pointed at her with her knobby finger after Selah had read the passage about people being filled with the Spirit. *"You,"* she had said simply, but firmly. The message was clear. Miss Genevieve wanted her to receive the baptism of the Holy Ghost, as well.

Selah sat with the book on her lap and looked out the window at the dwindling light. *"God, I'm still mad at You,"* she prayed silently. *"And I still don't trust You. But Genevieve did. She trusted You, even after You allowed Carlos to die. I don't know how she was able to do that."* Selah paused as the lump came into her throat again. Once again, she was crying as she had on the boulder by the creek. *"I know I said You didn't seem real anymore. But I don't see how I can live without You. I don't agree with everything You do, but I'm not You. You can see the end from the beginning. Maybe there really is a good reason for all of this, and I'd really like to know what it is."* She buried her head in the quilt on her bed in an effort to muffle her sobs.

In the kitchen, Jackson and Asha looked at each other over their plates, listening to the sound of Selah crying. Jackson sighed and pushed his chair back from the table. "Are you sure it's a good idea to talk to her right now?" Asha asked.

"I'm not necessarily going to do any talking," Jackson said. He went to Selah's room and knocked softly on the door.

Selah stopped crying as best as she could. *"What?"* she said in a raggedy voice.

Jackson opened the door and sat down on the bed beside her. Selah didn't look up. She had said so many horrible things. She couldn't bear to look him in the eyes. Jackson placed a hand on her shoulder and just sat there as she sniffled. She wished she could stop. It was strange how she could feel so grown up one minute and so immature the next. She kept expecting Jackson to say something, but he just sat there with his hand on her shoulder. There was something comforting about it, even though it didn't change anything. Miss Genevieve was still dead. Garrison was still gone. She had just made a complete idiot of herself. But for some reason, she felt better. She opened one eye and glanced over a rumple of the quilt at her father. His eyes were closed, and she could tell he was praying.

"Dad?"

Jackson opened his eyes and looked at her. Her hair was plastered to her cheeks, her face blotchy and red from crying.

"I didn't mean all those things I said."

"I know."

"But I told God I could never trust Him again."

"Is that true?"

"Well, I don't see how all things are working together for good to those who love God."

"Romans 8:28, huh?" Jackson said. "Did you know that some of the original manuscripts of the scripture read as 'God works all things together for good, or God works in all things for the good'?" Jackson seemed to study the permanent dirt stains under his fingernails as he tried to find the right words. "Sometimes when things happen and we can't understand why, I think it has to do with us living in a fallen world. Bad things happen here because sin entered into the world. Sin entered the world because God created man with a free will. He didn't want an automaton that would mechanically do His bidding. He wanted us to freely love Him and walk in fellowship with Him. Creating a being who had a mind of its own meant taking the chance that we would mess up. And, of course, we did. Which is why He came to save us. No one else could save us from our sins. Like it says in Isaiah 59, 'He saw that there was no man, and wondered that there was no intercessor; therefore His own arm brought salvation for Him; and His own righteousness, it sustained Him. For He put on righteousness as a breastplate, and a helmet of salvation on His head.'[75] God wanted us

---

[75] Isaiah 59:16-17a NKJV

to know that He knew, personally, what it was like to be down here in this mess. And He wanted us to know He wasn't just going to leave us down here by ourselves to wallow in it. God allows horrible things to happen because He is not willing to take away our freedom. But He can take those bad things that happen to us and weave them together to somehow cause them to work together for the good of His kingdom."

"For the good of His *kingdom*? Not for *our* good?" Selah asked.

"That's just how I interpret it. The overall plan of salvation to every tribe and nation is more important than whether or not we go through trials down here on earth. Just think about Job. If anyone had cause to complain, he did. Nothing that happened to him seems fair to me. But what did he say? *'Though he slay me, yet will I trust in him.'*[76] In the end, he got his health back, and he was blessed with more children and more wealth."

"But what about his children who were killed? God could have brought them back from the dead, and He didn't."

"No, He didn't. But do you think after spending several thousand years with them in Heaven, that it matters to any of them anymore? The few years we have in this life are just a drop in the bucket compared to eternity."

Selah sat up on the bed and pulled her hair back away from her face. "I still don't understand anything about this."

"Who does? Who *does* understand everything about this life? We don't *have* to understand everything. We just have to trust God. That's one of the basic foundations of faith—believing in things you don't understand. The important thing to remember is that God *does* understand and knows about everything that happens to us. It may seem like He is standing idly by while we suffer through it, but He is always there, working things together for good. The human race supplies Him with the threads and He sews them together—kind of like your Grandma Edna used to do with her needlework. When I was a boy and I would

---

[76] Job 13:15a KJV

watch her work on that stuff, I would wonder what she was going to end up with, because I was looking at it from the underside. When I would crawl up in her lap, I could see it from her point of view. It made sense then, like the scripture on your pillowcase." Selah looked at the pink and green lettering on the pillowcase her grandma had given her. It was Isaiah 26:3—"Thou wilt keep him in perfect peace, whose mind is stayed on thee: because he trusteth in thee."[77] She had been fascinated by the underside of it when she was younger, because it had looked like a sprawled mess of threads. The scripture was backwards and unrecognizable from the backside.

Jackson continued. "We can only see the underside of the tapestry God is creating, with the threads that stick out this way and that and the garbled mess of colors we hand Him. But in the end, when we sit on the other side of the loom, we'll be able to look down and see what He did with what we gave Him. There will be ugly things that happened that led to beautiful things. There will be threads of prayer that we never knew were used to create something truly wonderful. In the meantime, the best thing we can remember is that He is our Father, and He loves us. If we can remember that, and remember to crawl up in His lap on a regular basis, we'll certainly have a better view of things." He stroked Selah's hair and left quietly, closing the door back behind him. As he looked up, he almost ran into Asha, who had been listening at the door. She followed him into the kitchen.

"For someone who wasn't going to say anything, you certainly said something," she whispered. "How did you come up with all that?"

"I had a lot of help from the Holy Spirit," Jackson said simply.

Selah listened to the sounds of dinnertime as she sat on her bed. For the longest time, the world had seemed like the surface of a pond that was blown and rippled by the wind. The reflection of the clouds and trees in the pond was destroyed by the disturbance of the waters. But now the wind had died down, the surface was calm, and the world was coming into focus again.

---

77 Isaiah 26:3 KJV

"*I don't understand why things happened like they did, but even if You never tell me, I am deciding right now to trust You,*" Selah prayed. As she did, something heavy seemed to lift off of her. She looked down at the diary. "*You have given me the garment of praise for the spirit of heaviness,*" the words read. She put the diary back in the satchel and dressed for bed. She had a big day tomorrow, and she was going to need her rest.

30

SELAH awoke long before dawn. Asha wasn't even up yet, so Selah knew it had to be incredibly early. She had awakened several times in the night, and always her mind was on what she had decided to do before she went to bed. It had steeped in her a sense of determination for the tasks of the upcoming day.

Selah knew she had to go visit Payton Hamby. It wasn't a pleasant thought, but she needed to do it. She had verbally forgiven him with Miss Genevieve's direction and the help of the Holy Spirit, but now, *she* was the offender. She was the one who needed to apologize and ask forgiveness. A hundred excuses had already popped into her head as to why she should put it off or forget about doing it altogether, but she couldn't ignore the conviction of the Holy Spirit. She felt as if someone had placed their hand on her shoulder for reassurance, and had placed the other one in the small of her back to propel her forward. It wouldn't be easy, but it needed to be done.

She lit the candle by her bed and got out the Amplified Bible Miss Genevieve had given her. She had been neglecting her Bible reading for the past few days, and was surprised at the difference it had made. Of all the times to distance herself from God, she had chosen the time when she needed Him most!

"People don't need an excuse to stop coming to church or setting aside time to read the Bible and pray," she could hear Miss Genevieve say. "Some people who have been faithful all their lives but haven't had many struggles will stop seeking the Lord when they finally have a big problem. They get mad because they think He owes them a life of ease since they serve Him. I wonder what those people who were martyred for Christ would think of that view? And some people come to God when they are having trouble, but as soon as things start looking better, they drift away because they think they are doing fine again on their own. And some people just drift." At this point, Miss Genevieve would move her hands through the air to mimic a boat on a river. "You know what happens if you are paddling a canoe up the creek, and you stop paddling? You fall back. You go downstream. We can't just do nothing in our relationship with God, Selah. We have to spend time with Him everyday, or we'll lose momentum."

Selah was surprised how true that was. She had lost so much ground the last few days that she hadn't recognized until now that some of what she had been experiencing wasn't mere grief at the loss of her friend. It was the enemy feeding her lie after lie, which she had eagerly gobbled up in her weakened emotional state. What she needed was truth, not lies; so she opened up the Word of God and began to read.

She had decided to look at John 14:16-18, the verses Miss Genevieve had indicated she wanted her to memorize.

> "And I will ask the Father, and He will give you another Helper (Comforter, Advocate, Intercessor—Counselor, Strengthener, Standby), to be with you forever—The Spirit of Truth, whom the world cannot receive [and take to its heart], because it does not see Him or know Him, *but* you know Him because He (the Holy Spirit) remains with you *continually* and will be in you. I will not leave you orphans [comfortless, bereaved, and helpless]; I will come [back] to you."[78]

Selah marveled at how the Amplified Bible expanded on the King James Version's rendering of the Holy Spirit as a "Comforter." It had such a wider, richer meaning than "someone who gives comfort." As her

---

[78] John 14:16-18 AMP

Counselor, He could give her good advice. As her Helper and Strengthener, He could enable her to do things she could not do on her own. As an Advocate, the Holy Spirit would plead her cause before the throne of God. As an Intercessor, He would not only work on her behalf, but would work *through* her during prayer on the behalf of others. As her Standby, He could be relied upon in any situation, no matter how desperate. Selah read further into the chapter, and then turned to the book of Acts, where she once again saw the effects of people receiving the baptism of the Holy Spirit.

Daylight was near, and she could hear the rattling of breakfast pans in the kitchen. She put the Bible away and prayed for wisdom and the words to say when she went to visit Payton. She took time to thank God for giving her a new outlook on life. "Don't forget to thank Him, Selah," she could hear Miss Genevieve say. "We are always *asking, asking, asking.* How long would our prayers be if we took one day and decided we would only *thank* Him and not ask for anything?"

After thanking the Lord, Selah took time just to be still, to wait, and to listen. She thought about how He had guided her, protected her, and provided for her throughout all of her life. "I need more of You, not less of You, Lord," she said. "Especially now."

The smell of bacon wafting under her door proved to be the ultimate distraction from prayer time. She got up from where she had been kneeling and went to the kitchen. "Morning," she said to her mother, who was ladling pancake batter onto a griddle.

"Morning. Did you sleep ok?" Asha asked as she turned over one of the pancakes.

"Not especially, but I'll live," Selah replied. "I decided last night that I'm going to apologize to Mr. Hamby, and it didn't make for a very restful sleep."

Asha's eyebrows raised in surprise. "I would imagine not, but that's a very mature decision."

Selah leaned against the counter and watched the cakes bubble up before being flipped. "Mom, have you ever been filled with the Holy Spirit?" she asked suddenly.

Asha thought a while before answering. "Well, I know that when we ask Jesus to forgive us and become Lord of our lives, He puts His Spirit in us, but as far as the experience of being baptized in the Holy Spirit... no, I guess not. I've never spoken in tongues or anything like that."

"Why not?"

"I don't know. It just wasn't emphasized as something that was relevant for today. So I figured it was just something that happened here and there in the history of the Church. No one ever told me it was important, like prayer, reading the Word, and following the Lord in water baptism," Asha said.

"But Miss Genevieve spoke in tongues. And one of the last things she tried to tell us was how important it is to receive the Holy Spirit," Selah reasoned.

"I know," Asha said as she slid another pancake onto a serving plate. "I've been thinking a lot about that these past few days. She seemed determined to get her point across—using that comforter on her couch to try to get us to read about the Comforter that Jesus sent to His disciples after He left for Heaven."

"But the way I understand it, He didn't just send Him to His disciples. Peter told that crowd on the Day of Pentecost that the Holy Spirit is for all who have been called by God. Doesn't that cover everyone?"

"That's what it sounds like the Bible is saying," Asha said. "But we never spend much time studying those scriptures."

Jackson came into the kitchen and they all sat down to breakfast.

"I overheard you say you were going to apologize to Brother Hamby," Jackson said between mouthfuls.

"Yeah. I'm going over as soon as I take care of Maggie and the chickens. Or do you think it's too early?"

Jackson shook his head. "Payton is usually outside working on something by the crack of dawn." He mopped up a pool of molasses with his pancake. "I also heard you asking about the Holy Spirit."

"So what do you think about it?" Selah asked.

"My Grandpa Connor prayed in a different language. I didn't understand it, so I asked him one time what he was saying. 'I don't know, Jackie,' he told me. 'What do you mean, you don't know?' I asked him. He told me he didn't know because the Holy Spirit was helping him pray and he was just saying the words that came out. 'How does God know what you're saying if *you* don't even know what you're saying?' I asked him. 'God knows because He is the one who is helping me to pray.' Well, that was just too much for my nine-year-old mind to process. 'You mean God is asking *Himself* what to do?' I asked him. Grandpa Connor told me he knew it sounded silly, but the best way he could explain it was that God was helping him to pray in God's perfect will. Since he didn't know God's will for the particular thing he was praying about and he didn't want to just guess at it, he asked for the Holy Spirit's help. When the Holy Spirit prayed through him in a different language, he wasn't tempted to ask for things the way *he* thought they should be done. He was praying the way *God* wanted things to be done."

"I can understand why you were confused," Selah commented.

"Yes, but I loved my grandpa so much, I didn't let that oddity bother me. He was a man of integrity. He always did what he said he would do. If he had promised to take me fishing, he would do it, even when he was tired. That meant a lot to a nine-year-old boy."

"It meant a lot to a nine-year-old girl, too." Selah smiled at her dad, who had taken her on many a fishing trip until she was old enough to go on her own.

After the breakfast dishes were washed and the animals were fed, Selah headed up the road to the Hamby's place. Each step seemed to bring with it a heightened feeling of anxiety. Her hands were sweaty and her feet felt like they were made of lead. She stopped in the middle of the road and tried to get a grip on her emotions. She knew this was what God wanted her to do, but she didn't feel like doing it. Part of her was still afraid of Payton, and the other part was proud and didn't want to admit to doing wrong. She needed something to keep her feet moving. "For God is working in you, giving you the desire to obey him and the power to do what pleases him,"[79] she quoted. "God, if Philippians 2:13 is true, and You really want me to do this, then give me the desire to do it and the power to finish the job," she said.

"Sometimes when doing the right thing isn't easy, you have to take it one step at a time," Miss Genevieve used to say. "Just keep putting one foot in front of the other, and suddenly you realize you're already there at your goal."

Selah looked down at her boots, and instead of imagining how uncomfortable she would be when she got to the Hamby place, she began to just concentrate on the moment—the cracked leather of her boots, the way the morning sun made the grass blades cast shadows on the edges of the road, the crunching sound her footsteps made in the gravel. There was no point in worrying about what would happen when she got there. She had planned what she would say and had asked God for help. To worry would mean she wasn't trusting God to help her. "I told You I would trust You, Lord," Selah said. "And I intend to keep my word."

One step led to another step and another, until finally Selah found herself at the edge of the walkway to the Hamby's front porch. A few ginger-colored chickens eyed her suspiciously as she debated on whether to knock at the door or check for Payton in the field behind the house. Suddenly the front door opened and Addy came outside to shake out a rug. "Well, hello, Selah!" she said, with a look of surprise.

"Hello," Selah said shyly. "How are you this morning?"

"I'm doin' just fine. Is everything alright?" Addy didn't act as if she were talking to someone who had yelled at her husband the night before. Maybe she didn't know about it.

"I was actually wondering if I could talk to Brother Payton," Selah said.

"He's out checking on his old speckled cow. He thinks maybe she slunked her calf," Addy replied. "You're welcome to come inside and wait."

---

[79] Philippians 2:13 NLT

"Do you think it'd be ok if I went out in the field to find him, or are his cows pretty spooky?" Selah asked. Nothing was more annoying than having someone walk up and spook your cattle when you were trying to count them or check them to see how close they were to calving, but she would rather talk to Payton alone.

"I think it'd be alright, and he'd be glad to see you," Addy said warmly. "He told me he stopped by your place last night."

So Addy probably knew about the heated conversation, after all. Selah had never given Addy much thought before now. Her personality had always seemed about as exciting as dry toast. But after what happened last night, she was treating Selah the same as she always had. Thinking back on Addy's behavior in the past, she realized that she had always been decent to people and was quick to try to help in any situation. Selah decided those were good traits for an elder's wife.

"Thanks," Selah said, and headed around the back of the house.

There was a smaller fenced lot where Payton kept one or two cows when they were about to calve. She could see him standing by a patch of cedar trees at the lower end of the lot. The cows were closer to the house, where he had put out some hay for them. Payton seemed to be studying something on the ground. Selah let herself through the gate and made her way to the tree patch. Payton looked up and watched her for a moment, and then waved as he recognized her. "Good morning, Selah," he said when she was close enough to hear him.

"Morning."

"Looks like my old cow lost her calf," he said, looking down at the lifeless form crumpled in the mud. "Wasn't due for another month."

Selah looked at the stillborn calf. "That's too bad," she said. "All that effort she put into getting him that big, and now this." Suddenly, the image of Clucky and the chick came to mind. At least Clucky had something to show for all her effort, Selah thought. She found herself remembering the dream where Clucky had spoken in Miss Genevieve's voice. *"Marcescent!"* she had whispered. Dry, brittle oak leaves rattled over the pages of Selah's memory. The images fired through her mind in rapid succession. They all pointed to the same theme.

"I know now that you weren't trying to destroy her life's work. And I have to believe that her work wasn't in vain," Selah said. "Miss Genevieve, I mean," she added quickly, as Payton looked from her to the dead calf.

"Oh," he said, his brow wrinkled in a combination of confusion and amusement.

"I am so sorry about the things I said. I was wrong to say them. And I guess I was wrong about you." Selah met his gaze briefly, and then looked at her boots again.

"Well, it's alright, Selah. I know how close you were to her. If it's one thing I've learned being a senior elder here, I've learned that hurting people hurt people. You were hurting and you lashed out. It's a common reaction," he said gently.

"That doesn't make it right," she replied.

"Maybe not. But I forgive you, and there's nothing you can do about it."

Selah looked up at him quickly, to find him grinning at her. She grinned tentatively back at him. "I know I said I couldn't believe Miss Genevieve got me to forgive you for—for what you apologized for yesterday," she said. "I didn't really mean all those things I said. And I never thought about the stress you must be under. Miss Genevieve told me about how hard it can be to be in spiritual leadership—how you are always under enemy attack, and how we need to pray for our teachers and pastors."

"We were blessed to have a prayer warrior and a teacher like our Sister Genevieve. And just by listening to you, I can assure you, her work wasn't in vain," Payton said with genuine warmth.

He turned to look back at the calf. "I guess I better get this thing on the burn pile," he said rather sadly.

"I can help," Selah offered.

Payton started to object, but as he looked at Selah, he changed his mind. "Ok. You take one leg and I'll take the other."

Selah knew Payton could have dragged the calf fairly easily by himself. The load was ridiculously light for two people, but as they carried it together, a burden of a different kind grew lighter as well. Months of bitterness melted away.

"Brother Payton, have you ever received the baptism of the Holy Spirit?" Selah asked suddenly.

Payton looked down at her and chuckled. "That's just what Miss Genevieve asked me about a week ago. I had to tell her no. But it got me to thinking. And I've been praying about it ever since."

Selah looked at him intently. "I'll pray with you," she declared.

The two walked on in silence toward Payton's burn pit. The feeling of reassurance she had felt that morning had changed to a feeling of approval that rested warmly on her back like the hand of a father resting lightly on his child. *"I am watching over my word, to perform it,"*[80] a voice echoed in her spirit. Selah looked again at Payton. She wouldn't just *say* she would pray, she would make *certain* she did. She felt the fulfillment of Miss Genevieve's work somehow depended on it.

---

[80]See Jeremiah 1:12 RSV

31

SELAH massaged her forehead and squinted into the sunshine. It was the second day of her fast, and she had a slight headache. At times like this, when she wanted to eat something, she had to remind herself why she was doing it. "Lord, I want to know more about Your Holy Spirit. I want to experience Him for myself. I want more of You," she said.

The words fell flat. As she had so often experienced when she fasted, there was a lack of emotion connected to her prayers that disturbed her. She had to remind herself that she wasn't seeking an emotional experience, she was seeking discernment of God's will, a closer connection to Him, and a spiritual renewal for her community. She recalled all the stories Miss Genevieve had told her about the spiritual awakenings and revivals that had taken place around the world. Fasting and prayer had preceded each of these events. She wondered if Payton was fasting, as well, and if it would be more effective if several others were involved. But how could she encourage others to do it? Somehow it didn't seem appropriate for her to come up to the other members of the community and say, "Excuse me, but I'm concerned because our community is dry and spiritually dead. Why don't you stop eating and spend more time in prayer about this with me?" She felt it would be disrespectful to the older ones, and was certain those her age would just laugh at her.

She picked up the hoe she had leaned against the garden fence and continued breaking up the hard clods of dirt, preparing a seedbed for the lettuce and spinach her mother was going to plant. Genevieve had always tried to do things the right way, with the approval of leadership.

What was it she had said when Selah had suggested the community might listen if someone just came out and told them they needed to work on their spiritual walk? "I doubt it. But if we pray for them to be more sensitive to the Holy Spirit, they might listen to *Him.*" Selah hoed and chopped at the clods as she worked. A scripture was on the edge of her memory. It danced in the rhythm of the hoe blade. She strained to remember. It was something about the ground.

"Sow for yourselves righteousness; reap in mercy; break up your fallow ground, for it is time to seek the Lord, till He comes and rains righteousness on you!"[81] Selah nearly shouted the words as she remembered the verse. It was Hosea 10:12. This fasting, this praying, it was like hoeing. She was preparing the seedbed not only of her own heart, but the hearts of the people in the valley. She could pray for Payton to say the right things in the messages he preached, and that his messages would come alive to the listeners. She would pray for people to be sensitive to the Holy Spirit and hungry for the things of God. And she would pray for people to be filled with the Holy Spirit. The hoe rose and fell with her enthusiasm. Soon the soil was ready. "Lord," she prayed, "make the hearts of your people like this soft soil. Break up the hard clods of disinterest and make the soil of our hearts ready to receive whatever you want to give us. Make our hearts thirsty for rivers of living water!"

John 7:38 was the scripture she had remembered when she was sitting on the rock on the banks of Bear Creek, angry with God. The water was what had brought it to her mind then, just like the soil had reminded her of the scripture in Hosea. "You filled Your Word with examples rooted in the real world, in our everyday surroundings! You wanted us to have every possible chance at a connection with You, so You told us what You wanted us to know in ways we could understand," she mused. Selah liked to keep a channel of communication open between her and God. She found that even when she went through her daily routine, if she could just remember that the Lord was with her and she

---

[81] Hosea 10:12 NKJV

could talk to Him at any moment, it helped her to have a different perspective. Sometimes it was still difficult to feel His presence, but she didn't need to feel it to know He was there. She had the Word of God in her heart to remind her that He had said, *"I will never leave you nor forsake you."*[82]

The "living waters" scripture was about the Holy Spirit, she had discovered later, when she began a more in-depth study during her fast. The very next verse had confirmed it. "But this He spoke concerning the Spirit, whom those believing in Him would receive; for the Holy Spirit was not yet *given*, because Jesus was not yet glorified."[83] Ever since she had studied it out, she couldn't get the image out of her head: a person with a spring of water bubbling up and pouring out of his middle, flooding the people around him with life and power and joy.

She had spent many hours of her childhood wading in Bear Creek. It never went dry, because it was spring-fed. Even during the hottest, driest part of the summer, it still had a healthy amount of cool water flowing through it. During the spring and fall rains, it bounced and splashed from rock to rock, looking for all the world as if it were dancing for joy. And after heavy rains, it became a formidable force, able to sweep away fallen trees and forge new eddies through the brush along its bank, scooping up a large amount of gravel from one area and depositing it in another. There was no denying the power of water to change a landscape in a matter of minutes. "Lord, that's what we need. We need Your Holy Spirit to come into our lives and change the landscape of our hearts. Lord, that's what *I* need," Selah said. She knelt in the soil she had prepared. It was cushiony for her knees because it was mostly free of rocks after all the work she had done on it. "Lord, I asked You to make the hearts of Your people like this soil. Please make *my* heart free of rocks of self-righteousness to throw at others, free of rocks of preconceived ideas about what I should be that would impede the growth of Your nature in me. I want to know You more. I want the seeds

---

[82] See Hebrews 13:5
[83] John 7:39 NKJV

of Your Word and of Your love to fall on good ground in my heart," Selah prayed. She lifted her hands as a child would lift her hands to ask to be picked up and carried. "I need You. I love You," she continued. As she began to pour out her love for the Lord, she felt the comforting closeness of His presence. An expectancy began to build in her. It reminded her of the wind that comes before a heavy rain, when the sky would turn a foreboding green, and the gusts would bend the trees and scoot the dust in swirls along the road. She could feel a type of wind in her spirit. *"I wonder what type of rain a spiritual wind will bring?"* she thought as she prayed. She didn't want to stop telling the Lord how she felt about Him. The more she told Him, the more clearly she seemed to be able to tell how He felt about her. But the more she talked, the more she realized her words were inadequate. "I'll never be able to praise You enough, or to explain how truly great You are," she said, "but I want to try!" She thought of all the beautiful sunsets she had ever seen. "Lord, You are more beautiful than that," she said. She thought of the sound of the wood thrush as it trilled and warbled in a forest canopy. "Lord, You are more beautiful than that to me," she said. She thought of the pale purple coneflowers, blue larkspur, yellow primroses and bright orange Indian paintbrush on Connor Glade. "You are even more beautiful than that," she said. She grasped for words to describe the majesty she could sense in the King of Glory, and as she did, a word that made no sense to her came out of her mouth. It was almost as if she could see the word in her head right before she said it. She felt the urge to say it again, so she did. *"That doesn't make sense,"* a voice inside her said. She told the negative voice inside her to shut up, and continued her quest to praise the Lord. The feeling of expectancy was building in her now, threatening to explode. As she continued to concentrate on the Lord, she felt a wave of power rush over her, and she realized that as she was praising Him, she was doing it in another language. She stopped as her brain tried to analyze what was happening, but her spirit didn't want to stop. *"You don't need to understand everything,"* a gentle voice spoke quietly to her heart. *"You just need to trust Me."* Selah let down her defenses and surrendered her need to understand what was happening. As she did, the Holy Spirit flooded her soul. She had never felt such power and joy. It was just as Jesus had described it, like a river overflowing the banks of her heart. The more she praised Him, the better she felt. Her faith was soaring. She had never felt this close to the Lord before. Her loneliness was replaced by a sense of overwhelming, loving companionship. As she spoke in another language, she knew the desires of her heart that the Holy Spirit had placed within her were being communicated directly to the heart of God. She had told God she wanted more. She had asked and received, sought and found, knocked and the door was opened. It was incredible. How had she gone so far in her walk with Christ and not experienced this? She wanted to tell everyone about it. But there was time for that later. Right now, she just wanted to spend some more time telling Jesus how much she loved Him.

32

SELAH did not jump right up from the garden and run down the road to tell everyone she met about what had just happened to her. She wanted to tell her parents, but Jackson was busy helping Clive Coffelt on the other end of the valley, and Asha was at the community hall helping to plan a baby shower for Jannalina Breedon. Selah was left basking in the warmth of God's love and nearly giddy with excitement to tell someone. Of course, if Miss Genevieve were still here, she would be the first one to know. Selah wondered if maybe, somehow, she *did* know. Just to make sure, she decided to ask the Lord a favor. "Father, if Miss Genevieve doesn't know about this, would you mind telling her? I know she would love to hear about it," she said.

The next person she would have liked to tell would be Garrison. Even though he wasn't close to the Lord, he had been her best friend. Maybe he wouldn't have understood; but when he saw how excited she was, he would have been excited right along with her. Or maybe not, she wondered. "Lord, I know I've asked You about Garrison a thousand times, but would You please keep him safe, and draw him to You by the power of the Holy Spirit?" she asked. She didn't even know how to pray for him. Was he even alive? Something inside her told her that he was. But if he had made a successful transition to the society of the Old Country, was he being corrupted by their dangerous, anti-Christian ideas? She had no way of knowing. How could she pray for him if she had no idea how he was doing? And yet still she felt the burden for him that she had always felt.

The solution that came to her was so simple, she nearly slapped herself in the forehead. "And the Holy Spirit helps us in our distress. For we don't even know what we should pray for, nor how we should pray. But the Holy Spirit prays for us with groanings that cannot be expressed in words. And the Father who knows all hearts knows what the Spirit is saying, for the Spirit pleads for us believers in harmony with God's own will.[84] Romans 8:26-27, right?" Selah asked herself. Miss Genevieve had told her about this. She had said that when she didn't know how to pray, the Holy Spirit would help her to pray.

Well, why not? "Holy Spirit, I don't know where Garrison is, or what he needs right now, but *You* do, because You see and know everything. Would You please help me to pray for Garrison?" Selah asked. She closed her eyes and lifted her hands as she asked for help. As she did so, she thought about Garrison, and a strange thing happened. She wasn't thinking about all the fun they used to have, or the way he could turn everything into a joke, or even about the crush she had on him. She wasn't thinking about how *she* felt about him, at all. Instead, a new kind of emotion seemed to well up inside of her from the pit of her being. It was a sense of longing and urgency she had never felt before…and love —not sensual love, but love in its purest form. She felt it as if it were her very own emotion, and somehow she knew that it wasn't her longings and love for him that she was feeling. Suddenly she realized she was experiencing the way God felt about Garrison: His longing to be closer to him, to protect, nurture, and teach him. As she prayed, she used the words God gave her in another language; and the more that she prayed in tongues, the more of an understanding she seemed to have about how God wanted her to pray. None of the things she felt God wanted her to pray about made sense when she thought about Garrison's attitude when he had left the valley. She wanted to pray in English those things she sensed in her spirit, but she hesitated, because it seemed to contradict everything she knew about him. Again, she felt as if a gentle

---

[84] Romans 8:26-27 NLT

hand of reassurance was laid upon her shoulder. She couldn't hear God speaking in an audible voice, but it was almost as if He spoke directly to her spirit, saying, *"Follow My lead. If you are sensitive, and obedient, I will use you to affect the life of not just one individual, but of a community, and communities, and a nation."* Selah was stunned. She opened her eyes and swallowed hard. How could that be? *"Trust me,"* the voice said again. Miss Genevieve had always warned her to "try the spirits," as she called it. She had told Selah that if she felt like God was telling her to do something, she should always make certain that what she was being told lined up with the Word of God. Selah searched her memory of the scriptures and compared it to how she thought God was leading her to pray. None of it contradicted God's Word. In fact, it was confirmed by it. Hadn't Jesus told His disciples to go into all the world and preach the gospel to every creature? Hadn't Paul told the Ephesians in chapter six of his letter to them to pray on every occasion in the power of the Holy Spirit, and to be persistent in prayers for all Christians everywhere? Hadn't Jesus, himself, said to pray to the Lord who is in charge of the harvest, that He would send out workers into His fields? Selah pushed aside all that she knew to be true about Garrison when she had last seen him. "Father, I surrender my will to Yours," she said. She was praying in faith that what she felt and believed would eventually line up with what she said, just as she had done when she had forgiven Payton. "I don't understand how what You are asking me to pray for is possible, but I want to be obedient to the leading of Your Holy Spirit." She paused and took a deep breath. "Father, I ask in the name of Jesus that you fill Garrison with such a hunger for You that he cannot rest until he surrenders everything to You. I pray You would mold him and make him into a soldier for Your Kingdom, a light for all to see. Make a warrior of him, Lord, so that he will win many, many souls, snatching them out of the depths of sin and despair and bringing them into Your marvelous light! And Lord, use me how You want me to be used."

Selah stopped suddenly. When she had uttered those last words, something flip-flopped inside of her. It almost seemed like God was trying to tell her something about the way she should be praying for herself. But surely she had heard wrong. She imagined this was what Maggie probably felt like when she was being trained to go into the stanchion. As a calf, Maggie had not wanted to place her head in the confined area. She had thrown her head back and balked. Selah had been patient and had worked with her until the calf was over her nervousness and learned to associate the stanchion with the treat of a carrot or an apple. But until that time, Maggie had planted her hooves firmly on the ground and refused to budge.

Selah opened her eyes. Her concentration was broken. She wanted to be obedient, but she was afraid of what her obedience might bring. "I understand that You want to use *me* as a light for people to come to You, as well, but I don't see how that is possible," she said. "Unless You mean that I am going to reach many people through my prayers, which know no boundaries," she said hopefully. "I'm not sure I understand, Lord," Selah admitted. "Please show me somehow what You mean, because what I think You mean doesn't seem realistic." As she said it, Selah got the distinct impression that God was laughing. She looked down at the seedbed. How long had she been praying? It didn't seem like very long, but the sun was definitely higher in the sky. The overwhelming urge she had felt to pray had lifted somewhat when she had resisted how she felt the Spirit was leading her.

She put on her jacket that she had hung on the barbed wire fence and picked up the hoe. From all Miss Genevieve had taught her, she realized what she had just experienced was intercession. She knew without a doubt she had been praying God's will for Garrison, and then for herself, up to a point. She tried to tell herself that the reason she had stopped praying was because she wasn't exactly certain she was praying God's will for her life, but a doubt nibbled at the corners of her rationalization.

Whatever the case, she still felt elated and overwhelmed. She had just been baptized in the Holy Ghost and experienced Spirit-led intercessory prayer for the first time. And although she had originally wanted to tell everyone she met about her experience, she felt a hesitation in her spirit now. For whatever reason, she knew God wanted her to wait.

She walked up the path between the chicken yard and the corral to the house. Asha smiled at her when she came in. "You're back from the community hall?" Selah asked. She looked in surprise at the table, which was set for lunch. "Is it lunchtime already?"

Asha glanced at her as she stirred a pot of soup on the cookstove. "It is. Your dad is still over at the Coffelts' place. The tree that was down on their fence must have done more damage than they thought. Sara said most of their cows got out, so the Beardsleys were over there, too, trying to gather them back in. So what have you been doing all this time? How did the lettuce bed turn out?"

"It looks pretty good," Selah said, peeking around the wall of the kitchen to check the hall clock. It had been three hours since she left the house to start working on the seedbed. How was that possible? She knew it had taken her about an hour to work up the soil. Could she have really spent two hours in prayer and not felt the passage of time?

"What's wrong?" Asha asked as she noticed the look of confusion on Selah's face.

"Oh, nothing," Selah answered, and poured herself a glass of water from the jug on the counter. She smiled as the memory of her encounter with the Holy Spirit played out in her mind. She could still sense the presence of the Lord all around her. It was comforting and invigorating at the same time.

"Selah," Asha said, "Did you hear me?"

Selah looked up at her mother. She didn't even realize she had been staring off into space, her face still glowing with the experience she had just had. "I'm sorry, Mom. What did you say?"

"I said, what have you been doing? Who were you talking to out there? I could hear you saying something, but I couldn't hear anyone else."

"Oh. I was just praying," Selah explained. She grinned at her mother and drained the glass of water.

Asha regarded her daughter carefully. Something was different about her. She couldn't put her finger on it, but something had definitely changed. The sadness that had hung about her since the death of Miss Genevieve was gone. Something else was in its place, and it made her face shine. "You seem awfully happy about something," Asha pressed, intrigued by the change of moods.

Selah had never stopped smiling. She laughed now, because all the smiling was making her cheeks hurt. It wasn't a problem she had very often. "Mom, God is doing something amazing in my life."

"I believe that," Asha replied. "Are you going to let me in on what it is?"

"Well, for starters, I just got filled with the Holy Ghost," Selah said. She couldn't help it. It wasn't something she could hold in anymore, and she didn't feel like she was supposed to keep the information from her parents.

Asha's mouth dropped open. "Really? How do you know?"

Selah laughed again. "Mom, when you experience it, you will know. There's no mistaking it. It's like...it's just like Jesus said. It's like a river that flows out of the deepest part of you and spills out all over with joy and love and power. And when I was praying, I started speaking this other language—I don't even know what it was. But I could tell the Holy Spirit was helping me to pray in God's will, just like Dad said about Great Grandpa Connor."

"You spoke in tongues?" Asha's eyes were wide, and a smile played on her lips. "I'm thrilled for you, and a little jealous, and..." she stopped, and her brow furrowed. "You're sure? You're sure you really spoke in tongues?"

Selah laughed once again at her mother's consternation. "Yes, Mom. I'm sure. Once you experience it, you'll understand." She stopped suddenly as she reasoned that her mother might be afraid of such an experience. "You do want to receive Him, don't you? You don't have to be afraid of it. It's incredible. All of the sudden, you're closer to God than you ever dreamed you could be. It's as if you feel His thoughts and how

He wants you to pray about things. I feel like I could ask anything right now, and receive it, because I know now how to pray in His will."

Asha stared at her daughter, her eyes shining. "I knew something was different about you, even when you were coming up the path. Ever since Genevieve passed, it's as if you've been under a shadow of depression and anger. Even after you went to see Payton and got things cleared up with him, you just seemed weighed down by everything that's happened. And just now, when I saw you heading for the house, it looked like you didn't have a care in the world."

"Oh, I still have things I'm concerned about. I have a lot of cares. But I see now clearer than ever before that I need to 'cast all my cares upon Him, because He cares for me.'[85] I know He hears me. I know He has Garrison in the palm of His hand. And I know Miss Genevieve is having the time of her life in His presence, if it's anything like what I've just experienced!" Selah exclaimed.

The two sat down to their bowls of potato soup, and Asha continued to ask Selah questions. She had been slightly apprehensive at first, but the more she heard about the Holy Spirit, the more she wanted to hear. The two were still sitting at the table talking when Jackson walked in, a new hole ripped in the sleeve of his flannel shirt. "That ol' tree took a bite out of my favorite shirt," he said.

"Uh-oh," Asha said, but she was still smiling from her conversation with Selah.

"You're ok, though, right Dad?" Selah asked.

"Yeah, it just got my shirt. I didn't get scratched up too badly." He eyed Asha and Selah suspiciously. "Say, what have you two been up to? You're grinning like a couple of possums."

Asha looked at Selah for permission, and then back at Jackson. "Selah just got filled with the Holy Spirit," she said excitedly.

Jackson's eyes widened and his face crept into a cautious smile. "Did …are you serious?"

---

[85] See 1 Peter 5:7

Selah and Asha giggled at his response. "That was my first reaction," Asha said, "But it's true. And you can see it all over her. It's just like the old timers used to talk about. Listening to her, you can tell. She's had a God experience. And I, for one, am jealous!"

"Don't be jealous, Mom," Selah grinned mischievously. "For the promise is to you and to your children, and to all who are afar off, as many as the Lord our God will call,"[86] she quoted.

Jackson pulled up a chair. "I want to hear the whole thing. Start from the very beginning." He looked at Asha with mock pleading in his eyes. "And I wouldn't mind a bowl of that soup, since I'm already sitting down and I've been working so hard."

Asha smirked and ladled up another bowl, placing it in front of him before she sat down again. "Eat your soup, Mister. But you've gotta hear this."

Selah took a deep breath. "Well, if you want me to start at the very beginning, it was really when Miss Genevieve had the stroke and got me to read all those scriptures about the Holy Spirit," she began, because she realized that was truly the beginning of it all. The Word of God had stuck in the soil of her heart and sprouted, even when she had been angry about Miss Genevieve's death. So as her parents listened intently, Selah told of the power of God's Word to change her heart and the power of the influence of her parents and even of Payton Hamby. She told of the fasting and the praying and seeking the heart of God. As she talked, the light that had come alive within her grew brighter. Asha and Jackson found themselves captivated by the awareness that there was a deeper level at which you could dwell with God. And as they listened, their hunger grew.

---

[86] Acts 2:39 NKJV

33

During the following weeks, Selah continued to pray for a spiritual awakening in her community. She had told no one except her parents of her experience, but anyone who was paying attention noticed there was something different about her. Selah noticed the difference in herself in many ways. It didn't just include her prayer life; the influence of the Holy Spirit extended into every aspect of her personal life, as well. She discovered that she was less likely to be annoyed with the people who usually bothered her the most. In fact, she seemed to have a new appreciation for them and the good traits of their personalities, and a more forgiving attitude toward their negative traits. She was more outgoing, and found herself eager to reach out in love to people she had never spent much time with before. It was as if God had given her a new way of seeing things through the lens of His love. Even Jannica Breedon, who had said so many degrading things about Miss Genevieve, wasn't excluded from the scope of Selah's newfound affection.

"Is Jannalina still having any problems with morning sickness?" she asked Jannica one Sunday after morning service.

Jannica stared at her as if she thought it was a trick question. She and Selah had never been on very friendly terms. "No, she stopped having that about a week ago," she finally answered.

"Oh, that's great!" Selah replied. "I've been praying for her. Are you excited about being a grandma?"

Jannica still looked puzzled, but the question about being a grandma finally won her over. "Oh, I can hardly wait! And you know, I have several names picked out, but Jannalina and Kevin neither one want to hear them. They say they don't want to be influenced by someone else's ideas for a name. Do you wanna hear what I came up with?"

Selah nodded politely. Months before, she wouldn't have given Jannica the time of day. But now she found herself listening to the woman patiently. She could hear in her voice the fierceness of her devotion to her family. Selah could see how God could use this natural trait in Jannica for the woman to pray powerfully for her loved ones, and she wondered how much she prayed.

Jannica read off every name on a list she had pulled out of her purse, telling her a reason for each one and how she had come up with it. "You've got some really promising ones on there," Selah said when Jannica was finally finished. "Your family has always had a talent for creative names."

Jannica beamed at her. "Why, thank you, Selah. I think that's the nicest thing you've ever said to me."

Selah smiled back at her and was suddenly struck by how unfriendly she had been to this woman before now. *"Forgive me, Lord. I can see how wrong and selfish I've been,"* she prayed silently as she turned to leave.

She was about to head out the door when she felt a hand on her shoulder. "Now wait a minute, young lady," said a voice of mock disapproval. "Just where do you think you're going without talking to me?"

Selah turned around to see Payton, sporting the most stern face he could muster. She grinned and gave him a sideways hug. "Sorry, Brother Payton. That was a serious oversight," she said.

"Indeed," Payton said, breaking into a smile. He seemed to study her a while before he spoke again. It was a common occurrence lately. People would look at Selah when she said something and seem to do a double-take. "I want to know what's going on with you. How is my prayer partner?" he asked quietly. They had told no one of their joint effort to pray for a better understanding of the work of the Holy Spirit. "Are you still praying regarding what we talked about the other day?"

"Yes. And something happened. I've been waiting for the right time to tell you," Selah began.

Payton raised his eyebrows. "Well, I'm waiting to hear it. You've seemed different lately. Happier. And there's something else, too. Have you had a revelation of some sort?"

Selah's heart began to pound. She wanted so badly to tell him, but she was afraid he would feel left out if he found out she had been filled with the Holy Ghost when he hadn't. "I'm not sure how to tell you this," she said apprehensively. "I'm so excited about it, but I don't want to seem like I'm bragging." She had prayed for the Holy Spirit to show her the right time to tell Payton because she wasn't sure how an elder would react to her news, especially when it had been such a long time since anyone in the community had been filled with the Spirit. *"Lord, if You want me to tell him now, let him say something about being led by the Holy Ghost,"* she prayed silently.

"Selah, if God has told you something He wants you to share with me, don't resist the leading of the Holy Spirit," Payton said suddenly.

Selah's face glowed. "I got filled with the Holy Ghost!" she whispered excitedly. "I spoke in tongues. It wasn't like anything I'd ever experienced before! And He's showing me how to pray. He's using me to pray—praying God's will through me. I can feel His passion for people. It changed everything—the way I see people, the way I read His Word," the words came rushing out like a river from a busted dam.

Payton's eyes grew round and he looked around to see if anyone had heard them talking. Just then, Asha and Jackson approached.

"Did you tell him the news?" Asha asked.

"Yes," Selah said softly. She could tell Payton was unsure of how others might accept this bit of information, so she tried not to draw attention to herself.

"So it's true?" Payton looked to Asha and Jackson for confirmation, and then back to Selah. "Not that I don't believe you, Selah, but it has been so long since anyone here has been filled. I wasn't sure you would know if it had really happened to you or not."

"Oh, you know when it happens," Selah replied. "There's no mistaking it."

"I can hear her praying every morning down the path by the garden," Jackson said. "Sometimes it's in English, sometimes it's something else, but it's the real deal. Kind of reminds me of how Miss Genevieve used to pray."

"Why don't you come over this afternoon and we can visit about it?" Asha suggested. She could see that Payton was eager to learn more.

"I would love to," he agreed.

Sunday dinner was barely over and the dishes were still being washed when Payton showed up on the front porch. "Am I too early?" he asked.

"Not if you don't mind me making noise washing the dishes," Jackson said from his station by the sink.

"I just can't get it out of my mind," he explained.

"Neither can I," Selah laughed. "I studied out the scriptures Miss Genevieve showed me about the Holy Spirit, and I realized I wanted what she had. I wanted to be closer to God. I wanted more of Him."

"So how did it happen?" Payton asked.

"Well, I was fasting about our community because . . ." she hesitated. "Because I felt like we were spiritually dead and needed revival. And I began to see how I needed change in my life, too. I started thinking about the verse in John about how out of your belly will flow rivers of living water. I prayed about it, and then I started praising the Lord and telling Him how wonderful He is. It just sort of happened while I was praising the Lord," Selah tried to explain.

Payton seemed to consider what she had said. "The Lord has been leading me to fast, but I have to admit, I haven't done it yet. There's something in me that rebels against the very idea of fasting. I think it's my love of eating," he joked.

"But when your desire for more of God overtakes your desire to eat, then it won't matter to you anymore," Selah said quickly. "And the enemy will try to convince you that fasting isn't important. But you know it is, even though it's hard. If it wasn't hard, what would be the point? That *is* the point, isn't it? Denying your flesh so you can let your spirit man see more clearly?"

The three adults in the room looked at Selah without a word, and then glanced at each other.

"Did I say something wrong?" Selah asked tentatively.

"No, honey, not at all," Payton said reassuringly. "It's just that, I feel like I've just been schooled by someone fifty years younger. You haven't said anything wrong. I think the Holy Spirit is showing you things about how to pray and seek the Lord. I know you've been seeking God for me, too. Would you continue to do that? I would like to devote some time to fasting about this. I don't want to be left out. I'm the senior elder, for goodness' sake."

"I don't want left out, either," Asha said.

"Then that makes three of us. I'd like to join you in fasting," Jackson said to Payton.

"Well, alright, then. Let's do it," Payton said excitedly. The four of them agreed on which days of the week they would be fasting. "Let's meet at my house for dinner on Saturday night. We can have a prayer meeting before we break our fast."

"Sounds good," Jackson said.

Selah was elated. She could feel a sense of expectancy building again, and she wished Miss Genevieve could be here to feel it, too.

It was helpful having other people fasting with her for a spiritual renewal in the community. There was a sense of unity and peace binding the group together as they prayed and fasted for a common goal. Selah had grown to love the experience of having a prayer partner in Miss Genevieve; having three other partners in prayer made her feel like a member of a small army. Just knowing there was someone else who cared enough about the spiritual state of the community to fast for it helped her to feel stronger in her commitment to prayer. The four had a sense of accountableness to each other that kept them faithful to their task.

When Selah and her parents arrived at the Hamby house on Saturday evening, they found that their army had grown by one more member. "When I found out Payton was fasting, I felt compelled to do it, too," Addy confessed. "I pray for our church daily, but it's been so long since I fasted about anything—not since we fasted all those years ago during the drought." She smiled shyly and fidgeted with her apron as she looked at Selah. "I had a feeling about you the day you showed up on our walkway, Selah. It's hard for me to explain, but I just felt like you visiting us was the start of something good. You all may just think I'm jumping on the bandwagon, but I've been thinking about the state of our community, and I think we are too comfortable. When our parents and grandparents came here, we were on fire for God. Now we just come to church, sing a few songs, listen to the preaching, and have a social hour afterward. When I was a little girl, we had some services that lasted 'til midnight. Grandma told me about times when grown men had to crawl across the floor because the glory of God was so heavy they couldn't stand up. Today we're so distant in our relationship with God that we don't seem to care whether we experience His presence or not. It seems to me that a spiritual drought like we've got right now is even more dangerous than a drought that kills our crops. A spiritual drought can kill a harvest of souls. Anyway, that's why I decided to join you." She stopped speaking abruptly, the way quiet-natured people will when they suddenly realize they have said more than their normal quota of words.

Selah looked at her wonderingly. Addy wasn't of low intelligence, at all, as Selah had always assumed. She was a little backward, but she had spiritual insight and sensitivity. Selah was ashamed that she had dismissed her as someone who wasn't worth taking time to get to know. She had been taught it all her life, but she was finally beginning to see firsthand that no one in the kingdom of God was without merit.

The five of them joined hands in a circle. Payton, being the spiritual shepherd of the community, led them in an opening prayer before they found their own places to pray separately. "Father, we have come to seek Your face. We are hungry for more of You. We know our community has drifted away from You, and we were once close to You. We long to be close to You again. Forgive us of our complacency and our apathy. Forgive us of our insensitivity. Create in us a clean heart, oh, God. Renew a right spirit within us, so that we can once again be close to You. Let us become more aware of Your presence. Let us experience You in close relationship once more."

The prayer partners moved to different places in the room. Payton knelt in a corner, bowing so low that his face touched the ground. Selah paced back and forth at one end of the room, as she always did while praying. Addy and Asha knelt at chairs, and Jackson sat in a chair, his head in his hands. It was quiet for a long time except for the soft whisperings of people who had grown unaccustomed to praying in close quarters with others present. It was hard for Selah to concentrate at first, because she was distracted by the sound and the nearness of other people. *"Help me to be able to pray, Lord,"* she said silently. She began to think of her prayer place by the lettuce garden. There were distractions there, too, she reasoned. There were birds loudly proclaiming their territory, Maggie mooing to be fed, and chickens cackling. They could all hear her praying, and they didn't care what she said. *"But these are people,"* a voice inside her said. *"They can understand what you're saying. You're younger. They're going to judge you by what you say."* Selah stopped pacing. She had heard the demeaning tone of that voice before. It was the same voice that told her it was useless to pray because God never listened anyway. It often told her that what she prayed about wasn't important enough to bring before the throne of God. It spoke fear into her heart every time she was about to have a major spiritual breakthrough. *"And don't even think about asking the Holy Spirit to help you pray,"* the voice continued. *"If you start speaking in another language, they'll know you're just faking it. They'll pat you on the head and tell you how sweet it is that you want to be filled with the Holy Spirit. But it just doesn't happen in this day and age. That was just something that happened to the apostles."*

"You Liar!" Selah said in barely a whisper. "You are the father of lies, and you always accuse my brothers and sisters and me. I refuse to agree with you. I know you're trying to tell the others similar lies. Right now, I bind you in Jesus' name. I command you to leave, in the name of Jesus!" In her mind, Selah picked up a sword. She raised her hands and spoke into the quietness of the room. "God has not given me a spirit of timidity, but of power, love, and self-discipline.[87] We will come boldly to the throne of our gracious God. There we will receive His mercy, and we will find grace to help us when we need it."[88]

As she spoke, the mood in the room shifted. From his place in the corner, Payton spoke. *"Draw near to God, and He will draw near to you."*[89] Selah recognized the first part of James 4:8. Payton continued with the tenth verse of the same chapter. *"Humble yourselves in the sight of the Lord, and He will lift you up.*[90] Father, we have humbled ourselves, and we will continue to do so until we hear from You…until we experience Your glory. For we long for You as a dry and weary land thirsts for water." He stopped abruptly, and Selah could hear him weeping. Something about the sincerity of his prayer moved her deeply. She could feel his longing and the longing of the other people in the room. Everyone there desired more of God. She found she was able to concentrate now. The accusatorial voice of the enemy had left at her command in the name of Jesus and by the power of the Word of God that she and Payton had spoken.

"Thank You for hearing us, Lord," Selah prayed softly. "We love You so much." She kept talking to the Lord, telling Him how she loved being His child. The presence of God fell gently on her like a spring rain. She stood still in the room, listening with her heart and attuned to His Spirit. The sound of sniffling came from the place where Jackson sat. Asha and Addy could be heard from the places where they knelt, their soft, pleading prayers growing in volume. God's love was thick in the

---

[87] See 2 Tim 1:7 NLT
[88] See Hebrews 4:16 NLT
[89] James 4:8a NKJV
[90] James 4:10 NKJV

atmosphere of the Hamby house. Selah hadn't felt His presence like this since she had prayed with Miss Genevieve. It felt even stronger than their private prayer sessions, since there were more people praying for the same goal. "Now I understand what David meant when he said how good and how pleasant it is for brethren to dwell together in unity!"[91] she exclaimed. Her fear of praying with the others was completely gone. She lifted her hands and closed her eyes and began praying in a heavenly language that only God could understand. The others were quiet at first, but they began to praise the Lord as the realization dawned on them that the promise of the Holy Spirit was real. It wasn't just something that had happened to their grandparents. It was for all Christians everywhere, "as many as the Lord our God will call."[92]

Addy suddenly lifted her voice in spontaneous song. Selah didn't recognize the words or the tune, but they portrayed a deep longing for communion with God, and seemed to come directly from Addy's heart. The song resonated in their spirits.

Then Jackson began to sing another song of praise that was familiar to all of them, his rich baritone voice filling the room. The others joined him. After the song was finished, Selah continued praising the Lord in another language, and the others began praising the Lord from the depths of their heart in their own way. Selah didn't know how long this continued, but she did know that the gnawing hunger pains in her stomach had gone. She no longer cared how long she had been without food. Nothing could compare with the sweet Spirit of the Lord that rested in the room.

She was basking in the presence of God when she suddenly felt as if she was supposed to do something. She stopped and tried to listen sensitively to the leading of the Holy Spirit. There was a distinct urge for her to go over to Payton and lay her hands on him and pray for him to receive the Holy Ghost. Immediately she balked in her spirit. "Just like Maggie," she thought, as she remembered the other time she had

---

[91] Psalm 133:1 KJV
[92] See Acts 2:39 NKJV

resisted the Holy Spirit during prayer. "Lord, are you really telling me to do this?" she prayed silently. Still she felt the gentle nudging of the Holy Spirit for her to make her way across the room to where Payton prayed. "But, Lord, Payton is the spiritual leader here. I can't just go up to him and pray for him to receive the baptism. It's not my place."

"Oh, really?" she heard a voice in her spirit reply. *"What is your place in the kingdom? Can you rank each member in this room? What did I say about the child I showed to my disciples? 'Whoever humbles himself like this little child is the greatest in the kingdom of heaven.'* You *do not know your place. Your place is to trust Me and not to draw back in unbelief."*

Selah stood still, her heart pounding. "Lord, the enemy is trying to make me afraid. That is why I am resisting," she prayed.

"No. That's not the enemy. That is your pride and fear of rejection. If you will lay aside your pride and obey the leading of My Spirit, I will use you. But it's your choice," the voice said.

Selah hesitated, searching for a scripture in her memory where it wasn't appropriate for a younger person to pray for an older person, but she couldn't remember any. As she hesitated in her indecision, she could feel the presence of God begin to lift. "No, wait. I'll do it, Lord," she said suddenly. She didn't feel like it, but she willed herself to cross the room to where Payton knelt. As soon as she moved in obedience, she felt a strange but wonderful sensation. It was like power and confidence combined. She stood over Payton momentarily, and then said to herself, "Not by might, nor by power, but by My Spirit, says the Lord of hosts."[93] She knelt beside him and laid her hand on his shoulder. "Father, you know the desires of his heart," she prayed out loud. "Give him the desire of his heart. Fill him with your Holy Spirit, and with power." Selah then began praying in the Holy Ghost. *"Ok, God,"* she prayed silently. *"I did my part. Now please do whatever it is You want to do in Brother Payton. Now do Your part, and help him to do his part—to let go of any doubt or indecision."*

---

93 See Zechariah 4:6 RSV

To her astonishment, Payton suddenly crumpled in a heap onto his side, his hands trembling. "God, what's going on?" Selah whispered frantically. She backed away, trying to understand what had just happened. "Lord, did I do something wrong?" she asked. But she could sense no disapproval. In fact, if anything, the glory of God only felt stronger. As she stood there, debating in her mind what she should do next, Payton suddenly began speaking in another language as he lay on his side. *Apparently,* Selah thought, *the power of God affects people in different ways.* She looked across the room at the others. They were all lost in the presence of God. As her eyes rested on her mother, she felt led by the Spirit to go lay hands on her, as well. She made her way quickly to where Asha knelt and placed her hand on her head. Asha immediately slumped forward onto the seat and slid to the floor. She appeared to be unconscious, but a smile was on her face. Selah moved away and looked around the room. Suddenly, she felt as if her legs would no longer support her. She knelt quickly and what felt like a wave of power washed over her and gently tipped her on her side. "Wow, God," she said. "I don't know what's going on here, but it's powerful." As she lay on the brown, braided rug of the Hamby living room, waves of glory swept over her like Bear Creek in flood stage. She didn't know how long she lay there, but after a while, she heard Payton get up and stagger across the room to his wife. Soon afterward, Selah could hear Addy lifting her voice in praise in an unknown language. She could hear Payton make his way around the room, and soon she could hear Jackson's voice as he was baptized in the Holy Spirit. Her mother remained in what appeared to be an unconscious state that Selah suddenly remembered Genevieve had called "slain in the Spirit."

Selah wasn't certain how long they lay there. It could have been minutes; it could have been hours. The passage of time seemed different, somehow. When Addy finally got up off of the floor and wandered into the kitchen, Selah heard her exclaim in surprise. "It's after eight! We've been lying in there for three hours!" Selah laughed and steadied herself as she got up off of the floor. Addy looked at her and giggled. "You have a rug print on your face," she said. Selah laughed again in sheer joy. She looked at the others. Jackson and Payton were helping each other to their feet. She made her way to Asha, who was beginning to stir.

"Hey, Mom," she said as she smiled down at Asha.

Asha blinked and smiled dreamily. "Hi," she said, and took Selah's hand for support as she attempted to get up. She fell sideways and laughed at herself. Jackson and Payton helped her to a chair at the kitchen table. The five looked around at each other in wonderment. "What was that?" Asha finally broke the silence.

"The power of God," Payton said in awe. "And all I can think is, I want more of it. I want our whole congregation to experience this!"

"I've never felt the love of God like that before," Addy said. "It's like He just held us in His arms for a while and let us know how much He loves us. I can't wait to tell the ladies who are working on the quilt for Jannalina's baby."

"I wonder what they'll think at the men's breakfast?" Jackson asked.

Payton seemed to consider things before he spoke. "I've been trying to prepare the people to seek God for a move of his Spirit, in case you hadn't noticed."

Selah had noticed. His sermons had been about the early church in the book of Acts, where believers were led by the Spirit and operated in the power of God to witness and be missionaries and to pray for others to receive the baptism of the Holy Ghost.

"I'm not sure all of them are ready," he continued. "But I don't know how any of us can keep this a secret." He looked at Selah. "How in the world did you keep this to yourself for as long as you did?"

Selah laughed. "It wasn't easy. But I felt I was only supposed to let my parents know at first. I just tried to follow the Holy Spirit's leading."

Payton smiled at her appreciatively. "The way you did when you came and laid hands on me to receive the baptism?" he asked.

Selah looked down nervously. "I didn't want to at first," she admitted. "The urge to do it was so strong. I knew I had a choice whether or not to do it, but I was afraid you might get offended since you're in leadership and I'm not."

"Well, I'm glad you decided to listen to the Spirit instead of to your fear. I feel so strong in my faith—like I could ask anything in His will, and He would do it," Payton replied.

"That's how I felt when I first got filled," Selah said quickly.

"Well, I don't know when God wants it to happen, but I'm certain He wants the rest of the community to experience His power and His glory. Let's all pray together that we will all be sensitive to the Holy Spirit's leading and that the hearts of the people will be prepared to receive all that God has in store for them," Payton suggested. They all joined hands again, praying in English and in other languages as the Holy Spirit gave them the words to pray.

Afterward, they all stood around the table, smiling through tears, until Addy finally said, "Well, how about something to eat?" She stepped onto their enclosed side porch and brought in a platter of cold roast beef sandwiches. "Sorry about the cold meal, but I didn't want something to be cooking on the stove, filling the whole house with food smells while we were at the end of our fast," she explained apologetically.

"Good grief. Now I know without a doubt that we've been changed in the presence of the Lord," Payton said. "I wasn't even thinking about food."

"I was," confessed Jackson, eyeing the sandwiches hungrily.

Payton's laughter boomed through the house as he slapped Jackson on the back. "Selah," he said, once he had regained composure, "would you please pray over the meal?"

Selah looked up in surprise and smiled at her former enemy. "I'd love to," she replied.

Once the food was blessed, they all sat down at the table and devoured the sandwiches. "This is the best roast beef sandwich I've ever had," Jackson said heartily, and then glanced at Asha to see if he had offended her. Asha wasn't paying any attention. She ate her sandwich with the same dreamy smile she had worn since she got up off of the floor.

"Thank you, Jackson," Addy said. "But I think you're just hungry. This is that old stringy cow we butchered and had kept frozen until things started thawing out. I'll have to can the rest of her since the weather warmed up."

"You could make jerky out of her if she's too tough," Selah suggested.

Addy tilted her head as if to consider the suggestion. "I guess I could, but I'm not very good at jerky."

"I could help you, if you want," Selah offered. "I make a lot of jerky out of the deer meat we get."

Addy smiled. "Ok, Selah. It's a date. We'll have a jerky-making party."

Selah grinned. She was looking forward to getting to know Addy better.

It was nine o' clock when Selah and her parents headed for home. Jackson and Selah walked on either side of Asha, who was still a little unsteady on her feet.

"See you tomorrow," Payton called after them into the darkness.

"Tomorrow?" Asha asked suddenly. It was the first word she had spoken since their prayer around the table. "Oh, for heaven's sake!" she exclaimed. "Tomorrow is Sunday."

"So it is," Jackson mused. "I wonder what church will be like in the morning?"

Selah smiled as she breathed in the brisk night air, with Asha still leaning heavily on her arm. She wondered what church would be like, as well. One thing was for certain. The five of them would never be the same.

34

SELAH wanted to arrive early for morning service at the community hall that served as their church building, but from the very beginning of that day, things seemed to go wrong. When she went to feed Maggie, she was shocked to see the little Jersey had gone into labor and was having trouble giving birth. She had known Maggie was close to calving, but she had never had any trouble with any of her other calves. Selah hadn't even bothered to check on Maggie last night. She heard her moo softly from the corral when the three came home, but it wasn't unusual for Maggie to say hello, bovine fashion. So she had gone on to bed.

When Maggie wasn't there to greet her at the gate in the morning, she knew something was wrong. She walked around the side of the barn and could see the cow with her head down, trying to push. "Maggie, are you okay?" Selah asked as she approached. Maggie turned her head toward Selah slightly, her eyes dull with pain. "Oh, girl. We'll help you. We'll help you," Selah said gently. She went around to check on the calf's progress. Selah could see one hoof and a nose sticking out of Maggie's backside. The calf's tongue stuck out and was swollen, as if it were being choked to death. Selah dropped the bucket of feed and ran to the house.

"Dad!" she yelled as she flew through the door. "Dad!"

Jackson emerged from his bedroom, tucking in his best Sunday shirt.

"Maggie's having trouble calving. We're gonna hafta pull the calf!" Selah practically yelled.

Jackson seemed shocked for a moment, but managed to maintain an aura of calm. "Okay, then. Get the pulling chains and a bucket of warm water. I'll be out there as soon as I change clothes."

"Well, hurry!" Selah exclaimed, and ran to the barn to find the chains. They had never used them, but always kept them ready in case Maggie had any trouble. She found them hanging on a nail in the barn, covered with cobwebs. Suddenly she realized she had forgotten the bucket of water, and ran back to the house, the chains jingling in her hands. Jackson met her on his way to the corral.

"Where are you going?" he asked.

"I forgot the bucket," Selah said frantically.

Jackson grabbed her by the arm. "Selah, calm down. You'll be no help to me if you're a panicked wreck."

Selah tried to slow down her breathing. She knew it wasn't wise to get too attached to any animals they raised on their farm, but Maggie was more than just a milk cow to her. She was a pet. Knowing Maggie was in pain made it hard for her to think straight, but he was right. She needed to be calm so she could think clearly, and so she wouldn't make Maggie any more nervous than she already was. "Right," she said, taking a deep breath and exhaling slowly. "Do you think you could clean off the chains while I get the warm water?" Dust and cobwebs could be rinsed off with cold water from the pump, but warm water from the kettle on the stove would help to get Maggie as clean as possible before they pulled the calf. Selah handed the pulling chains to her dad and walked quickly back to the house, praying as she went.

She was about to reach for the door when her mother opened it and handed her a bucket, already filled with warm water. "I'll be praying for Maggie," she said. "If there's nothing else I can do, I really feel like I should go on to church," Asha said.

"Go ahead. And thanks for praying," Selah replied.

Selah went to the corral as fast as she could without spilling any water. Jackson was with Maggie where she had wandered over to the fence farthest from the barn. "Do we need to put her in the chute?" Selah asked.

"Probably so," Jackson said softly. The two gently urged the cow toward the chute in the barn. Maggie offered little resistance, whether because she was distracted by the pain or somehow knew they were only trying to help—Selah didn't know. "Bring me the bucket," Jackson said when Maggie was secured in the chute. He rolled up his sleeves. "You stand at her head and try to keep her calm."

Selah talked softly to the cow as Jackson washed the manure off of Maggie as best he could and rinsed off his hands, as well. "I can't see the other hoof. It might be trapped behind her pelvis," he said. Selah watched nervously as Jackson reached in to find the problem. "Something about the calf doesn't feel right," Jackson commented. "Selah, I'm afraid we might be too late."

"Well, we can still try!" Selah said desperately.

Maggie mooed loudly, and Jackson gritted his teeth as he attempted to get his arm past the calf's head.

"Wait a minute, Dad," Selah said. "Maybe I should do it. I have smaller arms."

"True," Jackson said, and traded places with Selah.

Selah took off her jacket, rolled up her sleeves and rinsed off her hands. She reached in past the calf's head, which was no easy task with Maggie still trying to push. Finally she could feel the rim of the pelvis. "You were right. The leg is trapped," she said.

Jackson looped a chain around the leg that was visible. "Selah, you're going to have to try to push the calf back up the birth canal so you can straighten out the leg that's bent. I put a chain around this leg so we can still have hold of it."

Selah grabbed the trapped leg and tried with all her might to push the calf back with her other hand. "I know we need to push it back in far enough to bring the leg into the right position, but she's pushing so hard I can't do it."

"You'll have to wait between contractions," Jackson suggested. "But I have a feeling I'll need to help you with this. I've helped the Breedons with calving before, and this isn't easy." Jackson talked soothingly to Maggie as he joined Selah. "Lord, we could really use your help here," he said, as he placed his hands on the calf's head to get ready to push it back in. When Maggie stopped having a contraction, he pushed as hard as he could. Selah's arm was going numb as she strained to keep hold of the leg and bring it into the right position. "Have you got it?" Jackson asked, as he continued putting pressure on the calf.

"Just a little longer," she gasped, as Maggie's contractions started up again. She had to work quickly. "Lord, help us!" she prayed. Just then, she was able to bend the leg at the knee and pull the hoof past the pelvis. "Got it!" she said.

"Ok. Hold it tight. We need to put a chain on that leg now," Jackson instructed. The two worked together, straining to pull on the chains during contractions. Finally, with a gush of amniotic fluid, the calf slid out in a crumpled heap.

"It's not breathing," Selah said, and opened the calf's mouth to clear it of any mucus.

"It may not be able to get the fluid out of its lungs," Jackson said, as he grabbed a piece of straw. He inserted the straw in the calf's nostril and wiggled it back and forth.

"What's that supposed to do?" Selah asked, panic creeping back into her voice.

"Sometimes it makes them cough and helps clear their lungs," Jackson explained.

When it was obvious this method wasn't working, Jackson took the chains off of the front legs and put them on the back legs. "Help me pick it up, Selah. There's a chance it's still alive. It could have fluid in its lungs and just not have the strength to get it out. We need to hang it upside down." The two strained to pick up the calf and hung it on the side of the gate. Jackson pressed hard on its sides in an attempt to rid the lungs of any fluid.

Selah had a sinking feeling. Nothing seemed to be working. Maggie was mooing from the chute as they worked, making a tense situation even worse. Finally, Jackson stopped. "Selah, it's dead. It was in the birth canal too long, under too much pressure," he said between Maggie's bellows. He unhooked the chains from the gate, letting the calf fall to the ground. Selah released Maggie from the chute, and the Jersey quickly turned around, sniffing and licking the lifeless form.

Selah sat silently in the muddy straw while Maggie continued to vigorously lick and nudge the unresponsive calf. An incredible sense of guilt settled on her like a lead blanket. "I didn't check on her last night. I was so caught up in the excitement of the prayer meeting—I didn't dream anything bad could happen after we all got filled with the Holy Ghost! How could this happen?"

"Sometimes things just happen," Jackson said.

"Why would she have trouble now? She's never had trouble before. If only I had checked on her. But I was so distracted by what happened last night. I didn't even think of it. If only I had checked on her!" Selah repeated, wishing she could go back and do things over.

"If only. But there's no point in saying that now, unless you enjoy feeling guilty," Jackson observed.

"This day is not turning out at all like I had planned. I wanted to go to church early and pray for the service. Instead, my cow needs help calving, and the calf is dead!" As soon as she said it, a realization began to hit her. It left a cold feeling in the pit of her stomach. "Dad, I don't think this was a coincidence," she said.

Jackson eyed her thoughtfully. "Do you mean you think the devil killed your calf?"

Selah remained silent and looked at him levelly.

"You can't blame everything bad that happens on the devil," he continued.

"No, but it sure seems strange that the only time my cow has trouble calving is on a Saturday night, right after we have a major spiritual breakthrough and we all wanted to get to church early the next morning to pray."

Jackson sat back on his haunches and looked off into the distance, toward the community hall. "It does seem a little odd," he finally said.

"Apparently, Maggie isn't the only one having trouble giving birth," Selah commented.

Jackson watched his daughter to see what she would say. Lately, she had been saying things that surprised him. He had a feeling this would be one of those times.

"You know how Paul said he was travailing in birth again until Christ was formed in the Galatians?"[94] she asked.

"I vaguely remember that," he admitted.

"Well, it's in Galatians somewhere," she mumbled. "I remember studying it out with Miss Genevieve when we were talking about revivals. Paul said he felt like he was going through labor pains because he was praying so hard for the Galatians to become mature in Christ and for them not to be destroyed by false teaching. Dad, the enemy doesn't like it that we're trying to birth a revival in our community! And he will do whatever he thinks will distract us or discourage us from praying for it."

"Well, I guess it's possible," he said slowly.

"Of course it is," Selah insisted. "But what a cheap shot—to target my Maggie and her unborn calf! I guess it shouldn't surprise us that the devil would do something like that. It's not like he plays fair."

"The truth is, he's not playing," Jackson said. "He hates humanity because God loves us. If he can find a way to get to us, he will. Since we are God's children, he can't do anything to us that God won't allow, but sometimes that means the things we love take a beating."

"Just like Job," Selah suggested.

"Good grief. I hope it doesn't get *that* bad," Jackson said.

"Well, you know what I mean, though. The devil told God it was no wonder Job was faithful since he was so blessed. He said it would

---

[94] See Galatians 4:19

be a different story if God allowed some bad things to happen to Job. So God told Satan he could do whatever he wanted to Job except kill him."[95] Selah paused. "You know, that sounds a lot like our little valley. Nothing *really* bad happens very often here. People still get old and die, but we don't have any of the diseases they had in the Old Country. Of course, Miss Genevieve's husband died in an accident, but for the most part, we're protected. I wonder why He decided to keep us so safe? I wonder if bad things did start happening to us all at once, would we curse God, like Job's wife suggested he should? Or would we be like Job? Would we say, '*Though he slay me, yet will I trust in him*'?"[96]

Jackson seemed to mull it over as his eyes rested on the dead calf. "I don't know. But I hope we never have to find out." He glanced at Maggie, who was lowing softly over her calf and licking the still form, waiting for it to move. "Sorry, Maggs. This one didn't make it," he said as he took hold of the chains and began dragging the calf outside.

Father and daughter walked to the barn door, with Maggie bellowing loudly, close at their backs. "Dad, maybe we should leave it out here in the corral for a while, so she can understand that it's dead," Selah suggested.

"I'm not sure how much a cow can actually understand something like that, but I don't see how it would do any harm," Jackson replied. He dragged the calf just outside the door and removed the chains. Maggie stood over it and began licking it again, just as if it were a live calf.

Something about the scene made a lump form in Selah's throat. "It's not fair," she said again, as she swallowed and blinked back the tears that had formed in her eyes. Jackson rested a hand on her shoulder, and Selah looked up at him with fierce determination. "If the devil thinks something like this will keep us from praying for revival, he's dead wrong. It may have kept us from praying for the service this morning, but it just makes me want to fight even harder. I will *not* give up. I've

---

[95] See Job 2:6
[96] See Job 13:15

made up my mind that I *will* do what God wants me to do, no matter what."

Jackson could see the resolve in his daughter's eyes. "I'm with you, Selah," he said quietly.

They went to the house to clean up. It turned out to be too late to make the church service, so Selah set about getting lunch ready. She wanted to go back outside after a while to check on Maggie. The cow had already delivered her afterbirth, so that was no longer a concern, but Selah wanted to be certain to start milking her as soon as possible. It had been a while since they had milk, and there would be an overabundance of it since Maggie's calf had died. Selah could almost feel the soreness in her fingers and forearms as she thought of all the milking she would be doing. She was almost ready to go back to the barn when Asha came through the door.

"Well, I guess the calf pulling went okay," she said brightly, as she sat down a mason jar of pickles on the counter. "Jannica gave me these to give to you. She said she had noticed at the last covered dish dinner that you fancied them."

Selah stared at her blankly. "That was nice of her. But actually, the calf pulling went awful. A leg was back. We got it in the right position, and it came out fine, but it was dead."

Now it was Asha's turn to stare. "Well, if the calf is dead, whose calf is out there sucking on her right now?"

Selah's brow furrowed in confusion and she burst out the kitchen door to the barn lot. There was Maggie, licking the tail of a wobbly little calf as it nursed. Selah stood there a full minute with her mouth dropped open. She looked at the empty place where they had laid the dead calf. Asha and Jackson trotted out the kitchen door to join her.

"Well, I'll be," Jackson said in wonder.

"So you thought it was dead?" Asha asked.

"We didn't think it was dead. It *was* dead. I was sure of it. Maybe it was just *almost* dead," Jackson said, as doubt began to creep in.

"It was not *almost dead*," Selah said firmly. "It wasn't breathing or moving, and we tried everything to revive it. And this isn't a coincidence, either. I think God wants us to know that if we're faithful, hard times will come, but so will the miracles! After all, how can you have a miracle if nothing ever goes wrong?"

Selah suddenly gasped for air as if she had been holding her breath. A smile spread across her face as she threw her head back and laughed toward the sky. "God, you are amazing!" she shouted.

Maggie flinched at the noise and seemed to glare at Selah from under her thick bovine eyelashes. "Sorry, Maggie," Selah said, "but you don't seem to know you have a miracle calf!" Maggie mooed softly and went back to her rhythmic licking of the calf's coat.

35

"So did anyfing happen at churf?" Selah asked, her voice muffled by the sourdough roll she had stuffed in her mouth.

"Selah, how do you expect us to understand you with a loaf of bread in your mouth?" Asha asked, exasperated with Selah's lack of table manners.

"Sorry mom," she said after she had chewed and swallowed. "But I'm just so excited to know if anything unusual happened at church this morning."

Asha ran her finger around the rim of her tin cup. "Well, the message was wonderful. Brother Payton just dived right in and started preaching on Acts, the second chapter."

"And?" Selah asked eagerly.

"It was a good message."

Selah and Jackson waited for Asha to elaborate, but she seemed to be having trouble choosing her words.

"Did the people receive it well?" Jackson finally asked.

"Well, it's hard to say. I was on the edge of my seat, but it seemed like several people were actually nodding off to sleep. Until he got to the part about Garrison."

"What?" Selah and Jackson said at the same time.

"Where is Garrison in the book of Acts?" Jackson asked.

Asha pursed her lips and pushed a green bean around on her plate with her fork. "Well, obviously he isn't. I really don't think Payton had planned to say what he said. He was making a point that before Jesus' followers were filled with the Holy Spirit, they stayed in hiding. They were afraid to come out because they didn't know what would happen to them, since their leader had been crucified. Even after Jesus appeared to them after the resurrection, we don't read about them making any evangelistic efforts. It's only after they received the Holy Spirit that we hear them preaching the Good News that Jesus, who was crucified and had risen again, was the Messiah who had come to save them all from their sins. He talked about how Peter preached a sermon in front of over 3,000 people, even though he had been so terrified before that he denied he even knew Christ. He said that the Holy Spirit had made all the difference. And then he asked what kind of an effort *we* were making to reach a lost generation. He said the only one of us who left the safety and comfort of home to enter a lost and dying world was Garrison, and he didn't leave because he was trying to reach the lost, but because he had an adventurous spirit and wanted more than we had to offer here. 'So, what *are* we offering?' he asked. 'Do we have anything to offer?' And then he slammed his Bible down on the podium and said, 'Brothers and sisters, we have the most precious treasure on earth, and we're guarding it like it's a secret we're trying to keep. We have life, and we're hoarding it to ourselves!' Well, you should have seen the ones who had fallen asleep jump when he slammed down that Bible! And the look on Seth Beardsley's face when he brought up Garrison…. It was definitely a different service. Not what I was expecting at all. And I don't think Payton was expecting it, either. I don't think he really meant to say what he said, because after the service, he was talking to Megan Scoffield to make sure he hadn't said anything about Garrison that would have upset her. I think he was actually as surprised as the rest of us."

"Did anyone talk to him about it after the service?" Selah asked.

"I heard Seth comment to him that it was certainly a different kind of message. And Riley Rosales went up to him, laughing so hard I could barely understand what he was saying. But he was congratulating Payton on taking everyone by surprise and even waking up Mrs. Cornwright," Asha explained.

"Well, that *did* take some doing," Jackson chuckled.

"So no one took him seriously?" Selah asked.

"I just don't think people knew *what* to think," Asha said.

Selah looked down at her plate. "I wish we had been there to pray beforehand," she commented. "I can't believe he said that about hoarding the treasure to ourselves. That's not exactly something people want to hear."

"I know," Asha said. "But it's true. That's what it seems like we're doing."

"That's how Miss Genevieve felt," Selah said.

"But it kind of sounds like he came across as condemning, or trying to make people feel guilty about it," Jackson remarked.

"The way I see it, if they feel funny about it, it wasn't because of a guilt trip. It's the convicting power of the Holy Spirit. I'm glad he said what he did," Asha told them.

"I just hope it wasn't too soon," Jackson said, his fork see-sawing over a piece of venison roast.

"We need to pray about this, that people will receive the message," Selah said. "And we need to pray that Payton is sensitive to the leading of the Holy Spirit."

"And that he uses wisdom in what he says and when he says it," Jackson added. Selah looked at her father thoughtfully, and then out the window. She had a feeling that whether or not it seemed wise, it may have been exactly what the Holy Spirit had wanted Payton to say.

She had her chance later that afternoon to ask Brother Payton how he felt about it. She was sitting on the stump by the smokehouse, reading over Miss Genevieve's journal, when she saw Payton walking along the fence around their front yard. He hadn't seen her, and had slowed down as he looked at their house. He hesitated, his mouth twisted into a worried frown, and started walking, and then hesitated again. "Hi, Brother Payton!" Selah called from her perch on the stump.

Payton looked around and finally saw her. "Well, hello! I was just coming to see how Maggie was doing. But I didn't want to interrupt anyone's Sunday afternoon napping," he said.

"So that's what you were doing," Selah said. "You reminded me of a deer that wants a persimmon but is almost sure someone is hiding in the bushes with a bow."

"I suppose that person hiding in the bushes would be you," Payton said. He was well aware of Selah's success as a hunter. Her jerky and summer sausage were well-loved commodities in the valley. Selah had used them often in the valley's bartering system.

"Mom and Dad may be napping, but I can come show you how Maggie and Miracle are doing," Selah said.

"Miracle?"

"Just wait 'til you hear the story, and I think you'll agree," she said, and related to him the events of the morning as she took him to the barn lot to visit the calf.

"It's a heifer calf. And I'm glad, because that way, we can keep her. Someday, she'll be Maggie's replacement," Selah said.

"That's the best calf-pulling story I've ever heard," Payton said. "Isn't it incredible how God cares about the things we care about?"

"And how he can use them to teach us things," Selah added.

"Indeed."

"So, speaking of teaching, I really hated missing your sermon this morning."

Payton grimaced and kept his eyes on the calf as it stumbled between Maggie's legs. "I'm afraid it wasn't very well received," he finally said. "It could have gone better. My zeal ran roughshod over my wisdom. There were some things I shouldn't have said, and I think I made some people uncomfortable."

"Miss Genevieve said that if you always feed a baby milk, he won't ever develop a taste for meat," Selah commented.

"I'm not sure this was meat. It may have been just a piece of gristle. The minute I said it, I wished I hadn't."

"The part about Garrison?"

"So Asha told you about it, eh?" Payton grimaced again and looked over at her. "The people here are good people, Selah. I'm not certain they deserved what I said."

"They deserve the chance to wake up out of their sleep. They deserve for someone to wake them up. They don't even know they're asleep! You're the shepherd! You have to watch out for them," Selah insisted.

"Yes, but I could have gone about it differently. I could have been gentle and more subtle."

"You've been being gentle and subtle for the past several weeks. You've been planting seeds of revival every time you preach. And I am sure some of those seeds have taken root. But have you ever heard about the seeds of a Giant Sequoia?" Selah asked.

"Is this a Genevieve story?" Payton asked, a smile playing on his lips.

"Yep." Selah loved remembering the way her old friend told stories. Apparently, storytelling was in Genevieve's blood, because this story was second hand, from her father. Selah began the tale. "Miss Genevieve's dad got to visit one of the Giant Sequoia forests in Central California. While he was there, he decided he wanted to bring home a seed cone from the one of the largest trees in the world. He figured it would be the most humongous cone you could imagine. But it wasn't. It was only about the size of a chicken egg!

"As he was walking the trails, he was surprised by the amount of fire damage he saw. Many of the trees had dark black blotches and holes that looked as if they had been burned into their thick bark. When he stopped at the Ranger Station in the park, he said to one of the rangers that it looked as if there had been some fires there in the past. The ranger told him, 'Yes. And it's a good thing. You see that cone you're holding there–the fire is what causes them to open up.' The heat from the fire was what dried out the cones and enabled them to open up and release their seeds so they could germinate. Without the fire, there would be no new life." She paused and looked intently at Payton. "No one likes getting burned. But sometimes it takes a little fire for new growth to come."

Payton stared at her as if he were seeing her for the first time.

"Don't be discouraged because you think you may have made a mistake in how you planted a seed," Selah continued. "God can use even our mistakes. But I don't think it was a mistake. I think it was orchestrated. All those little seeds you've been planting...who knows how big they'll grow to be? But we may never know if they aren't allowed to open up in the fire."

Payton still just stared at her, at a loss for words.

"Don't be too impressed," Selah said with a wistful smile. "I learned all that from Miss Genevieve."

"She had a good pupil," Payton said. "I wish she could have heard you tell that."

"Me too," Selah agreed. A sudden wave of sadness swept over her. They came less frequently now, but still left her longing for her friend. "I really miss her. I wish she could have heard your sermons about the Holy Spirit. She would have been so excited."

"Yes, I believe she would have been. But more importantly, she would have prayed for their effectiveness in the lives of those listening. She would have prayed for the anointing to be on me as I preach," Payton said solemnly.

"That's what we're all here for now—Mom and Dad and Sister Addy and you and I, and all who want to see people saved and set free," Selah said.

Payton's eyes sparked as he looked at Selah. "You're right. Miss Genevieve isn't with us anymore, but she left a mantle behind, just like Elijah did when God took him up into the whirlwind. Elisha was there to pick up Elijah's mantle and continue his ministry.[97] Who will pick up where Miss Genevieve left off?"

As he said the words, something leapt inside of Selah. She swallowed hard and her eyes watered. She blinked and looked away.

---

[97] See 2 Kings 2:1-14

"I believe everyone should have a ministry of prayer," Payton continued. "But Genevieve's ministry was even more than that, as vital as that is. She was an intercessor. She was a teacher. And at heart, if she had been given the chance, I think she would have been a missionary. Not everyone is called to do even one of those things. But she was called to do all of them. And I think she did all of them to the best of her ability, with all of her heart."

Selah was surprised to feel tears rolling down her cheeks. She still missed Genevieve. But they weren't tears of sadness or loss. A strange kind of longing was building in her spirit. She kept her face pointed to the ridge top across the valley to hide her emotions.

"I played a huge part in keeping her from fulfilling all of her calling–not just because of recent events, but from all those years of drilling into my little flock that we need to stay in the boundaries and protect our own from the evil influence of the Old Country. Someday I'm afraid I will have to answer for that," Payton said somberly. He put his hand on Selah's shoulder. "I've kept you long enough. I need to go back and get ready for the evening service. Seth's preaching tonight. I thought I might get there early to pray."

Selah rubbed her eyes and turned to smile at him. "That's a good idea," she said. "I think I'll ask Mom and Dad if they want to go early, too."

Payton studied her for a moment, noticing the redness in her eyes. "The more, the merrier," he said. "Genevieve would have liked that," he added, squeezing her shoulder.

"Yes. She would have," Selah said, her eyes drawn back to the ridge top. It wasn't until the sound of Payton's footsteps faded into silence that she realized she was staring in the direction Garrison had taken when he left almost eight months ago.

36

WHEN Selah and her parents arrived at the community hall an hour before the service started, Payton was already there, lying on the floor behind one of the altars at the front. His muffled voice could be heard as he wept and prayed for the lives of the people in the congregation.

Selah and her family found their own individual places to pray in various pews. Soon the room was filled with the soft sound of people pleading in earnest prayer. Every once in a while, a voice would be raised in intense intercession when the Holy Spirit moved on one of the group.

A half hour later, Selah heard the door open as someone entered the building. There was a pause before the door closed, and Selah could imagine someone standing at the entrance, wondering what was going on. Then the footsteps continued. They stopped at the pew she was occupying, and she could feel someone looking at her. When she slowly looked up, her face streaked with tears, she saw Seth Beardsley looking sternly down at her. "Did someone call a prayer meeting?" he whispered. "No one told me anything about it."

Selah regarded him carefully. He seemed on edge, even suspicious. She tried to choose her words with care. "Payton told me this afternoon that he was going to come early to pray. I thought it sounded like a good idea, so we all came early."

"You mean *Brother* Payton?" Seth said quickly.

"Ye-yes," she stammered. "I meant Brother Payton." Selah always tried to remember to refer to those in authority over her with respect, but since her friendship with the Hambys had grown so much recently, she sometimes slipped up and forgot.

"Your parents are taking suggestions from *you* now? It must feel good to have regained your integrity," Seth said, his words laced with a hint of sarcasm.

Selah swallowed and looked at him silently. She had tried so hard not to offend. What could she have said differently? She opened her mouth to try to smooth things over, but Seth had faced the front of the building and was looking in the direction of the prostrate figure behind the altar. His eyes narrowed as he walked toward the front. Selah saw him glance in the direction of her parents as he passed the pews where they were praying, but he didn't stop walking until he stood by the altar where Payton lay. Selah stretched her neck up above the back of the pew behind her to see what would happen. What was he doing, just standing there? Payton was so lost in intercession that he didn't even seem to notice the silent figure. Finally, Seth walked to the other altar, a mere five feet away, and began praying. Loudly.

"Our Heavenly Father, we thank You that we can come to You in prayer. We thank You for placing people in authority over us who watch over our souls. I thank You that Brother Payton is one of those people You have designated to watch over us. I pray You will continue to guide him and protect him from any influence of the Evil One." There was a pause as Seth shifted his weight on his knees, as one who was seemingly uncomfortable and unaccustomed with that position. After a few moments, he continued. "Please be with our young people, Lord. Help them to understand that, as their elders, we are the ones who make decisions for this community, and that we are making them for the safety of everyone within the boundaries of this valley. Help them to go through the proper channels when approaching those in authority over them with new ideas. We trust You, Lord. We stand firm in our commitment to obey the directive You gave us when we left the sinful world behind. As an elder, I have pledged to protect this community and guide them in the light You have given us. Thank You, Father. Amen." When his prayer was ended, Seth got up briskly and straightened his suit coat, turning toward the back of the building to smile grimly in Selah's direction. She ducked quickly behind the pew again, her hands shaking slightly. Payton had grown silent during Seth's monologue. Selah stared at the polished wood of the pew where she knelt. She could hear Seth's footsteps approaching again, and she closed her eyes, hoping he would keep walking when he neared her. But he didn't. He stopped at the end of her pew. Selah opened one of her eyes and looked up at him timidly.

"Prayer meeting's over, Selah," Seth announced, loudly enough for the others to hear. "Soon, members of this congregation will arrive, and I don't want them to feel uncomfortable because they were left out of a private meeting."

Selah could hear Payton stirring at the front of the church. He stood up slowly and made his way to the back, stopping a few feet away from Seth. Seth made no motion to look at him. Rather, he kept his eyes fastened on Selah. Her blood ran cold.

"This wasn't intended to be a private meeting, Brother Seth. As you know, everyone is always welcome to pray before service," Payton said amiably.

"I understand why you made a special trip to visit Selah, since she wasn't in church this morning," at this point, Seth glared at Selah before continuing. "But if you're going to invite someone to prayer meeting, shouldn't the elders be the first on the list? Unless, of course, it wasn't your idea in the first place."

The back door suddenly opened, and Mrs. Cornwright toddled into the building. "Good evening, everyone!" she said sweetly, oblivious to the drama being played out in the back pew.

Seth's eyes softened and he turned quickly to greet her. "Good evening, Sister Cornwright," he said in his most congenial voice. "And how are you? Did you have a restful afternoon?"

Selah stared silently at Payton as Mrs. Cornwright exchanged pleasantries with Seth. Payton patted her on the shoulder. "I'll speak to him privately later," he said reassuringly. "He just misunderstood what was happening here."

Selah nodded and stood up. She looked around to find her parents, who had already gotten up and sat down together in their customary place. She had a feeling Seth had done more than just misunderstand the nature of the prayer meeting. When he had begun praying, the whole mood of the room had shifted. They had been cultivating a spark before he arrived, fanning an ember to produce a flame. When Seth came in, it was as if he brought with him a bucket of ice water. It reminded her of the soggy logs Genevieve had been trying to get to burn the night before she had her stroke. "Hmmpf," Selah grunted in surprise at the thought. Seth was a soggy log. Not only that, he was a bucket of water used to douse the flames of revival. But it wasn't him, she realized, as the Spirit of God reminded her that he was one of those she had been praying for to receive the baptism of the Holy Ghost. He was her brother. She was not his judge. But there was a spirit behind his actions and his attitude, and it was not the Holy Spirit. "This is not acceptable," she said under her breath. "I will not just allow you to come in here and squelch a revival. When the enemy comes in like a flood, the Spirit of the Lord will lift up a standard against him.[98]"

"What did you say? I couldn't hear you," Jackson said.

"It's nothing, Dad. I wasn't talking to you. I'm just putting someone in his place," she explained.

"You mean Seth?" he asked.

"No. The devil," Selah replied. She continued to quietly quote scripture until the service began.

Jackson looked around furtively to see if anyone noticed Selah mumbling to herself, until Asha finally elbowed him. "I don't know what you two were talking about, or why you're looking around like a raccoon caught in the hen house, but stop fidgeting. You're driving me nuts. I'm still trying to pray, no matter what that bully just said."

---

[98] See Isaiah 59:19

"Asha!" Jackson exclaimed in a whisper.

"Well, that's what he is. A bully. He's acting just like Payton did a few months ago. And the very notion that holding a prayer meeting is a *new* idea to be guarded against! What's wrong with these people?"

"Mom," Selah said suddenly, interrupting her own prayers. "He's scared, just like Payton was. And he probably thought we were trying to go around him—to do something without him being a part of it. But it's more than that. We have to pray against the spirit that is working to undermine Payton's ministry and the revival we are praying for. Miss Genevieve had a name for it. She called it a Jezebel spirit."

"Because of how Jezebel worked against the ministry of Elijah?" Asha asked. "That makes sense."

More people were filtering into the building. Seth made a point to greet every one of them, giving them a firm handshake and a carefully cultivated smile. When it was time for the service to start, the song leader, Ethel Rosales, made her way to the front and nimbly stepped up to the platform, eager to sing. She was a tiny woman, but her size belied her voice. She could belt out a hymn like a rooster crowing. It wasn't always pretty, but it was on tune, and it was always from the heart.

Selah stood up and sang the hymns along with everyone else, but it was difficult to ignore the feeling of heaviness that had settled on her earlier. She continued to pray silently throughout the service. When Seth took the platform to preach, she wondered if he would say anything about what had happened before the service. But nothing was said about it. His sermon was about Joseph and his experience of being sold into slavery and thrown into a dungeon. "It seemed like everything was going wrong, but it was God's will all along," Seth said. He looked around the room until his eyes rested on Selah. "Sometimes we feel like we are trapped, and the status quo simply can't be God's will. But sometimes that is exactly what we need, because God is trying to teach us something. He is trying to mature us so that we can be useful in His kingdom. Joseph made a lot of mistakes starting out. He was full of himself. That's what got him thrown into a pit by his brothers. He was spouting off things about his elders that he should have just kept to himself. He didn't show a lot of wisdom; but he learned it the hard way, when he ended up in the pit, and later, in the dungeon in Egypt. When he learned to submit to the discipline of the Lord, things changed for him. We would do well to learn from his mistakes." He stopped and continued to look at Selah. Selah stared evenly back at him.

When the service was over, Selah intended to slip quietly out and avoid him, but Seth stepped quickly in front of her before she could walk out the door. "Selah, I hope you found the message to be instructive," he said with all the warmth of a cottonmouth.

Selah stared back at him, and was surprised when a scripture came suddenly to her mind. It was from 2 Corinthians 4:2. "...not walking in craftiness nor handling the word of God deceitfully, but by manifestation of the truth commending ourselves to every man's conscience in the sight of God."[99] She gasped inadvertently as she remembered it, causing Seth to take a step backward. He smiled quickly, misinterpreting the look on her face as a reaction to what he had just said.

"Don't be surprised when the Word of God hits its mark," he continued. "It is here for our instruction and reproof. 'All scripture is given by inspiration of God, and *is* profitable for doctrine, for reproof, for correction, for instruction in righteousness....'[100] 2 Timothy 3:16," he quoted.

Selah couldn't believe the timeliness of the scripture that the Holy Spirit had brought to her mind a moment earlier. Seth was handling the Word of God deceitfully, bending and distorting its meaning to his own devices.

"It certainly is instructive," she said, "and we must remember also how those who are in the position of teaching it will be judged more strictly and held accountable for what they teach."[101] The smile faded from Seth's face as she continued. "It's true that Joseph needed to learn wisdom in how and when he shared his revelations. But the thing that

---

[99] See 2 Corinthians 4:2 NKJV
[100] 2 Timothy 3:16 NKJV
[101] See James 3:1

stands out most to me about the story of Joseph is how God's servants are often misunderstood, but if they will stay faithful and trust the Lord in every circumstance, He will use them. It's like Joseph said to his brothers, 'But as for you, you meant evil against me; *but* God meant it for good, in order to bring it about as *it is* this day, to save many people alive.'[102] Thank you for bringing us the Word, Brother Seth." She nodded her farewell, and stepped out the door into the cool night air.

---

[102] Genesis 50:20 NKJV

37

Selah stood very still. She didn't have any idea where she was, or how she had arrived there. It was unlike any place she had ever seen, but she had heard descriptions of such places from the old timers. Gray walls surrounded her on every side, but when she looked up, she could see the sky. The ground she was standing on was covered by the same, smooth, gray surface that comprised the walls. It was strange not to see grass or trees. Well, she mused, maybe the gnarled black skeleton over to one side of the enclosure used to be a tree, but its life had long since ebbed away. It was protruding out of one of a few square areas on the walking surface which were not covered over by the gray stone. Apparently, these squares of dirt used to support vegetative life. Selah looked up at the sky again. It seemed the wrong color somehow, as if it needed washing.

Courtyard. That was the name for this place. An area created to provide beauty and relaxation—a respite from the pressures of the work that went on behind the great gray walls. Selah tried to imagine what it looked like when it was first completed. Did anyone still come here to relax? The stress of work might seem more attractive after just five minutes spent in this place.

A few tables had been set up to one side of the area. A short, somewhat familiar looking woman who appeared to be in her thirties was standing by one of the tables. She held in her arms a bundle of pages sandwiched between two thick pieces of plastic and held together by three metal rings. The makeshift book was precious to her, Selah thought, because she clutched it closely to her as she looked across the courtyard, anticipating…what? A friend? A coworker?

A door in the gray wall across from the tables opened, and a group of people appeared. They weren't like any other people she had ever seen. Physically, they were the same, but something was different about them. Something fundamental. Selah looked again at the short woman. She was looking at the people with a careful hope and an intensity of compassion that spilled over her calm exterior. This lady could see it, too—the difference Selah saw. Selah looked again at the group, which had begun to disperse about the courtyard. The difference was an emptiness. The difference was something they didn't have. Selah heard a slight shuffle and turned to see the lady placing the book on the table. This woman looked as if she wanted so badly to talk to the people, but for some reason, she didn't. Her lips almost formed the shape of words as she watched them, but then she shut her mouth and quietly backed away from the table and the book.

Even though she never made eye contact with Selah, Selah knew the book was meant for her. She walked over to it and looked through the pages. It was a study of these people—how they lived, their interests, their work, their pastimes, their families, their world. By looking at the book, Selah immediately felt their emotions, and was struck again by the emptiness she felt. Each of the people was trying to fill this void with everything from relationships to mind-altering drugs to all different forms of entertainment and consumerism. Nothing really worked, even though some of them thought it did at the time. What was missing? What were they craving that drove them to work so hard to make up for the loss?

A burly man with a scraggly beard lumbered over to the table. "Hey, there. Are you the new transfer?" His smile seemed genuine. "My name's Jeff." Jeff held out his hand in a gesture similar to a handshake, but as Selah did the same, he dropped his hand as soon as hers came within a few inches of his. He looked confused. "I'm sorry. I didn't get that," he said, and swept his hand up to hers again. She reached for his hand, and once again he dropped it before she could make contact. "That's odd," he said. "I'm not getting anything from you. Where did you say you transferred from? Maybe they're not compatible."

But Selah was no longer paying attention to the strange way they shook hands in this place. Her eyes were riveted to a space on Jeff's torso that appeared to be a window. It was a glass box contained in his body, and inside was a candle on an old, dusty candlestick. Cobwebs were spun carelessly from the wick to the side of the box. The candle had never been lit. Selah looked up into Jeff's eyes to find him looking at her.

"What's wrong?"

"You—you have a candle in your stomach," Selah said, immediately regretting it.

"Of course. Everybody does."

Selah looked around. Suddenly, upon closer observation, she could see that all the people in the courtyard had the glass boxes with the candles in their midsections. None of their candles were lit.

"I don't have a candle. Or a glass box."

Jeff looked at her and laughed. "Yes you do. Everyone has a candle and glass box to keep it in."

"No, really! I'll prove it to you!" Selah said, lifting up her shirt slightly. As she did, Jeff's eyes filled with amazement and his face took on a strange glow.

"Hey, Luis! Marta! Hey, Akeem! Guys, come here!" he called to the others. A group of people began to form around Selah. Their eyes filled with wonder; and their faces, too, seemed to shine like Jeff's.

"Is it so unusual that I don't have a candle in a box? Where I come from, no one does," Selah said defensively.

"I don't believe a word you say," said one of the women.

"Why not?" asked Selah.

"You don't even know what you have," she said. "Well, look! Look at your window!"

"I don't have a window," Selah started to say, but stopped short as she looked at her stomach. There, indeed, was a glass box in her midsection, too. With a candle. But hers was lit. The glow on the faces of the onlookers wasn't originating from them. It was a reflection of the light of her candle, which was growing in brightness so quickly that it began to cast large shadows from the people against the great, gray walls. The shadows grew in height as the candle grew in brightness.

"Cover it up! You're hurting our eyes!" an elderly man cried.

"Get rid of it! Snuff it out!" a woman screeched.

Chants of "Cover it up! Blow it out!" began to fill the courtyard. The light grew brighter until her eyes began to hurt. Maybe it would be better to cover it up. But Selah knew that she could never allow it.

She blinked and could see leaves moving back and forth in the light. The light was framed like a picture, and the leaves moved like dancers in the breeze.

Selah blinked again. The frame was the frame of her window, and the leaves were the bunchy blossoms of the overgrown redbud tree outside her bedroom. She had overslept, and the sunlight was pouring through her window and spilling across her face.

She slid out of bed, put on her clothes, and made her way to the kitchen. Asha looked up from her Bible readings at the kitchen table. "Well, good morning!" she said warmly, a slightly amused smile on her face. "Or should I say, good afternoon?"

Selah's eyes grew round in horror. "It can't be *that* late!"

"No, of course not, silly," Asha laughed. "But I don't think I've ever seen you sleep that late."

"I had a weird dream," Selah reported. She ducked her head around the corner to see the hall clock. It was only 8 a.m., but it was still three hours later than she usually slept. "I can't believe I slept so late."

"I think your father took pity on Maggie and already fed her."

"But I was going to milk her," Selah said crossly. Even though the milk would have colostrum for a few days, there was no way the little calf could keep up with the amount of milk that Maggie produced, and it was easier to milk when Maggie was occupied with her grain.

"She can always have a little more," Asha suggested.

Selah grabbed a cold biscuit from the storage bin by the counter and headed out the door.

"Bye?" Asha said tentatively.

"Bye," Selah muttered. She felt groggy and unfocused after sleeping in so late, and the dream was at the forefront of her mind. She was beginning to recognize when a dream was not just a dream. She went over it again in her mind as she walked to the barn lot. The familiar lady whom she had never seen before—who was she? The candle analogy

316

seemed pretty obvious to her, from a spiritual perspective. The people couldn't find anything to fill the void in their lives because they didn't know about Jesus. They all had a candle, but it wasn't lit. Selah's candle was lit because she *did* know Jesus. It reminded her of the first chapter of John, verses 4 and 5. "In him was life, and the life was the light of men. The light shines in the darkness, and the darkness has not overcome it."[103] She quoted the verses as she got a can of grain and rattled it to bring Maggie to the barn. Maggie walked hurriedly to the stanchion, her huge udder swaying with each step. Miracle trotted beside her and lost her balance as she kicked up her back legs in play. "You're still too wobbly to be good at being frisky," Selah laughed. She set to milking. Miracle seemed intent on getting in her way and nearly knocked over the bucket. Selah would normally have enjoyed her playful antics, except for the part about nearly spilling the milk, but she was having a hard time just thinking. Then she realized what was wrong. She hadn't even had time to pray or read her Bible. No wonder she could barely think straight. Going for eight or more hours while she slept without talking to the Lord or reading His Word was similar to going that long without food. Her spiritual stomach was empty, and she was ready for *spiritual* food.

Although she may not have been talking to the Lord during that time, she was certain that He had been talking to *her*. The dream meant something; and while she understood some of the symbolism behind the imagery, some of it was a mystery. She had never seen that place before, and usually the elements of a dream had some basis in the reality of the waking world. Maybe she had just pieced it together from things Miss Genevieve had said. Suddenly she stopped milking. Could the woman in the dream have been a younger version of Miss Genevieve? She was awakened from her pondering over the matter by Maggie's tail slapping her in the face. "Hey!" Selah grouched, and tugged on the tail. "I'll tie your tail to your leg if you don't watch it." Maggie stomped and nearly

---

[103] John 1:4-5 RSV

kicked over the bucket. "You old hide! Hold still. We're almost done," Selah admonished her. She finished the job and grabbed the bucket just before Miracle could buck into it. "You sure are spunkier than you were yesterday," Selah said to the calf, sticking out her tongue and rolling her eyes back in her head to mimic Miracle when she was stuck in the birth canal.

"Charming," said Jackson as he came through the barn door. Selah grinned in spite of herself and started for the house. She had heard that one of the Breedons' more cantankerous cows had rejected her calf after it had to be pulled. Maybe they could use some of the milk. But she wasn't going anywhere else until she sat down and at least read a little of her Bible. Asha was done reading, but she had left the Bible open on the table. Selah put down the milk and sat down to see what her mother had been studying. The words of Mark 4:21 jumped out at her. *"Is a lamp brought to be put under a basket or under a bed? Is it not to be set on a lampstand? For there is nothing hidden which will not be revealed, nor has anything been kept secret but that it should come to light."*[104] Immediately Selah thought of her candle in the dream. It had been covered up so that she didn't even know she had a candle, much less a candle that was lit and burned so brightly it almost hurt one's eyes to look at the flame. It had been hidden from everyone, including herself. What was the benefit of lighting a candle if you covered up the light? That was what the gospel of Mark was saying. No one does that. If you light a candle, you put it out in the open so it can be useful. You share the light. A lump had formed in Selah's throat. Once again, she was surprised to find her eyes filled with tears. There was a strange feeling in her spirit, an aching in her heart as she stared at the page.

"Selah, are you okay?" Asha said from the kitchen doorway.

Selah could only nod and wipe away the tears. "I really don't know why I'm crying, Mom," she said. "I have this feeling that…I need to do something, but I'm not exactly sure what it is I'm supposed to do."

"Does this have anything to do with the dream you had?" Asha asked.

---

[104] See Mark 4:21-22 NKJV

"I think so. This scripture you had been reading about letting your light shine, it goes right along with it," Selah said, and told her the dream.

Asha frowned thoughtfully. "I think you're right. That isn't just a dream. Maybe the Lord is trying to tell us we need to be interceding for the lost."

"Maybe. But we always need to be doing that. There's a sense of urgency about this dream. It feels like we're up against some sort of deadline."

"We *are*," Asha replied. "There is a deadline for the world. Someday Jesus will come back. We are living in the last days, and soon, time will be up. But there is also the deadline each one of us has. Every one has a last day. There is a deadline for every soul. What are we doing about it?"

Selah's heart felt like a newly formed sinkhole, caving in little by little. She got up from the table and picked up the milk pail. "I'm going to take this milk to the Breedons for their bum calf," she said, and trudged out the door, tears blurring her eyes. What was happening to her? She kept walking, the urgency growing with every step. Since she didn't know how to pray for something she didn't understand, she asked for the help of the Holy Spirit as she prayed for this need—whatever it was. By the time she reached the Breedon place, she had regained her composure. They were glad for the milk, as it was dicey business milking their spooky cow, even in the chute. Jannica had come up with a few more baby names. Selah listened politely. All she could think about was the dream. She left as soon as tact allowed and took a roundabout way home. As she was passing by the Hamby house, she saw the front door open. Seth Beardsley and the other elders on the board all stepped out onto the porch.

Seth stopped short when he saw her, causing Riley Rosales, who had been following close behind, to bump into him. "Morning, Selah," Seth said, and resumed walking down the steps.

Selah thought back on all the good times she had spent at the Beardsley place, playing basketball with his daughters and sons and the other neighborhood children. It was hard not to treat him differently now, but she made the decision she was going to think of the kindly Seth she knew as a girl instead of the grim-natured one who was watching her now.

"Good morning, Brother Beardsley," she said as warmly as she could manage.

"What's in the pail?" he asked.

"Oh, I took some milk over to the Breedons for their bottle calf."

"This isn't exactly what I would call a direct route from the Breedon place to your house," Seth said, a suspicious edge to his voice.

Selah laughed in an attempt at lightheartedness. "No, I suppose it isn't. But I had something on my mind and I wanted some time to think about it."

"Thinking about calling another prayer meeting?"

Selah was dumbfounded. She stood there, rotating the empty pail back and forth as it hung from her fingers. If she said, "No," then she was indicating she had called the prayer meeting at church yesterday. If she tried to explain herself, Seth might think she was lying. Her heart began to beat faster. Seth was supposed to be her brother. Why did she feel like a rat caught in a trap? Riley and the other elders watched rather sheepishly from the porch. Selah had the feeling that they would rather not be there.

It was Seth who finally broke the silence. "There won't be any more unauthorized prayer meetings. From now on, you won't be making any more clandestine visits to the Hamby house, and Brother Hamby won't be making his rounds, either."

"His rounds?" Selah found her voice.

"That's right. Brother Payton is going to take a much-needed break. A sabbatical, of sorts. He needs time to do a little soul searching…to reflect on the principles upon which this community was founded."

This seemed so familiar—the suspicion, the fear, the grappling for control. It was like a window into the events of last summer right after Garrison had left. The circumstances were different, but the emotions were the same.

"He can't have any visitors?" Selah asked.

"He doesn't want any visitors," Seth said coldly.

"I don't understand," Selah said, tension mounting in her voice.

"Well, see for yourself. I won't keep you," Seth said, and motioned for her to go to the front door.

Selah stared at him, and then set down the pail on the side of the road. She walked self-consciously across the yard to the porch with Seth and the other elders watching her all the way. Riley smiled apologetically as she passed him, his prominent Adam's apple bobbing up and down as he swallowed nervously. He was so kind-hearted and jovial, Selah was certain he didn't have anything to do with this situation. Maybe none of the other elders did either. She hesitated at the door and glanced back at Seth.

"Go ahead. Don't let me stop you," he said, motioning to the door again.

Selah knocked on the door. There was silence at first, and then Addy opened the door. "Oh!" she said as she saw Selah with the elders. Selah wondered if she had been watching at the window, waiting for them to leave. "Well, hello," she said, her voice a little shaky.

"Hi," Selah said. Addy looked miserable, like she could break down at any moment. "Is Brother Hamby available?"

"No, I'm afraid he isn't," Addy said, her eyes fastened on the elders.

"Maybe I could stop by another time?" Selah ventured.

Addy's gaze shifted to Selah. "Well, he's really involved in his studies and will be for some time. How about if we plan to see you when he's finished?"

"Do you have any idea when that will be?" Selah pressed her. She could feel Seth staring a hole in her back.

"Oh, not 'til jerky-making time, at least," Addy said, being careful to maintain eye-contact with Selah.

That was a strange response. Selah could feel an undercurrent in the conversation. There was so much more going on here than the words on the surface. "You mean this fall?"

"Well, there's no set date. I can't remember exactly when it was you said you were going to make jerky. But I would imagine he would be ready for visitors around that time," Addy said.

And then Selah remembered. She was going to show Addy how to make jerky from their stringy cow. But everyone on the porch would think Addy was talking about Selah making venison jerky from the deer she would get this fall. She wondered if Payton would approve of Addy's rather underhanded method of calling a meeting. "Ok, then. I guess I'll see you at jerky-making time," Selah said, and turned to go. "Tell Brother Hamby I said hello," she said.

Addy nodded and started to pull the door closed.

"Thank you, again, Sister Adelaide," Seth said from the bottom of the porch steps.

Addy smiled weakly and looked down as she shut the door. It was almost more than Selah could stand. She clenched her teeth to keep from saying anything that would only make matters worse and turned to go down the steps, avoiding eye contact with anyone. The elders followed close behind. She felt as if she were being escorted off the property. She started down the road at a quickened pace when Seth called out her name. Selah tried not to glare as she turned around.

"You forgot your bucket," he said, holding out the milk pail. "Wouldn't want you to have to come back for it later," he added meaningfully.

Selah retraced her steps and took the bucket. "Thank you," she said coldly, and turned down the road toward home. How did Seth manage to sway all the other members of the board? Payton was the senior elder. Shouldn't he have the final say? Miss Genevieve said things were a little different when they had an actual pastor. For some reason, after Raymond Coffelt passed away, the congregation hadn't elected a new pastor. They had opted instead to have a senior elder. It had seemed to work well up until now.

Selah was so lost in thought that she almost passed the front gate of her yard. She went quickly into the house where Asha was setting lunch on the table. "We had begun to think you had a dinner invitation," Asha said lightly, but the look on Selah's face stopped her short. "What happened?" she asked.

Selah plopped down in the chair and set the milk pail on the floor with a metallic clatter. "You aren't going to believe this. I was just passing by the Hamby's house when I saw Seth and the other elders leaving. Seth told me there wouldn't be any more prayer meetings. I think they told Payton he wasn't allowed to see anyone."

"What?" Asha exclaimed. "How does he think he can do that?"

"That's what I want to know."

"What do you want to know?" Jackson asked as he came into the kitchen.

"Can the members of the board dictate what a senior elder can and cannot do? Can they force him to take a leave of absence from the pulpit, and keep him from visiting the general population?" Selah sputtered. "Because I think that's what just happened to Payton Hamby."

Jackson looked momentarily shocked, and he rubbed his beard like he usually did when he was perplexed. "Traditionally, the board has always served in an advisory capacity to the pastor. But I guess since Payton isn't an actual pastor, if a majority of the board decided he should step down, he could be made to do that. What did Payton have to say about their decision?"

"I wouldn't know. I wasn't allowed to see him. But Seth said that Payton didn't *want* to see anybody. He even made me go knock on the front door to prove it."

"Well?" Asha prodded.

"Addy came to the door. She looked scared, but she managed to give me a secret message. She said Payton probably wouldn't be able to visit anyone until he finished his studies—which would be around the time I made jerky," Selah said with a sly smile.

"Well, fall is a long time awa—Oh!" Asha exclaimed, as she caught on to the plan. "The stringy cow. Your original plans were to start on her this week, right?"

"Yup. Addy told me earlier that she would have the meat marinating in the spices I suggested, and we could start on it Tuesday."

"That's tomorrow," Jackson said suddenly.

"Yes. I'll go before dawn so no one will see me." She paused. "It seems strange having to sneak around like this. I always thought that if you weren't doing anything wrong, you didn't have to hide anything. It goes against everything I've been taught to circumvent the instructions of an elder."

"It didn't stop Paul," Jackson observed. "When he changed from Christian persecutor to Christian preacher, he was disobeying the in- structions of the religious leaders in power. He even hid from them and escaped their detection by being lowered in a basket down the Damas- cus city walls."

"Yeah, but the religious leaders of his day were against the preaching of Christ," Selah said.

"Yes, indeed," Jackson said. "Funny how history repeats itself."

Selah looked at her father and swallowed hard. Someday, if they didn't repent, Seth and the other elders would have to answer for their actions. "I'm sure they think they're doing the right thing. There's this scripture in Proverbs that always seemed kind of harsh to me, but it seems to fit what's happening right now. 'There is a way which seems right to a man, but its end is the way to death.'[105] And Proverbs 3:5 warns us to not to depend on our own understanding, but to search out what the Lord would have us to do. I don't think Seth and the others are seeking the Lord and operating in godly wisdom. I think they are leaning on their own understanding and operating in fear."

---

[105]Proverbs 16:25 RSV

"I can't believe Riley would go along with all of this," Asha said sadly.

"Like I said, I think he's afraid. Seth is afraid of the outside world, and Riley and the others just seemed like they were afraid of Seth," Selah said.

The three sat down to a solemn lunch, chewing silently as they were each lost in their own thoughts. Asha finally broke the silence. "I can't believe it's come to this. Our families left a place that was trying to control their freedom, and now it's happening all over again." Selah thought about the brave families that left the Old Country to follow the Lord's leading to a place unknown. She was sure God hadn't intended for them to live in fear. It was like Miss Genevieve had said when Garrison left—the valley was like an ark of protection from the flood of the outside world. But the ark was never meant as a final destination.

38

SELAH tried to keep herself occupied the rest of the day so that the wait until the next morning wouldn't seem so long. She even cleaned out the chicken house—her least favorite chore—but it kept her busy. She had separated Clucky and her baby from the rest of the chickens because she was afraid the little chick would get picked on by the others. Clucky was a good mother, but everyone had their slip-ups, and Selah didn't want to take any chances. She had seen chickens do some incredibly hurtful things to each other. Pecking orders could be cruel. She gave an empty laugh as she realized how much humans could be like chickens—each one fearful of losing power and pecking on each other so that they, themselves, didn't end up at the bottom of the pecking order. Any chicken that showed a sign of weakness was pounced upon, and the feathers would fly. When the chickens were allowed as much free range as was safely possible, their stress level was reduced and the cannibalistic characteristics of the species was brought to a minimum. Selah was always glad when spring came and the flock could have more time outside. The only downside of free-roaming chickens was that the ones who strayed too far were easy prey for foxes, coyotes, bobcats, raccoons, hawks…Selah sighed as she thought of all the dangers. But maybe it was better than devouring one another. She sighed. Maybe she should write a sermon with a chicken behavior analogy.

When sundown finally came, she went inside and planned her visit for the next morning. She would take the metal racks she used for drying jerky so she could get Addy started on the process. But she would also take a jar of their favorite preserves—the strawberry kind that Asha made. She added the jar to her pack, which was stretched to a strange, angular shape by the metal racks. Her father had given the pack to her as a Christmas present to replace the old one she had given away to Garrison. The new pack was made of soft leather her father had tanned himself, and was larger than her old one. If it had been any smaller, it wouldn't have been able to accommodate the racks and the other treasures she wanted to bring.

She frowned. She wanted to take something else, but she wasn't certain what else to take. Looking through their kitchen, she realized that the Hamby's pantry was probably stocked as well as anyone else's in the valley. But surely there was something she could take as a special treat. She went to her room, wondering if one of Miss Genevieve's drawings might be an encouragement. When she walked through the door, her eyes rested on a small metal tin on her dresser. Inside were a few of Miss Genevieve's molasses chews which she had rationed out since last Christmas. They might be a little hard to chew by this time, but the sentiment would be what mattered.

She wondered about the condition of the Hamby smokehouse. They could always make the jerky on top of the woodstove, but smoking it outside would be less messy, and much tastier. If they used a smokehouse, they would need some green hickory or apple wood. Selah shook her head as she realized using a smokehouse might arouse suspicion, even if she was never seen. Seth would probably wonder what they were smoking, because Payton didn't have hogs to make ham or bacon and wouldn't have had occasion to visit someone who did. Of course, people smoked beef ribs and brisket all the time. If they dried the jerky over the stove in the kitchen, it would fill the whole house with the distinctive aroma, and if Seth came by for a visit, it might smell suspicious. Considering everything, the smokehouse seemed the less obvious of the two methods. Then again, maybe Addy had given up making jerky in the first place, and it was just a good way to arrange a meeting. Selah would bring the racks just in case and let Payton and Addy decide if they wanted to take the risk.

"It's certainly a lot easier to live when you're not trying to hide something," Selah muttered to herself, and set the pack at the foot of her bed. She didn't have much hopes of a good night's sleep, but if she was going to get up early, she knew she had better make an attempt.

She changed into her sleep clothes and knelt beside her bed. "Lord, this is so messed up," she prayed softly. "Please help us. We don't know what to do. Please show me what You want me to do in this situation. I know Seth thinks I'm being rebellious, and apparently, he thinks Payton is being dangerous in the way he preaches. I really thought we were headed for a revival, but it seems like some people don't want it. Lord, please change their hearts. Please open their eyes. Maybe Brother Payton's message came across as too evangelistic. Maybe Seth misunderstood." Selah stopped suddenly. Payton said he hadn't really meant to say anything about Garrison and how the community was hoarding spiritual treasure. But if what he said had been orchestrated by the Holy Spirit, as she had mentioned to Payton earlier, then it wasn't a mistake. Wasn't one of the main signs of revival that the lost were saved and people who were already Christians began reaching out to others with the good news of Christ? It wasn't just about being filled with the Holy Ghost or experiencing the power of God. True revival brought forth a harvest of souls. Since she was pretty sure everyone in the valley was a Christian, that meant reaching out to the lost who were outside the boundaries of the valley. The devil had to know that would be a result, so he was using fear of exposure to the State to control Seth, and Seth was using fear to control the other elders. "Lord, please help me to pray Your will for this community," Selah began. "Please have Your will in me," she added. As she asked the Holy Spirit for help in praying the will of God, she began to pray in a heavenly language directly from her spirit. As she prayed, she felt like she was pushing up against a wall. In her mind's eye, she could see it– a tall, dark wall of fear and oppression. It was a stronghold, she realized. What did the Word say about strongholds? She got up from her knees and retrieved the homemade booklet in which she recorded the scriptures she was trying to memorize. There in the section on spiritual warfare was 2 Corinthians 10:3-5: *For though we live in the world we are not carrying on a worldly war, for the weapons of our warfare are not worldly but have divine power to destroy strongholds. We destroy arguments and every proud obstacle to the knowledge of God, and take every thought captive to obey Christ.*[106] "Lord, Your Word says we can destroy strongholds by the weapons You have given us. In the name of Jesus, I come against the stronghold of fear, because Your Word says in 2 Timothy 1:7 that You have not given us the spirit of fear, but of power, love and of a sound mind. So fear is not Your will for us. I pull down this stronghold in the name of Jesus, who gave us freedom from fear. Hebrews 13:6 says 'The Lord is my helper; I will not fear what man shall do unto me.'[107] Lord, I believe the promises of Your Word for myself and for this community. We will not live under fear from the enemy or fear of any man, but in the light of the love of our Lord." Selah continued to pray in the Spirit for some time, until the burden for her community lifted somewhat. Her concerns about not being able to fall asleep were gone. She rubbed her eyes, crawled into bed and drifted asleep.

Selah looked around. She was in a large room filled with long tables and folding chairs. There was a spattering of people here and there, eating their lunch. Selah was drawn to one woman in particular. She was overweight and had dark hair and sad, empty eyes. Selah walked over and sat down across from her. "Hi," she said.

"Hello," said the woman in a dull voice. She picked up the sandwich on her plate and took a bite, chewing methodically. She seemed to study it for a moment before putting it down and looking at someone else's plate to see what they were having.

"Not very tasty?" Selah ventured, noticing the green, mushy substance between the bread.

---

[106] 2 Corinthians 10:3-5 RSV
[107] See Hebrews 13:6 KJV

The woman's head slowly swiveled back to look at Selah. "It's okay." She scrunched her eyebrows up in a quizzical expression. "I don't really mind working here. I've worked here for years, and I was always glad to have the job. But then they told us we had to have the procedure." She stopped talking, and again picked up her sandwich.

"What procedure?" Selah asked.

The woman dutifully took several bites of her sandwich before continuing. "They said if we wanted to keep our jobs, we had to have the procedure. They said it would help us work more efficiently and would even help us think better. But they didn't tell us everything."

"What didn't they tell you?" Selah asked. The woman continued as if she hadn't heard Selah's question.

"I've always been overweight, and I could never afford some of the implants people have to correct that. So I thought this was the chance to be thin and keep my job at the same time. They said it would help us to be healthier, more efficient workers and would take the place of some of the old implants. So I thought, why wouldn't I want that? But after I had it done, something was different." The lady stopped talking and took another bite.

Selah was losing her patience. "What was different?"

The lady looked up at her sadly. "I can do my job better than I ever could without it. I'm making my quotas, and I'm eating healthy—I don't even think about eating something like cake. But I can't whistle anymore."

"What?" Selah asked.

"Ever since the procedure, I can't whistle. I used to be the best whistler when I was a kid. But I can't even remember how to whistle now." The woman finished her sandwich and got up from the table. "I have to go back to work. Have a nice day," she said, and left Selah sitting in the lunchroom.

Suddenly, Selah was outside of a large building. She knew somehow that it was the building which contained the lunchroom, and it was also the building with a courtyard she had seen somewhere before. Standing beside her was a familiar looking woman. She turned to look at Selah. Even in her dream, Selah's heart jumped. It was Miss Genevieve, 50 years younger. She was looking at the factory entrance, which was an immense steel gate standing open in the great gray walls. "We're going in there, aren't we?" Selah asked.

"I can't go," Miss Genevieve answered. "But you can. Will you go?"

Selah looked back at the menacing steel gate. "I'm afraid they might shut the gate and I won't be able to get back out."

"That is a risk you may have to take," Miss Genevieve said. "But these people are trapped, and they don't know it. Someone has to lead them to freedom. Will you do it? Will you go and lead them out, before the gate closes forever?"

Selah's heart pounded in her chest. She might be their only hope. "I'll do it," she said. "I'll go."

"Good," Miss Genevieve said. "Now, get your pack." Miss Genevieve picked up the satchel of drawings and sermons she had given to Selah. "I may not be able to go, but you're going to take part of me with you," she said, and with a mighty heave, she flung the satchel at the open gate.

Selah realized that somehow she had become inseparable from the satchel. She felt herself flying through the air with it, soaring through the open door. When she landed, she was standing in a dimly lit corridor. All was quiet. As soon as she took a step, people began to step out of open doorways into the hallway. The farther she walked, the more people appeared. They did not attempt to block her way, but they watched her every move. Suddenly, one man stepped out from the crowd. She recognized Jeff. "Hey! Hey, you're the light bearer!" he said.

Selah looked self-consciously down at her stomach and pulled up her shirt to see if the candle was still there. As she did, a warm light filled the corridor and shined upon the faces of the crowd. A collective gasp was heard as all could see the light. "We knew you were different. But how did you light your candle? We've tried everything, and nothing seems to work," Jeff said sadly.

"Someone had to light it for me," Selah explained. "His name is Jesus, and He is the real Light of the world. He wants every light bearer to share His light with others." She opened the little door to her glass box and brought out the candle. It flickered in the drafty corridor, but it stayed lit. One by one, Selah went to the people in the crowd, lighting their candles until the hallway was ablaze with light. Suddenly, a shrill sound pulsated through the building.

"What's that?" Selah asked, as the crowd looked around nervously and began to mill about.

"It's the alarm. There's too much light in here. They say we work better if we stay in the dark. They're going to come put out our candles!" Jeff said frantically.

"No, they're not. They can't put out your candle." Selah shouted to be heard above the piercing alarm, but to no avail. Many of the crowd had covered up their candles in an attempt to hide as the factory security guards marched briskly into the corridor. The sound of the alarm ceased.

"What's going on here?" they demanded. Selah looked around and could see that all the candles had been covered again. Then why was the corridor still so bright? She looked down. It was her candle, and it was glowing brighter than ever.

"That's against the rules here," said the lead guard. "You'll have to put that out."

"Not a chance," Selah said, and slung her satchel over her shoulder. "Who is with me?" she called out. Most of the crowd looked down, but a few furtive glances from others told her that she was not alone. "Let's go!" she cried, and leapt away from the guards and toward the open door. The gate was beginning to close. Suddenly, Selah remembered how Miss Genevieve had thrown the satchel at the gate. She grabbed it and hurled it with all her might toward the exit. As she did, she felt herself flying there with it. She arrived before it could close and stood in the gap to hold it open. Several factory workers rushed out, and more gained courage as they saw the success of their coworkers. Selah held the gate open for as long as she could, but the guards were approaching. She had to leave if she wanted to escape. She started to pull herself free from the force of the closing door when she saw the eyes of the guard nearest her. They were desperate as he looked at her candle. She realized then that he wanted it, too. He wanted the light, and he couldn't leave the factory. She was his only hope. She looked outside the gate to the lone figure of Miss Genevieve, and then lunged back into the corridor, the gate slamming shut behind her. "You can't stay here!" said the guard as he bent over her where she had fallen. "You should have left with the others. You have to get up! Selah, you have to get up!"

Selah awoke to Asha hovering over her, shaking her gently by the shoulder. "Selah, you have to get up!" Asha said urgently. "If you don't leave now, you won't have enough time to reach the Hamby place before daylight."

Selah blinked, bleary-eyed, and stumbled out of bed. She had laid out her clothes the night before and put them on quickly. After grabbing her pack, she kissed her mother goodbye and closed the door quietly behind her so as not to alert their rooster. When she was out of hearing range, she started jogging, the jerky racks jangling slightly in her pack. Perhaps she should have left the jar of jam, she thought, as it smacked against her back with every stride.

The dream wouldn't let her go. She could still see the miserable faces of the people in the crowd as she jogged up the road in the darkness. The desire to help them welled up within her, swelling her throat and filling her eyes with tears. "It was a dream," she reminded herself. But the feeling wouldn't go away. The desperate faces seemed to appear before her in the gloom of the path ahead, looking to her for help. Selah had read accounts of Christians having dreams about people who were in trouble in faraway lands. Later, those Christians found out that their obedience to pray for them had brought about their deliverance. *"Lord, if these are real people somewhere, please help them. Send someone to help them!"* she prayed as she hurried down the road.

Her mother was right about the time it would take her to reach the Hamby house. She could easily travel in the dark because she knew the way so well, but by the time she reached the weathered little cabin, she no longer had to be careful about where she stepped. The outlines of trees, rocks and fence posts were beginning to take shape in the early light. She went around to the side porch and let herself in. The side door of the house opened up, and Payton stood silhouetted in the doorway. "Get in here, young lady," he said. "It's time to make some jerky." At that, he chuckled and pulled her quickly inside.

39

"I don't know what came over me," Addy said, as she brought out a bowl of meat strips from the ice chest on the porch. "I wanted so badly to let you know what was really going on, and I feel like I was lying through my teeth."

"What? About making jerky? Looks like we're about to make jerky to me," Selah said, with a wink. "But I think your meat strips are a little too thick. Can we use your cutting board? And if you have a meat hammer, it would probably help if we tenderized them a little."

"Oh, fiddle!" said Addy. "I thought I was getting it right."

"You did, mostly," Selah reassured her. "Besides, if you did everything perfectly, then I would feel unneeded. What would I have to teach?"

"You could teach several people I know a thing or two about twisting the Word of God to suit their own devices," Payton said. "Ol' Seth told me how you schooled him on that. Of course, he didn't say it that way. He made himself sound like the hero, while you were—"

"Payton! Selah doesn't need to hear all the details," Addy scolded him.

Payton scratched his receding hairline. "Quite right, Dear." He looked over at Selah. "Wisdom," he said, pointing at Addy with his thumb. "I've said more things out of line in these past few days than I have all year, I think."

Selah was enjoying their antics, but she wanted to hear what happened during the visit of the elders. "So, what is going on? Can they really force you to live in seclusion for a period of time?"

Payton looked at Addy, who glanced up at him as she continued to lay out meat strips on her cutting board. He cleared his throat. "Actually, it was *my* idea," Payton said.

"What?" Selah asked in disbelief.

"It's the perfect cover!" he smiled.

"What are you talking about?" Selah asked.

Suddenly, the normally sweet-natured Addy slammed the meat hammer down with a *thwack*. Selah and Payton jumped. "I'll tell you what he's talking about, Selah. He's talking about leaving the valley. I've tried to talk him out of it, but he won't listen. Can you talk any sense into him?" Addy's voice quavered slightly. She went to the wash basin to grab a wet dish rag and began busily wiping off the counters.

"Addy, dear, Miss Genevieve was never allowed to fulfill her calling. A big part of that was my fault. Now she's gone. Who's going to go? Who's going to carry the gospel to the people we left behind? Do you deny that those people need to hear the Truth?"

"No, Payton!" Addy said fiercely. "I don't deny it. Of course they need to hear it. My argument isn't with taking them the gospel. I just don't feel you should be a missionary unless you're called. And you aren't. You are called to be the shepherd of this community."

"An office which I have been denied, if you will recall."

"I thought you said it was your idea to take a leave of absence," Selah said.

"Well, let's just say I beat them to it. I knew what they were going to say, so I decided to bring it up myself. And then I thought to myself, 'You know, I could be gone for quite a while before anyone noticed.' Not that any of them would have the nerve to follow me," Payton said with a twinkle in his eye.

"But this isn't something to be taken so lightly," Addy protested.

"You've prayed about it, of course?" Selah asked.

"Of course," Payton said. "And I'm already gathering things together for my journey."

Selah felt a hesitation in her spirit. "How long did you pray about it?" She asked.

"Well, I didn't really come up with the idea until about a week ago," Payton began, but Addy interrupted.

"There. You see what I mean? He came up with the idea himself. He wasn't led by the Spirit or called by God. He's just feeling guilty because he thinks it's his fault Miss Genevieve never got to leave."

"Now, Addy, I admit I feel guilty, but I really have prayed about this," Payton said.

Selah's stomach twisted into knots as the two argued back and forth. Finally, she could stand it no longer, and stood up to get their attention. "Brother Payton, it is not your fault that Miss Genevieve never left."

The two stopped bickering and looked at her. "The truth is, she was planning to leave a few months before she died. But I talked her out of it. I just didn't think she could make the trip, and I felt like God had probably released her from that particular part of her calling anyway. The only way I could get her to see reason was to ask her to pray about it for a while longer. So we prayed and fasted off and on for weeks… for months. Neither of us ever felt a release for her to go back to the Old Country. I think the window of opportunity for her to minister in that capacity had closed. God was using her in other areas, which she worked at with all her might. And I don't mean to sound presumptuous telling you this, but surely you need to spend more than just a week praying about something this important." She looked over at Addy. "It's obvious that Addy doesn't feel called to go. What's going to happen to her? Are you just going to leave her behind? Or are you going to try to convince her to go with you? And if even if she doesn't feel like she's supposed to leave, don't you think God would give her peace about you leaving, if it was really His will?"

"Well, now…." Payton began, but his voice trailed off into silence.

"Just pray about it. Really seek the Lord about it. Try to leave your emotions, your guilt, your sense of what you think is right—leave them out of it. Otherwise, you might just be doing what is right in your own eyes instead of trusting God and acknowledging Him in all your ways."

Payton ran his fingers through his hair and walked to the other side of the kitchen to look out the window. He turned back around and cleared his throat. "You can't argue with the Word," he said simply. "Okay, Addy. Okay, Selah. I'll give it some more prayer. But will you pray with me?"

"Of course!" Selah said.

"Hallelujah," Addy said in relief. "Thank God you sneaked over here today, Selah. Now, let's get back to the jerky and stop talking about this before he talks himself back into leaving."

The two cut meat into thinner strips while Payton got the smoke house ready. "I'm so glad you got him to postpone it, at least," Addy confided in her. "I really don't think he's supposed to go."

"Neither do I," Selah said. The strange, heavy feeling in her heart had returned. She had been thinking of the dreams while they cut the meat strips. What had she told the young Miss Genevieve? *"I'll do it. I'll go,"* she had said. The memory hit her like the shock of jumping in Bear Creek's icy waters in mid-March. She finally understood. All the dreams were connected. The chicken with the voice of Miss Genevieve, which had poured all its effort into one chick who turned out to look like Selah; the dreams about the people in the factory who had unlit candles and longed for freedom and light—they were all pointing to one thing, to one big question she had been choosing to ignore. *"Will you go?"* She had been praying for God's will in her life and the life of her community. She hadn't been praying about it for just a few days, but she had started several months ago when she had been praying with Miss Genevieve. The weight she had been feeling on her heart was both a burden and a request. God had placed upon her an infinitesimal amount of the burden of His concern and love for the people of the Old Country, and its weight was almost unbearable. With the weight came the request. *"Will you go?"* She could hear it clearly now.

"Selah? Can you hear me?" Addy was saying.

Selah snapped out of her daze and looked up at Addy.

"Do you think this is thin enough?" Addy was asking, as she turned over the pieces of meat.

"Yeah, that's great," Selah said, still reeling from her sudden revelation.

"Good. I think Payton is almost ready with the smokehouse. We're smoking a brisket, as well."

Selah smiled and tried to bring herself back to the present, while Addy chattered on. "Smoked brisket is one of my favorites," Addy was saying. "I'm glad you're helping us make the jerky. I'm just sorry it's not made from deer meat. I just love that stuff. And Payton, bless his heart. He's a wonderful farmer and cattleman, but he's no hunter, that's for sure." She looked admiringly at Selah. "You've always been good at hunting and fishing and gathering wild berries and edible plants. If Payton and I got lost in the woods, the Lord would have to send ravens to feed us like he did for Elijah, or we'd just starve to death!" she laughed.

Selah laughed to be polite, but as she did, she wondered how Payton had been planning on surviving on his journey back to the Old Country. If it was the Lord's will, God would have provided a way. But it didn't seem like good planning to know absolutely nothing about how to find food if you ran out. "God gave us brains, and He expects us to use them," Miss Genevieve had often said.

Selah decided to broach the subject again when Payton was finished putting the meat in their little smokehouse. "Brother Payton, we've all agreed to pray about your idea to be a missionary..." she began, and paused as Addy shot her a look, "and I know it may be kind of a sore subject right now, but I just wondered—how were you going to survive until you reached civilization? From all the stories I've heard, the population has been confined to the larger cities. It took our families a whole day of travel by vehicles to reach the valley. It might take a long time to reach one of those cities on foot. What if you ran out of food? What if you couldn't find any water that was safe to drink?"

Payton seemed to size her up. "You know, Seth told me you have your head in the clouds, but he's never seen your practical side. Surely you must know I've thought about this. As far as the food is concerned, I may not be the hunter you are, but I know all about blackberries and persimmons. I think I could survive for a while eating off of the land."

"Blackberries and persimmons aren't available this time of year. Blackberries ripen in the summertime, and persimmons aren't ready 'til fall," Selah pointed out.

Payton's smile faded. "Well, I guess you're right. Hadn't thought of that," he said, and then brightened. "I do have the water thing figured out, though!" he said triumphantly, and headed out of the kitchen, returning in a few moments with a canvas bag secured with a drawstring. "This was with some of the stuff Miss Genevieve had." He glanced at Selah, as if trying to decide whether or not to tell her something. "I kept this for your safety, because you were so upset at the time that I wasn't sure it would be wise to leave it with you. You see, it was with the things she wanted to leave for you. But I was afraid it might give you ideas."

"What is it?" Selah leaned forward with interest.

Payton reached in the bag and carefully pulled out a pouch made of a strange material Selah had never seen before. The pouch was fitted with a strangely shaped nozzle. Payton grinned as he saw her quizzical expression. "It's a water filtration system," he explained. "Her folks must have brought it with them from the Old Country. You can even drink the water out of that scummy pond in my back pasture with this thing."

Selah looked at him skeptically.

"Believe it or not, he's right," Addy said, forgetting her irritation that they were discussing Payton's travel plans. "He brought back some water from there in a mason jar just to prove it to me. You just unscrew the filter, pour the water in the bag, screw the filter back on and squeeze, and, *voila!* Fresh, clean, drinkable water."

Selah looked at the water pouch wonderingly, as Payton reached inside the bag once more to retrieve another item. "This should be familiar to you," he said. It was a small tin box. Selah recognized it immediately. It contained a bar of magnesium with a strip of flint attached to one of the edges. Miss Genevieve had used it to start fires in her cookstove. Payton opened up the little tin and brought out the bar of metal, which was wrapped in a small piece of charred cloth.

"I remember it," Selah said.

"You can see why I didn't want to leave it with you at the time," Payton said. "You were so upset, you might have thought of carrying out her mission on your own."

"No one here would even *think* of doing that," Addy said, with the slightest hint of sarcasm to her voice, but when Payton and Selah glanced at her, she shrugged and smiled sweetly.

"Sounds like maybe *I* should keep them for a while, now," Selah said with a grin, but her heart was pounding in her chest.

"You know, that's not a bad idea," Addy said with a sweet tone, but she was staring hard at Payton.

"I'd like to show that water pouch thing to Mom and Dad," Selah added.

Payton studied the items and looked up at Addy. "Well, okay," he relented. "She did intend for Selah to have them, anyway. But if I get clear direction from the Lord to go, I'd really like to have them back. At least the water filter."

"Sure!" Selah said, trying to sound casual. She slid the water filter back into the drawstring bag, but she held the tin box for a moment as she remembered sitting in front of the stove with her old friend. "Oh, good grief!" she said, as she slapped herself in the forehead. "I forgot about the candy." The tin box had made her remember the little tin of molasses chews she had brought with her. She went to her pack and pulled out the tin. "I thought you might like some of these. They were always some of my favorite candies." She opened the box and offered them to Payton and Addy.

"Miss Genevieve's molasses chews!" Addy exclaimed. "What a treat!"

"I've been rationing them out," Selah said. "I think Sadie Beardsley might have the recipe, but I'm not exactly on the best of terms with that family right now."

Payton smiled sympathetically at her. "You know, I really think they'll come around," he said. "We just have to keep praying and have faith."

"And choose to love, no matter what," Addy sighed.

Selah nodded in agreement. After all, here she was in the Hamby kitchen, visiting with the man who had made life so difficult for her in the past months. Forgiveness and the power of the Holy Spirit went a long way in restoring relationships.

40

SELAH stayed at the Hamby cabin until after nightfall. When the yard disappeared into inky blackness, she got ready to leave. Addy insisted on loading her up with the jerky that was finished. "If you hadn't come over to help, we wouldn't have jerky in the first place," she claimed. Selah smiled gratefully and accepted her offer. She left the metal racks there so Addy could make more the next day. No one had come over to question Payton about what he was smoking in the smokehouse, so apparently, no one had suspected anything from Addy's comment about jerky-making time. Payton promised to pray about his idea to carry the gospel out of the valley, and to pay a visit to the Merrit household to let his friends know when he received clear direction for his plan.

Selah walked carefully down the road, glad for the absence of moonlight, since it made it easy for her to remain undetected. The pack she was carrying was light, but she carried another burden now, a burden for the citizens of the Old Country. She couldn't believe God had chosen *her*. Being a missionary would mean leaving the valley—her parents, her friends, and everything she held dear—to go somewhere strange. No looking for morel mushrooms in the spring, no hunting turkey or deer, no fireflies or cicada songs…just tall gray walls and empty people. As she thought of it, the arguments she had for staying in the valley seemed hollow, and her chest felt like it would burst. She couldn't let those people die not knowing the Truth. They had to be told that there was hope for the hopeless—a God who loved them so much He was willing to give up His glory in heaven and live as one of them, to teach them how to live, and to eventually become the ultimate payment for sin. "Someone has to tell them, Lord," she said softly. "Genevieve can't do it. Garrison won't do it. Payton *shouldn't* do it, because he's called to be a leader of this community. But here I am." Tears began to roll down her cheeks. "I'll go."

Suddenly, the weight on her heart seemed to shift a little. *"Come, take my yoke upon you and learn of me, for I am meek and lowly of heart, and ye shall find rest unto your souls. For my yoke is easy, and my burden is light."*[108] The words fell on her spirit like a gentle rain. So this was what it felt like to be called into the ministry, she marveled to herself. It was a heavy load, but God was carrying it with her.

Her thoughts were interrupted as she passed by the community building. There was a light inside, and several figures could be seen seated together around a table. *"What could be going on at this hour on a weeknight?"* she wondered. She slowed down and crept closer, careful to stay out of the halos of lamplight spilling from the windows. From her vantage point, she could distinctly make out Riley Rosales, Seth Beardsley, Clive Coffelt, Joe Breedon, and Joan Ferrel—all board members. The only one she couldn't see very well had his back to the window. Whoever he was, he wasn't a member of the board, because there were only six of them at any given time, and Payton was at home. Maybe that was it, she considered. Maybe they were asking someone else if he'd like to fill in the vacant spot while Brother Payton was absent from his duties. She was certain Seth would assume the role of senior elder, since he was the assistant to that position, but that would still leave a vacancy. Selah strained to hear what was being said. Something was wrong, because the man with his back to the window had become very agitated. She crouched low in the shadows and moved silently to the stunted, manicured cedar trees planted at intervals along the community building. Once she was just underneath the window, she could hear them.

---

[108] Matthew 11:29-10 KJV

"Don't take it personally. Anyone in your position might be blind to it," Joan was saying.

"We just want to know the truth," Seth said calmly. "Are you noticing any difficulties in that area? Any signs of instability or inconsistent behavior? Mood swings? Lashing out in anger?" Selah wondered who the poor man was, that his sanity was suspect. She hadn't noticed anyone in the community acting strangely—except, perhaps, for Seth.

The man remained silent, but was shaking his head throughout all the questioning. Suddenly, he stood up. "There is absolutely nothing wrong with my daughter!" he burst out. Selah froze. That was her father's voice.

"Now, Brother Jackson, there's no need to be upset," Seth said patronizingly.

"How could a man keep calm, when you accuse him of having a lunatic for a daughter?" Jackson bellowed.

"There's no need to raise your voice, Mr. Merrit," Seth said sternly.

"We didn't say she was loony," Riley protested. "I've always liked Selah. But she *has* been acting a little different lately."

"Yes, she has!" Jackson exclaimed.

"Oh, then, you *had* noticed?" Seth asked. His voice reminded Selah of a snake, coiling its way around every argument and twisting a person's words back onto themselves.

"Yes. How could I not notice? She's more mature, more loving and understanding—even to people she never got along with before." At this, Jackson faced Joe Breedon. "You know *that* firsthand, Joe. She and Jannica never got along. But now, they visit like old friends. Now tell me, what's wrong with *that*? That's a *good* thing!" Jackson argued.

"Uh, well, about that, Jackson…" Joe paused as he chose his words. "Jannica was really pulled in at first, but after I talked to her about it, she could see what we were worried about. It just wasn't the same Selah. Something about her is different. It's almost like she's *too* loving and understanding."

"You mean to say you think she is insincere?" Jackson asked incredulously.

"Now, I don't mean to insult anyone, but after Miss Genevieve died, she *did* get kind of a snippy mouth on her," Joan said archly.

"This whole interrogation is an insult. And what did she ever do to you, Joan?" Jackson asked.

"Nothing, personally. I just heard how she had spoken to some people who really took offense at what she said."

"Her best friend had just died," Jackson spat out the words. "She was hurting. She didn't mean to be short with people. Besides, she's a teenager. You all know how moody they can be. And if the only evidence you have of unstable behavior is second-hand information, you'd better think again if you think I'm going to take you seriously."

"Her unstable behavior started long before Miss Genevieve passed," Seth said. "She hasn't been the same since Garrison left. We all know how close they were. It had an effect on her. I think she's been planning to leave ever since. Her recent good behavior is nothing but a cover-up. You're just too close to the situation to see it clearly."

"Her recent good behavior is a result of her being baptized in the Holy Spirit," Jackson said through clenched teeth. "In fact, it's something you might try sometime. I think it's the only thing keeping me from storming out of here."

"So, you feel that you have received the baptism of the Holy Spirit?" Seth asked, his eyes narrowing.

"Yes, I have," Jackson said warmly. "And next to being saved, it's the best thing that ever happened to me."

"You are aware that emotions can be very tricky things. Sometimes we can misconstrue emotionalism for the Spirit of God moving upon us," Seth said condescendingly.

"This wasn't just emotion, although I did experience joy, peace, love, faith—some of the same things Selah has been showing. Interesting how those are all fruits of the Spirit,[109] isn't it?" Jackson said.

---

[109] See Galatians 5:22-23

"If they are genuine, then, yes. I'm just not certain that what Selah has been displaying is genuine. I think she's pretending, so we won't suspect her of anything. And Brother Jackson, you are mature enough in Christ to realize you should test all the spirits. Not every spirit you come across is Holy. I think Selah has been using your good intentions of getting closer to God and seeking revival to throw you off track. And not just you, but Sister Asha, and Brother and Sister Hamby, as well. Any attempts to seek the baptism of the Holy Spirit should have been approved by the board first, not just one elder. And the unauthorized prayer meetings—Jackson, don't you see that Selah is in rebellion?" Seth said, his voice a loud whisper.

"Selah didn't call the prayer meetings. We all just decided we wanted to seek the Lord—under the senior elder's direction, might I add," Jackson said. Selah could tell by the tenor of his voice that he was nearing the edge of his patience.

"Why weren't the other elders informed? Why wasn't the rest of the congregation invited? That sort of behavior is divisive. Don't you see where this is leading?" Seth asked.

"I don't see where you *think* it's leading," Jackson said pointedly.

Seth sighed and looked around the room at the other board members. "We really have been amiss," he said, as his gaze came to rest on Jackson again. "Here we are, laying all the blame on Selah. But the board has been talking it over, and we agree that some of her behavior could very well be influenced by an oppressive spirit—the very spirit by which she claims to be filled."

"*What?*" Jackson exclaimed. "Do you think she's possessed?"

"Well, we really don't know if it's gotten to that point yet, which is why we need to keep her confined for closer observation. Now, there's no need to worry, because we've all already discussed it. We had originally thought about taking turns hosting her in our homes, since we are more removed from the situation and are able to see what is really going on. But what would keep her from running away? And how could we be certain that the oppressive spirit wouldn't begin to have an affect on us? So what I proposed is that we keep her at the old Ferrel place. Joan and Mike have already been fixing it up, securing the door and the windows. It would only be for a few months, where we could keep her from leaving the valley and counsel with her long enough to get her back on the right track," Seth said matter-of-factly.

"You think you're going to lock up my daughter like a criminal?" Jackson nearly exploded.

"It's for her own good, and for the protection of everyone living here," Seth said firmly.

"We've never had a jail in the valley."

"We've never needed one before Garrison went haywire. And it's not a jail, Brother Jackson. It's more like a sanctuary. Just think if we had acted more quickly with that young man—the good we could have done if we had detained him long enough to instruct him with some wise counsel. This whole chain of events could have been broken before it got out of hand," Seth reasoned.

"Do you really think he would have listened?" Jackson asked.

"Well, at least we would have done all we could. And if he chose to ignore our counsel, we could at least have kept him from leaving and endangering the whole community," Seth hissed.

"In case you hadn't noticed, the State hasn't come to drag us all back to society," Jackson said coolly.

"Not yet," Seth said, "but it's only a matter of time. They're probably just in the process of observing us—deciding what to do. They may not even want to reintegrate us, feeling that quietly annihilating us would be safer."

Jackson backed away from the table. "I'm not listening to any more of this," he said wearily. "I can't believe you all don't realize how ridiculous you sound. This is ignorance gone to seed. I'm going home to my family."

"I don't think you understand, Jackson. What we're saying is that we want to help. *Some* spiritual matters need to be handled by those who have spiritual authority," Seth said slowly.

"And as a Christian who happens to be Selah's father, I have spiritual authority over her. No one else is going to raise my daughter for me, or lock her up, for that matter."

"Mr. Merrit, do you know where your daughter is right now?" Seth asked, a smile thinning his lips.

"At this time? Probably at home getting ready for bed. She gets up awfully early to milk her cow and do her chores. She's a good girl, Brother Seth. I don't understand why you all can't see that!" Jackson said, his voice ragged with frustration.

"Well, if she's home, maybe you won't mind if we pay a visit," Seth said. It was more of a statement than a request.

"Tonight? Yes, I do mind. Asha isn't accustomed to receiving guests at this hour, especially without any prior notice."

"We just want to make sure she's tucked into bed, safe and sound. Jannica said that you were the one who brought over the milk for their bottle calf today. No one has seen Selah at all, and for the past week or so, she always paces back and forth every morning by your little lettuce patch, talking to herself the whole time."

"Praying," Jackson said.

"Ahh. I see. She told you she was praying. Well, she wasn't there this morning. We thought maybe she had taken ill, but surely you would have mentioned this," Seth said.

"Are you watching her?" Jackson asked in disbelief. "What is this? Big Brother? Are we a totalitarian society now? Are you watching our every move? I know that those who have the rule over us watch for our souls, but I don't think that's what the writer of Hebrews had in mind."

Seth glared at Jackson and pulled out a little New Testament from within his jacket pocket, turning through the pages until he found the scripture he wanted. "It's funny you should bring up that verse, Brother Jackson. If you look at the whole thing, I think you will find it very applicable to our present circumstance. Hebrews 13:17—'Obey them that have the rule over you, and submit yourselves: for they watch for your souls, as they that must give account, that they may do it with joy, and not with grief: for that is unprofitable for you.'[110] Those in authority are required to watch over those whose souls are entrusted to them. But when those we watch over don't submit to our authority, they are only hurting themselves. I'm trying to help you. Having a balance is so important. I'm afraid your family and the Hambys may be weighing in a little too heavy on the side of prayer. We must have a balance between the time we spend in prayer and the time we spend in the Word. Too much time in prayer without being grounded in the Word can end up making people flaky."

Jackson stared unflinchingly back at Seth. "And too much time in the Word without enough time in prayer can end up making people legalistic."

Seth's face turned red as he stood to his feet and smacked his Bible down on the table. "Mr. Merrit, I am trying to help your family! I am concerned for you. Can't you see Selah is controlling you? That is manipulation and rebellion; and as Samuel told Saul, 'Rebellion is as the sin of witchcraft, and stubbornness is as iniquity and idolatry.'[111] Now, if you would lay aside *your* stubbornness and be so kind as to let us accompany you home."

"I'll do nothing of the sort. This is foolishness. Riley...Clive...are you really listening to this? This isn't God's vision for this community! We came here to escape persecution and to be able to bring up our children to love the one true God!"

"Brother Jackson, I don't think you are in a position to decide what is and isn't God's vision for our community. And, as I said, I am concerned for your family. But if you don't make the decision to submit to authority, your daughter isn't the only one we'll be locking up," Seth growled.

"Are you threatening me?" Jackson asked in a quiet voice. Selah shuddered. She had heard that quiet voice before, when she was eight years old, after Jackson had discovered she had thrown eggs against the

---

[110] Hebrews 13:17 KJV
[111] See 1 Samuel 15:23 KJV

inside walls of the smokehouse. Seth didn't know it, but he was skating on thin ice.

"Not yet. But I will if necessary. I realize that it is an odd time of night to pay a social call. But putting all social decorum aside, may I suggest that if you don't have anything to hide, you won't mind us pursuing this matter."

Selah had heard enough. Her father would probably think she was home by now, anyway, and might eventually relent to avoid suspicion. If that were the case, then she had better be there when they arrived. Beating them there wouldn't be a problem, but it wouldn't do to be out of breath. She stayed low to the ground until she reached the main road, and then broke into as fast a pace as the darkness would allow.

Her father would never agree to letting them lock her away, she re-assured herself as she ran. But what if he didn't have a choice? What if they locked him up for refusing to cooperate? Surely Seth wouldn't go that far. On the other hand, she had thought the board members were just going along with his plan because they were afraid of him; but from what she had heard, it seemed they were really afraid of *her*. What if their visit to make certain she was home was just a ruse? What if the real plan was to take her away tonight?

She could see the light of her family's cabin through the trees. *"Mom will know what to do,"* Selah said to herself hopefully. As she neared the fence around the yard, she stopped short. She could hear voices coming from the porch. Selah stayed in the shadows. There was a board missing in the fence that Jackson had reminded her to fix last week, and as she climbed through the gap, she was glad she had kept forgetting about it. She stalked as close to the house as she dared, using the old sitting stump beside the smokehouse for cover. Jannica Breedon and Janie Ferrel were there, as well as Seth's wife, Kiley, and his daughter, Sadie.

"We just wanted to let you know what was keeping Jackson," Jannica was saying. "I'm sure they won't be very long now. You wouldn't mind if we came in while we waited for them, would you?"

"Them?" Asha asked curiously. "Are they all coming here, at this time of night?"

"Well, Seth wanted us to come by and let you know what was going on so you wouldn't worry, and they said we could just wait here and they would all walk us home," Kiley said.

"It's an awfully dark night," Janie said. "I don't think there are any snakes out yet this year, but it makes me feel safer if Mom and I walk home together."

Asha bit her lip and shot a glance into the darkness of the yard. "Well, it is a little chilly out here," she said reluctantly. "Come inside and warm yourselves by the stove."

"*No!*" Selah cried silently. Now how would she be able to get inside? She looked at her bedroom window. Because of the root cellar under the house, the window was up just high enough to make reaching it from the ground impossible. Her heart did a somersault. When she was a kid and had stayed out too late at the creek with Garrison, she used to sneak in by climbing the overgrown redbud tree right outside of her room. She dashed forward to the tree and grappled up the branches until she was even with the window. In the summer time, she had kept it open, of course. Hopefully, opening it from the outside wouldn't be a problem. She leaned forward and nearly lost her balance, catching herself on the windowsill. It was then that she noticed her window was already opened. How strange, she thought. Asha always scolded her for letting out the heat on these cold nights, and Selah was certain it had been closed when she left that morning. She lowered her pack through the window to the floor and scrambled inside as quietly as she could, managing to bump her head against the frame on her way.

"Did you hear that?" Jannica's voice said from the kitchen.

"What?" Asha asked innocently.

"I thought I heard noise from down the hall."

"Oh, that. I guess I'm just used to it. Selah moves around a lot in her sleep. Sometimes I wonder where she's going after she scampers off to dreamland," Asha said—rather loudly, Selah thought. Had her mother noticed her hiding behind the stump? Had she guessed that she was trying to sneak back inside? She looked around the room, frantic as to what she should do. If Seth and the board really suspected she was operating under the force of some demonic spirit instead of the Holy Spirit, then they very likely would take her away tonight. The truth should soon become very obvious to an objective observer that Selah wasn't under any influence of evil; however, Seth and the board were currently not objective observers.

She could hear Asha laughing. "I bet she's gigging crawdads in her sleep. That's where I would be, if I were her," she said, in an unnaturally loud voice. Selah's breath caught in her throat. Asha knew she was there, and she was warning her to leave. She was even telling her where to go! Maybe her parents would meet her there later and tell her when they thought it was safe to return. What they didn't know was that she had been called to the mission field. She might not return for a long time. Selah looked around the room frantically. She had only minutes to plan. If she were going to be a missionary, surely she would need as many Bibles as she could carry. Of course, there were the practical items, like food, water, a change of clothes...and her bow, so she could get something to eat if it was a long time before she reached her destination. She already had the jerky and a water filter. It would have been nice to have some biscuits, but it didn't look like that would be possible. The door to her room was slightly open, and she could vaguely see the outline of her personal belongings by some of the lamplight from the nearby kitchen. Something wasn't right. Her bow wasn't in the corner. The drawers of her dresser were half opened, and some of her clothes had been dropped on the floor. She looked on her nightstand for her Bible. It wasn't there. She looked at the hook on the wall where she always kept Miss Genevieve's satchel. It was gone. Panic began to well up inside of her. Someone must have already been there and searched her room. That might explain the open window.

"You know, when I was her age, I felt like I had everything I needed down by the creek," Asha said from the kitchen.

Selah stood up and grabbed her pack, trying to decide what to do. Asha was obviously trying to get her to leave, but did she realize that most of the things she needed were gone? Maybe she should risk sneaking down the hall to her parents' room to get a Bible. She walked stealthily toward the door and was about to push it open when she heard a gasp. Sadie Beardsley was standing at her doorway, her hand reaching for the knob.

"Sadie, where'd you go? What're you doin'?" Kiley called from the kitchen.

Sadie and Selah stared at each other, wide-eyed, for a full second. "Oh, I'm just looking in on Selah," Sadie finally said, never breaking eye-contact. "You're right, Asha, she really does move around a lot in her sleep."

"Well, leave her alone, Sadie. I don't want you near her—because you might wake her up, of course," Kiley said quickly, but there was an edge of fear in her voice.

Sadie backed away from the door, mouthing the word, *"Go!"*

Selah stood in shock for a split second, and then rushed back to the window. The board members could be there any minute. She crawled through the window, dropped to the ground, and began running. Asha had clearly mentioned gigging crawdads, and she knew Selah's favorite spot, but to get there, she would have to take a circuitous route to avoid the road.

Maggie mooed softly as Selah ran past the barn lot. "Goodbye, old friend," Selah whispered. "Take care of that calf."

Her feet flew over rocky ground along the fencerow to the woods behind the barn lot. There was a path there that led to the creek. The hills and the darkness might slow her down a little, but she couldn't take a chance on being seen on the main road. She would get there as fast as she could, hide out in the thick brush at the rendezvous place, and wait for further instruction.

Branches whipped her in the face as she flew by. She was glad it was too cold for snakes yet, because with the canopy of branches overhead, she could barely see to put one foot in front of the other. Holding her hands up in front of her face protected her from getting a stick jabbed in her eye, but it didn't stop the limbs from tearing at her hair and the green briars from clawing at her clothes. She had spent many a moonlit night walking this path through the snow, but that was completely different from the near pitch-blackness she had been so grateful for earlier.

There was a rocky drop-off somewhere up ahead, but Selah couldn't tell exactly where she was on the path. It had to be coming up soon. She slowed down a little, momentarily confused. Suddenly, with her next stride, her foot stepped out into nothingness. Selah gasped as she fell headlong down a slope, banging her shin on a large rock as she fell. She rolled to a stop in the thick leaves and grabbed at her leg, resisting the urge to cry out. It could just as easily have been her head, she reminded herself. She realized then how much God had protected her as she fell. The actual path led to a steep rock wall with a scenic overlook of a sinkhole in the forest floor. She had always enjoyed scaling the wall in her adventures through the woods. Somehow, she had veered off the trail and gone far enough to the right that the cliff had dwindled to the slope she had just encountered. If she hadn't veered so far to the right, she might have gone over the little cliff and had more injuries than just a bruised shin. "Thank you, Lord," she whispered, even though she was in pain. "That could have been a lot worse." She clambered to her feet and continued on her way. Bear Creek was only about five minutes away, at this pace. She wouldn't let this slow her down.

In a few more minutes of running, she could hear the creek gurgling noisily as it always did this time of year when there was an abundance of water. She slowed her pace as the path grew thick with buck brush and river cane. It wouldn't take long to reach the crawdad gigging place. It was just upstream from here. An opening in the canopy of trees momentarily gave her a little more light. Suddenly, a tree on the side of the path seemed to come to life and reach for her. She shrieked in surprise, but a hand quickly clamped down over her mouth.

"Oww!" a voice cried out as she bit down on the hand. She knew that voice. It belonged to Paul Scoffield, Garrison's dad. "Stop it, Selah! It's me, Paul!" he whispered.

"What are you doing?" she whispered back at him. "You scared me to death."

"I didn't figure I could avoid scaring you, seeing as how I was waiting here in the dark, but I thought I at least could keep you from making a lot of noise. So much for that, I guess," he said, keeping his voice low. "Your parents sent me here ahead of you. They got your stuff ready ahead of time—everything they thought you might need." He handed her the satchel that had belonged to Miss Genevieve. It was bulging at the seams. "They said to say they were sorry they couldn't be here themselves, but this was the only way they could give you the best head start. And they had to take out the drawings to make room for other things you might need more. I'm not sure what they were talking about, but I guess you do."

"How did they know?" Selah said as she tried to catch her breath from her flight through the woods. "How did they know this was going to happen?"

"I warned them," Paul said. "I've noticed the way Seth has been watching you lately, and I overheard a few conversations when the elders didn't know I was in earshot. I even thought I might have seen Joan snooping around your house one morning, on the pretense of needing some eggs."

Selah remembered that morning. She had been praying down by the lettuce patch and had looked up to see Joan Ferrel watching her from the chicken house. Joan had then smiled and asked if Selah could spare a few eggs.

"I overheard them at the community building. They think I'm crazy, or possessed, or maybe both," she said.

"After the way they reacted with Garrison leaving, I knew they wouldn't trust you again. I didn't think Payton would, either. But

355

then he came by to see us after Genevieve died. He apologized for everything, and even told us he was wrong about being so dead set against anyone leaving the valley. Is it true that Miss Genevieve wanted to be a missionary?"

"Yes. But now I'm going in her place," Selah said, and felt a rush of excitement as she admitted it out loud.

"That's what your parents said when I came by earlier today. They were hoping to see you off, but it just didn't work out that way."

Selah wondered if the workings of her inner heart had been so obvious to everyone but herself. "How did they know? You're the first person I've told."

"That, I don't know. But if you don't get out of here soon, you may never get to be a missionary. They'll come looking for you here, since this is where Garrison crossed over the boundary. We just thought it was the best place, since he had been exploring and probably knew the best route." Paul turned and reached for something in the brush beside the path. "Here. You might need these," he said, and handed her the bow and a quiver of arrows that had been missing from her room.

Selah took them. She could imagine the frantic scene at her house after Paul had met with her parents. "Selah, you need to go now!" Paul said, an urgency in his voice.

"Then, they aren't coming?" Selah asked, her voice cracking.

"How can they, with board members breathing down their necks? They said you would probably try to hang around in hopes of seeing them, but it's just too risky. You need to put as much distance between yourself and this place as you can. Garrison told you something about a road, right? Well find that road and head down it!" Paul urged her, giving her a slight push toward the direction of the creek.

Selah still hesitated. She had thought she would be meeting with her parents at the rendezvous point. She had thought she would be able to say goodbye. Suddenly, she could hear voices.

Paul gripped her by the shoulders. "That's the search party the board put together. I can stall them for a little while, but you've got to get going!" His voice was desperate. "Listen, Selah. Garrison is out there somewhere. I know it. Find him for me. Tell him Megan and I love him, and we understand why he left. Tell him that maybe someday, more of us will be able to leave; but until then, we'll never stop praying for him —for both of you."

Selah embraced him quickly, her body tingling with adrenaline. She turned back down the path to the creek and headed upstream. The boundary tree was just ahead. She could hear voices in the woods behind her. "Hey, I was just looking for Selah. I heard you had formed a search party. Can I help?" she heard Paul holler. She stumbled through the spindly witch-hazel trunks, glad for the sound of the creek that would help muffle any noise she might make.

Ahead, she could see the thick trunk of the boundary tree. Suddenly doubt began to creep into her mind. "Am I doing the right thing?" she asked herself. "Lord, is this really what You want?"

In answer, a verse of scripture flashed through her mind:

> "Is this not the fast that I have chosen: to loose the bonds of wickedness, to undo the heavy burdens, to let the oppressed go free, and that you break every yoke? Is it not to share your bread with the hungry, and that you bring to your house the poor who are cast out; when you see the naked, that you cover him, and not hide yourself from your own flesh?"[112]

Selah swallowed hard and stumbled forward, past the boundary tree and toward the valley's ridge. God's Spirit gently reassured her as she went, bringing to mind the rest of the scripture:

> "Then your light shall break forth like the morning, your healing shall spring forth speedily, and your righteousness shall go before you; the glory of the Lord shall be your rear guard. Then you shall call, and the Lord will answer; you shall cry, and He will say, 'Here I am.'"[113]

---

[112] Isaiah 58:6-7 NKJV
[113] Isaiah 58:8-9a NKJV

She floundered up the slope, weighed down by the two packs and the awkward bulk of her bow and arrows. "I can't make good time like this, but You promised You would be my rear guard," she prayed. "Throw them off track, Lord. I need Your help."

"Here I am," the scripture reverberated in her mind. The voices behind her grew fainter. Her face grew wet with tears as she realized God was keeping His Word. She had called upon Him, and He had answered. He was guarding her back.

The slope was steep, and her lungs began to cry out for air, but she wouldn't let herself stop until she reached the valley's rim. Once there, she stopped and looked back over her escape route. A few lights were bobbing down the road to Miss Genevieve's old house, which was still vacant. No doubt, Paul had suggested she might be there and had put the search party off her trail.

She lowered her packs to the ground so she could distribute the load more evenly, stowing Miss Genevieve's satchel in her larger backpack. Her throat was dry, and she drank from a water skin her parents had provided. She drank deeply and refilled it with water she filtered from the creek, marveling how everything that had happened that day seemed to be planned by Someone who could see the events clearly from start to finish.

"He knows the end from the beginning," she could hear Payton's voice say, and felt the reassuring presence of the Lord like a father's hand on her shoulder. After a few moments' rest, she was on her way again —more slowly, this time, since she was walking out of the valley into unknown territory.

"I am trusting You with all my heart, Jesus," she said. "Please direct my paths."

As the night faded into morning, she could see the outlines of trees and the details of the forest floor in the gray daylight. She pushed on, past weariness and into a state of exhaustion. Garrison had said there was a road up here somewhere. Surely it couldn't be far.

Though it was probably only minutes, it seemed like hours had passed when she came to a sudden break in the forest. In front of her was a road that was wider than anything they had in the valley. It was made of a rocklike material. Grass and weeds sprouted through cracks in its surface. She could tell it hadn't been traveled in a long, long time. It stretched before her and disappeared northward into the distance.

Suddenly, the sun burst over the horizon to her right, spreading its rays like fingers to embrace the eastern sky. *"Then your light shall break forth like the morning,"* a voice said in her spirit. Her heart pounded as she shifted the weight of the packs. She set a foot down on the strange surface of the old road. She was a light bearer. It was time to share the Light.

Questions for Thought

Part 1

1. Why do you think Selah was accustomed to trusting and defending leadership? Why does she refuse to show disrespect to leaders, even though she feels wronged by them? (Hebrews 13:17, Psalm 105:14-15, 1 Peter 2:13-17)

2. How has society's attitude towards our elders changed over the years? What does the Bible say about the treatment of elders? (Leviticus 19:32)

3. What does the Word of God say about an increase of knowledge and sickness in the last days? (Daniel 12:4, Matthew 24:7-8)

4. What is wrong with today's belief that there are many roads to God? (John 14:6)

5. Many people say they don't believe in God because if He existed, He wouldn't allow bad things to happen to innocent people.
   A. Looking at the story of the fall of man in Genesis, how would you answer this argument?
   B. Why would God allow the existence of free will, knowing it would result in such pain and suffering, instead of creating beings who would always obey Him without question?

6. When someone tells you they have a "word from the Lord" or they have been hearing from God, how do you know if it's true? (Matthew 7:15-20, 1 John 4:1-3, Hebrews 4:12)

7. What should you do if you think God is telling you to do something? How can you be sure it is His will? (Psalm 119:105, 2 Timothy 2:15, 2 Timothy 3:16-17, Acts 13:2-3)

8. What does the Bible say about lying? (Revelation 21:8, Proverbs 5:16-19, Proverbs 26:28) What does it say about telling the truth? (Matthew 5:37)

9. Do passages of scripture like Psalm 91 mean that we can expect to lead trouble-free lives? When Christians are tortured or killed for Christ's sake, does it mean they have done something wrong or don't have enough faith to be delivered? (See Psalm 91:15, Romans 8:28, 35-39 and 2 Corinthians 4:8-12)

10. What does the Bible say about gossip? (Proverbs 16:28, 17:9, 18:8, 26:20)

11. Why should we ask God for things when He already knows what we need? (Luke 18:1-8, Matthew 7:7)

12. Is fasting still for today? If so, how should you conduct yourself during it, and what is its purpose or result? (Matthew 6:16-18, 17:14-21, Ezra 8:21-23)

13. What can you expect during a fast? (Ephesians 6:11-12, 2 Corinthians 10:3-6)

14. What is the most effective spiritual weapon to use against the devil, and what prominent figure in the Bible used this weapon during a time of fasting?

Part 2

1. Why is it important for new Christians to learn from those who are mature in Christ and rooted and grounded in the Word of God, instead of only relying on what they feel the Holy Spirit is telling them?

2. Should someone young in the faith always assume a teacher or preacher is correct in what they teach? (2 Timothy 2:15-18)

3. What is the "plumb line" for correct biblical teaching? (Psalm 119:11, Psalm 119:34, Psalm 119:66-67, and Psalm 119:105)

4. What do you think King David would say about the potential of people the world views as hopeless?

5. Knowing what the Bible tells us of the mistakes David made and the origin of his mighty men, how do you think God feels about second chances? (1 John 1:9)

6. There are many different ways people worship God. Often, discussions about what way is best will emphasize the differences between bodies of believers. What is the most important thing to remember when worshipping God? Who is the worship really for? (1 Samuel 16:7, John 4:23-24)

7. Is there a difference between the spiritual rebirth one experiences at the point of salvation and the baptism in the Holy Spirit? (Acts 2:1-4, 2:39, 19:1-6)

8. What are some of the benefits of receiving the infilling of the Holy Spirit? (Acts 1:8, John 14:16-17, John 14:26, John 16:13-15)

9. When seeking the baptism of the Holy Spirit, how can you be certain you are not giving entrance to an evil spirit? (Luke 11:9-13)

10. When one older pastor was asked if he thought a person needs the Holy Ghost to get into Heaven, he replied that we need the Holy Ghost just to go to the grocery store! What are your thoughts on this? Do you feel the baptism in the Holy Spirit is helpful and relevant for today? Do you have scriptural basis for your view?

11. Even though she's just a dog, Macy seems to be an instrument for God's purposes. Can you find any other instances in the Bible where God uses an animal to accomplish His purposes? (Numbers 22:21-33, 1 Kings 17:2-6, Genesis 22:13, Jonah 1:17, 4:7)

Part 3

1. What is the role of someone who takes part in intercessory prayer?

2. Sometimes standing in the gap is simply being faithful to pray for people or situations. It doesn't sound nearly as exciting as preaching, being a missionary, or giving a prophetic word, and it is often done in secret, with no recognition or reward except seeing our prayers answered, or simply knowing we have prayed in God's will. Can you think of a revival that didn't have a foundation laid in prayer?

3. What does the Bible say about forgiving others? Who is often hurt the most in a situation of unforgiveness? (Ephesians 4:32, Matthew 6:14-15)

4. Why is it important to do things in order, under the covering of spiritual leadership? (1 Corinthians 14:26-33)

5. How can you be certain you are praying God's perfect will? (Romans 8:26-27)

6. Who was Jezebel? How could some people be compared to Jezebel, in regard to the way they operate in their church?

7. How is it possible for a Christian to be deceived into working against other Christians and what God wants them to do? What is our ultimate, tangible authority in this life? (2 Timothy 3:16-17)

8. Why is it important to maintain both a prayer life and a study of God's Word?

9. What does the Bible say about God's Spirit in 2 Corinthians 3:17 and Romans 8:15?

10. Is it possible to want to do something for God that is both admirable and biblical, and yet not be *called* to do it? (1 Corinthians 12:27-31, Ephesians 4:11)

11. What does Romans 11:29 mean for someone who is called by God to do something? Do you think Miss Genevieve took into account Ecclesiastes 3:1 when she began planning her missionary journey?

12. Does the Great Commission only refer to those involved in foreign missions? What do you think Jesus meant by His command in Mark 16:15?

13. Who was Jesus teaching in Mark 4:21 and Matthew 5:13-16? Who was Paul talking to in Philippians 2:13-16? What types of people do these groups represent, and how does this relate to you?

14. What is your mission field?

AN EXCERPT FROM THE IMAGE BEARERS (BOOK 2)

IRA Owens removed his glasses and pressed his thumb and index finger gently against his eyelids. "Maybe I *should* get the vision implant," he mumbled to the grid-work of monitors in front of him as he attempted to rub the soreness from his eyes. "My eyelids feel like they're lined with sandpaper."

"I can't believe you're using those spectacles. You realize no one has worn anything like that for years. You're a walking anachronism, Ira," the woman at the station to his right commented. The images on the monitors in front of her flipped from one drone's visual feed to the next." I don't see how your eyes can take it, seeing the readouts the old-tech way."

Ira glanced at his sole companion in the Mid-south Sector Drone Readout Room. She was leaning back in her ergonomically designed chair, eyes closed, but he could see them moving back and forth as if she were in REM sleep, watching the direct feed of the monitors to the chip in her brain. "Now that I have the chip, I don't even have to open my eyes to see everything that's going on. If I think something is suspicious, I can immediately take host in the drone and move in closer for a better look. No more flipping switches and using hand controls. The drone becomes an extension—"

"—of your body, yes, I know." Ira finished her sentence for her.

"I wish you wouldn't interrupt like that. What do you have against the new tech? I guess I can understand some people being hesitant about the chip, because it's such a huge life change, but to not even get 2nd Sight, when you work in a job requiring you to scan monitors with your eyes for hours on end—it just seems a little stubborn or paranoid, like maybe you're one of those conspiracy theory people."

"Vicey, you know one of the main reasons I got the job was because I didn't have 'Sight. They wanted something uncomplicated and unconnected to fall back on, in case the tech malfunctioned. And I think that's why they haven't pushed for me to get chipped, either. Nevermind that I was head of the class in programming tech interface. Nevermind that I was in a think tank with Dr. Jo-Mo. They. . ." The gangly man suddenly shoved his glasses firmly back up the bridge of his nose and leaned forward to peer into one the monitors. "What is *that*? Vice, come look at this."

"You know I won't see it in time if I unhook, Ira. Just give me the link to your feed."

Ira typed a few commands into the console, his eyes never leaving the monitor. His companion tensed and leaned forward, although the images she was seeing were streaming through her mind, rather than in front of her face. "Is that a person? That's a girl!" she exclaimed, answering her own question. "How did she get there, that far from the outer docks? That's miles and miles away from, from anywhere!" Vicey chewed on her lower lip. "Well, what are you waiting for? Take the drone in closer. Bring her in."

Ira smiled wonderingly at the screen. "Why don't we just watch her for a while and see what she does? If she doesn't know she's being monitored, we might be able to get some answers just from observation."

"Again, the old-fashioned way. We could also just chip her and get all we need in a matter of minutes," Vicey said impatiently. "I'm calling it in."

"Very well," Ira said, with a hint of disappointment. "But I'll do it. It was in my region, after all." He sent the information to his immediate supervisor and continued his vigil at the screen. There was something different about this one. Not just the clothes or the antiquated pack she carried. It was something about the way she interacted with her environment. Most of the Discards or the Unhooked seemed completely at odds with their surroundings when they ventured into the Preserve. The Discards who had never transitioned from smart phone to vista-visor clutched their phones, holding them inches from their faces as they navigated through forests and abandoned towns. The Unhooked kept their visors on, eyes glued to the readout, unwilling or unable to comprehend the data being fed to their natural senses by the their physical surroundings. They reminded Ira of the old flatscreen movies about submarines traveling through the mysterious depths of the ocean. They were completely insulated from their environment. A few who had lost their visor or their mind—there wasn't much difference, after all—huddled on the ground and covered their eyes, overwhelmed by the emptiness and terrified of what could be hiding behind the nearest bush. But this girl seemed to be looking at everything around her, as if she were an integral part of her surroundings, rather than an intruder passing through in her own self-contained little world. She didn't seem to be afraid. She looked as if she were on a great adventure.

Ira frowned thoughtfully as he zoomed in on her face. She was talking to someone. So maybe she was connected, after all. But how had she escaped detection until now? His thoughts were interrupted by a voice in his earpiece. "Do nothing for now. Simply observe and keep the link opened to my channel." Ira frowned again. This was, indeed, out of the ordinary.

Unless. . . "That must be it," he said to himself.

"What's that, Ira?" Vicey asked. "What did they say?"

"They don't want me to interfere. They just want me to watch."

"But why would they do that?" Vicey exclaimed, rising slightly out of her chair. "Oh, of course," she said softly, a sly smile curving her lips. "That girl must be part of the operatives program Jo-Mo started."

"To fish out isolationist outposts?" Ira asked. "That's what I was just thinking. But to be honest, I always thought that program was a little far-fetched. That a whole community could survive completely unhooked from the State is hard to imagine."

"Well, for whatever reason, Dr. Moses thinks it's possible. And I bet you next week's download that this girl is one of his spies."

Ira seemed to deflate a little as he settled down into his chair. Why was he so disappointed?

The girl's face broadened into a smile as she stopped suddenly to watch a small hawk swoop down and snatch a vole out of the grass in the road ditch. She had to be plugged in. That's why she looked so happy and at ease. She wasn't alone at all.